# THE COMPLETE CASES OF KEN CARTER

NORVELL W. PAGE

# THE COMPLETE CASES OF

# KEN CARTER™

## NORVELL W. PAGE

### ILLUSTRATIONS BY
## JOHN FLEMING GOULD

ALTUS PRESS

BOSTON • 2018

# TABLE OF CONTENTS

HELL'S MUSIC . . . . . . . . . . . . 1

CITY OF CORPSES . . . . . . . . . . 39

STATUES OF HORROR . . . . . . . . . 97

GALLOWS GHOST . . . . . . . . . . 151

SATAN'S HOOF . . . . . . . . . . 209

THE SINISTER EMBRACE . . . . . . . . 263

SATAN'S SIDESHOW . . . . . . . . . 321

SILK DOPE . . . . . . . . . . . . 353

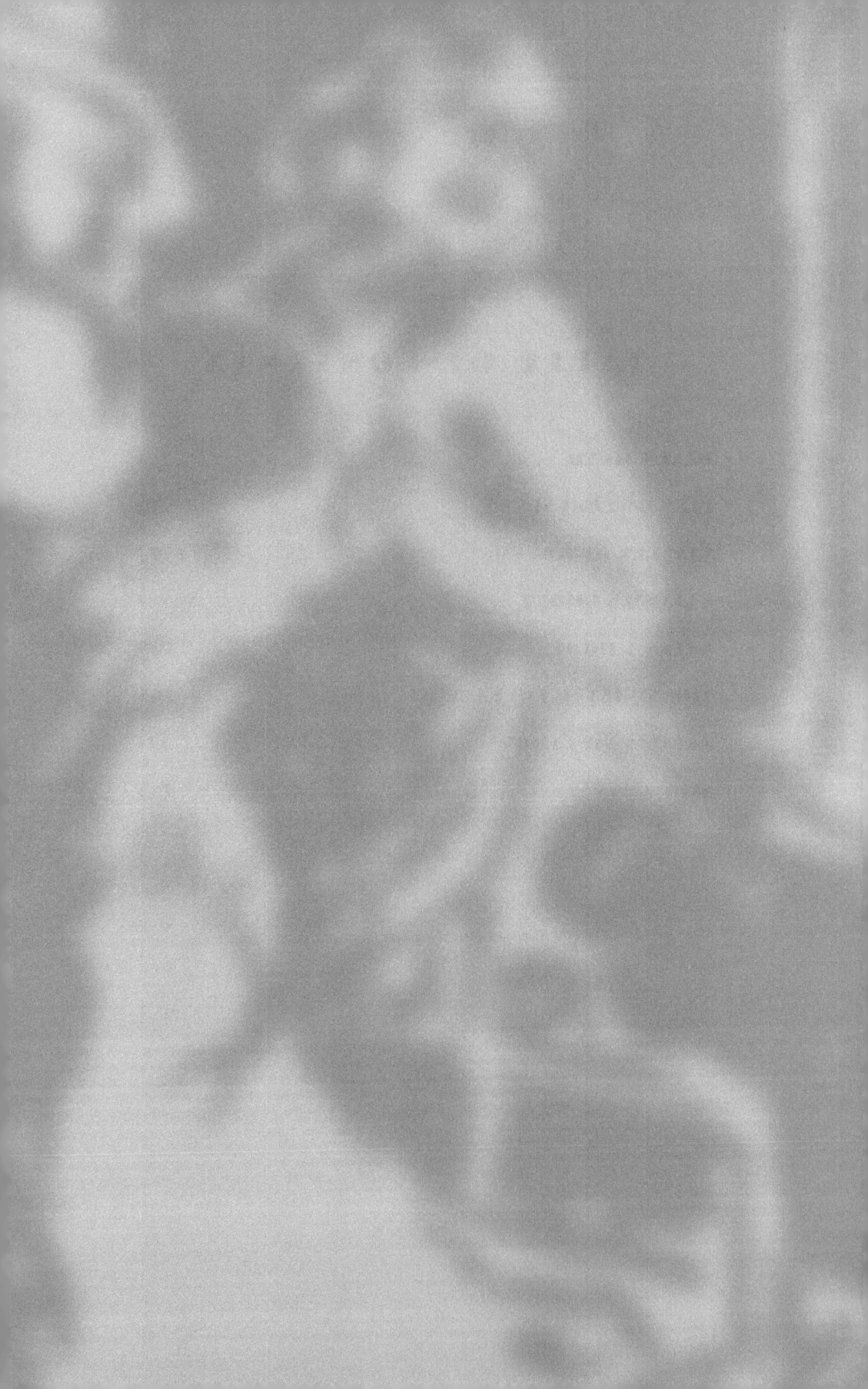

# HELL'S MUSIC

BLASTING ACROSS THE DECKS AND THROUGH THE CABINS OF THE *FRISCONIA* CAME THE DEVIL'S SONG OF DOOM. UNEARTHLY, LIKE THE PIERCING CRY FROM ANOTHER, SUFFERING WORLD, SHRILLED THAT MURDER MUSIC. AND LISTENING TO THAT GRIM RECITAL WAS DETECTIVE KEN CARTER. WITH THE LAST THROBBING NOTE THERE WAS APPLAUSE—THE CLAPPING OF DEATH'S BONY HANDS.

# CHAPTER ONE
# THE DEVIL PIPES

**S**TRIDING EXUBERANTLY along the dark-ened windward deck as the *Frisconia* thrust her prow into a bluster of March wind and rain, Ken Carter jerked to a halt in mid-stride. Pain stabbed his eardrums; his muscles quivered and knotted as if with cramp, and a thin, high note of unearthly music seemed to vibrate within his skull. The torture was exquisite, unendurable. Ken wanted to cry aloud in agony, but only uttered strangled sounds.

For thirty seconds the music continued. Then it was gone, and Carter wavered on his feet, his chest panting, blood throbbing in his temples, muscles aching. He gripped his head, and stood half-dazed, then heavily raised his eyes and looked about.

Frightened cries of women from within told him others had been afflicted. The deck was deserted. Dim lights at intervals made yellow pools that glistened on the wet boards. Beyond the rail crystal rods of rain slanted down, but that was all. What in heaven's name had sounded that horrible note!

It was terrible, unbelievably high and keen. It cut like a razor. Nothing human could have made it. It seemed incredible, like a piercing cry from another, suffering world.

Carter paced slowly on with frowning brows forward and around the end of the cabins. He checked then, remembering B Deck had been roped off on the starboard side so James Johnstone, who this day had quit office as governor of a middle western state, might have privacy in his suite.

Carter was about to turn back when, sensing a human presence, he glanced up sharply, nerves tingling and the memory of that stab of music at the back of his mind. The presence, he discovered, was a man and girl. They stood together against the forward side of the cabin.

Ken Carter started to retreat, then a vagrant beam of light fell upon the girl's face. It was white and startled, and the eyes were wide. Her features were delicate and her dress rich, a silken cloak with heavy fur. Yet the man who bent over her looked like a common sailor.

Apparently he had not noticed Carter's presence, for his attitude was tense and he continued to talk at the girl in low, positive tones. She said, suddenly, "No! No!" in a loud voice, and then the man seized her tightly in his arms, his mouth seeking hers.

Caution warned Carter to be on about his business, but even while he was thinking that he strode forward, clapped his hand upon the man's shoulder, and whirled him about.

He said, "Pardon me, miss, but is there some difficulty here?"

The girl cried out softly, "Oh, yes, yes!" and shrank back against the bulkhead, hands clasped at her throat.

The sailor turned a sullenly handsome face and snarled, "Naw, there ain't. Shove off before I sock you."

Ken Carter smashed his right across to the sailor's jaw, sending him down in a huddle against the foot of the bulkhead. The man showed no disposition to move, and Carter offered his arm to the girl.

"May I escort you to a more pleasant spot?" he asked.

Ken Carter saw the girl struggle.

The girl shuddered, and drew the smoky fur of her cloak up more closely about her white throat and nodded weakly. Carter took her slowly to a brightly lighted saloon. She seemed by this time entirely recovered, and adjusted her hair with steady hands, smoothing into place red-gold locks that the wind had torn awry.

She smiled at him calmly, a twisted little sideways smile that dimpled in her left cheek made her dark eyes a brighter blue. She opened her cloak, the smoky fur parted, and revealed herself slim and shapely in black satin. A broad sash of sage green delineated the smooth curve of her thighs.

She said, "Thank you so much."

Carter bowed gravely, proffered his card, and the girl read from it aloud, "Kenneth Carter," and looked up quickly from under the smooth burnished line of her brows.

She said softly, "It seems to me that I have heard that name before." She held out her hand straightforwardly, like a man. "I am Natalie Franklin, daughter of the captain. Thank you for helping me."

The pressure of her hand was firm and pleasant.

"Shall we go up to the lounge?" asked Carter. "I feel that something in the way of stimulants is called for after the—er—a—cold wind."

**THE GIRL** smiled her quirky little sideways smile again and said, "Yes, the *er—a—cold* was severe."

They walked slowly up the broad, winding stair. The girl allowed her coat to slip back from satin smooth shoulders, revealing a low V of décolletage, and looked up at Carter. He now carried his brown topcoat over his arm, showing the black and white formality of his attire, a tall, solidly set-up man with smooth black hair and gray eyes that were gravely intent.

"I can't help thinking," said the girl, "that your name is very, very familiar."

Carter, solemn as was his custom, bent toward her and asked: "When you were a very small girl did you often go to vaudeville?"

Natalie Franklin allowed her dark blue eyes to go very wide, in little girl manner, and cried, "Don't tell me, Mr. Carter, that you are an actor!"

Carter said, "Certainly not. I was a juggler."

The girl gurgled, "Oh, tell me more," but when Carter spoke she was staring straight ahead of her with eyes that seemed to see nothing. At the head of the stairs they paused a moment, looking over the lounge, and Carter became aware of a buzzing just back of him.

He whirled nervously, remembering that other earlier sound which the encounter with the girl and sailor had driven momentarily from his mind, and found himself looking at the steward's call board. There was a series of numbers laid out in precise rows; and beside each one was a little golden arrow. The arrow beside the number B-2 was turned up, and the buzzing was uninterrupted.

Carter exclaimed, "I say, Miss Franklin, we must do something about the steward service on your father's ship. It's beastly."

The girl languidly turned and glanced with him at the board, and a little gasp caught at her throat. Carter turned toward her quickly, with a "What's the matter?"

The girl's face was stiff. She swallowed with difficulty, and said, "Nothing."

"Do you know whose cabin that is?"

"Yes, that's ex-Governor Johnstone's room."

Carter ejaculated, "Judas Priest, where is a steward?"

A white-coated figure far down the passageway caught his eye, and he signaled with upraised hand. The man hurried toward him, face wreathed in obsequious smiles.

Carter jerked out, "Cabin B-2 is ringing, has been ringing for quite while."

The man said, "Yes sir, right away, sir," and started down the steps. Carter was at his heels. The girl called, "Where are you going?"

Carter, halfway down, looked back.

The girl's face was startled, and she was leaning forward, one hand clutching the railing in a tense attitude, the other stretched out as if to detain him.

Carter said rapidly, "That buzzer is still going."

The girl's voice was husky, "It must be just—just stuck."

Carter's face was grim. He said nothing further, but went on down the steps. There was a sharp tapping of heels behind him, and when he entered the long passageway that led forward to B-2, the girl's hand was on his arm. He said dryly, "Maybe the button is just stuck."

Natalie Franklin turned her dark blue eyes up at him and did not smile. There was a tightness about the sweet curve of her mouth. When they caught up with the steward, he was staring blankly at the door of B-2. He turned a worried face. "He doesn't answer, sir. I've knocked and called."

"Get the purser with his keys at once!" Carter ordered.

The girl moaned, "Oh!" and her hand was again at her throat. Carter turned narrowed gray eyes on her and asked, "Why are you frightened?"

The girl shook her head slowly, her gaze never leaving his. "I'm not frightened. Really, I'm not frightened at all."

Carter bent forward slightly. "I forgot to add that since I left the stage I have become a private detective."

The girl's expression did not change, unless a slight widening of the eyes could be called that, but her accelerated breathing caused her breast to lift jerkily the tightened bodice of her dress. She said again, rapidly, "I'm not frightened. Really, I'm not frightened at all."

The purser came swiftly, frowning. Carter explained, and the officer knocked and called:

"Mr. Johnstone! Mr. Johnstone! Are you all right, sir?"

They waited, but there was no answer. The silence became heavy, broken only by their breathing and the creakings of the ship.

Carter said tensely, "Open the door."

The purser inserted a key, pushed, and stopped dead, crying out hoarsely, "Oh—my—god!"

Carter shoved past him. The stocky body of ex-Governor Johnstone sprawled across a desk, clenched fist resting on the steward's call button. His body was horribly contorted, as if every muscle had been drawn taut as piano wire. Carter bent over him. The face was knotted, too.

His keen eyes swept the room. The windows were all closed, but through one Carter caught a momentary flash of a face, a sullenly handsome face.

"Judas Priest! The same sailor!" he muttered.

There was a sobbing cry and Carter whirled in time to see Natalie Franklin sink, fainting, to the floor.

## CHAPTER TWO

## MURDER MUSIC

**K**EN CARTER darted across the room, hurdled the crumpled figure of Natalie Franklin, and darted down the passageway. He whirled a corner, slid open a door, and burst out upon the deck.

A small man was leaning his back against the rail, a small man with broad, powerful shoulders. Carter panted, "A sailor! Did you see one ran this way?"

The man bent his head sideways, indicating the forward part of the ship.

"Yes," he said, "but I imagine you will have difficulty locating him."

Carter started forward, then hesitated. He could easily identify the man by having the crew of the *Frisconia* lined up. A search would be lengthy, and other affairs demanded his attention more immediately.

"Is there anything the matter?" the man asked.

Carter glanced at him again. The man had bushy black hair. Thick glasses made his eyes owlish and his brows and mustache were black and heavy. Carter answered slowly, "I don't know," and started for Johnstone's cabin, then saw two men in uniform walking aft along the deck with a sailor.

They passed under a light and Carter caught the glitter of golden oak leaves on the visor of the man's cap, and four golden bars on the cuff. It was Captain Franklin and the sailor—the sailor Carter had been chasing!

He took long-legged strides to meet the men and blocked their path. "Captain! I demand that sailor's arrest!"

The captain jerked out, "Later, later," and attempted to push by.

Carter seized him by the arm, biting out words. "He's mixed up in ex-Governor Johnstone's murder!"

Captain Franklin stopped short, turned a ruddy, worried face. *"Murder?"*

Carter rasped, "You're damned right, it's murder."

The sailor edged away. Carter grabbed his shoulder. "Captain, this man—"

The officer's white mustache bristled. "Hans, weren't you on guard outside the governor's window?"

Carter snapped, "He was off his post."

*"What!"*

Hans broke in vehemently, "You're not going to frame me, you—"

He jerked free and raced forward. Carter took two strides, shrugged and halted, gray eyes narrowed.

Captain Franklin barked, "Seize that man!" and his subordinate hurried off.

"He can't get away," Carter said grimly. "None of us can!"

The captain stared at him with puzzled eyes, stroking his mustache with his forefinger and thumb, then strode off down the deck, leaving Carter alone with the passenger. The short man ran a hand briskly over his bushy, uncovered head. "This is a terrible thing!"

Carter said grimly, "Thanks for the information," and walked away.

The man called mockingly after him, "Glad to help. Ransome is the name, Arnold Ransome."

Carter frowned and hurried to Johnstone's cabin. A guard had been posted and he was barred until he identified himself as a private operative.

There was nothing new to be learned in that room of death except that doors and windows had been locked on the inside, and that the ex-Governor's secretary had left him alive at 11:15, thus placing the death sometime between then and 11:35, when the purser had unlocked the door.

**THE SHIP'S** doctor could add little information. Johnstone had apparently been afflicted by a simultaneous cramp in all muscles, stopping his heart instantly. But as to what had caused such a condition, the doctor could not say.

"An electric shock," he said, "might cause muscular convulsion, but would leave the body relaxed in death."

When the captain left, he took Carter with him. Head bowed into the bitter sweep of the wind, Carter paced forward, blown rain misting into his face.

"Do you believe now, captain, that it is murder?"

Captain Franklin pursed his lips beneath his bristly white mustache. "Doctor doesn't know of anything that can kill a man like that."

Carter, thinking of that unearthly music, said slowly, "There are many things science does not know."

As if that had been a signal, the exquisite torture of that eerie note stabbed his eardrums, his muscles jerked as if with cramp, paralyzing him, and that thin, terrible music vibrated within his skull. Carter tried to cry out and could not. His body quivered and pain pulsed over him in waves.

The note stopped as abruptly as it had begun, and, trembling weakly, his breath laboring, Carter turned narrowed, speculative eyes to find the captain staring at him. Once more screams echoed over the ship, there was a muddled rising murmur of excited voices.

"In heaven's name," exclaimed Franklin thickly, "What was that?"

Carter said swiftly, "That is what I heard tonight just before they found ex-Governor Johnstone murdered!"

A sharp shout rang down the wind and Carter raced forward along the slippery decks, followed by the captain. Franklin cupped his hands, leaned over the rail above the well.

"Ahoy there! What is it!"

A voice cried back, "Jack Holly is dead, sir! He's lying all tied up in a knot on the deck!"

Carter and Captain Franklin glanced tight-eyed at each other, then drove down a companionway and out onto the deck. The full beat of the storm swept over them, drenching Carter's evening clothes instantly. He could feel the heaving lift of the *Frisconia's* bows beneath his feet as he stared down fixedly at the dead sailor, lying in almost identically the same posture as ex-Governor Johnstone.

Carter said grimly, "Do you doubt now that it's murder, Franklin?"

The captain stood on widely planted feet, staring down at the corpse, unmindful of the rain slashing into his ruddy face. "It's murder," he said. "But in God's name, how? What *was* that noise?"

"Noise, captain?" said Carter softly. "It sounded like hell's own music to me!"

Wind howled whining through braces and stays about the stump forward mast, chillingly reminiscent of that other, madder note.

Captain Franklin whirled about, cupped hands to his mouth. "Search the whole ship," he bawled. "Find Hans Mueller at once!"

## CHAPTER THREE
## THE THIRD KILL

**S EATED AT** his desk, Captain Franklin looked with worried eyes at Ken Carter and asked, "What am I going to do?"

Carter, lounging his tall, strongly built body, clad now in dry, dark tweeds, lighted a cigarette and said, "The first thing, of course, is to find that sailor, Hans Mueller. You've already radioed the owners?"

The captain looked down at his ruddy hands on the desktop and nodded. Carter narrowed his gray eyes. "You'll have to tell the passengers, of course."

Franklin closed his lips in a straight line beneath his bristly mustache. He stood, put on his uniform cap.

Carter said, "Before we go, captain, I want to have an understanding."

The officer turned at the door, frowning. "Understanding?"

"Yes. As I've told you, I'm a private detective. I'll be glad to cooperate with you in solving these crimes if your owners authorize it.

"If they do, well enough. The fee will be five thousand.

"If they don't, I'm going to act anyway. I may not have told you, but I am a man of sentiment. I always liked and admired the governor and he did me a favor once, though he may not have known it. A little private case I had.

"I'd like to act as your agent, captain, but whether I do or not, I'm going to catch Johnstone's murderer."

The captain said briefly, "Glad of your help. Retaining you right now, even if owners don't."

Carter rose. "That's that."

They went down to the saloon together. Before the huddled, panicky passengers, the captain made a simple statement of what had happened, that the former governor had been found murdered, that a sailor had been killed, and he mentioned the time. It was a silent, tense gathering. It was nearly two in the morning, but obviously no one had thought of sleep.

Men and women stood close together, casting frequent, terror-laden glances over their shoulders. Outside, the whine of the wind was wild and mournful; the *Frisconia* was laboring, lunging through a rising sea, and the floor of the saloon tilted slowly up and down.

Ransome was in the fore of the audience. He ran a hand briskly through his bushy black hair, blinking owlishly behind thick-lensed glasses, and said, "Pardon me, captain, but this is something that may be of interest. At about the time you say the governor and the sailor were killed, I heard an intensely high, almost inaudible musical note. It affected my eardrums. I wonder if there could be any connection?"

As he finished speaking, that hideous thin music that twice tonight had marked horrible murders shrilled through the air. Everyone in the room stood as if frozen. Strangled sounds squeezed from a few throats, but loud and clear, above even the whining of that unearthly sound, came a woman's piercing scream.

Carter tried to tear himself loose from the maddening paralysis, tried to dash forward, but until that hell's music ceased, he was helpless. It died abruptly and Carter reeled ahead.

The captain cried hoarsely, "Good Lord, that's Natalie's voice!"

He and Carter ploughed through the startled passengers, streaking toward the girl's cabin.

Behind them was a rising rumble of panic, women's hysteria and men's excitement. Ship's officers shouted peremptorily. The sounds faded behind as Carter's long-legged stride sped him to the girl's cabin. He was far ahead of the captain. He flung open the door. Natalie stood wringing her hands, her blue eyes closed, burnished smooth brows drawn down in a straight painful line. She moaned over and over, "Oh—oh—oh—!"

Carter said, "For God's sakes, Natalie, what's the matter?"

The girl opened vague eyes and looked at Ken as though she did not see him. Carter took both her hands.

"What is it, Natalie?"

She seemed to come out of a daze and said swiftly.

"That sailor—"

CAPTAIN FRANKLIN stumped in panting and there was a rush of other people. Natalie took her hands from Carter and held them out to her father.

"I'm awfully sorry, dad," she said, "I had a bad dream."

She seemed to realize for the first time that she was in deshabille, clinging black pajamas which left the creamy whiteness of her shoulders bare and revealed rather than hid her slim shapeliness. She snatched up a negligee and wrapped it about her, slapping the door shut. She ran to her father again and laid her ruddy-golden head against his chest, "Truly I'm sorry, dad."

She frowned at Carter with wide-open eyes, and seemed trying to convey some message. What she meant he could not gather, but it was obvious she did not intend to mention to her father the sailor, Hans Mueller, the man who had tried to force his attentions on her, whom Carter had seen from that room of death, and for whom the ship was being combed as a suspect in these two horrible murders.

But what had the girl meant by those two words, "The sailor—" Had the man been here? Carter frowned, his gray eyes worried. No chance to ask her now. He bowed gravely and said, "If you will excuse me, please?" and went out.

A purposeful half dozen men huddled in the passage, faces grim. At their head was Ransome, his bushy brows contracted.

"What can I do for you?" Carter asked.

Ransome said rudely, "Nothing. We want the captain."

Carter bowed, gray eyes narrow, and presently Franklin came out, heavy-shouldered, truculent. Ransome stepped forward.

"Captain," he said, "We demand you turn the *Frisconia* back to New York at once."

The captain's long jaw tightened, his mustache bristling.

"Demand?" he repeated quietly.

"Yes," said Ransome, "demand! Obviously there is some murderer loose on this ship over which you have no control at all. Apparently you've done nothing to apprehend him."

Captain Franklin said, "I'm in charge of this ship."

"We will radio the owners and have you removed," Ransome asserted aggressively.

Captain Franklin frowned, mouth corners tight. "Do as you please."

Ransome said acidly, "Perhaps the owners will display better judgment."

Carter shouldered forward, head down. He said roughly, "Shut up, Ransome!"

The captain grimly gestured him back. He glared at Ransome and the others individually, bowed with a click of heels like a Prussian guardsman. "Excuse me, gentlemen." He right faced and walked away, Carter following.

In the captain's sanctum, the tall detective and he faced each other grimly across the desk. Carter said, "You can't blame them. We've heard this hell's music three times now, and two men have died. Last time the murderer apparently missed." His jaw was tight, sharp vertical lines between his eyes. He said, "Hell!" and spun toward the door.

It flung open almost in his face and a man in blue uniform half-reeled in, bringing with him the raw dampness of the night.

Captain Franklin snapped, "What is it, Hendricks?"

The man gasped "Captain, captain!"

"What!"

"Captain, the radio is busted!"

Franklin gestured impatiently, his face angry. The man held out beseeching hands. "I heard a queer note of music like we heard when those two men were killed. My radio went dead."

Carter snapped, "What's wrong with it?"

The man turned dazed eyes toward him and said hoarse-ly, "The tubes are smashed."

"Spares, too?" Carter insisted, "They're wrapped in cotton wool and strawboard. They can't be broken."

The man jerked his head up and down violently. "Every damned one is broken. They seemed to have shaken them-selves to pieces."

**CARTER'S GRAY** eyes were narrow and hard. "Shaken to pieces—" he muttered, whirled to the captain. "That explains that third note. The murderer is cutting us off from the world for God knows what secret purpose of his own!"

Captain Franklin's voice was knife-like, "Repair that radio!"

The man's terrified eyes widened.

"I can't, sir! Everything we've got uses tubes."

Carter said, "Build a set."

"It will take hours!"

*"Get busy!"*

The man whirled, fright still straining his face, jerked open the door. *A seaman stumbled in, gasping!*

Carter's gun leaped to his hand. The man threw up defensive arms. He panted out, hoarsely, "Don't shoot!"

Carter's left hand seized the man's throat. "What do you want? Speak up!"

The sailor's chest was heaving. He got out the words, "Hans Mueller!"

Carter shook him. "Hans Mueller what?"

"We've—found—him."

The captain put both hands on his desk, leaned forward grimly. "Fine," he rasped, "Bring him in."

Carter gave the seaman a running start for the door and two minutes later he returned with two others, thrusting Mueller angrily ahead of them. Their faces were wet, their clothing disordered. Mueller's sullenly handsome face was grimy and bruised. Coal dust powdered his yellow hair.

"He was in a coal bunker, sir," the first seaman reported.

"And did he fight!"

Carter stepped squarely in front of Hans Mueller. "If you're wise, you'll talk."

The man growled sullenly, "I don't know nothing."

"Now I'll tell one," Carter jeered.

Captain Franklin said in a quiet but tense voice, "Let me ask a few questions."

Carter shrugged his wide shoulders, paced off across the cabin.

"Ask him why he wasn't on guard outside Johnstone's window," he threw at the captain and glowered at the captive sailor.

Mueller said angrily. "I wasn't! And you know why. That gi—"

His voice choked in mid-breath, sliced off. Shrill, horrible music hovered once more over the ship, quavering, piercing, unbearable. Carter felt it stab through his temples, felt his muscles contract and his breathing grew labored. His eyes were fixed on Hans Mueller and he saw him double up in a knot and collapse with a strangled cry.

A sailor standing directly behind doubled over with a moan, and then silence cut like a knife through the sound, and Carter, released, reeled back weakly, and dropped into a chair. He glanced swiftly toward the room's one window, but saw only windy rain.

The two seamen still on their feet staggered like drunken men, and, jerking open the door, fled with hoarse cries. Carter could hear their shouts picked up by the passengers. Screams and shrieks of panic swept the ship. He darted outside. The storm-battered deck was deserted. He returned, pounding hard heels.

The captain's shoulders drooped. He said heavily, "You better hunt another murderer."

Carter snapped, "I didn't say Hans was the murderer. I said he was tied up with him. He was, and his death proves it."

Captain Franklin reached slowly for his cap, dragged it on.

"I've got to calm those fool passengers," he said. "They'll be taking to the boats." He looked up at Carter under frowning brows. "You find the murderer. We've had enough horror."

Carter's mouth twisted in a thin, fighting grin, the only smile that ever came to his lips. His words were clipped. "I was going easy on you. I'll quit that. I'll find the murderer, but you may not like it when I do."

# CHAPTER FOUR
# DISCORD

IT WAS hard to believe that it was four o'clock in the morning, that so many tragic things could have happened in that short space of time since a little before midnight. The *Frisconia* did not look like four o'clock in the morning. It was ablaze with light, every cabin throughout the entire ship was illuminated. Passengers huddled together in saloons, in lounges, at the bar, and talked in whispers. At the slightest sound, they started.

Ken Carter, striding along the deck, knew word of this latest death had preceded him, but the captain had done his work well. The panic was quelled. Men looked at Carter belligerently. Women had fear in their eyes, and stewards scuttled from his path like frightened rabbits.

Carter passed the bar and it exhaled a burst of desperately drunken song. It sounded flat, frightened. He hard-heeled on down the deck, down a companionway, and rapped at Natalie Franklin's cabin. The answer was prompt, but faltering. "Who—who is there?"

"Kenneth Carter."

For a while there was complete silence within, then he heard the girl stirring, and presently the door opened two inches. The shoulder of a salmon satin negligee edged with marabou showed. Her voice was weary. "Please, I'm so tired."

Carter said shortly, "The murderer isn't!"

Her eyes flared wide. "Oh, what do you mean?"

Carter snapped. "Your secret is safe now. Hans Mueller is dead."

The girl drew a little shuddering breath and swayed back. Carter thrust in and the girl staggered into a chair. He shut the door, closed the window, draped over it a blanket snatched off the bed. He did the same at the door.

The girl asked tensely, "What are you trying to do?"

Carter glanced jeeringly back over his shoulder as he draped a comforter over the window. "I'm not trying to deaden the sound of what goes on in here."

The girl's eyes narrowed. The mockery of her sideways smile was not convincing. "I wasn't afraid."

She moved then to a chaise lounge, sat down carelessly crossing her knees, and Carter saw she still wore the clinging black pajamas. Her crank-sided little smile and the dimple were in evidence. She said, "Well, give me a cigarette and get on with the inquisition."

Ken Carter took a black and silver cigarette case from his vest pocket, offered it opened to her. Leaning forward to light it, he gazed steadily into her dark blue eyes. She let smoke roll slowly between her crimson lips, float up between them.

"When you screamed and I ran here, what did you mean by 'That sailor—?'"

Natalie met his eyes levelly. "Mueller came to my cabin, and threatened to harm me if I told of that—that scene on deck. Then he went out and I heard that," she shuddered, "—awful music and I thought he was trying to kill me—"

Ken Carter bent forward and shot out:

"Why did you want Governor Johnstone murdered?"

**NATALIE FRANKLIN'S** smile wavered.

"I didn't."

"Then why did you flirt with the governor's guard, and lure him from his post?"

The girl put both feet flat on the floor. Her hands clenched at her sides. "I won't be insulted!" she cried.

They stared bleakly into each other's eyes. Carter snapped out, "You are protecting the murderer. How do you know you won't be the next one he kills?"

The girl glanced, frightened, toward the window and the pink tip of her tongue touched her upper lip. "You're—you're trying to frighten me," she faltered.

Ken Carter said, "Sure."

Natalie Franklin hurled her cigarette across the room. "I won't stand for this! I won't! I won't!" She stamped her foot and threw herself full length on the chaise, shoulders twitching with sobs.

Carter, watching her closely, lit a cigarette. His tight, small smile played about his lips. Presently the girl's sobs eased. She twisted about, staring at him.

"God, you're hard!" she whispered.

Carter bowed suavely. "On the contrary, Natalie, I am a man of sentiment."

"Then why do you torture me so?"

Carter shrugged. "Answer my questions and I'll quit."

The girl gazed at him somberly, then slowly tilted back her head of burnished red gold, her dark blue eyes nearly closed beneath the bronze sweep of her lashes. Her sidewise smile dimpled her cheek.

"You stand there," she said, "and talk and talk—and talk—"

Carter looked down at his cigarette with amusement deep in his gray eyes, and flicked ashes on the silken rug. He asked calmly, "Are you inviting me to make love to you?"

The girl snapped to her feet. "You—"

Carter flipped his cigarette into a corner. "Going to talk?"

The girl's face was white with anger. "I'm afraid not!"

"Then you'll have to take the consequences. I don't need your confession. I was merely giving you a chance because, as I said," he bowed mockingly, "I am a man of sentiment."

He went out.

# CHAPTER FIVE
# THE MUSIC MASTER

**K**EN CARTER went directly to his cabin and began draping blankets and comforters over the door and window until he had nothing else to hang. He stuffed his ears with cotton and drew on a woolen cap that he bound in place with a scarf. He put on a sweater and three coats and sat down on his bunk to wait.

He cut off the steam in his quarters, but even then the heat became intolerable. Perspiration streaked his face and trickled down his sides beneath the heavy garments, but he bore it without so much as loosening the scarf about his head.

It was two hours later that he saw a faint stirring of the draperies across the window. He moved close against the wall and stood, eyes strained, tensely waiting. The blanket lifted at the corner away from him and for a while there was no further movement behind the draperies.

Waiting there, heavily muffled, Carter felt a thrill of fear like a cold slug crawling down his back. He knew that behind that curtain lurked the murderer who had sent three men to their deaths upon the ship, had struck with some unearthly weapon, a weapon that killed unerringly and paralyzed everyone near. And he knew that this monster was seeking his life!

Minutes passed as he crouched waiting, minutes that seemed like hours. Abruptly the blanket was yanked down, and a brass tube, two inches across and three feet long was thrust through the window, its yawning black muzzle focused on Carter's head. He saw a lean, strong hand clenched about its middle. Good God, this was the inhuman weapon that tortured men to death with music!

In this tense moment, when his life hinged on split-second action, his years of juggling stood him in good stead. His first task there had been to learn to analyze movements, to take them apart in fractions of seconds, and to figure their exact sequences. He had learned also that the quickest movement was that assisted by gravity, so that his dodge from before the muzzle of this strange weapon was half fall, half jump.

As he moved, his left hand closed about the lean wrist, the right about the deadly weapon, holding it at right angles to himself. All the strength of his back, all the weight of his body, he threw into one gigantic heave. He felt the muscles of his legs and hands leaping and twitching, and faintly he caught the piercing hellish music that had murdered three men. It hurt, but he had armored himself against its torture.

He wrenched again, heaving mightily, and dragged a man in through the window, a man with powerful shoulders, and a thick mop of black hair and bushy mustaches and eyebrows.

Carter panted out, *"Arnold Ransome!"*

He could scarcely hear his own voice.

Carter could tell from the strained expression of the man's face that he, too, was suffering from the paralysis of his inhuman weapon. He yanked the brass tube away and threw it across the cabin, and rapidly bound Ransome's hands behind him.

Not until then did he take the cap and scarf from his head, and the cotton out of his ears. Sweat was streaming down his face. He heard screams and feet pounding, and fists beating upon the door, and the captain's voice crying,

"Carter! Carter! Are you all right?" Keeping a firm grip on Ransome's shoulder, Carter yanked down the padding and opened the door.

"Here's your murderer," he said calmly. "Be careful of that brass tube on the floor. It kills!"

CAPTAIN FRANKLIN sat rigidly behind his desk. The two seamen thrust Ransome roughly forward, gripping his shoulders.

Ransome, owlish behind thick-lensed glasses, turned a mildly inquiring face toward them.

"Do you have to be so brutal about it?" he asked.

Natalie Franklin, fully dressed now in sports tweeds, crossed slowly to a seat beside the desk. Carter, his mouth a grim line, and still padded in his heavy clothing, snapped out, "Keep your hands on Ransome, and keep them on tight. He's slippery as a snake."

He laid the brass death-dealing tube gently on the desk. All eyes centered on it. Ransome regarded it with a beatific smile.

"Pretty, isn't it?" he asked conversationally.

Carter whirled on him. "You call murder pretty too, I suppose."

Ransome continued to smile. "We—ell," he said slowly, "It has to be done artistically, as I do."

"You confess to murdering Johnstone and those two sailors, then?" Carter pounded out.

Ransome raised his bushy eyebrows. "Of course." He turned his owlish regard on the detective's much-bundled body. "You know," he said softly, "I would have killed you, too, if I hadn't grown a bit careless. But you have a keen mind. I didn't expect you to insulate yourself against the sound waves."

Carter said slowly, "Sound waves, eh? I guessed some-thing like that."

Ransome nodded. "Yes, sound waves. Useful things they are, too." His smile became conceited. "I'm the music master. I know *all the notes.*"

Something in the mad, bland face of the prisoner drew the captain to the edge of his chair, narrowed Carter's gray eyes and sent a prickle of apprehension along his back.

"What—what do you mean?" Captain Franklin asked hoarsely.

Ransome's smile widened, his eyes glittered. He almost whispered, "I know the keynote of this ship!"

Carter stepped sharply forward, his hands reaching for the gloating face. *"You fiend!"*

The man threw back his head and laughed, a falsetto giggle. It sent chills through his listeners.

Captain Franklin said, "In heaven's name, what are you talking about?"

Carter whirled toward him.

"It means," he said, "that this maniac is threatening to destroy your ship with sound waves."

The captain snorted, moustaches bristling. "Destroy the *Frisconia* with a sound? Nonsense!"

Ransome was furious. "You doubt my power!" he screamed. "I will show you." His chest panted.

"Captain," Carter said seriously, "you must listen to this man. He has *murdered* with sound, don't forget that."

He whirled to Ransome, his voice sharp with hatred, but holding the respect that all strong men feel for an opponent worthy of their strength.

"What are your terms?" he asked shortly.

Ransome started to shrug, but the gripping hands of the sailors prevented. He glanced at the rough fists with a smile of sinister gentleness.

Captain Franklin's face was strained. "Carter," he asked hoarsely, "you believe this man?"

Carter jerked a nod, eyes never leaving the madman's face.

Franklin stared with truculent blue eyes at Ransome. "How," he sputtered, "how can you sink a ship with nothing but sound?"

Ransome eyed him with the glittering, unblinking stare of a madman. The silence of a full minute fell in the room and the breathing of the two sailors became hoarsely audible. Terror blanched their faces. Finally Ransome sighed.

"Very well, I guess I'll have to explain," he said, and with the bored, didactic manner of a teacher reviewing for the fiftieth time a well-known lesson. "You are all doubtless familiar with the way musical instruments like violins or guitars vibrate at the sound of a heavy voice, or nearby music? Yes, I thought so. Well, that is because the keynote of the instrument has been approximated."

Captain Franklin broke in skeptically, "You aren't comparing a ship and a violin, surely?"

**RANSOME SMILED** condescendingly. "Have patience, captain. There is another little lesson I'd like to call to mind. Remember in physics class—you did go to school, eh, captain?" the madman snickered at Franklin's red-faced indignation. "Well, in physics class you place two tuning forks of identical pitch on opposite sides-of the room and by touching one make the other vibrate. They have the same keynote. Well, in the same way—"

Captain Franklin interrupted, "Men and ships don't have tuning forks inside them!"

Ransome was slightly irritated. "If you don't keep quiet, your ship will sink before I get to the point."

One of the sailors gasped, "In God's name, captain—" Ransome turned an approving smile on him. The fellow shrank away, made a hurried sign of the cross with the hand that did not hold Ransome.

"Get on with it, Ransome. Hurry!" Carter urged. His fists were clenched at his sides.

Ransome said, "Oh, all right. You know that scientists have speculated for years on the destructive possibilities of determining the basic keynotes of skyscrapers and so on. Their theory was that if they could strike that note, strike it forcibly enough and with sufficient sustentation, it would shake the buildings to pieces. A German scientist—was Hecht his name?—achieved the fracture of thick glass with a tuning fork and a violin bow."

Carter leaned forward tensely. Ransome turned his owlish eyes toward him. "Ah, you have guessed it, I see!"

Carter nodded shortly, "You found the keynote of the muscles in the human body, and their contraction—"

Ransome broke in, "Exactly." His eyes glittered on the tube on the desk. He said, "There is a piece of thin steel inside that tube, nearly as long as the tube. That sliding piece on the side determines the note and a small electric battery causes continuous vibrations. By an intensive study of acoustics I have been able to make the stream of sound directional in intensity. It affects other people than the victim slightly, of course."

He frowned. "I hope I'll be able to perfect it someday, so that even this will be eliminated."

Carter rasped, "You won't live long enough to perfect anything, you murderer!"

**RANSOME RAISED** his bushy eyebrows. "You call it murder to remove that vermin, Johnstone? I've been planning this for years, biding my time to strike. My son was framed for a political crime, and for political reasons Johnstone refused to pardon him, although seven doctors certified the boy's death from tuberculosis if he stayed in prison. They were right. He died this morning—"

Carter heard a gasped breath and whirled to find Natalie Franklin limp in her chair. Franklin leaped to his feet, crashing his chair to the floor, went to her side.

"You fiend," he snarled. "Have you harmed my daughter?"

Ransome smiled gently, "Oh, I fancy she'll recover presently. This oration must have proved a bit trying."

Carter turned slowly back and stared at the man with narrowed eyes. "Yes, quite trying," he said softly. "Get on with your story."

"Ah yes, those sailors," Ransome went on. If it had not been for the glitter of his eyes, the smile would have been gentle. "They became curious about the brass tube which they saw me carrying along the deck. So I—" he shot forward his head like a striking snake. *"I showed them how it worked!"*

The words fell like lead in the room. The professor straightened slowly from his crouch, recovered his bland smile and glanced at the clock on the wall.

"My time is short," he resumed mildly, "I shall have to request that you unfasten my bonds."

Natalie had recovered slightly now. She sat erect, her face pale. Captain Franklin walked heavily around in front of his desk, his shoulders hunched. "I'll die before I'll turn you loose," he ground out. "You're a fiend from hell."

Carter frowned, gray eyes narrowed, lips thin, but Ransome only smiled more widely. "You're forgetting I can sink your ship. You're forgetting that while I was talking to you in the saloon, you heard my smaller vibrator. I had rigged it up with a time device in my cabin and timed my speech to coincide with it. A little trick to avert suspicion, which failed—" his eyes flashed sudden hate at Carter, "—thanks to my detective friend. Incidentally, I used it also to destroy the radio so my escape would be assured.

"Well, captain, I have hidden on your ship a giant vibrator and hooked it up with a time device. *It is tuned to the keynote of the Frisconia.*"

Captain Franklin's ruddy face drained slowly of blood. "Good God, Ransome, you mean—"

Ransome nodded, smiling gently. "My vibrator is timed to go off in twenty-five minutes, unless I reach it before that time. When it starts, your ship will shake itself to pieces. During that time everyone on board will be paralyzed." He giggled suddenly. "Terrible, isn't it, captain, to think of all those people drowning?"

The captain's voice trembled. "Take us to that vibrator."

Ransome raised his eyebrows. "I'm afraid you don't quite get the point, captain. There are certain little stipulations attached to my telling where the vibrator is."

Captain Franklin sagged into a chair. "Name them," he said.

"First," said Ransome, "you must drop this vibrator overboard. I will be generous and not demand to take it with me.

"Second, you must lower your motor launch and put me in it, free and unaccompanied, except—"

He paused and his glittering eyes glanced mockingly at the captain's strained face. Carter's eyes were slits of gray ice. He said, "You can't do that!"

Ransome's smile was evilly pleasant. "But you don't know yet what I'm asking," he protested.

The captain stared from Carter to Ransome with puzzled eyes.

"Please, please hurry," he urged.

Ransome's smile intensified. He shifted his eyes from the hate in Carter's face to where the girl sat hunched forward in her chair, swaying slowly from side to side.

Franklin jerked to his feet. "No! No! Not that! Anything but that!"

Ransome said mildly, "Natalie, your father is objecting to your going with me as a hostage."

**THE GIRL'S** head lifted slowly as he called her name. She stared at him uncomprehendingly, then hate flashed into her eyes. She jerked to her feet. "Cheat!" she spat out.

Ransome said, "I have offered to show your father the vibrator which will destroy the boat, provided he lets you go with me as hostage. Otherwise—" he paused, lips lifted again in that hideously gentle smile.

Natalie Franklin got slowly to her feet. Her face was white and without expression. She said dully, "Do what he says, father. I will go with him. You must think of your ship and your passengers."

Ransome said carelessly, "I won't harm her. I'll turn her loose when I reach shore. We're not far out. With extra petrol, I can make it easily."

Captain Franklin's face was haggard, his eyes burned deep in their sockets. His mouth was thin as a knife and his words came out with extreme effort. "You leave me no choice. Where is the vibrator?"

Ransome's perpetual smile was mocking.

"When I am safely in the boat, I will release a bottle tied to a string which you can haul aboard. A note in it will tell you where the vibrator is hidden. To stop it, just jerk loose an electric wire."

Franklin said hoarsely, "What guarantee have I that you will tell where the vibrator is and not trick me?"

Ransome shrugged. "None but my word. We have eighteen minutes to discuss the matter."

Carter said incisively, "We'll have to trust him, captain. There is no choice. I'll order the motor launch lowered."

## CHAPTER SIX
## DEATH'S FINALE

DAWN WAS breaking in red fury, the sea heaved sullenly, gray and ugly. The motor launch's engine drummed with muffled exhaust and Ransome stood in the slowly rising and falling stern.

"Remember!" he shouted. "No tricks, captain, or—?" He leveled a pistol at the ruddy gold head of Natalie Franklin.

The captain shouted hoarsely, "Hurry, man!"

Ransome laughed mockingly, but tossed overboard a bottle that glittered in the sunlight, and a seaman rapidly pulled in a line hand over hand, hauling it to the bridge.

The motor of the boat dropped a note and the launch began to move away. Captain Franklin snatched the bottle, smashing its neck on the railing and seizing the piece of paper it contained. He opened it with hands that he fought vainly to keep steady.

The launch was already a hundred yards away, gaining speed momentarily. Ransome stood on the deck, back to the cockpit, the gun clutched in his hand, his eyes fixed on the *Frisconia* rapidly dwindling behind him now.

Natalie Franklin was staring fixedly at the bottom of the boat. Neither of them saw the cowling of the motor lift slowly, nor saw a man's smooth black head and tall, compact body squirm out of the opening, saw Ken Carter wriggle free and stand erect. As he did that, his shadow fell across Natalie and she looked up sharply, muffling a cry that rose to her throat by shoving both hands against her mouth.

However small her outcry, Ransome caught it, and whirled, the pistol in his hand. Carter hesitated not a moment.

He sprang to the seat that ran along the port side of the cockpit and, as the gun swung that way, leaped again to the right side and then dived for Ransome's legs.

The pistol exploded, but the bullet went wild and before a second shot could be fired Carter was at grips with Ransome. He wrenched the pistol wrist savagely and the gun came free in his hand, but Ransome struck at the same instant and the weapon thumped on the deck and slid off into the sullen gray water.

Abruptly Ransome switched tactics and his fist drove into Carter's groin. Ken doubled up in agony and pitched backward into the cockpit of the boat. Ransome laughed triumphantly, bushy head thrown back. He fumbled in his pocket and drew out a small tube, a small brass tube like that larger one that had killed three men.

"Just a paralyzer," he jeered, "To make it easier to handle you. I tricked Captain Franklin, and—"

CARTER, BLANCHED with pain, struggled to his feet and reeled toward Ransome. Good Lord, could the madman mean he had not told where he had hidden the vibrator that would sink the ship? The tall detective staggered into a frantic charge, and Ransome squeezed the tube hurriedly before he had pointed it accurately. A piercing note shrilled around them, cutting into Carter's eardrums, stabbing into his brain, tightening his muscles, but in his desperate plunge he managed to seize the tube and twist its gaping muzzle, so the stream of hellish sound poured squarely at Ransome. The man let out a strangled cry, his face contorted horribly; his body knotted.

The eerie, pulsating note still vibrated in the air. Ransome's writhings jerked him free of Carter's enfeebled hands and the madman slithered overboard, sinking into the heaving, angry waters.

The stabbing, shrill note of the vibrator stopped, gone, it is to be hoped, from the world forever, but Carter still lay squirming helplessly on the floor of the deck, his body racked by pain.

The tension eased gradually and, weakly, he rolled over and sat up, still breathing in gasps. Presently this condition, too, was relieved, and he was able to raise himself up on the long seat that ran around the cockpit. He staggered up and spun the wheel, sent the launch racing toward the *Frisconia.*

Carter was thinking feverishly of the ship. If Ransome had tricked Franklin, had not told him where the vibrator was hidden, there was still a chance. If all electric power were cut off on the ship, it would stop the time device and the vibrator.

The girl sat across from him, chiseled features white and drawn. Carter said politely, "Sorry to break up your little plan of escape, Miss Franklin."

The girl's voice was wooden.

"Escape? I suppose it does look like that to you, but I do not care. Ransome probably was planning to kill me to protect himself when he got away from the ship. I knew that, but it made no difference, so long as father's ship is safe."

Carter jeered, "Really!"

"You don't believe me?" the girl shrugged. "Well, nothing makes any difference now. Ransome's son who died yesterday was my sweetheart, and Ransome tricked me into helping him kill Johnstone. He told me that Johnstone had the power of pardon up till last midnight, and got me to flirt with the sailor so he could reach Johnstone and—so he said—plead with him, forcibly if necessary, to pardon Frank. He told me that Frank was still alive. I'm sorry I tricked dad."

Carter shot a quick look at the ship, glanced at his watch. Two and a half minutes to zero hour. In two minutes they would be in hailing distance. He told the girl, "I shall not expose you. You were innocent in intent in helping Ransome to right what you considered a wrong, and you were ready to sacrifice yourself for the ship. I believe, too, that when you told Ransome I knew who the murderer was, you did it only so he could escape. I understand now your fainting in the cabin. That was the first news you had of your sweetheart's death."

The smile that had been so charming moved the girl's lips again, but it was wry and a little pitiful. She said, "You are generous."

Carter lifted her hand, saying, "Permit me," and kissed it. "It is not that I am generous. Just that I am myself a person of sentiment."

He straightened slowly and stepped back to the wheel. The *Frisconia* was a bare hundred yards away, still not shaken by that terrific, paralyzing hell's music.

He cupped his hands, "Ahoy, *Frisconia*, cut off all electric power!"

He could make out Captain Franklin's stocky figure on the bridge. The man's head was wagging vehemently. Carter shouted again and again without achieving any other result. He ran in against the *Frisconia's* side and clambered frantically up the ladder.

His watch told him there were only seconds left of that twenty-two minutes Ransome had said remained.

"In God's name, Captain Franklin, hurry," he panted.

The captain's face was beet-colored. He was cursing. He said, "That blank, blank, blank tricked us. His note said he didn't have any vibrator hidden aboard to sink the ship!"

# CITY OF CORPSES

AN ATTRACTIVE GIRL STUMBLED INTO A GHASTLY GRAVE, HER CREAMY SKIN TURNING A LIVID BLUE. TEN BLOCKS AWAY, A MAN DIED, BLUSHING BLUE. THE GRIM REAPER STALKED THE CITY WITH A BUCKET OF BLUE DEATH—AND PAINTED A LANDSCAPE OF STARK TERROR.... ALONE, BUCKING THIS MAD MARCH TO THE GRAVE, WAS KEN CARTER, THE DETECTIVE JUGGLER. COUNTLESS TIMES HAD CARTER JUGGLED LIFE AND DEATH—BUT NEVER THE FATE OF MILLIONS!

# CHAPTER ONE
# BLUE DOOM

**THE JUBILANCE** went out of Ken Carter's long-legged stride. Instead of twirling in the sunlight, his cane tapped somberly along at his side.

Fifth Avenue, gay with modish shops, had become for the lean-faced detective a place of sinister aspect. Even the July sun that bounced hot beams off the concrete seemed to have drawn a jaundiced veil across its face.

Ken Carter braced his well-knit body, threw back his head and his brown tailored shoulders resolutely. Still that prickling in his scalp continued. He moved his tongue in a dry mouth. The air tasted of death. He swore softly at himself.

Nobody else seemed to be worried. That young girl ahead now, tap-tapping high heels vigorously along, straight young shoulders jaunty beneath the white-flecked elegance of a silver fox.

What the devil! Was he seeing things, or *had that girl reeled?* She was not more than ten feet ahead of him and he frowned, keen gray eyes upon her back. There it was again! Her shoulders quivered, jerked. Her pace grew unsteady. Carter quickened his stride. The girl's daintily shod foot tripped, the golden blond of her head sagged.

Ken Carter sprang forward—too late. Tottering, reeling, the girl stumbled, recovered, stumbled again and plunged to the pavement on her face! Carter's outreaching hand just missed her arm. He dropped to his knees, his lean face grim.

Even so, fingers on her arm, he hesitated, that tingling warning of death racing down his neck. He forced himself to turn the girl gently over on her back. He snatched off his hat to fan her. The girl's lips were parted, her breath rapid, gasping. It was labored, as if she forced her lungs to work against some great oppression. Then, abruptly, the girl's breathing stopped.

It was as quick as that. One moment her breath whistled in her throat, the next moment there was a fearful silence, and no movement at all.

Frowning fine black brows above the intent gray of his eyes, Carter laid the girl gently down to the pavement, felt her pulse. There was none! He sat back on his heels, staring at her face, ran his hand worriedly up over his peaked forehead, into his dull hair.

Death. He had felt it tingle in the air and here it was, in the beautiful form upon the hot sidewalk of Fifth Avenue. Beautiful? Carter's gray eyes tightened suddenly. His body stiffened with horror, with crawling, cold horror. That bluish tinge in the

girl's lips! Was it *deepening?* Good God, it was!

As his eyes fixed with a terrible fascination upon them, the blue spread over the white clearness of her face, slowly at first, then rapidly until the entire countenance, from the golden blond of her hair to the soft V-neck of her dress was a *horrible, livid blue!*

**A WOMAN'S** scream quivered in the air, and Ken Carter jerked his head up, for the first time aware that a circle of men and women had crowded around him. The familiar swish and drone of automobiles along Fifth Avenue became audible again, but strangely unreal. The faces of the crowd about him were drawn and white. Mouths gaped.

In the background a rough voice ordered. "Move on with yez now!" and a policeman shouldered his way through the crowd.

He said gruffly: "Here, here, what is all this?" and then looked down at the girl. *"Holy Mother!"* he gasped.

Ken Carter pulled out a silk handkerchief and spread it gently over the horror that had been a girl's lovely face. The blue showed its sinister tint even through the cloth. He snapped to his feet, told the policeman peremptorily:

"Call an ambulance! Hurry!"

The cop squinted a fat florid face, grunted; "Sure, and you'll come along with me. You're the one with the girl when she fell."

"All right, all right," Carter jerked out impatiently. "But move, man, move! You can't leave this girl's body lying out on the sidewalk like this."

He plowed angrily into the crowd, jostling with his broad, strong shoulders. It was a relief to have action after the horror of that death. He thrust on, stopped suddenly with people muttering angrily at him. In the distance, the quaver of a siren swelled. The clang of a bell mingled with it.

Carter turned back, stood guard over the dead girl, brown felt hat down over scowling brows, gray eyes keen with thought. The girl's small white hand was clenched in agony against her throat, the light stain of nicotine on her fingers pitiful in its suggestion of bright life.

**THE CLANGOR** of the ambulance grew. Carter glimpsed its gleaming blue sides.

It jerked up short at the curb, the back doors burst open. A young interne, white-coated, fought through the crowd.

"Too late, doctor," Carter told him with clipped words. The young interne dropped swiftly to his knees, mouth hard beneath a straw-colored mustache. Then his movement slowed. He lifted the edge of the handkerchief almost fearfully, dropped it again with a shudder.

"My God!" Carter heard his hoarse voice. "Another one!"

Carter crouched beside him. "Another one? What do you mean?"

The doctor glanced at him out of the tail of his eyes, said nothing. The cop's belligerent voice, ordering, "Move on now, move on, I tell you!" cut into the silence between them, and the ruddy-faced ambulance driver shouldered through with a stretcher. The two bore the girl's poor body to the ambulance.

Carter frowned a moment after them, then strode over and said, "Listen, doctor, I—"

The interne slammed shut the doors, hurried toward the driver's seat. He said brusquely, "I can't tell you anything, mister!"

"Listen," Carter urged, "I saw this girl fall, and I was there when she died. Her breathing—"

"Yes?" the interne's voice was suddenly interested. "What was it like?"

Carter described the death and the doctor nodded slowly. "Yes," he said, "yes, every one I've seen today—"

"How many?" Carter asked quietly.

The interne muttered, "Ten." He looked up into Carter's intense face, eyes frowning, face drawn. "I'm worried," he admitted. "It looks—it looks like a plague. God, it sounds like the old days of the Black Plague in London!"

Carter shook his head sharply. "The symptoms aren't the same."

"You're a doctor, sir?"

"Just a student of medicine, among other things," said Carter. "I'm a private detective."

Carter looked down thoughtfully. Fingers bit suddenly into his arm. He jerked his head up. The interne's face was white beneath the straw-colored mustache. His left arm was pointing.

"Good Lord!" he gasped. "Another one!"

Carter whirled. A man reeled past. His mouth was open, his chest panting. His eyes had a glazed, unseeing look.

Carter felt again the tingle of horror he had known when he had bent over the girl.

He forced reluctant muscles into action, sprang toward the man, dragged him toward the ambulance. The man sagged to the pavement. The doctor snatched a hypodermic.

Carter tore at the fastenings of the man's shirt, watched his face. The lips were already blue. For a moment, after the hypodermic had gone home, the breathing was a little easier; then it rasped sharply again, grew hoarse in the victim's throat. The lips opened and sound rasped out.

"Lu—lu—luc—"

Then the breathing stopped. Like a horrible blush, the blue spread its livid, sinister hue over the man's face. Carter and the interne stared with horror-widened eyes into each other's faces. The interne sprang erect, dousing his hands with antiseptic.

**CARTER STARED** up narrowly into his eyes. "Luc!" he quoted slowly. "Now what in God's name could that mean?"

They snaked a second stretcher out of the ambulance, put the man in beside the girl. Sweat stood out in beads on the face of the interne. He dug in his pocket for a pack of cigarettes, offered them. Carter dug out his own monogrammed brand from a black and platinum case.

The doctor muttered: "I ought to be getting back to the hospital."

"If you don't mind," Carter said, "I'll go along. I'd like a talk with the autopsy surgeon."

The interne said, "Sure," and started forward beside the sleek blue body of the ambulance. The driver already had clambered to the seat. Carter, pulling at his cigarette, glanced over the gay expanse of Fifth Avenue.

Passers-by turned curious eyes toward the stationary ambulance, but few that had seen the two die still lingered. Two dead, and ten more. Even so many would make no difference to the city at large, but dozens, scores, falling with this blue death, with funeral fires ringing the city in smoke, with—

Carter snapped his cigarette away, slapped his cane against his leg, and started forward. Then his hand about the cane became a white fist, and his body tensed. *The young interne was clawing the side of his ambulance, his fingers like talons!*

Hoarse sounds rasped from him, and Carter sprang to his side, laid him on the pavement. The interne's eyes were strained wide. There was no vision in them.

His hands tore at his white jacket, at his shirt. "Nitro," he mumbled.

Carter gave him the liquid, filled a hypodermic, ears tortured by the whistling of breath. Then he heard the sound no more. There was a tension throughout his body. He had to force himself to look down at the young doctor. *His face was dyed with the blue death!*

Carter snapped to his feet, jerked up the doctor's limp body, shoved it into the front seat of the ambulance.

"Drive for the hospital, man!" he shouted.

## CHAPTER TWO

## THE MORGUE

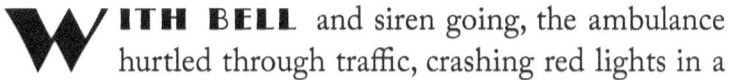ITH BELL and siren going, the ambulance hurtled through traffic, crashing red lights in a

wild dash across town. Every moment's delay might mean another lethal stab of this eerie blue death.

In a moment of partial silence, when their own siren died to a purr, Carter could hear the frantic shriek of other ambulances on runs. His face grew white and grim, and his mouth a tight line.

Buildings rushed backward on either side, and automobiles rushed frantically to the curbs from the ambulance's noisy path. It whirled beneath the elevated line, shot on across Eleventh Street and squealed brakes into a skidding curve as the driver shot into the arched entrance of the hospital and into the courtyard inside. He snubbed to a halt at a doorway.

Carter leaped out, dashed into the hospital. A blonde nurse, in starched white, jerked to her feet.

"Oh," she gasped, "not more of those—"

"Yes," Carter snapped. "The Blue Death. Where's the head surgeon?"

She wrung usually competent hands before her and wailed, "I don't know, I don't know. Every doctor in the hospital is working on the ambulances, going out on these horrible calls. We have over a hundred bodies in the morgue now."

"Find the head surgeon," Carter ordered. "It's life and death. I tell you, we must find him."

The girl cried helplessly, "But I can't, I can't." Carter seized her by the shoulders and shook her until her hair spilled down.

"Snap out of it," he ordered, frosty-eyed.

Gradually the nurse calmed. "Now," Carter ordered, "Find the head surgeon!"

An ambulance clanged in the street, droned hollowly into the courtyard, but the man who ran inside was an interne, not the head surgeon.

"Two more!" he rasped, and a white-coated orderly rushed in from the next room, waving a paper slip.

"Waverly and MacDougall!" he yelled.

The doctor was gone.

The nurse said helplessly, "They're all like that."

Carter turned to the orderly. "Listen, there are three dead in that ambulance out there, including the doctor." He turned to the nurse. "Telephone?"

She gestured toward a niche behind her desk, and Carter pounded to it, snatched up the receiver and grated: "City Hall! The mayor's office, right away!"

The operator's voice presently came back. "I'm sorry, sir, the line is busy."

Carter snapped, "Give me the traffic manager!" Got him and bullied and cajoled until Mayor Miller's pompous, slightly irritated voice boomed over the wire.

Carter identified himself rapidly and said: "Listen, you probably already know about this Blue Death."

Miller growled over the wire: "Do I know about it!"

Carter barked: "Every doctor here has completely lost his head, and is dashing about picking up corpses. You've got to get hold of the chief medical examiner and have an autopsy, chemical analysis, and a toxicologist examination immediately on one of these bodies.

"It's a thousand times more important to find out what is causing these deaths than it is to pick up dead people. Will you see that an order to that effect goes out?"

The mayor growled: "You're rather peremptory, young fellow, but you're the first man today who has had anything to suggest."

Carter broke in impatiently: "You'll do that at once?"

Miller growled, "Yeah, if these damned calls will let up long enough," and slammed down the receiver.

**CARTER DARTED** out of the office, pounded across the echoing courtyard to Eleventh Street, flagged a taxi. Grating out the number of his apartment on lower Fifth Avenue, he sat tensely, black brows drawn over intent gray eyes, tapping an initialed cigarette.

A hundred dead at one hospital! The symptoms of the Blue Death corresponded with those of no known disease, but at home he had a medical library which he felt sure would yield a clue to this horror if anything like it ever before had been known.

The taxi swung out of Tenth Street into Fifth Avenue and whirled to the curb. Carter sprang out, tossing a bill to the driver, dropping a barely puffed cigarette. He strode into the lobby and a man behind a desk said: "That's him now."

Carter whirled. A girl in sleek gray minced toward him. She had a small oval face in which brown eyes were large and serious. She smiled faintly and said hesitantly:

"I'm so glad you've come back."

Carter bowed politely, "I'm afraid I can't possibly see you today."

The girl had full, perfectly formed lips. She caught the lower one between white teeth, and cried out softly: "Oh, you must see me, you must! It's life and death to me."

Carter frowned, his face elongated by the twin peaks of his forehead. He took in her petite figure in its draped gown of heavy gray silk, rich black fur about her shoulders. Her face, beneath the cocky slant of a small black straw was white and drawn. She said slowly:

"I'm Sally O'Day."

Carter bowed again. "Miss O'Day," he murmured. His face was impassive, but his mind was racing. Sally O'Day! Her name had been linked many times in the Broadway gossip columns with that of the Mayor, Bertram Miller, whose secretary she was.

"Come up," Carter agreed, and crossed in three strides to the elevator, bowed her in. He stood frowning in silence while the elevator sighed up ten floors.

Conducting the girl to his apartment that looked out of the back of the building, he used a latch key, glancing up at the crack along the top. The thread he always fixed across the crack when he went out had been snapped. His apartment had been entered!

Going for a morning stroll, he had not thought it necessary to carry his automatic. He began talking cheerily to the girl about nothing in particular and snapped the door open, bowing her in. The living room they entered was furnished in luxurious but tasteful style, and Carter waved the girl to a seat on a Victorian settee while he crossed to his desk and secretly pocketed an automatic.

He sat then so that his back was toward the wall and he commanded all entrances.

"Now, Miss O'Day," he prompted.

The girl said rapidly: "We are quite alone?"

Carter nodded, suspicion at the corner of his eyes, and the girl sighed comfortably and leaned back and took a cigarette from her purse. Crossing her knees, she revealed legs shapely in gauze-thin gray silk.

Carter snapped fire to a lighter, held it while she sucked yellow flame to her cigarette. He tripped the lighter out, stood staring down at the girl, hands thrust deep into his pockets.

"Did you bring me some message from the mayor?"

The girl's large eyes widened. "How did you know?"

Carter gestured impatiently. "Please—I am in somewhat of a hurry!"

Sally O'Day nodded. "All right," she said. "What I came for is: the mayor and I have been receiving threatening letters from people who do not sign the letters at all. They want $10,000 or else, they say, they will kidnap me and—" She dropped her eyes to the cigarette she held in her lap, "—well, do unpleasant things to me."

Carter frowned. "I'm sorry. I have no time for the case."

The girl's upflung glance was startled. Her quivering lips opened in a circle of dismay. "Oh, but you must!" she said. "Bertie said you would!"

Carter's mouth was a thin, hard line. "I had the pleasure of talking with *Bertie* this morning," he ground out, "and I'm afraid my time is otherwise occupied."

"But this," exclaimed the girl, "is a matter of life and death—my life and death!" She jumped up, put an appealing small hand on Carter's arm. "Please, for my sake, won't you?"

Carter said grimly: "I must ask you to excuse me. People are dying all over the city, and, perhaps foolishly, I regard their salvation more important than your own. I am, you see—" bowing stiffly—"a man of sentiment."

The girl gasped, her eyes narrowed angrily.

"You'll be sorry for this." Her voice suddenly became coarse.

Carter said easily: "I'm sure I shall," and guided her somewhat forcibly toward the door. She jerked her elbow free. "Keep your hands off me!"

Carter, smiling thinly: "With pleasure!"

The girl clicked indignant heels across the hardwood floor and out.

Carter shut the door sharply, made a thorough search of his apartment, but found no one hidden, nothing missing. He shrugged at his fears, doffed his coat, and draped it carefully over a hanger in a hall closet, shoving its bottom past the tanks of an oxy-acetylene torch outfit. He thought again that the thing should be carted back to his office, then strode swiftly into his study, which opened off a bedroom.

Curios of his travel, sombreros, lassos, Chinese silks, a Moro knife, decorated the walls above long shelves of books. He selected a thick leather-backed tome and dropped into a deep chair behind a desk. Light from an open window came over his shoulder.

He reached absently toward a humidor of cigarettes, missed it and glanced at the leather-covered can. He was puzzled. Had it been moved? His hand started out again. Halfway toward its goal, it froze.

His sharp eyes studied a hairlike mark upon the side of the humidor. The lines crossed both top and lower portion of the humidor, but the lines' ends did not coincide. They were nearly an inch apart, yet when he had left, he had placed those lines exactly together!

CARTER LAID his book down and cautiously opened the humidor. Nothing seemed to have been disturbed. The number of cigarettes was exactly the same. He frowned, eyes narrow, lips firm and angry. He dumped the cigarettes on an ash tray and set fire to them. A pungent, chemical odor that knifed his nostrils filtered out into the room and he hurriedly raked out a dozen or so and put them back in the humidor. Doped or poisoned, they undoubtedly were; a chemist could discover which.

Frowning at the humidor upon his desk, Carter lounged back in his chair and was reaching for the book again when the phone buzzed softly.

He jerked up the receiver. "Carter speaking." Shrill sounds rasped in his ear and his hand tightened fiercely about the instrument. When he spoke, his voice was kindly but strained.

"Do everything possible for Jed's family. I'm footing the bill, of course." His voice suddenly went hoarse. "And I'll catch the crooks behind this Blue Death if it's the last thing I ever do."

He hung up slowly, staring straight ahead with sombre eyes in which cold anger burned. His assistant in his detective agency, Jed Harris, was dead of the Blue Death.

For long minutes Carter sat like that, then he caught up the book as if it were a weapon and began again. His black brows drew down in concentration. Half an hour later he cried out: "That's it!" and phoned Mayor Miller. Finally Miller's pompous voice answered.

"Listen, Mr. Mayor," Carter shot into the mouthpiece, "this Blue Death is not a plague, it's poison! And I've got a line on the kind of poison being used."

The mayor's voice rasped into the receiver. "The hell you have!"

Carter said slowly: "Have your surgeons examine the victims for a lack of red corpuscles in the blood. If they find there is, we'll be sure of the poison; and we can do something about it quickly."

Miller shouted over the wire: "That's fine, young fellow. Listen, I'm offering you ten thousand dollars here and now to work on this case. Okay?"

Carter smiled grimly. "Try to keep me from working on the case."

He returned tensely to his studies. Now and then he ran his hand up over the peaked forehead, into his dull hair. He muttered words like "exalgen," "mathacetine," "antipyretics." He put the book down, jumped up and hurriedly selected another, pored over that.

A sudden sound snapped up his head. He jerked about toward the door. A man stood there, a man in flashy, tight-fitting suit, a gray fedora pulled down over his eyes.

Carter saw these things but did not notice them; what he noticed, what narrowed his gray eyes and brought his black brows into a frown, was what the man held in his right hand. It was a gun, and its black muzzle was aimed directly at Carter's heart!

## CHAPTER THREE

## POISON SMOKE

**K**EN CARTER said calmly, gray eyes icy: "Good afternoon. To what do I owe the pleasure of your visit?" As he spoke, he swiveled his chair around toward his desk and put a hand slyly toward a drawer.

"Both hands on the desk!" The gunman snapped, and as Carter spread long fingers upon the wood, the man relaxed slightly. "You're a cool one all right. Get your hat and coat. We're going places."

"And doing what?"

The gunman waggled his square, heavy jaw and said: "That's my business. Get the hat and coat."

Carter smiled suavely into his visitor's ugly eyes. If the gunman had known the detective better, that smile would have been a flag of warning. Ken Carter got slowly to his feet, hands still on the desktop, gestured toward the humidor. "Help yourself to a smoke," he said, "then you can follow me while I slide into the required garments."

"Now I call that handsome," the man said. He lit up and with a nonchalantly held gun followed Carter into the next room while he opened a closet for his coat.

"No funny business," the gangster warned.

"I never go in for funny business," Carter returned gravely, shrugging into his coat. His eyes were narrowed on the beady gaze of the other. His body was alert, his weight on his toes. Years of juggling on the stage had taught him to analyze action in split-second divisions, had taught him swift, agile movement. Now he waited for the effects of the drug or poison he was confident was in the cigarette.

When it began to act, there was apt to be a moment of fast action. Abruptly he blinked. The breath of the gangster was speeding up. He detached the cigarette from his lip, glared at it suspiciously, and tossed it into a corner.

"Sa-ay, what kind of a smoke is that?"

"My own private blend," Carter told him lightly. "It has a good bit of Latakia in it. I should have warned you."

He was edging forward while he spoke, hands apparently lax at his side, but ready to flash into instantaneous action.

"Tastes like a reefer," the gangster muttered, then anger flamed into his eyes. His breath became hoarse. "You've tricked me, you—"

The gun flashed up, but Carter, timing movements to split seconds, ducked under its flaming crash, came up inside the man's guard and smashed his fist to his chin. The gangster arched backward, crashed over a chair.

He lay with his breath whistling in his throat. It mounted to a racing rattle, stopped. As the detective watched, that never-failing tingle of alarm trickling cold fingers up his back, the Blue Death spread its indigo blush across the gangster's face!

A cold smile twisted Carter's mouth. The death others had planned for him had overtaken one of their number. But it proved one thing conclusively. The deaths were the work of an organized group of men, or of one man heading such a gang. And that gang was on his trail!

He moved with long-legged alertness to his phone, called police to come and get the body. The sergeant's voice was empty of emotion, as if much tragedy had blunted his senses.

"You'll have to wait your turn. There's five hundred of these blue deaths already."

**FIVE HUNDRED!** Carter whistled amazement, ran his hand worriedly up over the peaks of his forehead, into his dull smooth hair. Five hundred dead. And only he, of all the city, had a suspicion of the causes behind these deaths, of the way they were accomplished, and the action he must force on the city would have to be jammed down Miller's throat personally. He'd like that!

Carter's thin, fighting smile played about his lips. He patted his gun in his pocket, yanked a brown Stetson down over his eyes, and strode from the apartment, raced to the street, shouting: "Taxi! Taxi!"

A yellow cab swerved to the curb. Carter started toward it, and fingers dug into his arm!

He whirled about, clenched fist flashing upward, but checked just in time. The man who grasped his arm was panting hoarsely, his lips were already blue with the approach of death.

Carter seized him by both shoulders. "Quick, man, what kind of cigarettes do you smoke?"

The man stared with glazing eyes, gasped: "Luckfield," and sagged to the pavement. Death brushed a blue sponge across his face.

Carter glanced up for his taxi. It had darted away. Women and men ran screaming from the corpse on the sidewalk.

Carter ran after them, found another taxi, hurled himself in. "Quick! The mayor's office! Twenty dollars if you make it in two minutes!"

The taxi screamed around a corner on skidding rubber and raced down Fifth Avenue, across the park, darted over and ripped down Rialto Street, skidded to a stop before the City Hall. Carter was out almost before the brakes had clamped on, spinning a twenty dollar bill into the man's hand. His feet stung as he slapped lunging along the pavement. He caught his balance, raced for the City Hall.

A policeman sprang into his path, shouting: "Hey, you!" but Carter ducked past him, plunging into the building. He knew where the mayor's office was located. His fist hit the door like a brick, slammed it open, and he plunged into the midst of a startled group of men.

They leaped to their feet, shouting hoarsely. Carter, his haste and excitement strangely at odds with his ordered svelte clothing, stood panting in the doorway.

A white-haired man on the far side of the room was smoking. Carter gasped: "Drop that cigarette!"

**THE MAN** stared blankly, and Carter hurled across the room, snatched the cigarette and threw it away. He whirled toward the group then.

Mayor Miller had reared his pompous bulk at the head of the table. Carter whirled toward him.

"I'm Ken Carter," he said, "the detective you hired to end the Blue Death. I have found how it is spread."

Miller leaned forward, mouth agape in a fat red face. He said in a hoarse voice:

"You have found how the Blue Death is spread?"

Carter gulped down his panting breath, and said: "Yes. Through cigarettes, through tobacco! Broadcast it to the newspapers, over the radios. Send the police around to stop all sale of tobacco at once!"

Miller stared at him and shook his ponderous head slowly. "That's ridiculous," he said.

"Ridiculous?" Carter slapped across the floor and pounded on the table. "Let me tell you what has happened."

And he told how the doctor in the ambulance had died after smoking, how the poisoned cigarettes had been planted in his own apartment, how the gunman had died by one instead of himself. How the man on the sidewalk had died. He pounded the top of the table.

"It's Luckfield cigarettes that do it. But there may be other brands poisoned, too. You must broadcast this order at once. Every second means more deaths."

The incoming mayor, Walker Hines, the man who in a few days would take over the office of the great city of Cornwall, turned a thin-nosed face toward Carter.

"That is absolutely ridiculous," he said.

The man from whom Carter had snatched a cigarette, a white-haired man with a white mustache, a big city politician, came forward with pale face.

"You say cigarettes cause the deaths—the *Blue Death?*" and the man said: "But man, that is impossible!" His breath was panting, hoarseness was in his voice. Carter snapped, "My God, man, have you any whisky here?"

A flask was offered in a shaking hand—too late. It was always too late with the Blue Death. It already tinged his lips. As he sagged toward the floor, men shrank from him, shrank from the indigo of the plague upon his countenance, strangely doleful beneath the bristling white mustache. The city's leading politician, dead, was a terrifying thing to them.

Carter whirled toward the others. "Will you believe now?"

**MILLER, SAGGING** his weight upon his arms on the table so that his shoulders hunched up like a strange bird, said: "Yes, we believe!" and groped for his telephone, shouted orders.

He straightened finally from his frantic work and Carter was lounging in a chair, head lolling back against the wall, eyes nearly closed.

Miller crossed to him pompously. "You have saved the city from a fearful thing, my man," he said. "I'm putting you in charge of all the police as a special commissioner."

Carter, his lean face weary, said, "All right, but this is only the beginning. We have saved a few lives, that is all. Don't think that whoever did this will stop now. We haven't checkmated the terror—only checked it."

Another pompous politician waddled up to Carter.

"I will give you a hundred thousand dollars," he said raspingly, "if you will capture this Terror, rid the city of this Blue Death."

Carter said wearily: "If you mean that, post a certified check. I've a notion I'm going to need a considerable rest after this thing is over."

He urged his tired body to his feet. "If you will have police check on tobacco thefts recently, they will find that two loads, including Luckfield cigarettes, were stolen in quick succession, and that in the second case the truckload of tobacco was found apparently intact."

Carter sent out for food, sat with the mayor at his desk. A secretary announced Sally O'Day, and the girl strolled jauntily in. At sight of Carter, stiffened and stopped.

"Come, my dear, you're not still angry with Mr. Carter? He has just saved the city."

Carter rose from the desk and bowed.

"Certainly I forgive him," the girl said, her large eyes lustrous in the small pale oval of her face, "Since it's you who ask me to, Bertie."

Carter said bitingly: "Honored, I'm sure."

Miller snapped to his feet. "What do you mean?" he rasped out.

"I am merely implying," Carter explained, "that it is no signal honor to be thanked by the mistress of a mayor who is being kicked out of office for his grafting."

Miller scowled, his red face suffused with angry blood, but his answer was singularly subdued. "I didn't want the renomination," he growled.

Carter said softly: "Of course not."

**AS THE** day drew on toward evening, the Blue Death was reported less and less frequently to the mayor's office, where Ken Carter awaited the news.

The politicians had moved into City Hall, and there Bertram Miller had invited his successor, Walker Hines, to share office with him, to help the battle against the Terror.

As the deaths grew fewer and fewer, the spirits of the politicians lightened, and finally at eight o'clock, when no fatalities had been reported for an hour, Carter went to a nearby hotel to sleep. A check-up by police had revealed the accuracy of his prediction that a stolen tobacco truck had been recovered, and they were bending every effort to locate the thieves, but Carter had little hope of their success.

He arose early, long-legging across to police headquarters, where the first report of any new deaths necessarily would be reported. No word had been received.

Carter strolled to a window. It was the moment before dawn, and the heavens had turned a delicate periwinkle blue. Usually that sky was the one that Ken Carter loved best, but not this morning—this morning, that blue vault seemed a reflection of the faces of all those corpses, victims of the Blue Death. Carter shuddered and turned away, and a telephone jangled.

The desk clerk cried out, "Ten people just fell dead in Madison Square! *The Blue Death again!*"

After that, the bell rang continuously. By noon eight hundred more had died, with their blue-tinted faces turned up to the sky. The city was mad with terror.

Business was at a standstill. People walked furtively through sunny streets, their pale, frightened faces strangely at odds with the bright summer weather. Each man stared askance at his neighbor, for despite Carter's broadcast statement that poison in cigarettes was causing death, the cry of plague was raised every time a man fell dead.

He had been unable to find the source of this new outbreak of the Blue Death. He insisted some new way of distributing the poison had been found. Police were frantically at work, trying to trace this new outbreak. Chemists were laboring to discover the poison, for despite the lead Carter had given them, they still had been unable to determine its exact nature.

Carter finally, wearily, left the mayor's office at one o'clock to go to lunch, striding across the open square around City Hall. The drone of motors struck his ears, and glancing up, he saw a low-flying tri-motor plane. It was far below the legal safety limit, skimming the tops of the skyscrapers.

As it neared City Hall, a stentorian voice bellowed from the ship, the same loud-speaking device that had been used many times for advertising. This time the voice seemed hollow, seemed to boom and ring with terrifying volume in Carter's ears. Everywhere people stopped in their tracks, turning up a sea of frightened faces.

"Listen, my slaves," bellowed the huge, pompous voice, "listen, slaves of the city of fear, this is the Blue Terror speaking. Tonight, at eight o'clock, your radios will tell you how the Blue Death may be driven from your city. Listen well, oh slaves, to the radio at eight o'clock."

Carter heard the message, dashed back for a telephone and bellowed orders for police planes to fly after this terror that dared to flaunt its identity in the faces of the populace it was decimating.

Hundreds of planes took the air. But the ship that had thundered its dread message had slanted sharply upward, its three motors roaring, and long before the first pursuing plane could take the trail, it had vanished into the vault of the sky. And the Blue Death still stalked like the grim reaper himself through the streets, and hundreds still died, and people slunk along like cur dogs that have been lashed for more reason they did not understand.

# CHAPTER FOUR
# DEATH SPEAKS

**I**T WAS a tense, terrorized group that gathered at the home of Bertram Miller that night to listen to the voice of the Blue Terror over the radio. Miller was ex-mayor now. He had retired ahead of time so the new city administration could cope with the panic sweeping the city. Mayor Hines, his thin-nosed face intent, sat with the rest.

Sally O'Day was there, drawing aimless circles with her forefinger upon the crimson silk of her evening gown, draping over long, shapely thighs. She was dressed for this terrible speech as for a ball. Death, her jaunty grace said, would not catch her sloppy or unprepared!

Four radios had been installed in the room, tuned on widely different wave-lengths, for it was a curious thing about the announcement of the Blue Terror that it had stated no spot on the radio dial at which its announcement could be heard.

Arrangements had been made with Washington that at 7:55 all stations in the country would go dead.

Bertram Miller, his fat face seamed, glanced time and again at his watch.

The sudden cessation of the radio babble at 7:55 was like the last gasp of a man dying of the Blue Death. The group in the room stared into one another's countenances.

Police Commissioner Rover, gruff and white-haired, a man risen from the ranks, was impassive, but now and then his high collar seemed to choke him, for he ran a finger between its sharp edge and his corded throat.

Sally O'Day glanced up from the meaningless circles on her knee and asked:

"Isn't it almost time?" Her voice started loud and finished in a whisper.

In that silent voice of the ether, squeals of heterodyning radios could be heard. Carter glanced at his watch, found it lacked but fifteen seconds of the appointed hour, and leaned forward to twirl the dials. The whine of a station's carrying waves shrilled into the silence, and a deep-toned, pompous voice like that that had thundered from the plane spoke:

"My slaves," it began slowly.

The words weighed like drops of ice pelting on the hearts of those who listened. Truly they were slaves! Slaves of terror that knew no bounds, a terror in which the fear of death blended with the panic of the unknown, of death that struck in horrid form.

"My slaves," the voice repeated, "relieving the city of Cornwall of the Blue Death is a simple matter. Ten million dollars ransom is all that is required. Get the money ready in small bills, not in series, and have it at City Hall. Then put a flag of my color—blue—upon the flagstaff of the City Hall, and I will tell you how the money is to be paid into my hands. When I have the money, and not before, the terror of the Blue Death will be lifted from Cornwall."

Miller jumped to his feet, his face almost apoplectic with rage.

"Ten million dollars!" he screamed. "We won't pay it! We won't!"

Carter sat calmly and looked up under lowered brows at him. Mayor Hines did not move, and Sally turned her large lustrous eyes toward Miller's face. The police commissioner cleared his throat, ran a gnarled finger along inside his collar.

He said: "Twenty-two of my boys died today."

Carter thought: "And one of mine," and there was an ugly light at the back of his gray eyes as he looked at Miller. "You're getting off cheap!" he said sharply. "Better get the money together at once and run up the blue flag."

Hines spoke up presently, tugging at his thin, long nose: "Why didn't we think to try radio message finders on that message? Locate where it came from."

Carter said: "We did!"

**CARTER STRODE** to a telephone in the hall, called a number.

"Carter speaking," he said. "Where did you locate that message?... I see. Very far?... Planes got off all right, I suppose? We should be getting reports within an hour's time, then.... Okay, thank you."

He turned from the phone, started down the dim hall, and stopped, eyes grimly amused. Sally was in the hall, her bright red dress a cry in the darkness, and there was a man with her, his arms about her. The man was not Miller. He had a long, tapered nose—Mayor Hines.

Carter sauntered forward and paused for a moment in the doorway. The two apparently thought themselves concealed in the shadows.

"Rats, I have heard, always desert a sinking ship," Carter said, "but I shall not betray you. I am, myself, a man of sentiment."

He passed into the main room. Miller was still on his feet, declaiming against paying the money.

"Calm down, Miller," Carter growled. "You don't think this message was sent privately to us, do you? Every man in the town who has a radio was listening in and it was sent over all wave-lengths. If you refuse to pay, the people will riot at your doors, drag you down the streets. There is no question of not paying. We must pay!"

A dead-pan butler bowed formally at the door "Beg pardon, sir, but the reporters want to come in."

Carter gestured assent, and the butler went out. There was an abrupt crash of glass from the window and a rock bounced into the middle of the carpet and spun there. Miller stared at it stupidly. Police Commissioner Rover jerked to his feet, his old face angry.

Carter said: "The people have spoken! If you want to hear more emphatic words, I suggest you go out on the porch and tell them you are not going to pay the money."

There was a howling murmur of voices in the street. Now and then a cry stood out sharply. There were thumps against the porch, more rocks being thrown.

"Go on out and talk to them, Miller!" Carter urged. "Calm the mob!"

Miller let his heavy, pompous body sink into the chair. "They don't want me," he muttered. "They turned me down at the last election. It's Hines they want."

The butler came back and bowed with his blank face, and a dozen reporters filed by him. Carter said, "Ask Mr. Hines to step in, please," and turned to the reporters.

"Mr. Miller," he said, "is against paying the ten million."

Miller ground out, "I'm against any form of connivance with criminals."

A reporter with a pale face, heavy shadows beneath his eyes, said softly, "Sure, sure, Miller, you always were."

Miller jumped to his feet, shouting. The reporter said gently, "Nuts," and turned to Carter.

"What's the decision of this august assembly?" he demanded.

**CARTER MET** the sophisticated young eyes with mild amusement, ran his hand up over his peaked forehead and through his dull hair. "At present," Carter said, "Mr. Hines, the mayor, is consulting the boss. When he comes back, he will tell us what our Board of Aldermen will do about the matter."

There was no amusement in what he said. It was a calm acceptance of fact. The reporter nodded. "Try radio triangulation?" he asked.

"Police planes are on the way now. We spotted the broadcast from a boat, apparently about fifty miles at sea."

The reporter raised brows. "Fool stunt," he said, "sending a message from a boat. Where is it?"

Carter said: "It probably isn't. By the way, we've traced the second outbreak of the Blue Death to three midtown restaurants. New employees who left tonight, dishwashers, apparently smeared the poison on eating utensils."

The reporter's eyes were sleepy. "Then why pay the ransom?"

"Exactly," thundered Miller.

Carter said wearily: "Oh, dry up," and turned back to the reporter. "This is why. There are too many ways the Blue Death could be spread. Sanitary paper cups. You can't close all restaurants. Chewing gum vending machines. Any confection on the market could be hijacked secretly and poisoned, and there's always the city's water supply."

The reporter's face was tense. "Hell!" he mumbled, "nothing like this ever got next to me before. A chap in the office got his tonight."

The butler shoved his wooden face in at the door. "Mr. Carter wanted on the phone."

Carter passed Hines in the doorway. "Boss says pay, eh, Hines?" and the mayor nodded and made an entrance.

Carter went to the phone. "Carter speaking…. Blew up the boat, eh?… Find anybody?… Probably skipped out by plane and left a time bomb. No, nothing further to be done about it…. The crowd in front of Mr. Miller's house is becoming rather unruly…. Reserves already here, are they? Okay."

He stalked back into the living room in time to hear Mayor Hines say pompously, "We cannot allow the straitened financial condition of the city to come before the health and welfare of its citizens."

The reporter broke in: "Sure, sure, you said that in every speech of your campaign. What we want to know is, are you going to pay the ten million?"

Hines glared at the man, looking with small eyes down his big nose, and spat out: "Yes!"

The reporter was halfway across the room in a stride. There was a stampede of others, and in a fraction of a second the room was clear of reporters.

Carter said shortly: "Now, Mr. Hines, if you'll make your little speech to the people outside, tell them we're going to pay, maybe they'll let us get down to the City Hall to raise the blue flag. Although that seems to me a rather useless procedure."

Hines bored into him with gimlet eyes. "Useless?"

Carter's gray gaze met his unwaveringly, a thin smile lighting his grim face. "Yes," he said gently, "The newspapers are probably already on the streets."

Hines said, "Oh."

**GETTING THE** money at midnight was a bit difficult, but when the aldermen had met hurriedly to obey the boss's orders, several banks were opened and the money was placed in an armored car and, ringed by motorcycles mounting machine guns, was taken to the City Hall.

In the next half-hour, a telegram was received from Philadelphia, which gave instructions where to leave the money. Carter told police to check on its source. The message said, simply:

PUT TEN MILLION IN MAYORS OFFICE BY TWO AM TURN OUT ALL LIGHTS ANYONE REMAINS INSIDE WILL DIE

It was Hines' full platform voice reading the telegram. He frowned. "This is ridiculous," he said, "and it puts me in a bad light."

Carter said: "Quite so!" and Hines got up and thumped his fist down on the table. "Are you trying to insinuate I'm tied up with this criminal?"

"No," Carter said slowly, "I wouldn't say tied up with the criminal."

The mayor leaned forward across the desk, his weight on his hands, and glared down his long, thin nose at Carter. "Just what are you driving at?" he demanded.

Carter raised innocent eyebrows: "Good Lord, mayor, I was simply agreeing with you!"

His lids veiled laughter in his eyes, and Hines straightened slowly.

Miller rumbled into action. "I'm going to stay in this room when the money's left in here. The crooks shouldn't be allowed to get away with this." He looked to Carter. "If I should be killed, I want Sally O'Day to have all my stuff out of the basement room, furniture and papers."

Carter nodded gravely.

Police Commissioner Rover was an old-timer. He carried his head grandly as he strode across and thrust out a gnarled hand to Miller's fat paw.

"By God, you're a man, Mr. Miller. I'll stay with you!"

Carter put a kindly hand on Rover's shoulder. "I wouldn't do it, commissioner," he said, "it might mean death. Miller feels like he has to because it was his office, but that doesn't affect you. The guard we've set up outside will be impenetrable. They can't possibly get in."

"Death, you say," Rover grumbled. "Well, Carter, I've always done my duty as I saw it."

Carter opened his mouth to argue further, but saw it was useless. Instead he clasped the commissioner's gnarled hand in his own. "Okay, commissioner," he said, "I'll draw the line tight outside."

The four men began then to stack the money in bundles on the table. Miller's fat hands were greedy over the greenbacks. Rover handled them reverently. Carter's movements were agile. So far as Hines showed, the money might have been scraps of paper, but his beady small eyes were bright.

When the money was arranged, Hines walked rapidly out of the room. Carter paused in the doorway. The two men, Miller, fat and pompous, the old commissioner, grim-faced, sat together beside the desk, guns in their hands.

Carter waved a hand, half a salute, at Rover. The old man smiled. Miller was staring fixedly at the ten million.

Carter turned out the lights and closed the door. Two police guards took their stand there.

**CARTER STRODE** scowling out of the building. There were four police at each door. There was a ring of them about the hall. He paced deliberately about City Hall, finding every sentry alert with a gun in his hand. Floodlights made the square as bright as day.

Ringed around its sides were motorcycles, with machine guns trained on the open square. No soul could get in or out of that City Hall without being detected. It would take a small army to enter by force.

Carter went the rounds of the sentries twice, circled the motorcycle guards, returned to the building. Nothing had been seen, nothing heard. He stalked to the mayor's office.

"Heard anything?" he asked the guards.

They shook their heads grimly.

Carter pressed close to the door, listening. Not a sound.

"Rover!" he called, "heard anything!"

There was no answer.

He called more loudly. "Rover! Heard anything!"

No answer.

He thumped on the door with his fists. No response. He kicked it and aroused only echoes. Tingles of apprehension raced down his back. His scalp tightened. He wrenched his gun from his pocket, turned it on the lock, fired, one—two—three—four times before the huge old lock was shattered, and the door shudded in at his strong-shouldered thrust. He switched on the light, then cried out. *The money had vanished.*

The money, yes, but what was on the floor? His eyes flashed to two bodies there, the pudgy pomposity of Miller flat on his back, Commissioner Rover doubled over in his chair. *Their faces bore the badge of the Blue Death!*

# CHAPTER FIVE

# THE DEATH TRAP

**C**ARTER WHIRLED to the guard at the door, his eyes cold. "You heard nothing at all?"

The cop shook a dazed head, staring open-mouthed at the bodies. "I ain't heard a thing."

The table was swept clear. There wasn't even tobacco ash there, though all of them had smoked furiously while they had awaited the Terror's telegram.

Carter bent solicitously over the still body of the commissioner. That blue had wiped every vestige of humanity from the man's countenance. There was a piece of cigar leaf on his lip and the detective, lean face drawn, bent over and brushed it away with his handkerchief. Jed Harris, whom he had loved, dead, and now the grand old commissioner. He jerked erect and, eyes bitter, strode from the room.

"Turn this building upside down," he ordered. "The Blue Terror and his men simply could not have got out of this City Hall."

Grim-faced police started the search, prodding every dark corner, investigating every locked office, every storage closet. Carter paced slowly up and down the hall, smoking his monogrammed cigarettes end to end.

A door jerked open, spilling out pale yellow light, and Hines stood in the opening. He waited until Carter was opposite him, then bit out:

"You're through. Get out!"

Ken Carter stopped his pacing, turned with a thin smile.

"I haven't yet started, Mr. Mayor."

Hines grinned nastily beneath the thin thrust of his nose. "That is precisely what I am complaining about. You are too slow in starting."

Carter's hands swung idly at his sides. No one looking at him would have guessed the white anger that burned within. His words clipped out:

"I'm in the case not for love of you, but to save the people of the city. And when I start to round up these murdering crooks, no one will stop me. Not you, nor all your pompous, grafting officials of the city!"

He spun on his heel and strode out, paused at the door. A police inspector stood there, face thin and dark.

"I'm ordered off the job," Carter told him. "That money is inside this building, and the man who stole it. Don't relax your guard."

As the two stood talking, a sheet-covered body that made the stretcher sag was carried past toward a shiny undertaker's coach.

"Miller was a brave man, sir," said the inspector. "Maybe we misjudged him."

Carter's eyes were still hard and angry. He said: "Sure," moving away.

**INSIDE THE** door of his apartment, Carter stood with weary, bloodshot eyes surveying the comfort of the room. His shoulders wanted to sag, but he held them erect. Ransom had been paid, the city freed, perhaps, from the menace of the Blue Death. But Carter would carry on. Jed Harris was not yet avenged. And that grand old man, Commissioner Rover, had yielded his life in the battle.

Yes, Ken Carter would carry on, but while the police guarded City Hall nothing more need be done. And meanwhile, he must rest. He moved heavily across the room, entered his study, and a point jabbed his ribs. The lean detective turned his head slowly, looked into a rat-like pointed face, down at a gun against his side.

He said wearily: "Well, what is it this time?"

"You're coming with me!" the man barked.

Carter muttered: "Okay," and leaned as if tired against the doorjamb a moment, then straightened and walked slowly toward his desk.

"Hold on," the gangster grated. "That's not the way out!"

Carter drew a cigarette from his pocket, lighted it with a lighter on his desk.

"There isn't any way out," he said calmly.

"What do you mean?" tensely.

Carter shrugged broad shoulders, leaned against the desk. His eyes, sleepy looking, were fixed on the door. The wooden portal stood open, but dull gray steel closed the opening. His pressure on the doorjamb had slid it out in oiled grooves, locked it in place.

The lean detective nodded toward it and the gunman whirled in a crouch, glaring at the gray steel. He struck it with the gun and raised a dull clamor, spun back, leveled the automatic in a tense white hand.

"Open that door," he snapped, "or I'll blow daylight through you."

Carter smiled thinly, exhaling smoke. "In that case," he said, "you would be forced to remain with my murdered body until police came. That door can't be opened from inside. A neat little safety device, isn't it?"

The man advanced with stealthy, animal-like steps, ape shoulders hunched. "You open that door," he growled out, "or—"

Carter spread his hands. "My dear fellow," he said, "you really must be reasonable. I told you I can't open the door from here. I can call the policeman at the corner and he'll open it, or you can shoot me and wait an hour until my office checks up and finds the door is closed. Which do you prefer?"

The man continued his menacing approach. He circled Carter, jammed the gun against the nape of his neck. "Wise guy," he growled, "you open that door or—"

The cold pressure of the gun muzzle sent an echoing chill down Carter's back. He had lied, of course. He could open the door. Perhaps it would be better to do that and chance getting the man afterwards? But he must have companions below stairs. Carter stood a better chance of escaping from this one than from the guns of three or four.

Carter continued to reason with the gangster calmly. "I don't especially want to die. Neither, I imagine, do you. As I said, that door is the only way of getting out, and I can't open it. You can imagine what chance you would have, caught in the room with me murdered."

Carter felt the cold steel waver fractionally away from his neck, jab close again. "You can't talk me out of it," the man muttered. "Anyway, I got pals coming soon."

Carter fumbled out words with a semblance of fear. "I told you the truth, honest. When your pals come, I'll tell them how to open the door from the other side."

The gun was removed from Carter's neck. The gunman hurriedly frisked Carter, slipped a gun from a desk drawer into his coat pocket.

"Okay," he said, "we'll wait for my pals. I don't think it's going to do you no good."

Carter, still pretending fear, his jaw sagging, trembling, said, "I said I'd go with you, didn't I? Put that gun away, will you? It makes me nervous."

The man laughed, and held the gun very obviously pointed at Carter. He walked around to the far side of the desk, draped a leg over its corner.

Carter lifted his lip corners in an artificial grin, hope springing at the back of his eyes.

"Do you mind if I do a bit of juggling?" he asked. "I used to work on the stage, you know, and it always calms my nerves."

Without waiting for a reply, Carter picked up two heavy books and a bookend and started tossing them into the air, one after the other, catching and whirling them in a criss-cross pattern, his white hands flashing with deft speed. The man followed his movements with admiring eyes.

"Sa—ay, you're pretty good," he sad.

**CARTER STARTED** flinging the books and bookend higher, snatched up a pen stand from the desk, and joined that with the other three. Carter's eyes, following the tossing objects, narrowed. He glanced at the gangster, following his play with open-mouthed stare.

While his left hand still threw objects into the air, Carter caught the book-end with his right and with an underhand fling, cracked it against the jaw of the gunman. The man slipped off the edge of the desk, gun flying from his hand and slithering across to clang against the steel door.

Carter leaped around the desk, grabbed the man by the throat. But his aim had not been as sure as he had thought. The bookend had caught the gunman only a glancing blow, and he jerked the gun he had taken from Carter out of his pocket.

Carter grabbed his wrist, and the two men stiffened, hunching up powerful shoulders, struggling for the gun stretched straight above their heads. Then began a furious battle. There was terrific strength in those crouching, apish shoulders. Carter's own body was like whipcord, and both men knew they were fighting for their lives. The gunman had the advantage. The weapon was clasped in his hand.

They reeled around the desk. A chair crashed to the floor. Behind him, Carter heard the steel door clanging beneath the beat of fists. Muffled voices called out.

These undoubtedly were the pals the gunman had spoken of. Carter's case was doubly desperate now. With despairing thought, he remembered the oxy-acetylene torch outfit in the closet. If the man found that, his steel door would keep them out no more than ten to fifteen minutes at most.

The gunman was shouting hoarsely now, cries for help. His breath was panting, whistling in his throat. He made a final, desperate effort and Carter reeled back toward the open window. His head struck the frame and saved him.

He jerked on the wrist, using it to restore balance. The gunman lunged suddenly toward him. Carted edged aside from the window, seized the man by his throat, and hurled him on his back across the sill, bending with him. The man's right hand opened in a frantic grab for safety, and even as Carter snatched for it, the pistol dropped downward, glinting blue in the sunlight.

The gangster wrenched and squirmed, slammed a hard fist into Carter's face and sent him reeling back, knocking loose his hold on the gunman. Screaming shrilly, he teetered on the sill, arms flailing. It was only a second he poised there, then he slid head foremost into nothingness.

**CARTER STOOD** laxly, shoulders sagging with fatigue. He panted for breath. But there was no time for this. If those gangsters in the next room had found that torch outfit—he whirled toward the steel door. As he stared at it, a small spot of steel near its bottom bulged and melted and blue flame sliced into view.

He staggered toward the gangster's gun, lying against the door. If he could reach that, he still had a fighting chance.

As he reeled across the room, the blue tongue of flame flicked over the automatic. The blue steel fused and melted.

Carter flinched back, snatched at his phone, but it was dead, the wires cut before his return.

Carter's eyes searched the room swiftly, scanning the souvenirs of his wild travels. A horsehair riata, strong enough to hold the plunging of a 1200-pound wild steer, hung among the trophies.

With a glad cry, Carter snatched the riata down, leaped to the window.

The three floors below him were occupied by a collection of valuable art objects, and he had steel-barred all the windows. If he lowered himself to those windows, he could only cling until he was shot off. The roof of the next building was level with his window and twenty-five feet away. But one chance remained, a chance only Ken Carter could have utilized.

Working frantically, he unrolled the long riata, opened its loop and whirled it within the room. Luck was with him. At the first cast the stiff loop dropped over a chimney on the other roof. Carter tugged the rope as taut as 180 pounds plus whipcord muscles could make it, and tied it fast to a steam radiator.

He sprang to his bedroom, yanked mattress and springs from the bed, ripped out four slats that he tied together, ends overlapping, into a pole perhaps eighteen feet long. He worked it through the doorway, out the window.

Then he climbed outside, holding himself by the frame, and balanced the long pole crosswise against his body. He kicked off his shoes, got the bite of the rope across his insteps, and then he hesitated. Below him were ten stories of space and only that slim rope stretched across the void. Almost certain death? Perhaps. And yet here in the room was no question of his fate. Those gangsters were here to *kill!*

Renewed shouts behind him! Carter stepped out upon the thin horse-hair *riata*.

Everything in him cried out against the peril of that endless rope that stretched above death. Carter fought his way resolutely to calmness. He forced his mind back to the days, a few years ago, when he had danced upon a slender wire stretched across the stage. But that wire had been springy with 1,000-pound tension, there was no side sway to it, and only his muscles had tightened this rope.

**A WIND,** insignificant at street level, was twenty miles strong here. It jostled as he moved out, out across that terrible abyss, one slow foot sliding forward, the other slipping behind.

Carter forced himself to a conception that he was back on the stage with a wire beneath him. Out yonder was an audience, demanding only to be amused. That racket at the steel door was only applause.

The long pole was heavy in his hands, but it steadied him against the thrust of the wind. He dared not look toward the safety of the roof ahead, dared not guess how far he had moved out the void.

The rope sagged in the middle of the twenty-five-foot stretch, and hills moved with him, one behind, one ahead. Always he stepped against an up-slanting rope. His weight carried the dip with him, but at the end of this climb, somewhere on that rope, he must go uphill.

There was no rosin on his soles to help him, as there had been on the stage. The slender horsehair cut into his feet, and now the shouts behind him were louder. The steel door must be giving way!

He lifted his head and risked a glance ahead. Ten feet to go, and a steep upgrade on the rope. Not used for months, it had stretched. He could feel its sidesway with the push of the wind.

Desperately he shoved his left foot forward, drew his right up behind it. The slant of the rope increased. He could feel the drag of it across his socks, pulling the silk against his soles. Another instant and they would slip. Would his balance stand the strain?

The cries behind him came out into the open. The men had burned through the door, were leaning out of the window. There was only one hope. Carter bent his knees cautiously, bounced once and sprang, hurling the pole ahead and up as he leaped.

For what seemed ten eternities, his body flew through the air. The brick parapet at the roof's edge shot upward before his eyes. God! Would he miss! His chest struck the wall. His grasping arms hooked up and over it, and, half-dazed by the force of the blow, he clung, dangling.

There were renewed shouts behind him, the crack of a pistol. Brick dusted off by his arm. Carter muscled his body slowly up with aching arms, raised a knee, and edged it over the parapet. Another shot rang out, and Carter felt his shirt jerk.

With a final expiring heave, he pulled his body up, rolled over and dropped behind the parapet. Chest panting, he crawled across the gravel toward a trapdoor in the roof. Bullets fanned his ears. He dropped flat, peered back. The parapet was too low. Unless he lay absolutely flat, he was exposed to gunfire.

That trapdoor was twenty feet away. To reach it, he must expose himself. Even if he dashed for it, there was no way of telling whether it could be opened. And behind—those guns waited.

# CHAPTER SIX
# BLUE TERROR'S TRAIL

**T**HE EIGHTEEN-FOOT pole that had balanced Carter across the abyss lay just within reach of his hand. He drew the pole toward him slowly, inched it forward until its end was under the rim of the roof scuttle. He twisted it, and though the ropes that bound the slate strained and groaned, the scuttle was gradually raised.

It took him five minutes to ease the edge off the trapdoor frame. He braced the pole against the side of the scuttle and then, with a sudden shove, cleared the opening. There was nothing for it now but to dive across twenty feet of bullet-swept roof.

He sprang up, made a dodging dash. Shouts echoed behind. Gravel cut his unshod feet. He leaped into the opening, landed with flexed knees and pitched forward on his hands and face in a poorly lighted upper hallway

He heaved up, panting, jerking his hair from his face, found an elevator, and shot it to the basement. There was a courtyard behind the apartment. Carter went through that, over a fence, and out through the basement of a residence into another street.

Newsboys were howling extras in the street:

"Blue Death kills continue!"

"Reprisal for guard at City Hall!"

"All police withdrawn!"

Guard off City Hall and the Blue Death rampant again! Carter cursed low in his throat, grabbed a taxi and raced to the square. A moving van was backed up to a Carson Street entrance of the hall and furniture was being carted out. The detective dropped from his taxi at the corner, ducked into a store and bought shoes, a sweater and a hat.

He put them on swiftly, strolled out again. He was working a lone hand now, deprived of police help. He could not seize and search the truck. He doubted if it could be successfully followed.

The moment he showed himself in pursuit, the entire gang would turn on him, kill him as ruthlessly as hundreds had died of the dread Blue Death. And they would be watching for a trailer. Yet he was certain this truck would lead him to the Terror.

He thought swiftly, pacing along the opposite side of the street, and peering into the windows of a five- and ten-cent store. Suddenly his eyes brightened. He strode in and bought three cans of scarlet paint, hurried to a phone booth and called a friend at a near-by flying field, got him to hop off at once for the Cornwall River off Carson Street in an amphibian.

Then he grabbed an elevator and was swished up six stories. He flashed his badge to a dubious girl in an office and she permitted him access to a window.

The truck was still at the curb, but its load was being lashed fast and, even as Carter watched, the driver cranked it and leaped to the seat. The detective's lean, powerful hands had been busy.

Every can of red paint had been opened and its contents poured into the paper bag in which they had come. As the truck neared, he swung the bag out with the nice calculation of timing and angles that his juggling days had given him.

The brown bag flashed through the air in an arc and burst over the top of the truck, spreading an irregular stain of crimson.

Carter barked, "Thanks" at the girl, darted to the elevator and out, grabbed a cab to the river. The plane was floating off a ferry slip. Carter dived in, swam with a brisk overhand stroke and pulled himself aboard.

Before he was fairly in his seat, he yelled: "Get going," and the plane skipped across the water, dodged a tug, and slid into the air between a ferry and a liner idling toward the sea. They rose swiftly and Carter gestured toward the city.

It took him ten minutes of searching with glasses, but they picked up the scarlet blob atop the truck, and keeping it spotted, circled in the blue for two hours while it made its trundling way out into the open country, turned in the drive of an elaborate mansion.

For some miles, Carter had noticed a sleek car trailing the truck. He had assumed that it was the gangster car, but when the truck turned in, the car sped back toward the city. He frowned and studied it through the glasses, but could make out nothing. At the detective's signal, the amphibian was dropped to a landing field near the mansion. Carter, scrambling out, said briskly:

"If I find what I want in that house, I'm going to wave this blue shirt of mine out a window on this side. If you see it, get the police here as fast as you can."

**CARTER CUT** through the under brush with a silent speed that proved him no novice at woodsmanship, and scouted the house from the edge of the wood. The truck was almost unloaded and he watched the men carry the last furniture into the house before the truck was trundled around to a barn. All the men went into the house. Carter circled so he could approach from the barn, made a final unobserved dash and ducked into a basement window.

He dropped down silently into almost pitch darkness and crouched there until his eyes became accustomed to the dim shadows.

Light filtered in from dusty windows and he made out rickety stairs leading upward. They sagged under his feet, made mournful creaking, but, gun in hand, he cat-footed up and listened at the closed door at the top.

No sound reached his ears. He peered through the keyhole. Nothing within the range of his vision except a kitchen table, and over against the far wall, a stove.

Carter tried the knob softly. It gave beneath his hand and he pushed into the kitchen, gun ready. Sounds reached him now. A deep-throated rumble of voices and now and then a shout of laughter or the icy clinking of glasses. The gangsters of the Blue Terror were celebrating.

Carter found a narrow stairway that twisted upward and made his cautious way along it. The second floor hall was high and dark. An open door let in a pale blob of light.

The grumble of voices below stairs was more distant here, but still helped to cover the creaking of his footsteps. He soft-footed down the hall, stopping to listen at every doorway. At last his cautious investigation was rewarded.

He heard a girl's trilling laughter and a man's pompous voice declaiming, "A cinch, darling, a cinch. And once we get to France, no one will dream of connecting me with Cornwall or the Blue Terror. This last outbreak of the Blue Death we engineered will do marvels to cover our escape."

Carter crouched and peered through the keyhole. He could see neither speaker, but there was a table piled with money. He straightened swiftly, retreated to the room, which stood open and entered it softly. He ripped off sweater and shirt, and crept swiftly to the window. He peered out. His friend's plane was not in sight.

Carter waited, watching the sky. Footsteps trooped back and forth below. A man strolled across the lawn and Carter ducked from sight. Just then the amphibian, swinging in a low arc, came into view from behind the eaves. It circled languidly. Carter almost cried aloud. Would that gangster never get out of sight in the woods?

Finally the man vanished behind a tree, and Carter hoisted the window cautiously, thrust his shirt out and jerked it back and forth.

**HE WAITED** then through an eternity of seconds while the plane circled through slow glides, then his heart leaped within him as the plane bee-lined toward the city. His signal had been observed!

Carter slipped back into the hall again, crept to the room where the man and the girl had the money. He crouched again and heard only the girl humming a light song. What was his best move, Carter wondered. Should he crash in and brace the girl and the man, take command of the money and wait for police to come?

He would not have long to wait, he knew, for the flier was to land at the first village, send help from there and phone metropolitan police. Some would come by plane. Or should he slip out into the woods again, and hide?

His pride resisted the latter. He had made the find. The capture was his alone. He would not wait until they came and took possession, took credit, too. Besides, there was always the chance that the Blue Terror, the king of them all, might slip through his fingers.

Carter got lightly to his feet, his lips drawn back in his fighting grin, and wrenched open the door. The girl smothered a scream and caught her mouth with her hands. It was—*Sally O'Day!*

Her lustrous eyes, wide and frightened in the pale oval of her face, glanced swiftly from Carter's grim, purposeful face to the pompous, florid-faced man who sat fumblingly erect on the side of the bed. It was—*Miller!* Ex-Mayor Bertram Miller, who had lain on the floor of the mayor's office with his face tinted by the blue stain of the Terror's death!

## CHAPTER SEVEN
## DEATH STRIKES AGAIN

**M**ILLER SAID heavily: "So, it's you." The girl said nothing, but continued to press her hand to her panting chest. Carter did not reply. There was no surprise in his face and his eyes were cold. Miller sat there blinking at the leveled, ready gun. He said, "Well, you caught me, Carter. I was afraid you would."

Carter smiled without mirth. "Yes, you tried hard enough to stop me. I was forced to kill another of your men last time."

Miller shrugged sluggishly to his feet, and Carter eyed him intently, muscles tense in his bared brown arms, gun hand alert. That was a mistake, that close regard for it left Sally uncovered, Sally who stood unmoving, without a sound. She acted swiftly now. Swaying her petite figure forward, she lunged and seized Carter's gun wrist.

Miller dived across the room.

"Atta girl, Sally!" he barked.

Carter yanked savagely at the gun, twisting it to get it away from the girl. He hesitated to shoot her. He could see a mental picture of himself, clicking heels, bowing. "Madame, I am a man of sentiment." He sneered at the picture, but he couldn't squeeze the trigger.

Miller charged with his fat chin against his chest, small eyes ugly. Good, the man was going to use his fists. Then Carter must be between him and his gun!

Miller seized Carter's gun wrist, and the girl jerked free, darted back and began to creep like a primitive cat up toward Carter's flank. Was that where Miller's gun was?

Carter threw himself bodily backward, pulling with all his weight and strength on that grip upon his wrist. He didn't wrench free, but he yanked Miller forward, struck the girl with his shoulders and sent her sprawling.

He slammed his left into the man's paunched body and Miller let go with his right hand and swung a sledgehammer blow.

Carter jerked his head under it, and fat but extraordinarily powerful fingers gripped his throat. Carter tore at them with his left hand, but it was futile. His lungs strained and blood drummed in his ears. Darkness swarmed before his bulging eyes. Desperate, he dropped his gun and grabbed Miller's strangling fingers with both his hands.

The roar in his ears was deafening now. Miller's fat, demoniac face seemed to float before him in a blue aura. Carter seized one of Miller's fingers with both hands and tried to shred it off. The man fairly whimpered with pain, but tried to squeeze on, flailing at Carter with his other fist. But the pain was too great. Just as Carter felt his lungs must burst, the fingers tore loose from his throat.

He sucked in air gratefully and the battering of Miller's fists seemed inconsequential.

Something of his old ability to analyze action came back to him slowly as his head cleared and he ducked under Miller's blows, side-stepped them, smashed his own fists into the paunchy stomach of his opponent.

Finally, with a well-timed punch on his pompous jowl, he knocked the man to the floor, out cold.

He stood panting, one hand on the edge of the table where the money was piled in a great gold and green heap. There was a heavy paper knife beside it that had been used to open the covers, and Carter stared at it, blinking dazedly.

**THE GIRL'S** shrill voice broke in on his gasping. She was cursing him in oaths no woman is supposed to know. The detective glanced at her. In the small, competent grasp of her hand, outlined against the dark yellow silk of her dress, she held Carter's automatic! Its huge muzzle was leveled at his heart.

Carter's head was hanging, his dull hair sprawled forward over his forehead, a disheveled figure, shirtless and with undershirt torn. He stared upward under his brows with gray intent eyes, and his hand closed upon the paper knife.

"Fool!" the girl spat at him. "To think you were man enough to take us alone!"

He saw her eyes go flat with murderous rage, saw her trigger finger whiten with tension.

In the split second before she fired, he threw himself to the floor and rolled. The bullet whizzed overhead and Carter, flat on his back, jerked up his left hand and hurled the paper knife.

Knife-throwing too, had been one of his tricks upon the stage, and the blade flew straight and hard, but not point first. Carter's sentiment again. The handle caught the girl between the eyes, snapped her head back and hurled her to the floor with a small, frightened moan.

Carter scrambled to her, snatched the gun. What was *that?* He whirled toward the door, crouched behind the table with gun ready. Trooping footsteps in the hall! Then quiet. Carter could almost hear the tense breathing of many men. The knob twisted slowly and the door eased forward, then was hurled open. Carter's gun leaped up, then he shouted.

"Hold your fire! It's me, Carter!"

He straightened slowly. The man in the door was in police uniform and had a dark, lean face; the inspector who had been on guard at the City Hall. Suspendered, rough-clad men with shotguns were behind him. And another man in natty civilian clothes. Beady eyes stared hostilely down a long, thin nose—Mayor Hines.

Carter growled: "How in hell did Hines get here?"

The inspector said: "We met his car on the road. I flew out, picked up the posse your friend had organized, and here we are."

Carter nodded, and asked: "What happened to the gangsters downstairs? I made enough noise to wake the dead!"

"Not quite," the police inspector said grimly, "Not when it's the Blue Death. This guy must have poisoned them so he could take all the money. Who is this Blue Terror anyhow?"

Carter stepped aside, hard laughter in his eyes, and the inspector squeezed in, stopped dead with a low oath.

"Good lord, it's *Miller*. I thought he was dead."

Carter said, "Just a neat little trick to escape detection. When he and the commissioner were in the room together, waiting to guard the ransom, he gave Rover a poisoned cigar, then hid the ten million dollars in some secret place in the chimney or floor, which also had an opening in the room below.

"Then Sally O'Day, to whom he left all his furnishings, took the money out of the trap door. I'll admit that when I saw him with his face blue on the floor of the office at City Hall, I was thrown off the trail for a while. Then, later, I remembered a scrap of tobacco leaf on the lips of Commissioner Rover when there were neither ashes nor cigar butts lying around. Miller was too careful there, removing too much evidence."

The inspector muttered: "That was damned smart."

"I had been suspicious of Miller from the first," Carter went on, "because the first attempt to kill me was made after I phoned him and indicated I was going to take care of the investigation.

"My reputation scared him, I guess. He also sent the girl to try to lure me into another case, so I wouldn't interfere with his extortion racket. Further, after I called him and told him it was poison and not a disease, after the girl had failed, he sent a gangster to get rid of me.

"All of which convinced me he was guilty, but left no way of proving it. My only chance was to catch him red-handed with the money, and his trick of feigning death threw me off for a short while."

Hines broke in sharply: "Good God, Miller isn't unconscious. He's dead."

Carter sneered: "Not again?"

**AND THEY** whirled toward him. His face was horrible with the *badge of the Blue Death!* Beside him lay a small phial uncorked and Carter, bending cold-eyed over him, ascertained that this time he was really dead.

He glanced toward where Sally O'Day lay and found her eyes wide open. When she saw she was detected, she scrambled to her feet, smoothing the yellow silk gown over svelte hips.

"He's dead this time, Sally," Carter said grimly. "The undertaker who got him out of City Hall for you won't be able to deliver a living corpse this time."

"So what, Mr. Sherlock?" she jeered. "I'd have left him long ago except for his money, and he knew it." She tossed her head defiantly. "Sa-ay, can't anybody give me a cigarette?"

Hines stepped forward, offering his with a flourish, and the girl put one to her artificially perfect lips, sucked smoke into her lungs.

"All of what you're saying is true," she told Carter, talking out smoke. "But you still don't know the poison he used."

Carter grunted. "That's true. It's an aniline derivative, akin to exalgen and mathacetine, all members of the acetanehde group, but venal in action. One of the aniline analgesique antipyretics. But it's more powerful than any poison of that class ever developed before. This drag destroys the red corpuscles and causes that blueness of the skin. There is no antidote since its exact nature is unknown.

"I checked up on Miller at college. He was a brilliant chemistry student there. A bit of a genius. I think he must have gone completely mad to do as he did. I suspect that behind it was the fact that he was being kicked out of office as a grafter, whereas much bigger crooks got away with it. Brooding over fancied wrong has driven more than one man mad."

Carter glanced up quickly at the girl. Her face was pale, her breath rapid.

He cried out: "Good lord, have you poisoned yourself, too?"

The girl gasped: "I haven't—poisoned—myself. I've been—poisoned!"

Carter cried aloud: "That traps you, Hines! I saw your car following the truck out here. The police met you on your way to town. You were spotting the girl for future collections, and I'll bet you and she had a deal. I saw you flirting with her in the hall at Miller's home. Now she's a danger to you, so you kill her."

Hines shouted: "You're crazy!" but Carter ignored him.

"You were planning to grab this money and get rid of Miller. You thought when you gave her the cigarette, that the drag would kill the girl before she could accuse you and she'd be thought a suicide too. You must have got those poisoned cigarettes from downstairs, where Miller murdered all those men."

The girl's breath was painful to hear now. It was hoarse and whistling.

"That's right, too, Ken Carter," she gasped out, "and—with—my—dying breath—I accuse him!"

She stabbed a terrible white hand at Hines and Carter whirled toward the mayor, sprang across the room at him, then checked, staring with his grim smile lighting gray, intent eyes. The man was calmly exhaling smoke from a cigarette out of his long, thin nose. The girl let out a little ranting scream and sank down, a crumpled yellow heap.

Hines, lounging against the wall, muttered hoarsely: "So ends the Blue Terror," and slid down to the floor, still sitting grotesquely erect. The swift, horrible blush of the Blue Death crept over his face.

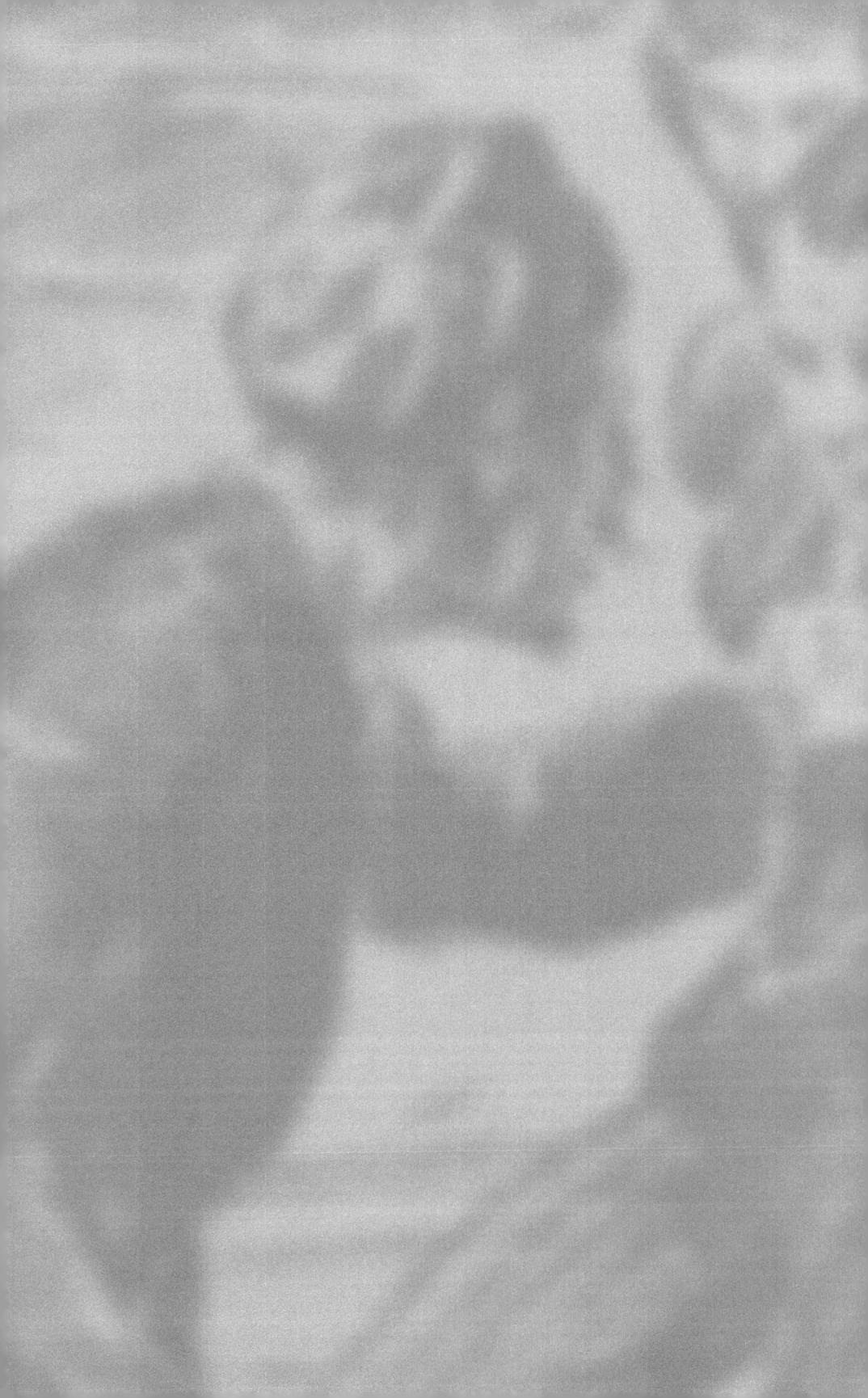

# STATUES
# OF
# HORROR

DIRE WARNINGS—PROMISES OF
DIABOLICAL DEATH—AND VOICES
IN THE NIGHT CAN'T MAKE A
MAN GIVE UP A FORTUNE. BUT
ONE GLANCE INTO ACHMED BEN
HASSAN'S PRIVATE CLOSET
WOULD MAKE A MAN GIVE UP HIS
SOUL. FOR A GIRL STOOD IN THAT
CLOSET. A GIRL WITH GOLDEN
HAIR AND AN EXQUISITE BODY,
BUT HER FACE WAS A HORRID
MASK OF FEAR. AND THAT BODY—
WAS A STONE STATUE!

# CHAPTER ONE
# DEATH SHADOWS

**THE HALL** was dark and still. Fragments of light spattered into it from far off, but only deepened the sinister shadows. No whisper of the before-dawn traffic, fifteen stories below, penetrated here. Ken Carter, crouched beside a suit of rusted Asian armor, felt more than saw movement close by. Straining eyes and ears, he snaked out his gun.

He heard nothing. There was not even the sibilance of feet on the thick carpets. Nothing brushed the suits of armor, the cluttered exhibit cases lining the walls. Yet Carter knew the assassin he had awaited throughout the weary night had come. Some sixth sense trickled cold drops of warning down his back.

The invader's progress was as sure and swift as a bat flitting through a cavern. Carter, with cautious breath, automatic in his hand, cat-footed up the hall.

At its remote end, a feeble glimmer of streetlight sifted through a small window and grayed the darkness. Against it Carter spotted the crouched figure of a man. His outline was vague and enormous. The figure seemed to glide rather than walk, and once more Carter thought of a huge bat. He drew a flashlight from his pocket and crept after that shadowy, somehow horrible shape drifting so silently down the hall, down the hall toward where Colonel Hawks slept, toward where his daughter, Myra, cowered behind a locked door.

Ken Carter had taken the job with his tongue in his cheek, reading with amusement the blackmail letter Colonel Hawks had received. Couched in stilted phraseology, it had demanded two hundred thousand dollars on a threat, if he refused to pay, of turning his daughter, rather terribly, into dead stone.

The letter had gone into gruesome detail:

> *First the little toe of that perfect foot will become a trifle stiff;*
> *then unmovable. If you were to touch it, it would be cold and hard*
> *as stone, and there would be no feeling in it at all, nor life. It will*
> *be dead, a dead member on a living person. Swiftly, but not so*
> *swiftly but that your daughter shall know the fear of its spread, the*
> *stone death will creep up her feet, up her perfect, symmetrical limbs,*
> *past the jewel-like curve of her hips, and the gripping, icy cold of*
> *the stone death will march ahead of it, turning her heart to water.*
> *I do not think that you, her father, will enjoy the spectacle of your*
> *daughter turning into a statue before your eyes.*
>
> *Or is your money more precious to you than your daughter's life?*

The signature was exquisite, a flourish not readily legible: Achmed ben Hassan.

The threat seemed ridiculous, and in spite of the fat fee offered, Ken Carter had started to turn it down. But beneath those smooth words there had seemed to lurk a venom, like vicious snakes masked in the brilliance of tropic flowers.

Snakes and bats. Certainly there was something equally horrible and venomous about that creeping shadow down the hall. Ken Carter felt a dread of approaching it, a shrinking from cold, writhing coils in the dark.

He forced himself to stride faster now, cutting the distance between himself and the half-seen figure. The flitting shape had merged with the shadow of the right-hand wall; its motion ceased at the door of Myra Hawks.

Every muscle of his tall, athletic body tense, Carter eased closer and closer to the door. He smiled grimly at the idea of its being opened, except from within. Colonel Hawks had loaded upon it a half dozen different bolts and locks, and in its middle an iron rod braced diagonally down to the floor. If every other lock snapped, that one would hold.

Only feet away now from the crouching shadow, Carter could hear muffled, metallic fumbling. Suddenly a gray strip of light showed and widened. Carter fought back the gasp of amazement that rose in his throat. The locks had been opened! Good Lord! The man had done the impossible! Cold dread gripped him, but he leaped forward, slashing the darkness with the white gleam of his torch, gun poised.

**THE SHADOW** man did not whirl to give battle. He sprang forward into the girl's room, thrust the door violently to close it. Carter was too quick. His foot jammed over the sill, his powerful shoulders heaved. His shout boomed through the house:

"Miss Hawks! On your guard! Colonel Hawks! Help! Quickly!"

Strength that matched his own rammed the door against him. His gun was in his hand, but he dared not fire. The girl's bed was directly across from where he battled through a wooden panel against the crushing force of this shadow man.

Suddenly Carter rolled his shoulders across the door to the edge. Something struck the middle panel. Blue glittering steel crunched through the wood where his back had been. The needlepoint of a dagger glinted. Carter gasped out a strangled cry, eased away from the door. It slammed shut. Instantly he heaved against it again, flung it shuddering inward and dived in close to the floor. Flame lanced from the gun of the invader, but went high.

Myra Hawks, her face a white blur above the bed across the room, found her voice. Shriek after shriek tore through the house. Shouts and pounding came from a distance.

Colonel Hawks' bellowing voice, and the answering cries
of servants.

Pale slabs of moonlight lay upon the floor, streaming
through two iron-screened windows on either side of the
bed, laying a lattice-work of silver and black. Again Carter
was forced to hold his fire, for the shadow stood now
directly between him and the girl. He saw a bright glitter
of steel. The man turned, flung himself at the girl.

A swirl of bed coverings. The girl's screams soared. She
sprang from the bed, cowered against the window.

Carter hurled himself at the shadow, a human projectile.
A glitter of steel streaked toward the paralyzed girl. His
hands seized the man's collar. His feet struck and he braced

and spun like a hammer thrower, hurling the invader full length upon the floor.

Ken Carter dropped upon him. He felt muscles like steel. The man threw out a hand toward the girl, trying even while battling for his life to strike at her. For an instant the thing that glittered was framed in cold moonlight, and Carter saw it was a hypodermic needle.

He seized the wrist and the man's hand bent slowly over so that the point jabbed toward Carter's pinioning fist. With a low curse, Carter jerked his hand away. The needle stabbed toward his body.

**HE LEAPED** back, snatched out his pistol. The man sprang toward the girl again, needle outthrust. Carter plunged with him. His flashlight smashed on the man's wrist. The needle dropped and the man huddled over it.

The girl's mouth opened in a throat-splitting scream, she plunged sideways, hands outthrust. Light flashed suddenly in the room. Colonel Hawks' voice filled it.

"Myra! Myra dear, you aren't hurt!"

Carter, gun leveled, stood with tense muscles. He shouted suddenly and dived upon the man, hurled him flat upon his back, seized his wrists. The right one dangled limply, broken. The left hand clutched an all-metal hypodermic. The plunger had been thrust all the way down.

The man, prostrate beneath Carter, smiled. The skin was dark, as if browned by tropical suns. His piercing eyes were oddly jubilant.

"Thees time you win, *effendi*," he said in a slurred accent. "But you will not again. There are too many of us too willing to die. It would be wise, Colonel Hawks, if you pay."

Carter wrenched the hypodermic from his grip. The man let it go willingly now, and Carter sprang to his feet, yanking the fellow up, too. Long black robes billowed from his shoulders. He wavered on his feet, flung out his left hand and braced it against the wall.

"If you want me to stand, effendi, " he said, "you will have to balance me very carefully against the wall."

Ken Carter's mind flashed to that threatening letter, the emptied hypodermic. Good Lord! The emissary of Achmed ben Hassan's had inflicted on himself the stone death intended for Myra Hawks!

As he stared awestruck at the assassin, the man's chest suddenly ceased to pant, and a horrible rigidity spread over his face. The mouth was still open, as if in speech; amusement sparkled in his eyes; then, suddenly, they were expressionless, stony.

Carter reached out a slow, fearful hand toward the man's throat. His fingers flinched back from the touch. Achmed ben Hassan's assassin had turned to stone!

## CHAPTER TWO
## THE STONE DEATH

FROWNING AT the figure of stone that so recently had been a living creature, Ken Carter retreated two slow half paces. The assassin stood rigidly, propped up against the wall like a disused board. No rigor mortis could act so quickly. Carter inspected the hypodermic.

It was all metal and the needle could be detached and screwed point inward for safe carrying. He slipped it into his pocket and turned.

The girl had drawn a scarlet mandarin cloak close about her slim body. Her narrow white feet were bare in satin mules. Colonel Hawks, bending over Myra, raised his leonine head with its flowing white hair.

"Sir," he said, "I have you to thank for my daughter's life."

The girl's face was pale, but her low voice was firm. "I cannot thank you enough, Mr. Carter."

Carter bowed suavely. You could not have told from the faultless perfection of his brown tailored suit that he had been battling for his life and the life of this lovely girl.

"You do me too much honor," he murmured. "Miss Hawks, you had better occupy some other room tonight."

"There is still danger?" she asked quickly.

Carter shrugged his broad shoulders. "No way of telling. This man tried mighty hard to kill you. He didn't mind dying if he could do that."

Colonel Hawks snapped out: "I'll see you safely to the guest room myself, Myra."

The girl shook her head slowly. Her eyes on Carter's were fraught with some meaning he could not determine, as if she warned him. Carter spoke slowly:

"Before you do, colonel, I'd like to ask Miss Hawks a few questions."

The man's maned head shook emphatically. "In the morning, perhaps, not now."

"I'm all right," the girl said mildly.

Hawks' arm went about her shoulders. "Come, my dear, I'm the best judge of that," he said, and led her away.

Carter frowned after the two. The girl's evidence might be very useful in his immediate inquiry, but the police would have to be called and he'd get a chance then to learn the girl's message.

He searched the assassin's body, but found nothing, and strode swiftly to a telephone and called the police. He hung up and paced back up the hall toward the bedroom, stopped as if turned to stone in his tracks, then broke into a pounding run. Once more the girl's screams made the night horrible!

**THE LONG,** dim hall stretched interminably beneath Carter's speeding feet, but finally he reached the room where the screams sounded, hurled himself against the door. He bounced into the room. Against the windows a man crouched.

Carter's automatic spoke. The answer was mocking, hard laughter. The man sprang to the window sill, outlined like a huge bat, and suddenly was gone. Carter punched on the light. The girl's screams died to a whimpering moan. She tossed from side to side in the bed. Carter pounded to the window, stared down. Fifteen stories below a dark, still blot stained the pavement. Another of the assassins had killed himself!

Carter whirled to the girl. She still rolled from side to side, but there was this difference: there was no life in the movement of her feet and legs. They were like inanimate logs fastened to her.

"I feel so cold, so cold!" she wept.

Colonel Hawks plunged into the room.

"For God's sake, what's happened?" he cried.

Carter darted past him, raced to the phone, yelling for an ambulance, slammed back into the room. The whimpering had ceased, and Colonel Hawks was a crumpled, beaten figure by the bed, his leonine head bowed above his daughter's body.

The lines of her face had stiffened in a horrid mask of fear. Even her hair seemed rigid as stone. The marble-like gaze of her eyes struck into Carter's heart, accusing him. She and her father had depended on him for protection and he had failed.

Carter's long face was haggard and thin, his eyes burned. Colonel Hawks stiffened beside the bed, jerked up his head, glowered at Carter.

"Get out!" he said hoarsely.

Carter's eyes jerked to his. Colonel Hawks repeated slowly:

"Get—out—of—here!"

Carter said calmly: "I can't blame you for feeling that way."

The man took a full stride toward Carter, fists clenched. "Will you get out of here? I hire you at enormous fees to protect my daughter and myself, because you have built a fabulous reputation. But you're just a cheap crook like the rest of them. Get out of here!"

Carter's eyes bored into Hawks' and his whole body was rigid with anger. He had failed, it was true, but he felt sure no human ingenuity could long resist Achmed ben Hassan, whose servants killed themselves lest they betray their master.

Anger burned in him like white-hot iron. "Okay, Colonel Hawks," he said. "I'll leave, but nothing on earth can keep me from following this case to its end. And I'll catch this Achmed ben Hassan. He has discredited me and he preys on women and—" he bowed gravely "—I am a man of sentiment."

He whirled and strode out of the apartment, slid behind the wheel of his Hispano Suiza. His high forehead wrinkled with thought, he shot the powerful car out toward the open country. He had a problem and long drives helped him think clearly.

His foot was heavy on the accelerator and the drone of his motor was a song of speed. Apartments swept past him, then smaller homes, interspersed by trees.

He became aware then that bright twin headlights were on his trail. Carter shot his car more rapidly ahead. The machine hung on. The last of the houses were past now, and he rolled through lonely park lands that invited speed. The Hispano took the challenge, roared like a comet. But those dogging headlights hung on.

Carter, a grim smile on his mouth, loosened his automatic in its holster and eased up on the accelerator.

His quick eyes flung ahead, spotted a low bridge. He spurted, slewed to a stop just beyond the arch, backed onto smooth grass at the roadside, cut motor and headlights. He sat waiting, tensely, gun in hand.

**EVERY SOUND** in the world seemed to cease with the stopping of the Hispano's motor. There was no distant mutter of an engine. The bridge cut off the sound, Carter thought. He had been too far ahead for the assassins to have seen him stop. Nevertheless his tenseness increased as he cranked down the special windshield flat against the cowl to clear the decks for battle.

He sat so for some minutes, and still no following car appeared. Carter twisted about and searched the skyline above the bridge. Nothing moving there. Nothing moving anywhere. Just the still, sinking moon in the sky, and in the distance the rasping double croak of a tree frog.

Carter cursed under his breath, unfolded his long lithe body from beneath the wheel, and toiled up the rise to the bridge.

The grassy slope was slippery with dew, studded with shrubs, and Carter, struggling up its steep incline, bent almost double. The gun was alertly ready in his fist. The bridge gave him a wide sweep of road dully lighted by the moon.

The highway was a white, unspotted river. Nothing there that might be a car. His eyes pierced the shadows. The car might have been parked in the edge of the woods, with lights out. Achmed ben Hassan's assassins might be creeping upon him even now.

Carter snorted at his fears. That car must have turned off into some side road he had missed. He strode back and half-slid down to his car. He jerked open the door, heard the soft pad of furtive feet. He whirled too late.

Strangling silken folds jerked tight over his face, around his throat, and throttled him. A sweetish odor dogged his nostrils. He twisted his gun behind him and fired. A man screamed in pain, then the gun was wrenched from his hand. The silken garrote tightened. The odor choked him. Carter was sinking, sinking, into blackness.

## CHAPTER THREE

## SLAVES OF ACHMED

TINKLING LUTE strings, faint as an ancient memory, was the first sound Ken Carter consciously heard. His senses drifted slowly back, but with rare presence of mind he forced his eyelids to remain closed, trying to orient himself. He continued his deep, regular breathing. Delicate, flowerlike perfume wafted over him.

He realized he lay upon soft cushions; his fingers, moving fractionally, snagged on silk. He heard girls' voices nearby.

Queer, he felt no headache from that attack on the road, no pain in throat or lungs. He slitted his eyes and peered out through the mesh of his lashes. A wall straight ahead of him was twenty feet away and hung with exquisite tapestry. To his right was an arched opening through which sunlight streamed.

The whispers at his side had ceased, and only the archaic tinkling of the lute continued. Carter rolled his head over slowly, then blinked in bewilderment.

Lolling on cushions beside the heap of luxurious silk on which he lay were two girls of dark and exquisite beauty. Their eyes were large and dark in pale, fair faces, and jeweled fillets bound their locks.

As Carter gazed in amazement, the two girls rose and swept slow salaams and he realized with a start that their clothing consisted of jeweled plates about their bosoms and diaphanous skirts that hung low on softly curving hips. They stood with hands folded modestly and downcast eyes, and one spoke in a low, musical voice:

"Master, we are thy slaves."

Carter squeezed his eyes tightly shut, opened them again. The girls were still there. He thrust himself up from the cushions, sitting erect with an effort, and frowned upon the two unbelievable beauties.

"In God's name," he asked softly, "who are you?"

"The handmaidens of Allah," the one who had first spoken replied, and Carter cried out:

"Achmed ben Hassan!"

The girls before him showed by no slightest change of expression that the name meant anything to them, and Carter went on.

"You will tell me next, I suppose, that I am in Paradise, or whatever the Mohammedan equivalent of that is."

The girl, startled, peered into his face with wide eyes and said:

"Surely thou art no unbeliever!"

Carter frowned, swore under his breath, got abruptly to his feet.

The girls bowed, "What is it my lord requires?"

"Let me speak with Allah," Carter said grimly.

The girl salaamed again and said: "This way, my lord," and moved off with a slow, gliding step that was almost music. Carter saw her feet were bare and that the nails were stained with henna.

Following her with lithe, strong strides, he swiftly studied the building. It appeared to be Oriental in every respect. It was plaster and stone. The doorways were low and the rooms draped with gorgeous rugs and silk. Windows were eastern arches, and across them were iron lattices.

They reached finally a huge carved door, and the girl salaamed again and stepped aside. Carter stopped and regarded her.

"Your name?"

"Elandi, master."

"You go no farther than this?"

"It is forbidden, master. We are thy slaves and none other may look upon us."

Carter frowned and ran his hand up over the twin peaks of his forehead.

"Not even if I order it?"

"If you order it, master, I will go."

Fright trembled in the girl's voice. Carter asked softly:

"Why are you afraid?"

**THE GIRL** trembled even more and folded her arms so that her right hand lay upon her left shoulder and her left upon her right. She said, "If you will come, I will show you why."

Carter hesitated, then nodded and she led the way through a side passage that grew increasingly dark. The blackness suddenly seemed to turn green and gradually a pale green light diffused into the air and they entered a small long chamber.

At the other end was a cabinet. The girl stopped in the doorway, and her trembling was more noticeable than ever.

"If you will look in that cabinet," she said, "you will know why I dare not disobey."

Carter, something in him rebelling at all this mummery, sped across the room, sprang up low stairs to the cabinet, thrust out his hand to the door.

But even so, with his hand outstretched, he paused. Might this not be some trick, some device of Achmed ben Hassan, who sought to get him within his power?

Ken Carter snorted at that foolishness. He was in Achmed's power! He grasped the knob of the doors. At the touch, the doors folded back. Within the cabinet stood a girl.

Golden hair streamed over her shoulders, her body was exquisite, but her face was twisted into gargoyle ugliness by fear. The eyes stared wide, the mouth was open as if to scream. But there was no life in her. She might have been a statue, a stone statue, except for the golden, cascading loveliness of her hair.

Another victim of the creeping death of Achmed ben Hassan!

Anger swept in a white-hot tide over Carter as he stood there, and he strode across the room. A voice boomed into it, a voice that might have come from anywhere, and nowhere.

The girl prostrated herself on the floor, terror-stricken. Carter stopped tensely, fists clenched, head thrown back defiantly. The great voice boomed out:

"I challenge thee, Carter! Death with the girl in the cabinet, or life with the girl on the floor!"

Carter's eyes ran swiftly over the ceiling, searched the walls. He strode across and tore aside a tapestry—only blank stone behind it. The voice boomed laughter.

"You have until tonight to decide. What you wish, you need only ask for—and the girl is thy slave."

Carter crossed to her. "Get up!" he bit out, and the girl, still cowering, rose to her feet.

"Take me to Allah," he said.

She gasped out: "But that was the voice of Allah!"

A grim smile lighted Carter's face. "I want to see him face to face."

The girl's eyes were wide, her head began to shake slowly from side to side, then violently, and she protested:

"No! No! It is not permitted. The sight of Allah means death."

"Just the same," Carter insisted slowly, "I want a look at him. If that's Allah, he talks a whole lot like a human being. Lead on, Elandi."

The girl started tremblingly down the passage and the green luminance of the chamber of death faded into blackness. And then there was a distant gleam of sunlight and they were back in the chamber where Carter had first regained consciousness.

"Listen," he said shortly, "this isn't the place you were taking me at first." The other girl had vanished now, and the lute music had ceased, and Elandi stood in the middle of the room, her arms hanging at her sides, palms forward in a gesture of supplication.

"Allah is everywhere," she said. "If he wishes you to see him, you may. If not—" she lifted one shoulder in a small shrug, moved toward him on gliding, dancing feet, her filmy skirt swaying. She put her hands upon his shoulders. The nails were hennaed and her dark hair was scented with musk. Her voice sank to a whisper.

"Do you yearn for death? Why not forget whatever it is that the voice of Allah has warned you against? Why not live here," her whispering voice became a fragrant breath that fanned his mouth, "with me?"

Carter raised her chin with a hand, and his eyes, studying hers, were weary.

"Nice child," he said.

He led her to the couch, looked down with a strange, hard smile on his face.

"I am going," he said, "for a little walk."

# CHAPTER FOUR
# TWO MEN DIE

CARTER'S LONG-LEGGED stride sped him across the room, out the exit he and the girl had first used. Hallways and trick entrances confused him, but eventually he stood at the heavy carved door behind which the girl had said previously was the voice of Allah.

He seized the knob and the door swung inward, revealed a long, high room at the far end of which stood an empty golden throne. A dozen men strolled about. One or two glanced at him curiously, but none spoke.

Carter's long stride was slow and determined. He marched up the center of the room, straight up the low steps, and sat upon the throne.

For a moment there was absolute silence, the men frozen into statues of amazement. There was a sudden surge and shrill cries and they raced to the room, jammed about the foot of the throne steps. They did not seem to dare to advance farther.

Carter leaned forward, putting his elbow on his knee, and regarded the men with apparent disinterest, his face calm.

"I'd like to have a little chat with Allah," he said. "What hocus-pocus do you use to call his attention to the fact that I'm here?"

A great voice boomed out suddenly overhead. There was anger in it.

"Down, fool! Down upon your knees, and pray for forgiveness!"

Carter leaned carelessly back in the throne and crossed his knees.

"Sorry to disappoint you," he said casually, "but the floor looks mighty hard."

The men before him had dropped down and their foreheads were bowed until they touched. One straightened and raised his hands above his head, crying:

"Oh Allah, what shall thy servants do to avenge this insult?"

"Horseradishes," Carter grunted and strolled down the throne steps.

"Listen, you bozos, this is all a fake. That lad has got a radio up there and he's broadcasting, and that's all this voice of Allah business amounts to."

The great voice trembled with fury now. "Seize him!"

A half dozen men leaped on Carter and dragged him down, pinioning him flat on his back on the floor. A man with a sour, blackened face drew a long knife and laid its blade against Carter's throat. He gazed at the wall above the throne as if awaiting orders.

The full resonant glow returned to the voice.

"Carter, you are a brave man, and a foolish one, and overbold. Still, I would use your brain in my business. Will you serve me—or die?"

Carter twisted and stared up at the vacant throne, and short laughter barked from his lips.

"Neither!" he said sharply, and felt the knife prick his throat. His narrowed, dark eyes glared into those of the man who gripped it.

"Listen, fool!" he said "If you strike without orders, you're going to be in a hell of a tough spot."

The man grinned savagely and turned his head heavily and stared up above the throne. Carter's voice rose peltingly.

"You are not served by men, but by skulking dogs. I could conquer any three of them at one time."

He looked around at the angry circle of faces, bent intently over his recumbent form. "Run on and play with your paper dolls," he growled.

The voice was mild and vague. "Youseff."

The man with the knife looked up. "Youseff, kill thyself."

THE MAN blinked his small black eyes once, took two steps out into the room, faced the throne and thrust the knife to the hilt in his breast.

He stood swaying a moment with his hand on the hilt of the weapon, an exaltation in the small eyes fixed on the empty throne. Then his knees gave and he twisted and fell to his back.

"Mohammet," came the soft voice again, "hurl thyself from that window!"

A man ran across the room and dived over the high railing. Carter's eyes were twin points of anger.

"Are you men or slaves," he flung at his captors, "to kill yourselves at the mere whim of this fake?"

The booming voice of the unseen master, gentle now, was the only answer:

"Is there any living king, Carter, who is served as I am? Can you afford not to ally yourself with one so powerful? I grant you ten minutes to think. If you refuse, they will be your last ten minutes of life."

Ken Carter cried hoarsely: "Then call off your pack of dogs, and let me think!"

The men snarled over him, but the voice called them off and Carter got slowly to his feet and paced the long throne room. Arched windows showed a sunset, but a wall hid the earth. Against the varicolored west, a humpbacked monoplane was flying, heading south, and the hum of its motors came distantly.

A blond man with blue, kindly eyes strolled up to Carter and said: "You have five minutes left."

The double carven doors at the other end of the room burst open and Elandi ran on little dancing feet into the room.

The men shouted angrily and converged on her, but the booming voice of the unseen filled the room again, halting them. The girl glanced with wide frightened eyes about the room, saw Carter and ran toward him with outstretched arms, seized his coat with her little hennaed hands and turned beseeching dark eyes up on his face.

"The voice told me to come in here," she said swiftly, "and I am terribly afraid, for women are not allowed in the throne room. It means their death."

Carter patted her on the shoulder. "I'll take care of you, child," he said.

The blond, slight man with the kindly blue eyes said softly. "You have one minute left."

Carter thought desperately, ran his hand up over his high-peaked forehead into his dull hair. Suddenly powerful hands seized his arms and wrists. The girl uttered a little smothered cry and Carter jerked angrily in her direction and saw that she, too, was held by two men.

They were marched with the slow, solemn pace of a sacrificial parade back to the throne and the deep booming voice sounded again.

"Well, Carter, my ally or my enemy?"

Carter threw up his head defiantly.

"Just a moment, Carter," came the voice. "You speak not alone for yourself. If you die, the girl dies also. It is a little custom of ours. I know she means nothing in particular to you, but she is woman, and you are an American.... A man of sentiment, I have heard. Now, Carter, your decision."

Ken Carter turned his head slowly and looked at the girl, and found a dagger presented at her breast. Her face was white and her eyes pleaded. Strangely, it was her little, henna-tinted feet that moved him. They looked so like a child's. Carter squared his shoulders and glared at the throne.

"You hold all the trumps," he said slowly.

# CHAPTER FIVE
# ACHMED STRIKES

**K**EN CARTER straightened aching shoulders, glanced about him. The interior of his Hispano Suiza was wet with dew. The windshield was misted.

Carter dragged a hand heavily across his high forehead, leaned forward against his clenched fist and tried to think. He remembered perfectly a girl with bare feet and hennaed nails and eyes that cried for help. Or was it all a fantastic dream?

Carter felt rapidly through his pockets and came upon a long thin roll of vellum. He opened it and with frowning eyes read:

*Hear and obey. If you fail, you die.*
*Achmed ben Hassan.*

A bitter, thin smile twisted his lips. Achmed had drugged him, hasheesh probably, and had him transported back to his car. And he demanded obedience. Carter's smiling lips became hard. He kicked the starter and sent the Hispano roaring toward town.

One thing stood clearly out in his mind, the picture of a humpbacked monoplane speeding across a sunset sky. He knew the Stinson had a profile like that. There was a bare chance that through this knowledge he might locate the aerie of Achmed ben Hassan.

Carter sped straight to his home, a high, quiet penthouse he had taken after gangsters had wrecked his previous quarters during his terrific battle against the Blue Terror.

On his way he bought a newspaper, and once in the lofty aloofness of his apartment he read it hurriedly. The date told him he had been in the stronghold of Achmed forty-eight hours. Its pages told him other things, too. The death of Colonel Hawks' daughter—she was actually his ward, the story stated—had revealed a widespread black-mailing plot by Achmed ben Hassan.

Dozens of letters such as the one Hawks had received had been sent out, and many had paid with the threat of horrible death hanging over them. Authorities were working madly to checkmate the assassins.

Carter phoned his office and ordered his corps of assistants to place every single-motored Stinson in the country at sunset the day before. He hung up on their excited questions about himself and snapped suddenly out of his chair, whirling with his gun in his hand. No one in sight. Yet he had heard glass tinkle in breaking and a thump on the soft, thick carpet.

Carter's swift eyes spotted a stone in the middle of the floor with paper tied around it. He darted through French doors to the roof. The sunlight was dazzling. No one in sight, and except for the rumble of distant traffic, there was no sound, no drone of airplane motors. The nearest building was a hundred yards away.

Carter slowly holstered his gun, strode back into the living room, picked up the stone. The paper tied about it was a note.

The note said:

> It would be wise, *effendi*, if you would ally yourself with the police, then frustrate all their plans where the pursuit of Achmed ben Hassan is concerned. It is for this that your life and brain were spared. Remember, if you serve well and faithfully, there are countless rewards. If you fail, there is the Stone Death.
>
> *Achmed ben Hassan.*

Carter cursed under his breath, ran his hand swiftly up over the dual peaks of his forehead into his dull hair. His dark eyes were angry, an ugly light in them. The phone rang. Carter still stared down at the ornate chirography.

There was a postscript. It stated that when need arose, someone would make contact with him for his "report." Carter shredded the note with the previous one and set them afire on an ash tray.

The phone rang again more insistently and Carter crossed to it in quick long strides.

"Carter speaking."

"Thank God you've come back," a man's voice poured words into his ear. "We want to hear your version of the Hawks murder and you must help us, too. Gregory Delaney has been threatened now."

Carter asked quietly: "Who's speaking?"

"Inspector Littleman," the voice snapped back and Carter remembered a small lean man with a dark, intent face.

"You want me to go to Delaney's house?"

"At once!" Littleman barked. "You fought these assassins at Hawks' house. You know how they work. Your help in guarding Delaney will be invaluable."

**A PRIVATE** automatic elevator dropped Carter to the street. He sank back into the leather cushions of his Hispano gratefully and the deep-throated motor dragged him swiftly up Fifth Avenue, across to Columbus and up Riverside Drive to the great stone mansion of Gregory Delaney.

A picketed iron fence surrounded grounds thick with shrubbery. A policeman clanged open the gate and Carter nodded and strode quickly past, keen eyes noting the layout of the grounds. A thousand hiding places in those shrubs, but the black outline of the fence was clear against the opposing buildings.

He spotted Littleman's small, wiry figure in uniform and nodded briefly to the lean-faced inspector of police.

"We have three hours before dark," Carter said rapidly. "Let's have floodlights rigged to cover those fences all around the grounds. Then if we post enough men around, the assassins can't possibly get in—or away."

Littleman nodded and issued orders.

"And that's about all we can do," Carter said. "Checked the servants yet?"

Littleman nodded. Something white struck and bounced in front of them and the two men crouched, snatching ready guns. Nothing to be seen, no one near. Carter's brow was wrinkled angrily. Littleman picked up the paper tied to a rock, read slowly:

> *The penalty of treachery is death.*
> *Achmed ben Hassan.*

A warning to him, Carter knew, but Littleman frowned over the message, shrugged it aside. The two redoubled their efforts to fortify the Delaney mansion.

When darkness fell three hours later, Carter was making a round of the sentinels, churning his way through shrubbery, searching every inch of the mansion's grounds.

Silence lay over the place on the Drive. Clouds rolled overhead and the earth sucked down darkness like a blotter sucking ink.

Carter nearly stumbled into a shoulder high clump of spirea, circled it on wary feet. He cursed softly to himself. The backglow of the floodlights, revealing the black bars of the fence, only made his own task more difficult.

He was on edge, his nerves taut. He felt slightly super-stitious about Achmed, as if the man were a doom upon him. He was conscious also that police were keeping him closely under eye. He wondered if Colonel Hawks had repeated his charges of criminal neglect or attempted to connect him with the assassins.

His swinging hand struck a barberry bush and he whistled, jerking it away and sucking it, glaring down at the thorny shrub. Something metallic gleamed within it and he leaped back.

His spring was just in time. Two men exploded from the bush with upraised knives. His years of juggling, of split-second analysis of motion, stood him in good stead now. He plunged to the right. As the knives slashed down, his left fist shot out, hurled one man against the other.

They tangled, plunged to the ground. Carter whipped out his gun and slashed down on the nearest head. Police sentries shouted, three ploughed headlong through the shrubbery.

The second man, protected by his unconscious com-panion's body, slashed at Carter's legs. The tall detective danced out of range, weaved about, seeking an opening. Suddenly he leaped backward. The unconscious body seemed to spring at him from the ground. It caught his ankles and he half stumbled.

Police were just behind him now, shouting loudly. Carter, off-balanced momentarily, saw the second man leap to his feet, saw steel glitter in his hand as it swept back and Carter fell face down on the ground. Steel whispered above his head. A choking scream shivered up into the black night.

Instantly Carter was on his feet again. The man flashed away over the grounds. Carter, pursuing, darted a glance over his shoulder. A policeman was a swaying figure against the white floodlights, his hands tugging at a knife in his chest.

**CARTER RACED** on through the shrubs. The murderer had disappeared.

Inspector Littleman's short, striding legs brought him panting to Carter's side. They dashed back to the prisoner and the stabbed policeman. The officer was dead.

Littleman ordered the grounds searched, handcuffed the prisoner and, with Carter, herded him up the marble stairways of the mansion to an elaborate drawing-room.

Carter thrust the prisoner into a chair. The man was dark-visaged, hawk-nosed. He glared savagely, handcuffed hands buried in his sleeves.

"Where's your plane?" Carter demanded.

The man bared long yellow teeth in a snarling smile, said nothing.

Carter said softly: "You don't fear death, I know, but many things can happen to a man before he dies." He spun on his heel, long-legged across the room, borrowed a cop's nightstick. He wrapped it in newspaper, came back and thrust it under the prisoner's nose.

"We have a new sort of nightstick," he said softly. "Shall I—demonstrate it to you?"

Littleman growled, "Here, give me that. I know how to use it." He crouched and snapped it against the dark-faced man's shins. It rang hollowly, like a stick on concrete, and the prisoner gave no sign that he felt the blow at all.

Carter's eyes narrowed. He sprang to the man and seized both his wrists, wrenched the hands out of the sleeves. A metal hypodermic needle clattered to the floor. The prisoner smiled mockingly.

"Not even the scourge of Allah could hurt me now," his words grew blurred. The mocking leer froze on his mouth.

"This is the Stone Death, Littleman," Carter said heavily. "Achmed's men all kill themselves to protect him."

They went through the man's clothing, but found only another of those carefully penned notes and a six-foot strip of leather which widened to about two inches at its middle and had a loop at one end. Carter held it up.

"That explains how Achmed's notes are delivered. A sling, and a powerful one. It could hurl a rock 150 to 200 yards with great accuracy."

"More damn fool things mixed up with this case," Littleman growled. "Here, let me see that letter."

He opened it, glanced at it swiftly, then peered up with eyes hard as agates. His hand flashed under his coat, jammed a long-nosed revolver into Carter's middle.

"You're one of Achmed ben Hassan's men we'll make talk," he bit out.

## CHAPTER SIX
## A MURDER MISTAKE

CARTER SUBMITTED to search by two policemen Littleman called, but his eyes were ugly in his thin long face. His voice rasped:

"You will explain this, Littleman, or I'll have you kicked off the force!"

Littleman laughed shortly. He seemed to swell with triumph. "I've suspected you for a long time, Carter. You solve cases too easily. You couldn't do it if you weren't in with the crooks you trap. And I've noticed this: men you capture always die."

Carter glared. "You don't even capture any, Littleman."

Littleman's doubled fists drove hard toward Carter, pinioned helplessly by the two policemen. The inspector's face was red with fury. Carter said wearily: "Oh, stow that!"

Littleman glowered at his captive and said heavily:

"This last note we took from Achmed's assassin goes like this." He drew the paper from his pocket and read somewhat laboriously:

*This is the price, Carter, of those who betray their master.*
*Achmed ben Hassan.*

Carter jerked his head impatiently.

"Can't you see it's just a trick?" he demanded. "Achmed is clever as hell. He's just trying to make trouble between you and me so his assassins will have no trouble in getting to Delaney."

Littleman laughed nastily: "I'm afraid it's no use, Carter. I'll just put you where you can't help out your master. Judson, there's a radio car in the drive. Take Carter to headquarters. See that he gets ahold of no one and tell them to keep a guard on him to keep him from killing himself."

Carter grinned thinly: "You needn't worry, Littleman, I'm going to survive just to get back at you for this!"

Judson growled: "Okay," and Littleman returned Carter's stare with hostile intensity.

"And look out for this guy, Judson. He's slippery as an eel, and dangerous."

Judson said: "I'll take care of him," and he slipped a handcuff on Carter's left wrist and locked him to his own right arm.

"He won't get away from me, Inspector," Judson said. "Come on, you!" and he jerked the handcuff and strode off across the room with Carter at his side.

The lanky detective made no resistance. His eyes were nearly closed and there was tense anger in the stiff abrupt swing of his shoulders. The cop climbed into the car first, still handcuffed to Carter, and the tall detective folded his lanky body into the seat beside him. Carter clicked the door, stared down at his feet and said laconically: "Home, James!"

Judson glared at him out of the corner of his eye and then down at the handcuffs fastening Carter's left hand to his right. He lifted their two hands toward the dashboard to turn on the ignition, but didn't do it and let the hands fall back to the seat between them again and looked at them.

Judson muttered under his breath, and Carter said: "I beg pardon? I didn't hear you," and the cop growled, "Oh go to hell."

Suddenly he began to smile. He pulled Carter's arm over so that the handcuffs were against the steering post, then rapidly unlocked the bracelet about his own wrist and fastened it to the steering post of the car.

Carter watched him with amusement at the back of his eyes. The cop leaned back with a sigh of relief, then reached over Carter's arm to turn on the ignition, reached under his arm to shift gears. Carter said dryly: "That was a very clever stunt, Judson. It makes everything so convenient."

The policeman growled and tugged his visored cap down over his fat, ruddy face.

"Chief said not to take any chances with you and I'm not," he said, and spurted the car down the drive, waited while two other policemen opened the gate, then shot on downtown.

Carter began to squirm in his seat as the car shot down the Drive, pushed over to Columbus Avenue and then over to Fifth. "Listen, Judson," he said. "As a favor to me, would you mind going down some other street than Fifth? I don't fancy having my friends seeing me handcuffed like this."

Just then the lights went red and Judson, with a grunt, whirled left, down a dark, deserted side street. Carter swayed to the right, then lurched to the left, jamming the elbow of his handcuffed hand over both of Judson's. His right hand cut off the ignition, balled into a fist, and flashed to Judson's jaw.

Carter had trouble getting strength behind the blow. Judson was only dazed, and Carter was compelled to slam his fist again to the policeman's jaw before he was out.

The car coughed to a halt. Carter's swift fingers found the handcuff key in the policeman's pocket, unlocked himself. He hauled the policeman to his side of the seat, handcuffed him and gagged him with two handkerchiefs from his pocket.

**WITHIN A** minute and a half after he had jammed his elbow into the cop's side, he was driving the car swiftly toward his own apartment. He switched the radio on and immediately it began to squawk:

"General alarm," it said, and even in the stereotyped tones of the announcer there was excitement. "Pick up man six feet tall, Arabian or Syrian, dark face, scar on nose, last seen near Delaney mansion wearing long black robe from shoulder to ankle. Wanted for the murder of Gregory Delaney."

Carter's eyes narrowed. So the assassins had got through the guard after all, and killed Gregory Delaney! That made the charge against him accessory in murder. It meant, too, that the inspector would check his arrival at headquarters and when he failed to show up would broadcast an alarm for him, too.

He shot the police car to the curb near his apartment, hurled out the cop, who was mumbling dazedly now, and shoved him into the private automatic elevator that lifted them to his penthouse.

Once in his home, Carter whistled gaily, mixed a sleeping draft that he forced down Judson's unwilling throat.

Judson spluttered angrily: "You'll pay for this. What are you trying to do, poison me?"

Carter said grimly: "No. Just shutting your mouth for a while."

He shoved the policeman into a chair and stood guard over him until his head began to nod in sleep. Then he swiftly unlocked the handcuffs, took Judson out of his uniform and put him in Carter's own bed, handcuffed him there.

"Sweet dreams!" Carter muttered, and carrying the uniform, strode into his study, where he phoned his office to get the report on the check-up of Stinson planes.

His assistants had located a dozen in use at sunset the previous day, but seven had been headed in the wrong direction. Three others were too far west and of the rest, one had been on the way to Washington, and the other over the Big Smoky Mountains of eastern Tennessee.

Carter said: "Have Cary and Daniels go immediately to Newark airport and get the Lockheed ready for me."

He hung up, hurriedly donned the police uniform. The trouser legs were a bit short and there was too much room around the waist. Carter smiled grimly.

"Too bad Judson can't admire me in his uniform."

He hustled into the bedroom for a last look at the sleeping policeman. He switched on the light and spotted the white flutter of a piece of paper on the man's chest. Carter sucked breath between his teeth, crossed the room in a stride and a half and crouched over the note.

*The penalty of treachery is death.*
                    *Achmed ben Hassan.*

He touched the man. He was like stone. Achmed ben Hassan had murdered the policeman, thinking he was Carter!

Carter spun to the window, made a whirlwind search of his apartment and roof, and found no one. The murderer had vanished as completely as life had gone from Carter's prisoner on the bed.

Carter's fists clenched. He must, he must find Achmed ben Hassan now, rip the mask from his murdering features! For Judson's death meant an open and shut murder case against Carter.

## CHAPTER SEVEN
## ACHMED'S AERIE

**C**ARTER STOOD for a moment staring down at the stiff body of the man who had died in his stead. A hard, tight fighting smile lifted his mouth, but his eyes were like brown agate.

He dropped the elevator to the street, sent the police car skittering around a corner and down Fifth Avenue. He switched on the radio again.

Squawks and routine orders came from the instrument as he raced past apartment houses, past shops and office buildings, weaving through a clutter of night traffic.

Then abruptly there was a new squawk on the radio, "General Alarm. All cars Manhattan and Bronx, Brooklyn relay. Kenneth Carter, private operative, wanted in the murder of Gregory Delaney escaped while on way to headquarters with Patrolman Judson."

A word picture of Carter ran into great detail. His smile was bitter now. Carter shot down into the noisy rush of Holland Tunnel, over the express highway. The police car and his uniform shot him past the tollgate, up to the private hangars of the Newark airport, alight with purple flood lamps.

His low-winged red Lockheed Orion was outside the hangar with motor idling. One of his men stood beside it, arguing with two men in police uniform. Carter shot the police flivver up beside the Orion. The two policemen turned to him with relief. They were state troopers, Jersey men.

One jerked his thumb over his shoulders. "This bozo has a special dispensation supposed to exempt him from police interference."

Carter growled: "Yeah, he'll lose that now," and stalked across to the side of the plane.

If the operative's pudgy face showed any sign of recognition, Carter could not identify it as such. The man glared at him as sullenly as he had at the two New Jersey officers.

"There's supposed to be two of you," Carter growled, "Where's the other one?"

"None of your damned business," the man growled back at him, and Carter turned to the two Jersey policemen.

"Do you mind holding this bozo? I think the other guy's inside the plane."

The Jersey policeman said: "Sure," seized Carter's man by the shoulders and eased him over to one side. The door of the Orion was closed. Carter jerked it open and, bent over, walked forward. His man sat hunched down in the forward compartment so that he was invisible outside.

As Carter entered, the man whirled and jabbed the nose of a heavy automatic toward his face, recognized Carter beneath the visor of the police cap, and sputtered, "Well, for God's sake, man, what are you doing in that outfit?"

Carter said swiftly: "Get out of that, Daniels."

Daniels eased out of the single cockpit and Carter slid in. His hand jerked the throttle and the Orion bellowed into movement.

Daniels shouted in his ear: "You're heading down wind!"

Carter's mouth was grim. He nodded slowly, leaned forward and adjusted the propeller pitch to maximum climbing power. A long field and light load. That would help, but he was taking a big chance with the Orion's small wing area.

Sharp cries outside drowned in the roar of the motor. The airport starter dashed forward, waving his flag excitedly, pointing to a big Curtis Condor racing nose-on toward the Lockheed.

**CARTER KICKED** the rudder over, reversed it to check, shot down with the wind. A glimpse of the frightened face of the Condor's pilot, then they were gone.

The Orion's tail seemed nailed to the ground. The edge of the field was closer now, beyond it high-tension power lines stretched their steel-meshed net. Carter's jaw clamped. His eyes were pinpoints. Not a chance of taking off if he turned now. Hell, he couldn't turn now. Too near the edge of the field, going too fast. Daniels was shouting in his ear. He couldn't understand. It didn't matter.

At long last the tail lifted sluggishly. The motor was grinding, laboring. Carter tested the stick. The Orion hopped like an ungainly bird. He heaved on the stick, sent her nose up almost in a stall, nosed down and then almost muscled the Orion into the air as the markers of the field's edge slid past under the tires.

The steel net of wires loomed ahead. The motor labored. Carter's mouth was a grim white slit. With every nerve of his body he fought to lift the wind-logged ship. The wires flashed toward them. Carter pulled up the nose and waited for the snagging crash. Fractions of seconds dragged past.

Carter blew out breath between tight teeth, whirled the Orion in a steep bank and rode the lift of the wind upward, upward. Clouds at 5,000 feet. Carter dove into them, nosed south. His face relaxing, he leaned forward and switched the lever to maximum speed pitch for the propeller. They'd have a tough time flagging down the Orion now.

He raised his head, jerked a nod at Daniels. "Take her," he shouted. "Wake me when we pass Greensboro."

Daniels' face was strained. He smiled faintly.

"Pretty work," he yelled back and took the wheel.

Carter slipped off the police uniform, drew on tight-legged riding breeches and a flying suit. From weapon racks he selected a heavy automatic, a pair of glasses, and stretched out on the special seats of his Orion to sleep.

Carter woke shortly after dawn of his own accord before they had passed over the North Carolina town, and swept the country below with glasses while the Orion followed the path of the Stinson he had spotted from Achmed's aerie. He searched for a high-walled place in which would be Moorish windows covered with iron grill.

**IT TOOK** twelve hours of flying to find the place, high in the Big Smokies. Tangled virgin forest stretched on all sides of it for miles, but high on the promontory where the big Moorish building sprawled was a dinky landing field.

The Orion could never sit down there, or, having landed, could never take off. Carter doubted that anything but an autogyro could use that field. Carter swiftly strapped on a parachute pack, went forward to Daniels, He shouted:

"I'm going to bail out. Fly across the field. After I jump, hit for Raleigh. Get men to back me up. I've got to get down there so they won't get away. Whoever you bring better wear parachutes."

Daniels nodded, banked the ship in a slow circle. Carter heaved open the door against wind pressure, stepped out at four thousand feet. He shot down and down and down and didn't yank the rig ring until he was within 1,500 feet of the surface. Even so, a half dozen men spilled out over the field beneath him.

Carter's keen eyes were grim and he reached up to the shrouds of the parachute, pulled down on one side until air, slipping out from under the bell of the 'chute, slid him off to one side of the field into the trees.

Dangerous business, diving into trees that way, but landing on the field meant capture, and the woods would delay those henchmen of Achmed.

His side-slipping had been cleverly done. The men had rushed toward the near end of the field to meet him. By his side-slipping he had sent the 'chute back over the hangar and a hundred yards into the woods. He spotted a small clearing filled with second growth pine, as close together as quills on a porcupine's back. They broke his landing.

Carter sprawled to the ground, scrambled up unhurt. No time to unbuckle the harness. He snatched out a knife, slashing the shrouds, darted off through the pines. They grew slightly above his head, and the thick, intermingling needles allowed no more than two or three feet visibility.

Once out of the second growth, the forest became park-like, huge, straight pines, whose branches did not begin until fifty feet above the ground. Underfoot a carpet of pine needles, brown and slippery. Difficult woods to hide in.

Carter heard now the crashing of men, working through the second growth he had just quitted. He could see the hangars, a dark blotch against the sky. He took out his automatic, streaked back along the edge of the pines, ran swiftly toward the field again. The soft needle-carpeted earth gave off no sound.

There were two hangars, and Carter reached the first without having been spotted. He slipped along the side, peered in through the great open doors.

There was no one in the hangar, but there were three five-passenger cabin autogyros, like huge poised insects with their long rotors. Carter went swiftly to work, dumped a drum of gasoline down to the ground and rolled it slowly across the hangar so the gas covered the ground beneath the 'gyros. When most of the gasoline was out of the drum, he pushed it slowly toward the doorway, leaving a wet trail. Outside the hangar's door he touched a match to it.

Swift flames streaked across the floor and in a few seconds had wrapped the ships in red and yellow tongues of fire. Carter darted swiftly into the second hangar. No time here for elaborate preparations. He shoved a gasoline drum to the ground beneath the centermost of the three more 'gyros, wrenched at the gasoline plug.

There were wild shouts in the woods now. Carter dragged down a second drum. The plug stuck. He shot a hole through the drum, dragged it to the door, touched a match to the trail and fled.

He sprinted toward the sprawling building on the hill. It was a veritable castle. The high wall had doorways at regular intervals and a twisting path ran up the steep slope toward it, thick woods to either side.

Carter plunged into the woods. Those men on the field would have too much fire-fighting to do for a little while to bother him. There was a sullen roar and Carter whirled in time to see the roof of the hangar lift, the walls fly sideways. Patches of liquid flame spread over the field, flashed into the woods.

**THERE WERE** shouts now behind the wall toward which Carter panted through the cover of the woods. Gates flung open and men pounded down toward the field, a full twenty of them.

When no more men had come through the gates for a full minute and a half, Carter crept toward one and through it. Luxurious gardens spread within the wall. Flowering clusters of shrubbery were higher than his head. There was a profuse blossoming of roses and other exotic plants that Carter did not identify.

Abruptly he darted aside, crouched between two huge spreading bushes of Japanese quince, their thorns prodding him. He had caught a slight movement along the path, and as he crouched a huge Negro came into sight. He was naked to the waist but his legs were clothed in baggy golden silk and there were fantastic, brilliant shoes on his feet.

These were not the things Carter noticed. The right hand of the Negro grasped a scimitar with a heavy curved blade over four feet long. The man's movements were stealthy and his eyes swung from side to side, searching the shrubbery.

But dusk was filling the garden now, and Carter's clothing was dun-colored. The man, advancing with that long stride, crouched forward with that vicious blade in his hand, passed within five feet of where Carter crouched between the quince bushes.

He went around the corner of the building and Carter slipped out again and advanced toward the house. Around the third floor ran a shallow balcony, whose arched windows, covered with iron lattice, had been the clue by which Carter had identified the building from the plane.

As he slipped along, searching for some entrance, he heard a soft call and glanced up sharply, gun muzzle pointing with his eyes, to find a girl bending over the railing of the balcony. It was Elandi, his "slave!"

Her call was musical, as if she sang. A rope came writhing down from the balcony and she beckoned with a white hand.

A trap? But why bother? They could easily surround him in the garden. Carter took his gun between his teeth, tested the rope with a tug, and swung upward, hand over hand.

A hoarse shout below him in the garden. He twisted his head. The huge Negro was leaping in great strides across the garden, the scimitar raised.

He quickened his climb, twisted a leg into the rope and grabbed his automatic from between his teeth. The scimitar swished by beneath his feet.

The Negro howled unintelligible things, whirled back the blade again. Carter saw he would throw. His gun spoke, too late. Already the scimitar glittered through the air! But the blade required an expert to throw. It turned in the air. Its hilt struck Carter's hand, knocked the automatic to the earth.

Even while the sword and gun clattered to the ground, the Negro swayed on his feet. He toppled and fell like a redwood tree, mighty even in defeat.

Carter turned back to his climb, hauling himself with creaking muscles up the last ten feet. He caught the balcony rail, hauled himself over and stared into the venomous muzzles of three revolvers.

## CHAPTER EIGHT
## ALTAR OF ALLAH

BEHIND THOSE three pistols were the grimly determined faces of three assassins. The girl, after her treachery, had disappeared, and below him in the garden were heard the shouts of other men, returning from fighting the fire in the hangars.

Trapped—completely trapped, and at odds that were completely impossible. He had only one trump now. These men had no way of escape, now that the autogyros were burned, and land and hillside were clear for the landing of the relief that his operative was speeding in his swift Lockheed Orion.

Play for time was his cue—time was his only salvation. He smiled pleasantly into the muzzles of those three revolvers and said:

"Well, it looks as though you have me."

One of the men had a short upper lip and buckteeth, and when he spoke the upper lip was squeezed back and his teeth showed yellow and vicious as a wolf's. He said grimly:

"Yes. And this time you will not escape!"

He shoved his revolver into his robe and strode forward, assisting Carter over the balustrade. He leaned over and shouted down to the men below.

"The throne room. Allah summons you all to the throne room."

The three men closed about Carter. The screen of a window slid aside and they entered a room luxurious in Persian carpets. They strode along dim halls where Carter's hard heels echoed through the sly sibilance of slippers, where jeweled lamps cast a lurid glow. Finally heavy, carved doors swung open.

There were twenty men in a semicircle about the room, but only a sinister silence greeted him. Behind them he could see a low, white-draped, bier-like couch. His three immediate captors took him deliberately to it. At the couch's head an assassin stood with the huge, heavy scimitar that the Negro had vainly hurled at him.

Two men stepped forward and wordlessly began to strip Carter. He moved his arms unnecessarily, tossed at the men offers to do things for them, to unfasten the buckles of the 'chute harness, anything to play for time. He managed to delay them, but got not one syllable of response.

Finally he stood totally stripped, a leanly muscled, powerful man. A twist of white silk embroidered in gold was bound about his waist. Strong hands gripped his arms suddenly, and almost before he was aware of their intentions, he was spread-eagled upon the white bier.

The man with the huge scimitar strode forward. Carter wrenched his head about, saw that the man was stripped to the waist and that his shoulder muscles bulged with the lift and heft of the blade.

The man stood grimly at the head of the couch, put the tip of the blade on the floor and leaned on its hilt, his hands almost beneath his chin.

Carter forced his tensing muscles to relax, and calmly began to whistle a little tune. A man's fist struck across his mouth, and a deep voice boomed out:

"Silence and respect in the room of Allah!"

It was again what Elandi had called "The Voice of Allah."

A man began to intone guttural noises in a language Carter guessed must be Arabian, and the booming voice of Allah made responses. Finally it spoke in English.

"Kenneth Carter, you are to die, a sacrifice to wipe out your debt to Allah."

**CARTER KNEW** then that the platform on which he lay was an altar. The man with the scimitar moved. Carter's eyes flashed to him, saw him tense, and lift the big blade. Muscles pulled in the man's arms and he threw the blade back over his shoulder and then looked toward the wall above the throne, awaiting a signal.

Muscles swelled and corded in Carter's own arms against the tight grip of his captors. That blade, swishing down, would split him in two, from chest to the top of his head. Carter's face was drawn, his mouth corners strangely lifted in that narrow fighting smile of his.

There was a sudden clamor at the wooden door and Carter jerked his head about hopefully. The police? Oh, but not yet. They couldn't have come yet. It was not the police. The doors swung inward suddenly wide and through them rushed the small white figure of Elandi.

She waved above her head a thin, long knife and ran on swift feet across the floor to the throne and knelt.

"Allah, oh Allah, thy servant craves a boon, a chance to wipe out my disobedience. Let me execute the sentence of death upon this dog."

Men stood angrily over the bent figure of the girl, but no one touched her, and all stared at the wall above the throne, waiting, waiting for the decision of Allah upon the invasion of this girl.

Carter could not see her where she crouched, as he lay with his head straight back away from the throne. But the man with the scimitar had not moved. He stood still with his arms tensed back, ready to swish down with that murderous blade.

The voice of Allah was slow in answering, but finally its tone boomed out: "It is permitted."

The girl, with a glad little cry, sprang up and ran across to Carter's side. She was a little thing, and her eyes were warm, staring at Carter. There was no hostility in them, only friendliness.

She was dressed as she had been when Carter had first seen her, jeweled plates upon her breast and flowers in her hair. She raised the blade above her head and the voice of Allah broke in again rather hurriedly:

"No, no, not that way. And not the scimitar. Let it be the Stone Death."

The words fell like ice on Carter's heart. He saw movement and a man strode up beside the altar with a small glittering needle in his right hand. But even as he came near, the girl's dagger flashed down, a gleam of light striking not Carter, but the man that held his arm.

The man uttered a strangled cry and fell, and Carter sprang from the altar, fighting the man who gripped his other arm, and wrenching free. He felt a small hand upon his arm, and the blood-stained knife of Elandi's was thrust into his hand.

He charged the man with the scimitar, wrenched the huge blade from him, grasped it by the handle, and whirled. The blade was superbly balanced, its edge like Swedish razors. Two men fell at its first whistling sweep, a man with a knife dropped to his knees and thrust up under its swing.

Carter chopped down and the man's arm was severed at the shoulder. The scimitar flashed on, a glittering flame in the hands of the naked white giant. There was a shrill scream behind him, and Carter, with a whirling sweep of his blade to clear away his assailants, turned to see that Elandi had been seized by the man with the needle.

His hand was on her throat and her small body was arched backward on the altar, and the needle was going slowly toward her breast.

The scimitar slashed, sliced through needle and hand, and the man whirled back, blood spouting from the severed arm upon the girl. The voice of Allah boomed out suddenly:

"Down, down, all of you. So that I may slay this dog."

**THIS TIME** there was no doubt about the location of the voice. It came from behind the throne. Carter realized instantly that he would be helpless out of the protecting, close-pressing ranks of his attackers.

The voice of Allah had hardly ceased, the men were just dropping to their knees when he sprang forward, mounted the throne dais and struck violently against the wall behind it with the heavy hilt of his sword. It gave and Carter drew back and hurled himself against the same spot. A door pivoted beneath his thrust.

Darting into the opening, Carter dived sideways. Gun flame lanced at him from the dark, a lean hand thrust out between dark curtains and Carter swung the scimitar back and hurled it. His years at juggling stood him in good stead. It flew strong and true, and the revolver clattered to the floor.

Carter charged after the flying weapon and sprang upon the man behind the curtains. He was large and powerful and despite his wounded hand, gashed by the scimitar's blade, struggled violently against Carter.

They fought in almost total darkness, the only light filtering through the narrow door that Carter had forced. The heavy curtains swirled about them. A fist caught Carter in the face and hurled him violently back. He writhed aside as the man thumped down with his knees on the spot where Carter had lain. Carter jumped up and sprang on the man's back, linked his arms beneath his, and strained back.

"Give up, you fool," he grated out, "or I'll break your arm."

Sounds that might or might not have been words issued from the man. Carter, his grip on the man's arm rendering him helpless, dragged him toward the narrow door.

If he could show these assassins their conquered master, they might surrender, save the police a terrific struggle when they arrived.

Dragging the captive along, Carter became conscious of a stony chill in the man's arms. They were rigid and hard beneath his grasp, and Carter, with a sudden feeling of nausea at his stomach, dropped him to the ground.

He hit solidly and in the light of the small doorway Carter saw that his position remained entirely unchanged, that his face was twisted hideously with fear.

Carter put his hand slowly to the man's throat, and it was cold, as rigid as stone, and suddenly Carter understood. The blade of the scimitar that had gashed through the hypodermic needle about to kill the girl had slashed the man's hand immediately afterward! Poetic justice. The master of the Stone Death had died by the Stone Death, and from the virus intended for one of his victims!

Carter whirled and grabbed up his scimitar again, dashed for the door and saw the girl's small back in it. He peered over her shoulder and saw that she grasped an automatic and that she held at bay five or six assassins. Many others lay dead in a welter of blood where the scimitar had slashed, and others lay dead with bullets.

Clamor at the doors again. They swung wide and men in uniform with leveled guns dashed in. Carter stepped out into the open past the girl, his arm about her shoulders, and recognized Daniels at the head of the charge.

"Fine work, Danny!" he called.

Then he saw that the men behind Daniels were New York police.

"Danny," he said, "you didn't get all the way back to New York?"

Danny laughed and said: "No, they captured me in Raleigh, and I brought them along here to capture you."

Inspector Littleman strode forward, his keen dark eyes puzzled. He glanced at the shambles on the floor, to the girl with the gun in her hand, and the tall giant with the dark-stained scimitar.

"It looks as if we'd have to add to those murder charges against you," Littleman growled.

**CARTER TOOK** two swift strides forward and poised the scimitar. He grinned like a boy.

"Want to fight, Inspector?"

The police officer growled something unintelligible and demanded, "What the hell is this business, anyway?"

Carter said quietly: "Did you ever hear of Hassan ben Sabbah?" and Littleman growled, "No."

Carter said rapidly:

"He was called the Old Man of the Mountain. He lived in the tenth century and organized bands of assassins whom he tricked into believing they had gone to heaven for a few days, giving them everything that the Mohammedan expects to find in heaven.

"Then he gave them another dose of hasheesh and sent them back to earth in his service. If they served him, they went back to heaven when they died, and heaven to them had been such a delightful place that they did not hesitate to die at his command.

"Apparently this lad, Achmed ben Hassan, the same bloke these boys called Allah, had convinced them by means of a similar trick. You'll notice that all his servants are Syrian. I deduced this from his treatment of me when he kidnapped me and brought me to this castle originally. That was where I was, Inspector, just after Myra Hawks was murdered.

"He was using his assassinations to exact a tribute from the wealthy, just as Hassan ben Sabbah in the old days exacted money from the princes of the world."

"Yeah?" said Littleman. "Well, where is this guy Achmed?"

Carter's smile went from his face. He ducked his head toward the narrow opening behind him. "Achmed's in there, dead."

"Well, haul him out and let's see him."

Carter said, "Haul him out yourself. He died of the Stone Death that he was accustomed to inflicting upon other people."

"And what is this Stone Death?" Littleman demanded.

Carter said: "I haven't had any chance to puzzle out the exact nature of the injection he gave, but what he accomplished was to set up a condition of rigor mortis in the living body, stopping circulation of blood and stiffening the muscles so that the body became like stone.

"Cyanide poisons, especially prussic acid, cause early rigor mortis, often within an hour after death. Sometimes, in case of violent exertion, this occurs even sooner. Achmed undoubtedly used a cyanide in some terrible new form, ferreted out with his deep knowledge of the East and its secret poisons. He induced rigor mortis in the living body, turning people almost literally to stone.

"This business of death creeping from the feet upward was nothing unusual. In deaths by poison, especially those that affect the heart, the feet and hands always go numb first."

Littleman grunted, "You're so wonderful," and shouldered past Carter. "If you're squeamish about hauling out this Achmed guy, I'll do it."

He stepped in through the narrow entrance and flashed on his light. Carter heard a low curse of amazement and stepped in with him where the white light of his flash bathed the dead face of Achmed ben Hassan. The light showed a leonine white head and a face with the bristling white mustache.

"My God," cried Littleman, "It's Colonel Hawks himself!"

Carter smiled grimly and said:

"I'm not surprised. When Hawks hired me, his worry about his so-called daughter seemed vaguely unreal to me, and at his house I learned Myra had insisted on me and she tried to tell me of some suspicion, but she didn't get very far with it because Hawks wouldn't leave us alone.

"Then, when the assassins came, they opened the door with six locks on it as easily as I could open my own front door if I had a latch key. These men are human beings, and unless they had assistance—such as Hawks giving them the keys—they could not have opened the door. He must have feared his ward would give him away and took this means to kill her and avert suspicion from himself.

"Another thing that convinced me was the fact that Hawks was very slow in answering when I shouted for help while battling the assassins in Myra's room. Then, too, his house was full of relics of Asia, a tipoff in itself."

Carter felt a small warm hand on his arm and turned to find the brown soft eyes of Elandi looking up into his.

"Am I forgiven, lord?" she asked Carter.

He threw an arm about her shoulders.

"Forgiven? Yes, child—but I'll never forget."

# GALLOWS GHOST

DOWN OUT OF THE BLACK MAW
FLOATED THE GRISLY GALLOWS.
A TRIBUNAL OF TERROR SAT IN
JUDGMENT OVER THE LIVES OF
THE MIGHTY. AND A FIENDISH
EXECUTIONER DROPPED HIS
VICTIMS OUT OF THE NIGHT.
TO THE VICTIM'S BREAST WAS
ATTACHED A PLACARD. THAT
PLACARD CRIED VENGEANCE FOR
AN ANCIENT HATE.

# CHAPTER ONE
# THE HANGING JUDGE

**A LONG** line of luxurious cars filed past the entrance of the Cornwall Ball Park, stopping one by one to discharge a glittering array of wealth and fashion. Great red and white posters beside the gate announced a charity performance of Aida.

Ken Carter, lolling back on the deep cushions of his Daimler sedan, watched it all through grave, narrowed eyes. There was a sultriness like Egypt in the air and black night pressed close upon the sparkling gaiety. Voices were somehow subdued, the fretful impatience of auto horns seemed blunted. Ken Carter unfolded his long body, stepped nonchalantly to the pavement. His broad-shouldered height was emphasized by the black and white formality of full evening dress.

He nodded casually to several acquaintances—the governor's party was just passing—and sauntered toward the gates. Masses of people were held back by police beside the entrance. Carter's eyes skipped over the faces, spotted no one dangerous.

He moved on toward the gate and was presenting his ticket when a running, writhing murmur swept the crowd. It was a whisper at first. It deepened rapidly to a clamor, swelled to an excited roar.

Carter turned away from the gate. Damn this heat! Even the shout of the crowd was blunted, as if all were intimidated before the marching horror of some terrific catastrophe. Striding to the curb, Carter gazed at the crowds. Faces were upturned, stiffened upthrust arms gesticulated, and mouths were strained open in a vast inchoate roar.

The closeness of the night seemed to rise up within Carter. His throat choked. He threw back his head and stared where the crowd pointed. Vagrant gleams of light thrust up into the dark funnel of the night picked out a round, gleaming shape. Carter narrowed his eyes. It was a parachute with a man dangling from it!

Suddenly white light blazed behind the figure, outlined it vividly. The man of the parachute swayed loosely and Carter made out a floating magnesium flare such as is used in emergency landing of planes, drifting down on a smaller parachute behind him.

There was something odd about that swiftly descending figure. Something odd aside from the robes that flapped about it. A man in robes, descending in a parachute! Suddenly Carter cried out, dived into the crowd.

"Make way!" he shouted. "Make way!"

Frightened faces jerked toward him. A shudder ripped the packed masses. A few people shoved and pushed to get out of his path, then others struggled out of his plunging way.

Ken Carter raced to get under the parachute. From the swaying limpness of the body, he knew the man must be unconscious. And landing unconscious in a parachute meant at least broken bones and bruises.

The parachute was dropping more swiftly now. It was within the white circle of the many lights about the ball park, so that Carter caught a gleam of white hair above the rustling black robe. Some air current had caught the parachute now, making it sidedrift, so that Carter had to run to keep pace with it. It was up only fifty feet now, now forty, now thirty.

The dangling body whirled around. Screams of horror tore from the crowd. Carter felt his throat tighten and he muttered a curse, and halted his race to get under the parachute.

The face of the dangling man leered down at the crowd. It was terribly white in the glare of lights, the tongue thrust far out between the teeth as if in leering mockery. The eyes, bulging and awful, seemed to glare down with an independent light, and the neck seemed inhumanly *stretched*.

Carter realized suddenly what had struck him as odd about the figure hanging from the parachute. No harness was strapped about the black-robed figure. The shrouds converged higher up. They converged on the man's neck!

The body thudded to the ground. Wind caught the parachute and swept it aside. Only half collapsed, it dragged the robed man.

**CARTER SPRANG** forward, seized the parachute and forced it flat, darted back to the body. He dropped on a knee beside the man, ran his hand underneath the black robe, thrusting aside a white placard that dangled there.

No heartbeat. Well, he had expected none. He drew a silk handkerchief from his pocket and spread it over the horrible glaring eyes and the mockery of that strangled tongue. He glanced then at the shrouds of the parachute.

As he had seen from the ground, they converged on the man's neck. Underneath his left ear was a hangman's knot. And the rope about the man's neck was a noose.

Carter straightened, took off his high silk hat and ran a hand up over the high forehead and into the dull hair.

Police had fought their way through the crowd now, formed a circle around the body. Numbly Carter's mind switched back to the white placard he had thrust aside. He stooped and turned it over, laid it upon the black-robed chest. In large black letters was printed on it:

A CORRUPT JUDGE—NUMBER ONE
MOREHOUSE

One of the policemen knelt beside the body, lifted the handkerchief. He sprang up suddenly to his feet.

"My God!" he cried. "It's Judge Sidney!"

Carter watched him narrowly and gazed again at the placard, at the signature, "Morehouse."

Somehow the name struck a familiar note, but he could not quite place it. A hand touched his shoulder and Carter turned, recognized a member of the governor's staff. He nodded briefly, "Hello, MacHenry."

"Listen, Carter, what's this over here?"

Carter said, "A murder."

MacHenry's young, florid face paled. "Murder?" he cried.

He heard his name called, turned and saw the stocky, broad-shouldered figure of the governor. He had raised a hand and was gesturing impatiently.

MacHenry turned. "Mr. Carter, would you mind coming over to tell the governor about it?"

Carter murmured, "Not at all," replaced his high hat firmly on his head, and thrust through the crowd that jammed now more tightly than ever about the body.

MacHenry led him directly up to the governor. His young voice was thin with excitement. "Your Excellency, Mr. Kenneth Carter."

Carter removed his hat, bowed.

"Mrs. Samuels," MacHenry went on.

Carter bowed again to a gracious dark woman, the governor's wife.

**GOVERNOR SAMUELS** moved a hand jerkily, cutting short the formalities. Thereby, the impression of dynamic power was increased. He had a barrel chest, a wide body that tapered down to narrow hips. Immaculately creased trousers ended in small, gleaming shoes. The whole man seemed to run down to those two points. He had a fighter's bulldog jaw, a stubby, pugnacious nose. Black eyebrows were heavy above gleaming eyes.

"You were there, Mr. Carter. You can tell me about it?"

Carter bowed. "Yes, Your Excellency."

"Get going then," the governor bit out.

Carter explained in detail the manner in which the man had been killed, but when he came to the placard, he paused.

"It's Judge Sidney," he said.

The governor cried, "Sidney!" in a low, tight voice. "My God, he would have been the next presiding justice of the supreme court."

Carter said grimly, "Our murderer strikes high. There was a sign on Sidney's chest that read, 'A corrupt judge, number one.'"

Governor Samuels stared at him bitterly.

Carter went on, "And the signature—"

"What, did the murderer sign his name?"

Carter said grimly, "He did. The name he signed was, 'Morehouse.'"

The governor's face did not change, yet his eyes were like those of a man who has been struck violently in the face.

"Morehouse," he muttered.

Carter saw the governor's wife put a white hand on his arm. "John," she said, and her voice was tight, "John, isn't Morehouse the name—"

The governor turned toward her with a jerk. "Never mind, Nellie."

He turned back to Carter. "Going in now?"

"A little later," Carter said. "There are a few more things I want to check up on."

MacHenry, hovering at the governor's elbow, put in hurriedly, "Mr. Carter is a private detective, you know, governor."

The governor stared at him fixedly with his small fighting eyes. "No—no, I didn't know that," he said, continued to look at Carter for a moment or two, said, "Join us in our box, won't you?" then turned and thrust toward the gate.

MacHenry delayed a moment. Now that the governor's party had moved off, Carter saw a girl who had remained in the background. She came forward now, a pale blue, fur-edged cloak drawn about her shoulders. In the dark V of the fur, her face was vivid, lips like poppies, hair like black silk. She said severely to MacHenry,

"You haven't introduced me," and her teeth gleamed in a dancing smile.

McHenry's florid young face flushed. "I'm so sorry, Miss Ballin. May I present Mr. Kenneth Carter. Carter, Miss Ballin is secretary to the governor."

The girl held out her hand man fashion, raising her chin as she smiled. The light fell upon her eyes and Carter saw that they were bright blue.

"I am afraid I must ask you to excuse me," Carter murmured. "I'll see you presently."

He bowed and MacHenry fussily offered the girl his arm and they moved off toward the gates. The girl turned her head about and smiled slowly with her red mouth.

Carter momentarily forgot the urgency of his business. He stood, a lone, aloof figure in the midst of the crowd, distinguished, broad shouldered, head slightly bowed. Under his brows he watched the retreating couple. The girl's movements were lithe as a wild animal's, like a cheetah stalking.

Then an ambulance clanged and Carter struggled again through the crowd. A white-coated interne knelt over the body of the judge. Carter bent beside him. The interne looked up, recognized Carter.

He said, "This is the most fiendish device I've ever seen. The man's arms were tied. A hangman's noose about his neck. Evidently he was tossed out of some plane and the ripcord jerked. When the parachute opened, it snapped his spine."

Carter straightened and stared almost apprehensively up into the black, close vault of the sky. He shook his head sharply, once. He felt strangely that this was not the end of the affair. The sultriness of the night, mingled with the horror of this murder, put his hair on end, sent chills of cold dread racing over his body. He muttered a curse, turned to a policeman.

"You know where to get hold of me if they want any of my evidence about this thing."

The cop said, "Sure, I know."

**CARTER STRODE** off toward the gate, threaded his way along the ramps, through a tunnel, and down to the governor's box, where a place was made for him, between Samuels and the girl, Miss Ballin.

The governor jerked an alert, somehow worried face about. "Found out anything new?"

Carter said slowly, "The interne said death was instantaneous."

Governor Samuels turned back toward the pageant before them. He grunted, "That's a lot of help."

An usher touched Carter on the shoulder.

"Beg your pardon, sir. A gentleman here wants to see you."

Carter excused himself, walked swiftly to the mouthway of one of the entrance tunnels. A man with snow-white hair above a wrinkled young-old face, stood there. A soft black hat was in his hands. He had piercing blue eyes and there was a youthfulness about his face despite deep lines of care.

Carter said slowly, "You wanted to speak to me?"

The man stared at him with frosty eyes. "I heard you mention Morehouse," he said, "and I thought of something that might help you."

Carter nodded his thanks. "Go ahead," he said.

"It's just this," the white-haired man said. "I'm an old newspaper man, and I remember a connection between this Judge Sidney and a man named Morehouse. It was ten, maybe fifteen years ago. A woman named Amelia Morehouse was on trial for murder. She had killed a politician. Judge Sidney was the trial judge. The present Governor Samuels was the prosecuting attorney, and Amelia Morehouse was hanged."

Carter's eyes sharpened. He nodded swiftly.

"This woman's husband swore vengeance," the man went on. "He had to be expelled from the court, shouting for justice."

Carter said, "Yes, yes, there might be a connection. Thank you a lot. Now, if you'll just give me your name—"

The man shook his young-old head slowly. "It would be of no service. The information is sufficient."

Carter stared a moment and said, "Thank you." The old man turned away. His shoulders were bent, but there was a swing of easy power in them. Carter took a swift path paralleling that of the gray man. Near the gate he found two detectives.

"Listen," he said swiftly. "That man with bent shoulders and white hair. He just gave me some information about the murder that makes me suspicious. Could you tail him?"

"Aw, let's just pinch him," the man suggested

Carter shook his head swiftly. "That would do no good."

A police Cadillac drew up in front of the gates and a lean man with a brown, intent face clambered out. Carter strode rapidly toward him

"Inspector Littleman."

The police inspector glanced up. There was no welcome in his face. He scowled. "What do you want, Carter?"

Carter said rapidly, "Can you put two men on that man's tail?" he pointed towards the bent old figure. "I think we might get valuable information from him about this murder."

Littleman met Carter's stare for a moment. There was no love lost between the two, but each respected the other, and after a moment Littleman ducked his head.

"Okay," he said, called two plainclothes men to shadow the man.

Carter rapidly detailed the information the old man had given him and Littleman puckered his lips in a soundless whistle "Say, that sounds pretty good," he said.

Carter nodded. "See you later," and whirled back toward the gate, sauntered to the governor's box. The girl turned mocking blue eyes upon him.

"It must be awful to be so popular you can't even see an opera," she said, "without being interrupted."

There was merriment in her voice and Carter turned a frown into a smile.

"It is especially troublesome," he said, "when the company is so charming."

He turned to the performance. The first act was drawing to a close and a robust tenor was bellowing into the dark night air.

Suddenly Carter's eyes flicked upward. Was he seeing things or was that a parachute? His eyes focused on the white blur in the air and abruptly again a magnesium flare spread its dazzling light, outlined a dangling body that hung limply by a too-long neck.

# CHAPTER TWO

# THE THIRD MURDER

**S** CREAMS TORE into the night at the sight of this new horror, this parachute-swung corpse. Ken Carter heard Governor Samuels curse under his breath, heard MacHenry start up in muttering excitement. Carter hurdled the front of the box, sprinted across the field. The roar from the stands drowned out the music. The tenor faltered on a high note, gazing wildly into the blank sea of faces before him. Then he stared upward, spotted the floating parachute almost over his head, and fled with a shout that was half a scream.

The body was rotating slowly as it drifted down and at every turn the white corpse glistened in the white light as if drenched with death dew. The blackened, out-thrust tongue was horribly suggestive of an impertinent child mocking its elders. It was as if the corpse knew what terror it created, as if the murderer had sent a mocking message to police, to possible further victims.

When the body thudded down, Carter was upon it at once, easing the parachute and the noose around the man's throat. The neck dropped loosely to one side at an impossible angle and Carter ceased abruptly his efforts at resuscitation.

The man's neck was broken. It would be, of course. A man dropping from a plane fell sixteen feet in the first second; in the next second thirty-two feet, and in the next sixty-four, until the speed of the plunge was nearly one hundred and fifty miles an hour. Then the parachute would rip out of its casing, snap open with a miniature explosion like a toy cannon and that one hundred and fifty miles an hour plunge would be stopped with the suddenness of a man snapping the flick end of a whip.

It was as if a gallows were rigged at the edge of a five hundred foot cliff and a hundred foot rope was fastened to the man's throat.

Carter straightened slowly, stared down at the corpse. A placard lay upon the breast of this one also.

It read:

A BRIBED JUROR—NUMBER TWO
MOREHOUSE

Carter felt the crush of the crowd behind him, heard the angry shouts of policemen holding them back. The orchestra was blaring unheard music into the night, trying to slow the panic rush.

Carter could not force his way through the pack and it was three-quarters of an hour later that he regained the governor's box. It was empty.

Carter, frowning, strode swiftly along the darkened ramps of the stadium, made his way to his car.

"Home, Giulio," he ordered.

He sat lost in thought, smoking cigarettes end to end, and was totally unconscious of the streets through which the Daimler slid so smoothly. He glanced up in surprise as the chauffeur swung open the door before his apartment building. He entered a private elevator that shot him to his penthouse.

Carter unlocked the door and snapped on subdued lamps around the room. They spread a luxurious glow over the quiet elegance of the room—low, comfortable chairs and divans, small tables and the rich, deep nap of silken Chinese rugs.

He tossed off hat and coat, slipped hurriedly into a silk lounging-robe and strode immediately to his filing cases. He had here a record of the world's criminal life dating back two-score years. He dug through the index rapidly. Ah, here it was. Morehouse, No. 12,579. Carter snapped out a fat envelope, hurried to his desk, and tumbled out a neatly printed card, bundles of yellowed newspaper clippings.

He skimmed through the records of the Morehouse murder, snatched those of the trial.

It had been fourteen years ago and the reputation for integrity which Samuels had established as district attorney in that case had been a powerful factor in thrusting him toward the governorship.

Hurriedly Carter scanned the slips. He was convinced now that revenge for the woman's death was behind the series of murders and he sought the name of the next probable victim.

He could see but one answer: Governor Samuels must be the next man to die.

**FROM THE** story, it seemed the trial had been fair. The woman had been a member of an anarchist group, and the killing had been an assassination. But this, of course, would have no influence on the disordered mind that had planned these atrocities. Undoubtedly Morehouse, for it was certainly he, had waited until his intended victims were at the apex of their careers before he struck.

Carter snatched up a phone. The wire led directly to his office, where someone was perpetually on duty. A voice answered instantly.

"Carter speaking," he said. "Locate the governor, get him on the phone. Ring me back at once."

He hung up, drew out a platinum and enamel case and selected one of his private brand of cigarettes from it. He lit up with a lighter that matched the case, stretched out a foot and drew a footstool to him, rested his heels on it. He threw back his head, gazing with narrowed eyes through the updrifting smoke. A bell buzzed at his elbow and the governor's abrupt voice challenged him over the wire.

"Carter speaking. Governor Samuels, I want to warn you."

The governor's voice was choppy. "I know all you're going to say. I knew it couldn't escape your keen mind. And you're right, Carter. That Morehouse has marked me to die. I'm at the Ritz-Carlton. Will you come here at once and organize these numbskull police into an efficient guard for me?

"Name your own price. I've heard enough of your wonderful work before this and I believe no other man could protect me. You don't know the fiendishness of this Morehouse."

Carter said grimly. "I suspect it, at any rate. I'll be over in three-quarters of an hour."

Carter hung up slowly, got to his feet and turned. His eyes narrowed against the rising smoke of his cigarette. There was no start, no jerk of muscles as he beheld what stood behind him; yet any ordinary man must have cried aloud at the sight of that ghastly, horrible figure, at the threat of a revolver leveled at his body.

**CARTER TOOK** the cigarette from his mouth and deliberately surveyed the tall, black-robed and hooded figure. There was a mad gleam in the eyes that peered through the black holes of the hood. The hand that held the gun was like a rock.

Carter asked calmly, "To what do I owe the pleasure of this visit?" The man said nothing, but retreated two paces, beckoning with a bent finger and raising the gun threateningly.

Carter looked down at the tip of his cigarette, raised his eyebrows. Somehow it made his high forehead seem even higher.

"I take it," he said calmly, "that you want me to go with you?"

The hooded head nodded.

Carter began talking. "I'm sorry, but I really do have an engagement," he said. "I don't really see how I can go with you."

He watched the gun rise slowly and level at his heart.

"In fact," he went on, slipping his right foot underneath the footstool, "You come at a most unfortunate time. I was chatting over the phone with a friend and he asked me to join him for a late party. Can't we postpone—"

With a swift heave of his right foot, a smooth precision that years as a juggler on the stage had given him, he threw the footstool sharply into the air. At the same time he plunged forward and to the left of the hooded man. The stool caught the gun.

Poo—ow!

A bullet plowed harmlessly into the ceiling.

The stool had been hurled with considerable force. Striking the gun did not stop it. It slammed the gun into the hooded face.

The robed man fell back a pace.

Before he could level the gun again, Carter was upon him, an arm clamped about his throat from the rear, his right hand gripping the gun wrist.

In the vise of Carter's hand, the gun arm was drawn up and back in such a way that the elbow was turned inward toward the man's head. A groan squeezed from the man.

Carter's teeth were clenched tightly. He put all his strength into the upward heave. The breath of the man labored beneath the hood, came hoarsely.

Suddenly his hand relaxed, and Carter, with a heaving twist, hurled him half across the room, snatched the gun. But the man phenomenally recovered his balance. His reeling tumble across the room increased his speed, and he darted through the outer door just as Carter fired.... A miss.

Carter plunged across the room, saw by the dial that his private elevator was moving downward. To use the stairs would be useless, he knew. The man would discard his robe in the elevator and when the door opened below would be gone.

Carter whirled, shrugged, stared down at the gun and went to his apartment dressing room. He rapidly changed into dark tweeds, thrust the captured revolver into a drawer, and slipped his own heavy automatic into a clip beneath his arm.

Grimly, he slipped to the outer door and peered through a tiny aperture in its middle, searching the hall. It was empty. There was no doorway where a man might hide except the fire exit. That was closed.

Gun in hand, Carter crept out into the hall, pressed the button for the elevator. His eyes never left the fire exit. He heard the whine of air escaping under pressure from the elevator shaft, heard the click of the elevator stopping, the door sliding to one side.

Eyes still on the fire exit, he yanked open the elevator gate and stepped inside. A hand seized his wrist. Carter sprang backward and at the same time his elbow jabbed against the buttons that operated the elevator.

His enemy's grasp was on his gun rather than his wrist. Carter heaved backward, suddenly released the gun, and slammed the elevator door. Instantly the cage was in motion, dropping downward.

**CARTER DARTED** back to his apartment, got another gun and began to race down the fire stairs. It was fifteen stories to the street. He went down two steps at a time, one hand gliding along the rail to balance himself. He knew his best speed must put him on the ground floor far behind the elevator, but he plunged on, darted out into the small private lobby in which the elevator had its exit.

The cage was down. The gate stood open. It was empty, and the hall was empty.

Carter smashed the light in the hall and crept through utter darkness toward the outer doorway. A car sputtered into motion. Lead smashed through glass.

Carter threw himself flat, opened the door from that position and snaked through, moving gingerly on fragments of glass. He raised his automatic and blazed away at the fleeing car. The auto rocketed on, skated around the corner into Fifth and was gone.

Carter darted out, gun in hand, eyes shooting desperately up and down the street for a taxi. None in sight.

He ran with a quick breath to the corner. The nearest cab was blocks away. The fleeing car had already twisted another corner and disappeared. He heard a police whistle skirl in the distance. Radio patrol sirens already were whining.

Carter shoved his gun back into its clip, walked rapidly toward the trundling taxi, flagged it. The cab snaked him past shrieking police autos and deposited him a few moments later at the Ritz Carlton.

Carter's jaw was angrily clenched as he strode into the lighted doorway and bitter, ugly light lurked in his eyes. He strode into the governor's suite without ceremony, his usual suavity gone.

Samuels started to his feet, strode forward. Carter bit out words: "I want to see you alone at once."

The governor met the bitter, narrowed eyes. His gaze narrowed, but he nodded. MacHenry was with him, and the girl, Miss Ballin.

"Come Kathleen," MacHenry muttered to the girl, his young florid face excited. The girl, raising bright blue eyes to Carter's face, smiled at him.

"Oooo, is the cheat big man all excited?" she mocked.

Carter did not look at her. When the door closed behind the two, he said to the governor, "There is a leak in your office, among your present staff."

He told briefly what had happened.

"Obviously someone knew your intention to engage me before you phoned, for when I turned from the phone, there was a gun leveled. It could not have been coincidental."

Governor Samuels rolled his broad, pugnacious shoulders, stood erect with his head thrown back. "Couldn't it have been an echo of some other case you've worked on?"

Carter smiled grimly. He said slowly: "Most of the cases I work on are murders, and murderers rarely survive my cases. In fact, I can't recall any survivors."

Samuels stared at him. The beginning of a smile twisted the tight corners of his mouth.

He seemed pleased, said slowly, "I'm not willing to concede a leak in my staff yet. I called your office and home five or six times in the half hour before you phoned me. It is possible the leak might have been at the switchboard of the hotel, or even in your own office."

Carter glanced up fiercely, saw Samuels was smiling. The governor said, "I'm sorry, but it's just as easy for me to imagine a traitor in your office as it is for you to find one in mine."

Carter acknowledged that briefly. "Nothing we can do now. Are we leaving at once?"

"Only waiting for you to arrange our escort," Samuels said.

**IT WAS** half an hour later the governor left the hotel. Ahead of them rode six motorcycle police. There were two automobiles ahead of the governor's car, and two behind him. On the running board of the last car three men were clinging, detectives with guns ready in their pockets. A decoy car.

The governor was in the midmost car of the train, a man on either side of him, Carter in front beside the driver. In this fashion, with the sirens of the motorcycles whining a way through city streets, the motorcade traveled at high speed over the roads to Capitol City.

They were roaring along a stretch of highway with shallow ditches and woods on either side when white light blazed out ahead. Carter seized the wheel and sent the car jolting across the ditch, crashing through a wooden fence. The chauffeur shouted, but Carter plunged on until the auto was jammed among the trees. Governor Samuels sat bolt upright in the rear.

Carter leaped out, automatic in hand, darting through the trees. A magnesium flare was drifting down on a parachute and as Carter watched a man's feet descended into a circle of radiance. A man's feet, then his dangling body with a long, stretched neck, with a white placard on its breast.

Carter, with a quick shot, blew the magnesium flare to bits, yelled to the automobiles to extinguish lights. Darkness like a coal mine descended over the road, absolute silence too. Through it came the distant powerful drone of overhead motors.

Carter moved cautiously forward, heard the thump and saw the ghostly white collapse of the parachute as the body fell. He did nothing until the overhead drone of the airplane had faded into silence. Then he flashed on his light, staring grim-faced down at this new victim of the vengeful Morehouse.

The placard read:

A TOO AMBITIOUS POLICEMAN—NUMBER THREE. SAMUELS, YOUR TURN IS COMING.
MOREHOUSE

Carter flashed the light on the man's face and started with a low oath. Despite the horrible contortions, he recognized this as one of the two detectives put on the trail of the bent-shouldered young-old man who had approached him at the opera!

# CHAPTER THREE
# VENGEANCE STRIKES

**K**EN CARTER whirled to the nearest motorcycle policeman. "Load this body into the first car," he directed. He darted back to the auto where the governor sat.

His Excellency's face was white; his bulldog jaw clenched. He said savagely: "You don't need to tell me. I saw it."

Carter said grimly, "There are some things about it you don't know yet. Listen. We won't wait for this car to get out of here. This may be some trick to delay us for an attack."

He organized a squad of men, whose bodies completely protected the governor. In dead, ominous silence they marched in a compact mass to another car.

Within a minute and a half after the body had been found, the convoy was speeding on again toward Capitol City. They reached the spreading white governor's mansion without further difficulty.

The place was turned into an armed fort. Every corridor had its pacing sentry. There were double guards outside the building, and no man entered it unless identified and approved by MacHenry.

Carter called the newspapers and gave them the information on the latest murder, told them that it threatened Samuels. The governor had protested against this, but Carter pointed out publicity would make the movements of the murderer more difficult. A completely alert police force scattered throughout the state would make it easier to strike when the moment came.

It was now four in the morning and Governor Samuels went wearily to bed. His face was haggard. Even in so short a time, he seemed to have lost weight. His face had become gaunt, the strong bones outlined more rigidly. His wife showed her mettle plainly. Worried she was, but she held her head high. The girl, Kathleen Ballin, was quartered also in the mansion, as were all other members of the governor's personal staff.

When everything possible had been done to protect the governor from the threat of vengeance and death, Carter finally went to sleep, but every two hours he roused himself to make a circle of the guard, to check on the sentries pacing the halls. He did not neglect to have a state trooper behind him, at Samuels' insistence.

Carter was making the round again at ten o'clock when Governor Samuels came downstairs toward his office. He stopped the lean-jawed detective in the hall.

"Nothing happened last night, I take it?"

Carter shrugged. "All quiet. All we can do is maintain this guard while we try to track down Morehouse. Apparently he's working with at least one accomplice, because I'm positive it was Morehouse I talked to at the opera, and a few moments after a body was dropped into the street. I've given police a detailed description. Their efforts in tracing him would be more effective than my own."

Samuels said grimly, "You take care of me. We'll let the police take care of Morehouse."

Carter nodded, and Governor Samuels turned and strode off to his office. His shoulders were still squared, his barrel-like body carried erectly, but there was a drag to the determined tread of his feet. He jerked open the door of his office, started in and then fell back with a low, hoarse cry.

Carter was upon him instantly, jerking him away from the door, plunging in with a drawn pistol. Then he too halted, staring.

For dangling from the high chandelier was an effigy of a hanged man. Just a suit of clothes stuffed with straw and paper, but it was horribly threatening. The placard on its chest read:

A HANGING PROSECUTOR. NUMBER FIVE.

Carter whirled into the hall, mustered the sentries of the previous night. No one but members of the household had moved about, they insisted. MacHenry and Miss Ballin, the governor's wife, the governor himself, Carter. Five of them had been moving about the halls at various times, but none of these had entered the governor's office in the night.

Carter turned to a sentry. "Get MacHenry down here at once."

**GOVERNOR SAMUELS** behind him said wearily, "There's no use doing that."

Carter paid no attention to him and the guard stomped off. A servant came to the governor's ring and was ordered, "Take that thing down." Samuels gestured stiffly toward the hanging figure.

The man stared at the thing with widening eyes, then muttered, "Yes, sir," and entering the office, began work on the figure.

Carter stood rigidly, eyes fixed on the stairway until MacHenry clattered his light-footed way down. He walked, smiling, up to the detective asking, "You sent for me?"

Carter's mouth shut grimly. "I did." He turned toward the governor's office, pointed toward the still dangling figure.

MacHenry ripped out a low oath.

"Exactly," said Carter dryly. "That thing was swung there despite an impenetrable guard. You passed on every visitor admitted to the mansion."

MacHenry's fair face flushed. "Are you hinting I'm responsible? I thought you knew me better and were my friend," he said angrily.

Carter's grin was acid. "I'm a detective," he said shortly. "When I'm on a case, I have no friends. Listen, whom did you let in yesterday to hang this thing here and terrorize the house?"

MacHenry drew himself up stiffly, eyes flashing.

"That won't do any good," Carter said grimly. "Answer my question."

MacHenry's breath came swiftly. He said fiercely, "I permitted no enemy of the governor to enter the house."

"I asked you who hung this effigy of the governor?"

"I don't know."

Carter took two slow paces forward so that he glared down into MacHenry's face.

"I'm giving you one more chance to come clean, then I'm ordering your arrest as an accomplice in these murders."

MacHenry whitened. He opened his mouth to speak, but no sound came out. "You're mad," he whispered finally.

Carter placed a hand on his shoulders. His voice became deep, formal, sing-song. "Arthur McHenry, I arrest—"

Suddenly Governor Samuels jerked his energetic body up from his chair, thrust forward.

"Hold on, Carter," he said swiftly, "I think you're making a big mistake."

Carter turned his heavy gaze on the governor. "Well, I don't," he snapped.

"Please," said Samuels, "I'd trust MacHenry with my life. I'm sure you're mistaken about his being responsible. Why, one of the sentries might have been reached and done this thing."

Carter stared at him unbelievingly.

"You gave me charge of this case," he said firmly. "I demand the right to handle it in my own way."

The governor lifted a hand wearily. "You're right about that, of course, but I'm sure that you're making a mistake about MacHenry. I don't blame you for being suspicious of him, of anybody for that matter, but please—"

Samuels looked squarely into Carter's eyes and the man's face was lined with worry. Carter hardened himself to insist, gazed into the governor's eyes again and cursed under his breath.

"Okay," he said, "We're both being fools, but I'll let you have your way." He turned his hardened eyes on MacHenry. "But see that you don't get yourself in a bad spot again, or the governor and every other official in the state can't save you."

MacHenry glared at him. "You're a fool," he spluttered. "I'm not guilty and I'll do what I damned well please."

He slammed into the governor's office, cleared now of the dangling dummy, and left Samuels and Carter face to face. Carter shook his head angrily, spun on his heel and strode off, found the sergeant of the guard.

"Hereafter," he said tightly, "I want one of your men to keep an eye on MacHenry at all times. Understand?"

The sergeant saluted wordlessly, strode off. Carter paced on up the hall slowly, looked up and saw a woman coming down the stairway. It was the governor's wife. She had a jaunty hat upon her head and a fur thrown about her shoulders.

"You weren't thinking of going out, Mrs. Samuels?" Carter asked.

She raised finely arched eyebrows at him. "Why not?" she asked. "Surely the danger threatening John does not extend to me?"

"Nevertheless," Carter said gravely, "I would much prefer that you shouldn't go."

Mrs. Samuels drew up stiffly, threw back her dark head. She was a dignified woman, just under forty, haughty, somewhat spoiled, and intent upon having her own way. She brushed by Carter, threw open the door of the governor's office.

"Really, John," she said, "this is too absurd. Mr. Carter is trying to insist that I do not leave the house today."

**SAMUELS WAS** seated at his desk, staring blankly at the papers before him, obviously without seeing them at all. He said dully, "Do as you wish, my dear. Mr. Carter was only trying to protect you."

"At least, Governor Samuels," Carter bowed jerkily, "you will give me the privilege of resigning this case." He turned on his heel and strode off.

"Oh, Carter," called Samuels wearily. The detective turned haltingly, stared coldly at the man. The governor got slowly to his feet, his shoulders no longer pugnacious. They drooped. Flesh sagged upon his face and there were dark circles under his eyes. Overnight he had aged ten years. He came forward slowly.

"Don't desert me, Carter. If you leave, I may as well kill myself. This man is determined upon his vengeance."

Carter said, still stiffly, "How can I protect you if you if insist on countermanding the precautions I deem necessary for your protection?"

Samuels said slowly, "I think it inadvisable to keep Nellie here. People must not think we are cowardly. She is in no danger at all and it does not seem to me that it would hurt for her to go out. It you insist, couldn't we send a guard with her?"

Carter's back was like a ramrod. There was anger deep in his eyes. Yet, looking at Governor Samuels, he could not maintain his irritation. He thought to himself, "I'm a damn sentimentalist or I'd chuck this case and walk out." He smiled in self-mockery.

"Very well," he said aloud, beckoned to a state trooper. "Mrs. Samuels is going out. Go with her. And never let her out of your sight for an instant. I hold you responsible."

The policeman saluted smartly. He had a sun-tanned, eager face. "Right, sir."

Carter smiled at his stalwart back as he marched off. He felt that Mrs. Samuels would be protected.

**HE SENT** word then to Kathleen Ballin that he would like to talk to her. She came swiftly down the long high stairs of the hall, trim in a suit of herringbone gray. She alone, of all the household, seemed unworried. The smile on her poppy red mouth was mocking "What does the dreat big detecatiff want with the little girl?" she asked.

Carter refused to smile back. "Miss Ballin," he said coldly. "Mrs. Samuels has just left the house with a police-man guarding her. I want you to follow Mrs. Samuels also, keep her under close surveillance, and the moment you see any suspicious thing, call the police."

The girl's face grew grave. "You think she is in danger?"

"I think anyone intimately connected with Governor Samuels is in danger. This Morehouse is absolutely mad. Hurry."

The girl sped back up the stairs, reappeared a moment later with hat and furs, hurried out of the mansion.

Carter resumed his patrol of the halls, keeping the guard on the alert, glancing in every half hour to see that the governor was all right in his high, stately office. He was looking into the governor's office for the sixth time since the governor's wife had left, when the telephone bell pealed.

It was a long, sustained ringing, not ordinary automatic machinery buzzing. MacHenry, laboring at his desk in the corner, snatched up the phone.

"Governor Samuels' office."

His eyes widened then and he stared in horror at the mouth of the phone. His face blanched.

Carter crossed to him in two strides. "What is it?" he demanded.

MacHenry thrust the phone at him. The detective slapped it to his ear, said, "Carter speaking. What is it please?"

The excited jabber of a man came over the wire. Carter cut it short. "Speak more slowly." He caught words now. "Mrs. Samuels is kidnapped. Her guard was killed."

Carter said tightly, "And Miss Ballin?"

The voice jabbered back. "Struck over the head, unconscious in the hospital."

"How long ago was this?"

"Fifteen minutes."

Carter felt Governor Samuels' hand bite into his shoulder.

"What is it, for God's sake?" the governor's voice quavered.

Carter spat, "Just a minute," over his shoulder, barked into the phone. "Every effort being made to trace the kidnappers?"

"Yes," the man at the other end of the wire admitted. "There's small hope of success. The attack was made on a taxi on a lonely street. The taxi driver was out cold. Mrs. Samuels had been gone perhaps ten minutes when a policeman on the beat found the taxi, revived the driver, and found out what had happened."

Carter said, "Okay," turned to the governor.

His face was a rigid mask.

"Be yourself, Samuels," Carter said harshly, and told him what had happened.

Samuels seemed to shrink visibly in stature as Carter spoke. He said nothing but moved slowly as if on paralyzed limbs to the chair behind his desk, dropped into it.

"This is the end," he said dully.

Carter said grimly, "Yes, this is the end. But not the way you think. Morehouse has gone too far now. After all, it is not your wife, it is you he wants. Before long you will get a message saying your surrender is the price of your wife's life. When that happens we have them."

The governor's head came up slowly. There was the beginning of animation in his eyes.

"I'll follow you," Carter said swiftly. "We'll strike before Morehouse is ready."

A shout rang outside the window. Carter strode across, threw it open and leaned out. A guard saluted swiftly, pointed upward.

"A parachute, sir, with a man in it."

Governor Samuels staggered to the window. "Are you sure it's a man?" he croaked.

Carter stared upward. "It's a man," he said quietly.

Samuels groaned, "Thank God," and dropped heavily into a chair.

Carter vaulted the window sill, raced toward the spot where the parachute was settling. No mistaking the work of that madman. This corpse, too, was noosed about the neck. It lay stretched upon the sun-glaring roadway, a placard upon its chest.

A LYING WITNESS—NUMBER FOUR.
MOREHOUSE

An envelope was fastened to the placard. Carter seized and ripped it open. The letter began abruptly:

> *Samuels:*
> *If you want your wife to live, you must surrender in her place at 2 A.M. Drive your car alone along the Mulligan Road. If you are followed or permit the police to interfere in any way, your wife will be hanged as you hanged my wife.*
> MOREHOUSE

Carter strode back into the mansion, put the letter in Samuels' hand. The governor looked up heavily. "You were right."

Carter nodded. "I am convinced Morehouse never means to turn your wife loose. Consequently, whether I follow you or not makes no difference at all. I am going to follow you, alone. I believe that way we will have a much better chance of success than if we threw a dozen police patrols along the line, because Morehouse will not suspect. We will take you to wherever his hidden headquarters may be."

Samuels agreed dully. "Whatever you say. Every time I have disagreed, something terrible has happened."

During the course of the long afternoon, Kathleen Ballin returned home. There was a small white bandage upon her forehead. She could add nothing to the story of the capture. A hooded man had shot the policeman, clubbed the driver over the head, and hauled Mrs. Samuels out. Kathleen had been struck down attempting to interfere.

Dinner was a morose and terrible affair that night and afterward Carter and the governor talked for a short while, then Carter went up to his room to sleep for a few hours. Nothing could be done before 2 A.M.

Carter had been under terrific strain. He felt enormously tired. His feet dragged, and without undressing he dropped upon his bed. When he awoke, early red sunlight was streaming through the window. Carter leaped from his bed, ran through the halls. It was 6 A.M. Governor Samuels had disappeared!

## CHAPTER FOUR

## TRAIL OF DEATH

**I**T **TOOK** Ken Carter ten minutes to check the sentries around the house and learn that Governor Samuels left the house at 2 A.M. exactly as Morehouse ordered, that he had forbidden police to follow him and gone off alone in his car.

"Four hours start!" Carter muttered. He clenched his fists at the hopelessness of pursuit.

Dozens of cars must have passed along that way since Samuels had gone. It was a main highway, one that inter-urban trucks and buses would use. No; it was useless to follow now.

Carter's first thought was MacHenry. He called the sergeant of the guard, learned from him that not a man in service overnight had left the grounds. The same was true of the servants. Kathleen Ballin, MacHenry, and the governor's other employees were all in the building. The only persons missing were the governor and his wife.

Carter's eyes grew narrow. MacHenry. He opened his mouth to order the secretary's arrest. But wait. There was a better way. He spoke abruptly to the sergeant of the guard, a Scotsman with a dour, long face.

"Sergeant," Carter bit out words, "I have an unusual order. I want you to keep the night guard on duty all day, too."

A slight frown crossed the sergeant's wrinkled brow. "That'll be hard on the lads, sir. Is it necessary? I have a relief."

Carter said grimly, "It's necessary that these same men stay on duty."

The sergeant's lips tightened. "Very good, sir."

"One more thing," said Carter. "I have no objections to anyone in the house leaving, but he must leave by this front door. Furthermore, no one is to know that this order comes from me. Understand?"

The sergeant saluted, marched away.

Carter went slowly down the wide front steps of the mansion, entered a small hotel across the street and got a room on the front. He put through a call to his home office and ordered that seven of his best operators fly immediately to Capitol City and come to his room.

He next ordered a car hired and parked out front for him, sent for breakfast, and, sitting well back from the window, watched the entrance of the executive mansion.

In a little over an hour his seven operatives were trickling into the room. They were as queer a group as ever-assembled under one leadership.

There was a stocky, bandy-legged little Jew not more than twenty years old.

There was a bronzed Westerner with a horsey roll still in his leg and a predilection for wide-brimmed hats.

There was a gravely polite Japanese whose protruding upper teeth were perpetually bared in smiles.

Another had the broad-toed shoes and stocky, red-faced impassivity of a policeman.

A tall, weathered man with squint eyes and a mop of black hair was the pilot.

He lounged next to a square-built ruffian with a broken nose and a cauliflower ear, who spoke with a meticulous Oxford accent and exchanged gay badinage with a girl in a trim blue dress piped in red, with a silver fox scarf across her shoulders and a pert sauciness of face that matched the blazing red of her hair.

The girl said pertly, "Well, chief, the gang's all here."

Carter was cold-faced. His jaw was hard and his gray eyes were unamused. Beneath the high sweep of his forehead they moved individually from member to member of his force.

He said briefly, "The governor's wife has been kidnapped. Samuels went away at two this morning to ransom her with his own body. I was to trail him, but my dinner was drugged last night and I woke four hours after he had left. Every trace of him is gone now."

Each of the group showed sharp interest.

"There have been repeated evidences of inside work," Carter went on. "Someone in that house drugged my food last night—unless it was the governor himself. That I do not believe. He had gone counter to my judgment on several occasions and trouble resulted every time. He said last night that he was satisfied to follow my way. I believe he meant it.

"I suspect the governor's secretary, MacHenry, but we absolutely cannot let any chance slip. Therefore, there is this to do. Whenever anyone leaves that house today, one of you will follow him. We will save Samuels and his wife at all costs. These murders are crimes of vengeance. I do not believe that vengeance will be exacted on Samuels and his wife until that person comes to the scene. Understand the situation?"

Quick nods answered his individual glance. Carter turned back to the window.

It was twelve o'clock before the front doors of the mansion opened and one of the governor's secretaries came out. Carter, without taking his eyes from the window said, "Jordan."

The tall, tanned pilot strode out.

**A HALF** hour later a flustered woman came from the mansion door. Her dress indicated plainly she had been used to the servants' entrance. Carter said, "Cholmondeley," received a "Righto," for answer, and the broken-nosed man stepped forward.

Three more operatives were dispatched behind two more office employees and a servant, and then MacHenry came from the mansion. Carter called "Jo," softly, and the redhead crossed to his side.

Carter said swiftly, "That man is MacHenry. Don't lose sight of him, Jo."

The girl's hand rested lightly on Carter's shoulder. Her heels tapped out of the room. There were left now Carter and the tall Westerner.

Carter said, "Buck, I'm a little worried about Jo and this lad, MacHenry. Suppose you follow Jo. I'll be here to take charge. If you get a break, call me."

Carter took one of his interminable cigarettes from the platinum and black case, took out an automatic lighter and snapped it. The device did not work and Carter, a vague irritation stamping his forehead, struck a match. One of his operatives would be back soon to take up the next trail, he hoped, otherwise he would have to go. And he wanted to remain in touch, stay here to take command when the right trail was struck.

Five minutes later Kathleen Ballin strolled out of the mansion across the street. She was dressed as on the day before in chic gray. Carter rose immediately, drew on a soft brown borsalino. No help for it. He'd have to go. He left a brief note to Jordan to take charge and hurried to the lobby.

The girl strolled along toward the hotel and Carter slipped into a cigarette store which opened off the lobby. The girl walked past the cigarette store. Carter bought a pack of cigarettes. The girl still stayed outside. The man behind the counter peered through thick glasses. "Was there something else you wanted?"

Carter looked blankly about, spotted a can of fuel for cigarette lighters and purchased that. He hung around, filling his lighter, and when he finally had done that he saw the girl was moving off up the street, swiftly now and with apparently definite purpose.

Carter dropped the can of fuel and lighter into his pocket, slid back into the lobby of the hotel and entered the car he had hired and parked out front. He hopped in, slid slowly forward. If his guess was right, the girl would soon take an automobile or taxi, and it was with a feeling of elation that, an instant later, he saw her enter a garage. He drove on slowly past and within two blocks the girl's swiftly driven car passed his own. She shot directly for the open country, took the Mulligan Road, the one Morehouse had told Samuels to follow!

Carter frowned heavily. There must be some mistake. This lovely girl with the murderer? He shook his head, but trailed behind, falling far back when the road led through remote sections, closing up when they passed through small towns. When dusk, hours later, began to creep from the valleys toward the hilltops, Carter closed up. The towns were left behind now and the girl was penetrating into the mountains.

He was alone on the trail, no chance to send for help. Carter shut his lips grimly as he drove on. Well, he had played a lone hand before.

**IT WAS** a mile and a half farther that he saw the lights of the car ahead switch sharply to the right and slant downward, flash among trees. When he reached that point, he saw a narrow private road wound downward. Two miles away, in the depths of the valley, he caught the black gleam of a lake. Carter had no way of telling how far down this road the girl would drive, but he could tell that the road was rarely used. His guess was it would not lead farther than the lake shore.

He drove a hundred yards back down the highway, parked the car on the side, then strode briskly down the narrow road toward the lake.

Beneath his arm the heavy pistol nestled, and in his hand he carried a flashlight which he used sparingly now and then to be sure he was on the right track, and that the marks of the girl's car were in the road.

The way was lonely, rough, and dark. Kathleen Ballin must have been forced to cut her pace to a crawl. Carter had been walking about twenty minutes when he heard the sound of a motorboat on the lake below. It was no more than a half mile distant now, and he hurried down the road, afraid to use the light, making his way by watching the gap in the trees overhead.

Minutes later he brought up violently against the back of a parked auto, threw himself to the ground, and snaked out his gun. But in the car all was silent. Slowly Carter got to his feet, examined the car by intermittent flashes of his pocket torch. It was empty, and it was the car the girl had driven.

Carter turned to the right and, slowly through the dark woods, groped his way to the lake shore, gazed out across the water. The puttering of the motor boat died. Over the black water Carter made out a dim yellow gleam of light that marked an island in its midst. It was perhaps a mile to the island. Carter could swim it readily, but it meant running the risk of ruining the cartridges of his gun with water, leaving him unarmed.

He groped along the edges of the lake, found where a small stream trickled into it, and hidden under the branches of the trees was a rowboat. It was a dinky thing, tied only with a rope, but there were no oars and no paddle. Carter hurried back to the car, ripped out a floor board and climbed into the small boat. Using the floorboard as a paddle, he propelled it laboriously across the lake.

It was a moonless night and only the pale stars cast down a glimmer on the water's surface. But the dim yellow gleam of light ahead guided him. It was slow work. Carter stripped off his coat, transferring the fuel can and lighter to his trousers pocket against emergency, and set to work in earnest.

Luckily the night was windless, there was little or no current in the lake, and after three-quarters of an hour of strenuous work, he beached the small boat at a remote end of an island, fighting clear of the wharf that was near its middle.

Once on shore, he slipped along the lake's edge until he reached the wharf. It was the work of a few moments to tear loose wires until the boat was useless, then he slipped toward the house, still guided by that vagrant gleam of yellow light.

The island was overgrown with trees and vines, but when he had struggled through these he came suddenly upon a clearing in which stood a huge gaunt pile of a house. The gleam of yellow came from an uncurtained window and Carter circled, crept up on the house from its dark side, and clambering upon a ledge, raised his head slowly above the window sill.

The lamp that cast the light dangled from the center of the ceiling, an oil lantern, and Carter raised up, saw the top of a man's head. The hair was black and stubborn and peering still more daringly, he gazed into the haggard countenance of Governor Samuels.

The man's eyes were staring, fatigue lined his face, and there was a look of utter despair upon it. He did not see Carter; his eyes were staring straight ahead. Carter raised even further and saw that the governor's arms were bound behind his back. He was standing, very tensely and stiffly as if he dared not move, and then Carter saw the reason.

The floor had been totally removed from the room, and every rafter, too, except one in the precise middle. Across this a thick but narrow plank was balanced and the governor stood at one end. Carter frowned in puzzlement. Why was the governor standing so stiffly, what weighted down the other end of the plank at which Samuels stared with horror and despair on his face?

Carter moved his head slowly sideways and he saw!

At the other end of the plank on which the governor stood was his wife. She, too, stood in rigid immobility. Her arms also were bound behind her, but there was this difference in their situations. About her neck was a hangman's noose, fastened to the ceiling. If Samuels so much as moved, the board would teeter and *his wife would swing off into space and be hanged!*

# CHAPTER FIVE
# POISON PIT

**K** EN CARTER could not restrain a gasp of horror at the sight of the governor and his wife and the torture device that this mad Morehouse had rigged. He was forcing Samuels to hang his own wife!

There was no possibility of escape. Samuels feared even to shift his footing, lest the board on which he balanced shift and the tight rope drag his wife off. Her face was strained and white, her bodily pose was stiff. Obviously both Samuels and his wife had been standing for hours in this position. Obviously, unless Carter effected a rescue, Mrs. Samuels was doomed.

But Carter could not see that, aside from a tumble into the dark pit, Samuels would be injured. He peered down into the depths below and saw something that made him shudder inwardly. The vagrant yellow gleams of the light overhead penetrated into the darkness and suddenly Carter understood the musty odor that clung around the house. For the cellar beneath Samuels and his wife was a den of snakes!

Dozens of them writhed around the floor and coiled in iridescent folds. No man could fall upon them and live. It was a fiendish trap, a thing to stagger the imagination.

Carter stared fascinated at the two victims, saw hate writhe across Samuels' face, such hate and rage as Carter had never before seen. The governor shouted curses, but retained the rigid pose of his body, lest some slight tremor of his might make it worse for his wife. When Samuels had finally raved himself into silence, the calm voice of another man called from a slight distance.

"You weary me a great deal, Samuels. You take so long to die. So I have rigged up a little bell which will permit my daughter and me to sleep, and yet allow us to pleasure in your death." The voice laughed. It hissed through the night like a snake.

Samuels' breast was laboring, his breath harsh between clenched teeth.

"Ah," came the mocking voice again, "I can see that you have guessed it. As you have discerned, Samuels, the bell is fastened to the rope that goes about your dear wife's throat. When her weight falls upon the rope, the bell will jangle and my daughter and I will hurry down. So be assured, Samuels, that at least you will not have to die without company."

Mad, hissing laughter rang out now. Samuels' choking voice was raised. "For God's sake, Morehouse, have mercy," he pleaded. "Kill me if you will, but let my wife go free. She has done nothing to deserve this."

Morehouse's voice howled back at him, "Neither had my wife. She was a sacrifice to your ambition!"

Samuels said deliberately, "You know that wasn't so."

Suddenly Carter caught movement in the room and dropped to the ground. He heard the words exchanged a while longer, then silence fell upon the house. Carter slipped around toward the back of the building where Samuels had faced when he had pleaded for his wife's life. He found an old rotting stairway and up this made his cautious way.

**A DOOR** at its top was closed. Through the keyhole, yellow light fell. Carter squinted through it. A huge Negro sat in a chair facing an open doorway.

Carter grunted. That didn't help him, but it did explain something that had puzzled him, that was how Morehouse had managed to dump a body down on the ball park opera when both he and the girl were on the scene. Evidently this Negro had done it.

The Negro had a gun in his hands and now and again Carter heard his hoarse voice jeering at the two on the plank. Carter turned the knob slowly, a fraction of an inch a minute, and pressed upon the door. It yielded!

Gun in his hand, Carter eased the door open and thrust inside. But the draft of the open door gave the Negro warning. He sprang up, whirled with gun leveled. It was too far to leap and Carter dared not fire. It would bring the house down about his ears and Carter did not know how many men Morehouse might have above stairs with him.

Carter's juggling years, his amazing accuracy of eye and split-second judgment of action, stood him in great stead then. Like a flash he drew back his arm and hurled the revolver squarely in the face of the Negro. It caught him between the eyes and with only a grunt of sound the Negro stiffened, his arms went high and he pitched backward through the open doorway and vanished into the pit of snakes! His own gun—and Carter's—went with him.

Carter heard him thud below, darted across the room at top speed and checked in the doorway. He signaled frantically to Samuels for silence and peered down into the pit. Cruel the Negro might be, but Carter had no wish to kill him in this horrible way. But he saw that already he was too late. A dozen snakes, coiled, were striking viciously at the prone man. As Carter watched, one jabbed fangs three times into the Negro's throat.

Grimly Carter stared down at him. He was beyond all human help now. One snake bite might be treated successfully, but dozens, such as this man had received, were beyond all hope. Carter smiled grimly at Samuels, put a finger to his lips and shook his head.

Hope beyond all believing blazed on the man's face. Carter stared around the room, saw that a narrow ledge ran across the wall toward the rafter on which Samuels and his wife were balanced. Along this Carter made his cautious way and finally the straining eyes of Samuels' wife could see him too. She had not dared move her head lest she disturb the balance of the plank. She heaved a deep breath and whispered, "Oh God! Thank God! Thank God! Thank God!"

Samuels whispered anxiously, "You've got someone with you?"

Carter shook his head slowly and hope faded from the governor's face as if a sponge had been wiped across it.

"Then we are no better off," he said, "we are still doomed. It took two men to get us on this plank, one to balance each side. There is no possible way you can reach Nellie without overbalancing the plank so she will fall off and be—be—" He couldn't say the word.

**CARTER SMILED** calmly. "There's a way," he said and made his slow way to the room where the Negro had stood on guard. His torchlight flashed around the room then and picked up a huge butcher knife on a table. With this, Carter edged once more along to the rafter across which the death plank was balanced.

The rafter was narrow, but that presented no difficulties to Carter. Balance is part of every juggler's training and Carter had walked tightropes in his day. He made his way easily along the rafter until he reached the plank on which the two stood. Then he mounted that, with one foot on each side of the center of gravity, steadied the plank. He said quite calmly then, "You can relax your positions a little now. I am in a position to counteract what you do."

Gingerly at first, then more confidently, Samuels let himself relax, shifted his feet a little, and Carter, with pressure of one foot or the other, counteracted it easily. He turned to Mrs. Samuels.

"Kindly relax," he said, "I am going to cut that rope about your neck at the ceiling with this knife. You must not be so tense that the release of the slight drag of the rope on your neck would throw you off balance. You understand?"

Mrs. Samuels nodded wordlessly. Her lips moved in silent prayer.

Carter balanced carefully. Never in his life had he aimed with more caution. Many times had he outlined a young girl standing against a board with flashing thrown knives. It had been years since then. He hoped desperately he had not lost his skill.

He balanced lightly on his toes, drew back the knife and threw. The blade flashed cleanly through the air, somersaulted once, and its blade bit the rope where it was fastened to the ceiling. It severed, but for one small strand which could be easily snapped in two.

Carter could have cheered. "Now both of you walk toward me slowly." He stood in the middle of the plank, with a hand outstretched toward each. Samuels and his wife took slow steps forward. The rope tightened about the woman's neck, but she walked on, straining against it, and suddenly it snapped. There was a loud jangle of bells above and Carter remembered painfully that Morehouse had told them of an alarm that would go off when weight went on the rope!

But now he could reach out a hand and touch both of them. His pocket knife came into use and he rapidly cut their bonds, led the two of them back across the rafter, helping them balance, to the ledge and thence to the room where the Negro had stood on guard. Heavy feet pounded overhead.

Below them the Negro twitched and moaned, and suddenly, coming out of his coma, reared to his feet, saw the snakes striking at him and went mad with fright.

He screamed, shouted, hurled curses into the air. He found his gun on the floor and blazed away at the snakes around him. Carter, unarmed, dared not wait to try conclusions with Morehouse. He did not know how many men were with him.

He shouted to Samuels, "Through the door; quick!" and the governor and his wife reeled out, Carter right behind them.

As they dove down the steps, a gun blazed within and lead whined over their heads.

# CHAPTER SIX
# A FOILED ESCAPE

**C**ARTER LED Samuels and his wife at a pounding run toward the end of the island where he had left the rowboat. Floodlights flashed on from the house itself, seemed to illuminate the whole island. Carter crouched in underbrush, dragged the two down with him.

Feet raced toward the wharf, and finally, desperate, Carter slid from cover and, braving the lights, led on to the wooded end of the island. A figure rose ahead of him, white light blazed into his face, and Carter dived forward. The person behind the light fell with him to the ground. Silk and soft mesh were under his hand and a woman's scream in his ear.

Carter cursed, snatched the light and leaped to his feet, throwing the light down on the woman on the ground. It was Kathleen Ballin. Her black hair was disheveled and hung about her face, her red mouth was twisted. Scream after scream tore from her. She was unarmed and Carter left her lying there, raced on with the Samuelses. The girl followed, screaming at the top of her voice. An answering shout rang out from the old mansion.

Carter was panting heavily now. The governor and his wife were gasping for breath. Carter sent them on and turned back toward the girl. She kept warily just out of reach and continued to scream. Finally Carter, in desperation, ran at her. She dodged, whirled and ran, but Carter was upon her again.

He spun her about, clamped a hand across her mouth.

"Shut up," he grated out.

The girl bit his hand, screamed again when he jerked it away. Desperately, Carter ripped a sleeve off his shirt, bound it around her mouth as a gag, and, throwing her over his shoulder, jolted off after the governor and his wife.

The glimmer of water showed between the trees. Carter trotted toward it, smiling grimly. Success was near now. Morehouse and his gang would have plenty of difficulty finding wire to rig up the motor boat in time to do them any good.

At last he broke through to the short narrow beach, found the small boat he had left there.

Carter tossed Kathleen Ballin into the bow of the boat, gestured to Samuels and his wife to enter, then stiffened, a frozen statue of amazement, listening. Unmistakably, up the shore of the island, he heard the splutter of an outboard motor.

It coughed once, died, caught again, roared out steadily. Carter cursed savagely. Evidently Morehouse, in addition to the engine, had an outboard motor for the boat. The girl in the boat raised her head, tore off the gag and screamed again. Carter turned swiftly to Samuels and his wife.

"Can you swim?"

The governor nodded.

"Swim a mile?"

"Three if necessary."

"Your wife?"

"She swims equally well."

"Fine, now listen," Carter heaved a breath of relief. "I'm going in this rowboat with the girl. Morehouse will think she and I are you two. While I decoy them with the rowboat, you two must swim ashore. You'll find an automobile at the head of the hill road. Here's the key. When you get there, drive for help with all speed."

"But you," the governor protested, "they'll catch you. You'll be dead before I could get help."

Carter said grimly, "You forget, I've got the girl for hostage. Now get going or all this work will be wasted."

Samuels hesitated a moment, then thrust out his hand. Carter gripped it silently, and then, with reluctance, Samuels led his wife out into the black water. They began silently to swim toward the distant shore. From the opposite direction, the bark of the motor drew rapidly nearer.

Carter piled into the boat and shoved off. The girl was screaming words now and Carter snatched up the torn sleeve and bound it across her mouth again, drew her hands behind her and used his belt to bind them. Then he thrust her forward in the boat.

"Stay there," he growled at her, seized the board paddle and shoved off into the lake, stroking frantically.

He had not gone twenty-five yards when he spotted the motor boat curving out into the lake. A hand torch beam flickered here and there on the surface of the water, picked up Carter in a moment.

"Surrender," a man's voice boomed over the water. "Surrender or you die."

**CARTER MADE** no answer, paddled desperately on. He must delay capture as long as possible so that the governor and his wife might have plenty of time to escape.

So far as he could discover, there was only one man in the boat, but that man was armed, and Carter was empty handed. He paddled on.

The crack of the revolver whipped over the lake and lead whined overhead. Kathleen, forward in the boat, was struggling, kicking around. Finally she surged to her feet. Behind Carter the gun blazed out again. Breath gasped out of the girl. She swayed, then crumpled to the bottom of the boat.

Carter dropped to his knees beside her, felt hurriedly for her pulse, ripped the gag from her mouth. Breath rattled from her throat and suddenly there was no breath at all. Carter felt frantically for her pulse. The girl was dead.

Carter's mouth drew down in a thin line. Morehouse's vengeance was carrying him a little farther than he had intended. His move was obvious now. He would slip overboard from the boat, try to dive beneath Morehouse's craft, and take him from the rear.

A bullet plucked Carter's sleeve. He rolled over the gunwale and slid down behind the boat, clinging to its edge. The pistol spoke twice more and lead plunked into the boat. The beat of the motor was quite near now and Carter pulled his hand from the edge and trod water, waiting.

He heard the hollow thump of the boats colliding, heard Morehouse's hissing laughter of triumph. Suddenly the man gave a low cry, then a horrible shout of rage.

Now was Carter's chance. Taking a deep breath, he ducked beneath the surface, pulled himself swiftly beneath the rowboat, under the motorboat, and finally popped up on the far side. He put his hands on the edge of the boat and peered over. Morehouse was crouched over the farther gunwale, his head bowed, shoulders bent with despair. Carter sank low in the water, then yanked himself up and with a desperate heave swarmed into the boat.

Morehouse whirled, jerking up a revolver. Carter charged, striking savagely with a clenched fist. He slipped and fell flat on his back.

Morehouse leveled the pistol at his head.

Flame spat into his face. Red and white lights blazed within his brain. Black darkness settled upon him.

## CHAPTER SEVEN
## PARACHUTE GALLOWS

WHEN CARTER came back to consciousness, he heard the sound of a spade grating on earth. His head ached throbbingly, and trying to raise his hands to it, he found they were bound together. His feet too were bound, he discovered, raising them experimentally. Evidently Morehouse's bullet had only grazed his skull, knocking him unconscious, but causing no serious injury.

The grating of the spade continued and Carter, rolling his head over, saw the slouched shoulders of the old man and his white hair, bent over a hole he was digging. Presently he straightened, lifted from the ground the body of Kathleen Ballin, and lowered it gently into the pit he had dug. He stood for a moment gazing down upon her, then slowly and methodically began to fill in the grave.

When it was finished he walked heavily back to Carter, stood over him with an electric torch blinding him. The back glare was in Morehouse's eyes, and they were mad, red with maniacal bloodlust. The young-old face was harsh with hate now.

"You have torn the governor and his wife from my grasp," he said bitterly. "By now they will be back in some city, will have the police on my trail. You, Carter, have caused me to kill my own daughter—Kathleen was my daughter, you know, the child of the woman Samuels hanged—and so it is you who shall pay the penalty in Samuels' place. You killed the Negro—a good pilot. He dumped over the judge and some others."

Morehouse strode off, leaving Carter lying on the ground, and Carter rolled his head over again, saw a monoplane tucked back under the trees. The madman climbed upon its wing, reached into one of the two cockpits and drew out a parachute.

With this he came quickly back toward Carter, detached the harness of the 'chute, drew out the ends of the shroud, and to them fastened a quickly fashioned hangman's noose. This he looped about Carter's throat.

"I'm sorry to keep you waiting, Mr. Carter," he said in mocking apology, "but the truth is I didn't think I'd have need of any more of these parachute gallows of mine. I had intended only four deaths that way, but, see, I'm thoughtful of you. I give you my own parachute, so that if we should meet disaster in the clouds, you at least will be protected."

He laughed again, and the hissing of it made Carter's flesh crawl. The man drew the noose tight, the knot under Carter's left ear, then he lifted the detective's lean 180-pound body as casually as if he had been a child, put him upon his shoulder, and stalked off toward the airplane.

He stuffed him into the front cockpit, the parachute behind him, and Carter realized then why his hands had been bound in front. The man was taking no chances with his meddling with the parachute and injuring it so that he would fall to his death rather than be strangled by the 'chute.

Still chuckling insanely, Morehouse fastened a light cord to the rip ring of the parachute, fastened a coil that must have contained a hundred feet to this and then secured the other end within his own cockpit.

"You see," he said suavely, "you will be unable to pull the ring of the cord yourself, so I have rigged this automatic rip for you. It will ensure safety in case you should be thrown out and in your—shall I say astonishment—be unable to locate the rip cord yourself."

Carter smiled mockingly up into the madman's face. "It is kind of you," he said, "to take so many extreme measures for my comfort."

Morehouse snarled and struck him in the mouth.

"Your comfort, bah! If it were not for the fact that I want Samuels to know of your death, to realize I am still free and will strike again, I would bury you alive there beside my daughter, whom you caused me to kill."

Carter said grimly, "I perceive that you too are a man of sentiment, Morehouse. I should scarcely have expected it."

The man contorted his rage-filled face, but did not strike again, then climbed into the rear cockpit.

There was the whine of the compression starter and a moment later the motor hummed and the propeller was flashing ahead of them. Carter could see the black outline of trees against the sky, made out the wind-filled direction sock on the top of a tree and saw the plane already was headed into the wind.

**AFTER A** few moments of preliminary warming up, Morehouse opened the throttle of the machine. It bounced across the field gathering speed. Carter felt its tail pick up suddenly and the madman jerked the nose into the air, climbed a moment, then leveled off until the plane picked up speed again, zoomed again. It was all done in the dark, but the man must be intimately familiar with the field. He had cleared the trees by a score of feet and now the plane was sent in a steep climb off into the southeast.

Carter did not know whether Morehouse intended to drop him over Capitol City or over Cornwall, but he suspected it was the former. If his guess was right, Carter would have a little more than an hour to contrive some escape. He squirmed in the cockpit seat. The unaccustomed parachute at his back was uncomfortable and, in moving about, something pressed against his side, something in his trousers pocket.

Suddenly Carter remembered the cigarette lighter he had dropped into his pocket "for emergency." He strained his bound hands and tugged at his coat. After minutes of awkward twisting, he managed to get hold of the lighter. He bent forward now in his cockpit, his body almost completely filled the opening, so there was little draft. He maneuvered his fingers and flicked the lighter into flame, wedged it between his knees with the flickering yellow flame burning upward, then held the ropes that bound his wrists in the fire.

Three times he was forced to strike the lighter and wedge it between his knees before he could ignite the rope and his straining wrists snap it apart. It was only a few instants then before his hands were free and he had reached down and released his feet.

He was free of bonds now, but he still was in the forward cockpit, unarmed, and the madman out of reach behind him with a gun, was in a position to see any movement he might make. He peered over the side and beheld the twinkling lights of a city not more than ten minutes flight ahead. Thinking quickly, Carter realized it would be impossible for him to overpower the man behind. He must allow himself to be dumped from the cockpit and take his chances on thwarting this fiendish parachute gallows, a dim hope.

Carter's mouth was grim. If he had to die, he would take this monster with him, foil his further attempts on the governor. Eagerly he ripped what remained of his shirt into fragments, wadded it into a ball, then he dipped into his pocket and found the container of cigarette lighter fuel. They were over the city now and settling downward, the time was short.

Carter saturated the piece of cloth with the liquid. Using a small key, he ripped open the seat beneath him that was stuffed with curled hair. He stuffed the saturated cloth into the opening so that half of it lay against the cloth side of the plane and half within the cushion. Then he got his lighter ready. They were settling low over the city now, circling wide and shooting back at top speed.

CARTER KNEW then that the madman was preparing to barrel roll and drop him to the ground. He struck the lighter, thrust the flame down among the saturated cloth. It burst into flame. Carter stepped on the seat and plunged over the side.

As he fell, he seized the rope about his neck, pulled it in until he found the spot where the cords of the shrouds came together. He twisted the ropes swiftly about his hands. Scarcely had he tightened his hands in the shroud, flexed his arms with all the strength of his muscles, when he felt the tug of the rip cord fastened to the plane. An instant later heard the small explosion of the opening parachute.

The jerk on his arms snapped them straight out, ripped at his hands till the ropes bit into them. He felt the bones snap sickeningly, the noose tightened about his throat stranglingly, and half dazed, his arms strained and numb, Carter swung, choking. Desperately he fought against the paralyzing weakness, began to tense his arms. The pain in his hands was incredibly intense, but his life depended on persevering.

Slowly, painfully, he drew himself upward. The noose loosened and breath whistled through his clamped teeth. On and on until he twisted one arm through the shrouds, got the ropes under his armpits and freed his tortured hands.

The city swam up toward him. For seconds Carter hung so; then, somewhat recovered, twisted his head and peered upwards.

He could not see the plane from which he had jumped, but he could see the red flare of the fire lighting the sky. Then, suddenly, it streaked into view, plunging toward the river.

Carter drifted on downward, his movement scarcely perceptible and watched the flame-wrapped plane dive on. As he gazed, he saw a dark figure rear up in the cockpit, suddenly fall clear of the plane. Body and flame streaked down toward the river, then the plane veered sideways, struck Morehouse. There was a tearing scream, then they dove together into the black water.

Moments later the ground shot up and, flexing his knees feebly, Carter landed in the street beside the river. He took his head laboriously out of the noose and staggered toward the bank.

The gleaming black bosom of the river was unbroken except for a few rippling waves still lapping from where the plane had crashed. Carter leaned weakly against a warehouse, heard sirens wailing in the distance. Police and ambulances on the way. Staring out across the river he muttered,

"The sky has rained its last floating corpse."

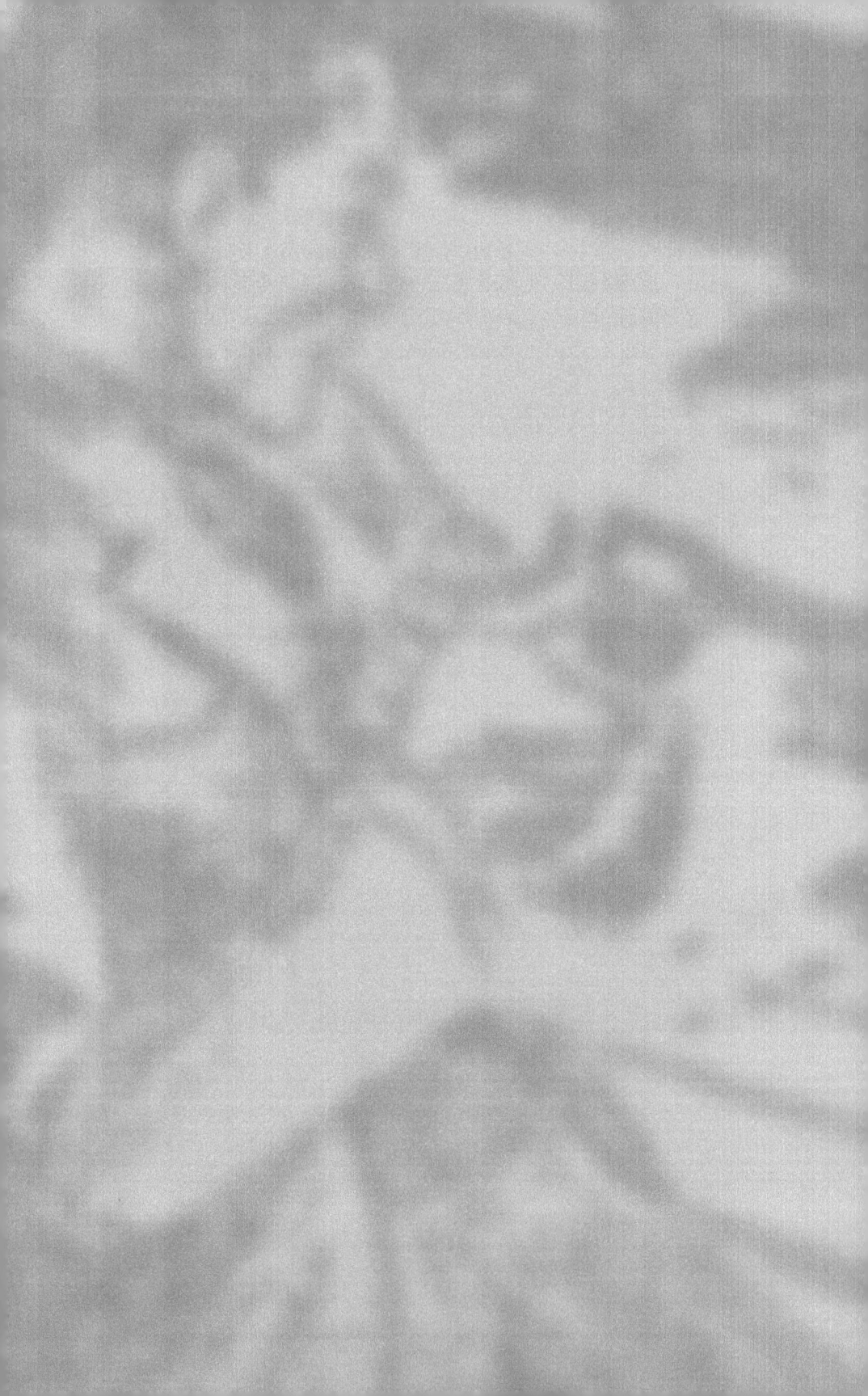

# SATAN'S HOOF

SINISTER SUPERSTITION HELD
SWAY OVER THAT NEW ORLEANS
RACE TRACK. AND THE CURSE
REACHED OUT AND TOUCHED
DETECTIVE KEN CARTER WHILE
ON A VISIT HERE. HE WAS
SHUNNED, FEARED; COULDN'T
EVEN GET A BELLBOY TO HANDLE
HIS LUGGAGE. THEN CAME THE
MIGHTY TREAD OF SATAN'S HOOF,
WITH ITS WAKE OF MANGLED
MURDER. KEN CARTER WAS STILL
FEARED—BUT NOT SHUNNED
BY THE BLOODY FINGER OF
SUSPICION.

# CHAPTER ONE
# THE MAD COLONEL

**T**HE LIGHTNING blazed blue white, glittered on rain that sheeted across the taxi windows. On its heels the thunder crashed like a cannon, a typical New Orleans downpour. Ken Carter saw with relief the hazy yellow lights of the Royale Hotel. The taxi swerved to the curb.

Carter swung his lithe, long body through the Niagara that poured down between the taxi and the marquee, looked around for a bellboy to take his bag. There was none. Frowning, Carter lugged his heavy suitcase toward the door. He caught a fleeting glimpse of a black face.

A boy ducked out and leaped for his bag. Once more lightning, like an unbelievably huge flashlight, poured electric glare into the street. The boy snatched back inside again.

Carter cursed and slapped open the door on the verge of harsh speech, then saw that fear trembled in every inch of the boy's coal-black body, actual paralyzing fear. But fear of what? Carter frowned and strode long-legged, high wide shoulders squared beneath his tailored brown topcoat, across to the marble counter behind which a dapper, wax-mustached clerk smiled. The huge gilt and crimson lobby seemed dusty.

The Royale was not the finest hotel in New Orleans, but its cuisine was noted and Carter appreciated good food. He scrawled his name across the register and the clerk dinged a bell with a slapping hand.

Carter followed the black boy, lugging his bag now, toward the elevator. An upright old man with a clean-shaven, flushed face and jet-black hair sweeping back from heavy brows smiled at him and moved into his path. Carter stopped, peering at him inquiringly. He heard a thump and looked about in time to see the boy, having dropped his bag, scuttle across the lobby and behind the elevator cages. His face, glancing back, was panic-stricken.

Carter was thoroughly angered now. He said, "If that rain would let up for ten minutes, be damned if I wouldn't go to another hotel. These bellboys are absolutely crazy."

The welcoming smile faded from the florid face of the upright old man. He frowned his heavy brows.

"It's the curse," he muttered, and a worried fright crept into his face. Slowly he forced himself to smile again, though his eyes remained clouded. "Thank you, Mr. Carter," he said, "for coming so promptly. If you will come up to my room, we can go into the thing in more detail."

Carter frowned, "I'm sorry. I don't understand."

"I'm Colonel Hartain," the man said, "Colonel Jove Hartain."

Carter still stared at him. The hotel must be full of mad people, he thought, these pesky bellhops who jumped at a whisper and dashed away, and now—

"I'm sorry," said Carter, "the name doesn't mean a thing to me."

"Then why are you here?" Colonel Hartain's voice sharpened.

Carter said calmly, "I came down for a vacation."

Carter felt fear feathers
brush his spine.

"When did you leave New York?"

"I really can't see that it's any concern of yours," Carter said, turned his shoulder to the man and snapped his fingers for a bellboy. He might have been alone in the Sahara Desert, a paralyzed deaf mute for all the attention he attracted from the bellhops.

Colonel Hartain's voice at his elbow was harsh. "You're very rude, young sir. If I didn't need your help so badly, I'd have nothing further to do with you. I can only assume that you did not get my telegram."

Carter said, without turning his head, "I did not."

Hartain moved around in front of him. There was a pleading in the depths of his pale blue eyes that was not evident on his face.

"But you will help me?" the Colonel asked. "They've put the curse of the Devil's Hoof on me. They've frightened my stable boys so that almost all of them have quit. There isn't a Negro in the hotel who doesn't run when I come near."

**CARTER WHIRLED** suddenly toward him. "Then I suppose you're responsible," he said, "for my not being able to get a bag upstairs."

The man nodded his head ruefully. "I reckon so."

Carter said, "Look here, I don't mean to be rude, but I came down here for a vacation, to have a bit of a fling at the races, and I can't take any case right now. If you like, I'll wire for some of my men to come down here. But I, myself, can have absolutely nothing to do with it."

The man put his veined, puckered old hand on Carter's arm and Ken saw for the first time that he carried a cane in his left hand and leaned heavily upon it. He concealed it half behind his leg, as if ashamed of his infirmity.

"You don't understand," the man said. "I've told you I'm Colonel Hartain, Colonel Jove Hartain. I have a racing stable and some enemies of mine have put the curse of the Devil's Hoof upon me. They're trying to force me out of the big race."

Carter said firmly, "I'm sorry, but that's the best I can do."

He saw anger stir in the colonel's face, stepped back a pace, picked up his handbag and started for the elevator. The Negro boy slammed the door in his face and although the car was empty, it shot upward. Carter cursed and dropped his bag upon the floor. He heard a sharp footfall behind him. A rasping voice, hoarse with anger, grated in his ear.

"Traitor!" It was Hartain's old voice, vitalized by rage. "You've sold out to my enemies, have you?"

Carter whirled just in time. Hartain, his face crimsoned by anger, his pale blue eyes flashing, had raised his heavy cane and it was swinging in a swift arc toward Carter's head. Carter skipped lightly aside, seized the cane as it whistled down and wrenched it from the man's hand.

Hartain took another step toward Carter, then his left leg gave way under him and he collapsed on the floor. Still no one came near them. There wasn't a Negro on the floor. A few men standing remotely on the far side of the room stared, but none offered to interfere.

Carter bent in commiseration over the feeble old man lying helpless on the floor, put his hands under the older man's arms and lifted him. Hartain struck out ferociously with his fist at Carter's face. Then someone small slipped between the two men and Carter looked down with surprise upon blue-black hair, upon a small head that did not come to his chin. A girl's low voice came in upon their anger.

"Father, father," it said. "You mustn't act this way. Stop now, father. It isn't good for your heart, you know."

Above the gleaming blue-black of the girl's head, Hartain still glared at Carter, but as the girl continued to talk, his anger faded and he dropped his pale blue eyes.

"Come, father, come upstairs with me. It's getting late. You must rest."

The man said, "All right, Frankie," and with a hand upon her shoulder began to limp slowly away.

Carter strode after them on positive feet and said, "Just a minute please."

**THE GIRL** stopped and anger darkened her black eyes as she turned upon him. Her mouth was red as ripe cherries and scornful. She said sharply, "I want nothing to do with you. Tussling with an old man."

Ken Carter bowed ironically. "I can appreciate your viewpoint, being a man of sentiment," he said. "But I do object to being hit over the head with a cane even by an old man. However—" he proffered the cane extended over his crooked arm like a sword— "I gladly surrender the spoils of war."

The girl took the cane with her left hand, but the scorn did not leave the smooth olive oval of her face. She turned away and Carter watched her march away, proud and erect, every line of her sweetly curved body radiating her scorn and anger, as she helped her old father across the lobby and slowly up the stairs.

Carter glanced rapidly about him. The bellboys still were not in evidence. Angrily he strode across and slapped the marble counter.

"Listen," he said, "either you get your bellboys in hand, get them to take my grip upstairs and operate the elevators, or something worse than a Devil's Hoof, or curse, or whatever it is, is going to descend on their benighted heads."

The clerk was pale behind the pointed ends of his waxed mustache. He said, "Yes sir! Certainly, sir! Right away, sir!"

and ducked out under the counter himself, skipped across the lobby to a small corridor and herded out a bellhop, talking at him vehemently as the two crossed back to Carter.

The bellhop rolled white-rimmed eyes, but took the bag. He kept a good ten feet ahead of him all the way to the elevator, where he stood in a remote corner. Carter eyed him speculatively. His fright was genuine, but the cause of it was obscure to Carter. He was familiar with voodoo, but this Devil's Hoof was something new.

Carter spoke so abruptly the boy jumped.

"Do you know anything about the Devil's Hoof?"

The Negro's agitation increased. He glanced sideways out of his big eyes, then jerked them hurriedly away. His teeth began to chatter. " 'Deed I don't, sir. 'Deed I don't. I don't know nothin' about nothin'."

The car stopped and the boy skipped out quickly, darted ahead. Half between anger and amusement, Carter followed.

"Are you sure, Rastus," he called after the boy, "that you don't know what the Devil's Hoof is?"

Carter heard a gentle chuckle and whirled to stare at a man who stood in the open door of a room.

"I suppose you have met Colonel Hartain," the man said.

Carter nodded. "I did. There isn't a boy in the hotel now who will come anywhere near me since I did."

He stared into the face of the man. It was quizzical. The hair was snowy and long, and he wore an imperial and a mustache, white, too. He chuckled again.

"I'm Colonel Whittier Jackson," he said, and Carter proffered his card.

"I reckon I could tell you about the Devil's Hoof if you're interested," Colonel Jackson said.

"I wish you would."

"Well," said the colonel, "it's like this. The Negroes long have had a superstition that when it thundered, it was the devil riding his horse across the skies against a host of angels. Lately there's been a new twist to the thing. The door of Hartain's stable was found smashed with a hoof mark upon its center. A hoof mark larger than any horse known, even bigger than a Percheron, and the story got around mysteriously that Hartain was cursed.

"He has the idea that it's some trick being worked by racing enemies of his, but the Negroes take it much more seriously. The other night the door of his room was smashed, crushed in the middle by a huge hoof. The print was plain on the soft wood and naturally the Negroes are somewhat worked up about it. I think the colonel is worried too."

**CARTER MUTTERED,** "The Devil's Hoof, eh? Well, I hope it stays 'way from my do'."

He laughed and the other man laughed, too. "That goes for me, too," he said. "I have a few horses myself."

Abruptly Carter felt that eyes were upon him, and glancing over the colonel's shoulder, looked into the green eyes of a woman. She was standing where the bright overhead light shone down on red hair that was like fire in the dull sobriety of the hotel room. She had drawn about her a plainly cut negligee of heavy green satin that emphasized every inch of her superbly mature body.

She moved slowly forward as she met Carter's eyes, neither hurried nor slow, but with a luxurious lounging pace of sheer graceful animality.

"This is my wife," the colonel said. "My dear, this is Mr. Ken Carter of New York. A detective, he tells me."

Carter bowed slowly, his face expressionless.

The woman dragged out words. "So this is Ken Carter. Boy! Have I heard of you!" Her voice was a drawl, but it was not a honeyed Southern accent. It was a drawl from farther north, where Ken Carter was much more intimately known—and feared.

She lifted her arm with slow grace, offered a tapered white hand to Carter. The slashed long sleeve of her negligee parted over it with a startling sense of nakedness.

"You do not come from the South," Carter said.

The woman let her head sink forward slightly, turning her green eyes upward to stare at Carter beneath the smooth black line of her brows.

"You seem to know everything, mister," she said, "and you're a regular devil with the ladies, I guess."

Carter smiled grimly. "Then you better beware of my hoof."

Out of the corner of his eye, Carter saw Jackson's face grow long, a startled glance flickering across his face.

The woman only laughed lazily, tilting back her head. Her throat line was exquisite.

"Look in on us sometime," she said, and the colonel also extended his invitation.

Carter bowed again and went on, found his boy had thrust the key into the lock of his door and fled. His bag rested by the entrance.

Carter stared down at it a moment, then shrugged and unlocked his door. It was too late now to hunt up another hotel, but in the morning he would certainly leave this place, find headquarters where superstition did not have quite so wide a sway.

Grumbling to himself, Carter pressed open the door and stepped inside. He reached out a hand, fumbling for the switch, and suddenly the lights went on. He blinked at the glare, and looked into the red-masked faces of two men who leveled revolvers.

## CHAPTER TWO
## THE PRISONER

**C**ARTER STARED from one man to the other, from one gun muzzle to the other, and said casually, "To what do I owe the honor of this visit?"

The men's eyes, glittering through the slits of masks he realized now were made with bandana handkerchiefs, told Carter nothing. He said cheerfully, "You won't mind if I remove my hat? I was brought up quite well and it makes me uncomfortable to wear my hat in the house."

He took his hat in his right hand and tossed it into the air. It whirled and, descending accurately—Carter's long years of juggling on the stage stood him in good stead now—it flopped squarely into the face of one gunman.

In the instant it settled, Carter dropped to the floor, plunging against the legs of the second man. The man did not fire, but hacked down savagely with his gun barrel. The blow caught Carter on the shoulder. Sharp pain shot through him. He jerked the gunman's legs and they went down in a huddle.

The lean detective sprang immediately to his feet, snatching for his armpit gun. But he got no chance to use it. The second gunman had flicked aside the hat that had blinded him and rushed with a down-slashing gun.

Carter dodged that with the swift, split-second balance of movement that his juggling training long ago had given him. He drove his left fist into the pit of the man's stomach. He hurled him back a full two feet, strangling, gasping for breath. Once more Carter grabbed for his gun.

His feet were jerked out from under him. He threw his head forward to escape a blow on his back when he struck the floor. Almost before he landed, the still panting gunman he had punched leaped feet first toward him.

Carter twisted in the air, rolled, dodged the feet. The gun slashed down again, glancing off the back of Carter's head. He stumbled to his feet, half dazed, jerking up almost with a reflex action of his roll. He was reeling. The room was swaying before him. His gun was in his hands now, and staggering through squinted eyes that refused to focus properly, he leveled it at the man who crouched before him.

"Hands up!" he ordered grimly. "You don't dare shoot, but I do."

Carter heard a soft movement behind him. He tried to whirl, but the daze of that terrific blow to his head was still upon him and his feet stumbled. Another blow fell hard and this one did not glance. Carter sank with a low moan, unconscious to the floor....

When Ken Carter recovered consciousness, he was hunched down on the floor in the tonneau of an automobile that was bounding over a rough road to a continuous accompaniment of lightning flashes and rolling thunder, as if the machine bumped tireless wheels over cobblestones.

Carter, opening his eyes slowly, peered about him in the darkness. Lightning rimmed the dark figure of one man on the back seat. Carter saw a gun in his hand. Cautiously, Carter moved his hands. Bonds held them and they were powerful and tight. He could not make them give a fraction of an inch.

His feet were tied, too. Carter struggled quietly against the ropes for a while and finally, finding it did no good, demanded, "What's the meaning of this?"

Instantly his face was painted with white light from a hand torch.

"Come around, have you?" the man jeered.

"What is the meaning of this?" Carter demanded again.

The man chuckled behind the hand torch.

Carter's teeth set grimly. "Crooks don't get away with treating me like this."

The man laughed again in the darkness. It was a giggle, a high and crazy tittering, but there was nothing funny in it. It made chills creep up and down Carter's back.

"Mister," said the man, "just you rest easy about that. You're not going to have any chance at all to make us pay up."

Carter said grimly, "So it's murder, is it?"

The man giggled again and the sound of it got under Carter's skin and made it crawl.

Suddenly the auto lurched more violently than usual, skidded in a half circle and slid to a stop.

"Well, here we are," the driver called back and the man on the back seat threw open the door at Carter's feet, then piled out into the driving rain. Carter made out a faint yellow light. Then lightning danced across the sky and he saw vividly a decrepit cabin built of logs and slabs of wood, with a sagging roof that cringed beneath the lash of wind-tossed tree limbs.

The yellow oblong of a door opened and there was a vague huddle of shadows before it. Presently the men came trooping back again, a third person with them. A giant of a man bent over Carter, caught Carter beneath the arms and with no apparent effort lifted him out of the car, slung him across his shoulder like a sack of meal and splashed off again toward the cabin.

Carter was immediately wet to the skin from the flailing rain. Rage consumed him. He was furious at this ill treatment, angry at the absolute craziness, the inexplicability of all that had happened, but he did not take it out in futile threats. He had warned the men once.

**SUDDENLY YELLOW** light fell around him and the beat of the rain stopped. He was inside the cabin. The man who carried him let him gently down upon the floor against the wall. Two other men tramped in and the door shut. Carter glanced quickly about. Obviously a Negro cabin. A rickety table against the wall, boxes and a couple of feeble chairs completed the room's furnishings, except for the straw pile in the corner that was a bed. On the table a dirty-globed oil lamp burned smokily. The dampness drove odors out of the walls, out of the very floor. The cabin smelled like an animal den.

The two men who had brought Carter still clung to their red masks, but the third man, the Negro whose cabin this apparently was, had not bothered to cover his face. It was savage in the extreme, beetling low brows, a flat nose, thick lips.

The giant who had carried Carter threw a clean blanket, got from heaven knew where, over Carter's body and peered down at him, for once without that insane giggle.

"You'll do lots better if you don't try to escape," he admonished. "Just you stay quiet and in an hour or two, maybe come morning, you'll be turned loose again."

The man strode over to the other two, talked in an undertone, then plunged out into the rain. Carter presently heard the motor, heard it fade away, then nothing but the beat of the rain. The two men left behind built a small fire of chips on a stone hearth and crouched over it, talking in mutters.

Carter gradually let his head sink forward, and assumed the deep regular breath of slumber and waited with slitted eyes. The bestial-faced Negro glanced toward him presently and grunted words like animal sounds. The other man peered at him and the Negro yawned prodigiously, and flopped on the pallet.

Carter could have laughed aloud with triumph. His eyes darted excitedly about the room, seeking something with which to sever his bonds. They lighted finally upon an old dull hatchet against the wall.

Softly, Carter began to snore, still keeping his watch upon the man who crouched by the fire. He was hunched down on his hams, head sagging, his hands clasped behind his neck in the forlorn posture of primordial man. Carter steeled himself to patience and waited an hour of slow seconds before he dared to stir.

Then, finally, he began to wriggle snakelike across the floor toward that hatchet. It took ten minutes of cautious effort to reach it, then Carter backed up against the wall and groped for the edge of the blade with bound hands. It was the work of a few instants then to saw through the rope.

**CARTER HAD** barely finished when the Negro on the pallet reared up on an elbow, glaring across the room with his small animal eyes. Instantly he was up and charging across the cabin. Carter had no time to unbind his feet. His hand snaked behind him, seized the hatchet and, with a thrust, he was leaning against the wall on his tied feet, the hatchet poised.

With his feet free, Carter would have felt himself a match even for this powerful Negro, but as he was and with his arms still half numb from their lashing, he would not stand a chance. Gripping the hatchet, he shouted peremptorily:

"Stop there or I'll bury this hatchet between your eyes!" The Negro hesitated in his rush. Carter leaned forward, the hatchet ready to hurl.

"The blade will strike the bone between those eyes of yours," he went on, "but it won't stop there. It will bite into your brain. And after that you won't know anything. You will be dead."

The Negro was nonplussed by this form of attack and he wavered, trying to decide what to do, those small eyes of his shifting from side to side.

Carter suddenly leaped forward, jumping with both feet at once, and brought the head of the hatchet slamming behind the Negro's ear. It was a blow to kill an ordinary man, but the Negro did not even fall at once. He swayed while his eyes glared, lost his balance and tumbled. The sound of his fall jerked the second Negro to his feet with a loud cry. He snatched a gun from his pocket.

Carter was wavering, unbalanced on his feet. As his second captor leveled his gun, he dropped to his knees. The bullet whined above his head and before the man could aim again, Carter had hurled the hatchet with the deadly precision of his years of juggling. It circled once in the air and struck on its blade between the man's eyes.

His head was hurled back upon his shoulder, his back arched and he pitched backwards, striking the stone fireplace as he fell. The gun exploded again and fell from his nerveless hand.

Carter dragged himself on hands and knees across the room, snatched up the gun, and with it resting beside him, went rapidly to work upon his bonds. The huge Negro he had struck with the blunt end of the hatchet was stirring again, legs twitching like those of a dog in a dream. The legrope knots were stubborn.

The Negro got to his knees dazedly, touched his head with his hands and began to stare about as Carter finally loosed the rope.

Carter's feet were numb. He managed with great difficulty to manipulate them into a walk until he could lean against the wall, clutching the pistol in his right hand. The Negro reeled to his feet, crouching, his powerful shoulders hunched, fingers opening and closing menacingly and his small, glittering eyes flicking about the room toward the body of his companion, the hatchet blade embedded in its skull.

A whimpering moan came from his throat, his huge teeth were bared by thick lips. He began to run back and forth like a dog and suddenly he was upon the body of his companion and had wrenched the bloody hatchet clear. He held it high and charged.

Carter fired squarely into the man's body. He grunted, checked, and charged on, jerked down his mighty arms with the hatchet aimed at Carter's head. The detective ducked sideways, firing again, but his numbed feet played him false and he swayed as he pulled the trigger.

**THE BULLET** went wide and smashed the lamp on the far side of the room. There was an instant's darkness, then the odor of kerosene permeated the room and suddenly flame leaped up, enveloping half the wall of the cabin.

Outside wind and rain still whooped and the distant mutter of thunder continued. The wind moaned into the cabin and the flame danced and quivered in an ecstasy of light.

The Negro's hatchet, missing Carter by inches, had embedded itself in the wall and he struggled furiously, whimpering little moaning sounds from his mouth as he fought to wrench it free.

Carter backed on stumbling feet toward the door, but he was still five feet from it when the Negro wrenched the hatchet free again. Blood was bubbling from the wound in his body where Carter's bullet had pierced. He pressed the palm of his huge left hand against it and lunged once more toward Carter with the raised hatchet. This time Carter did not dodge. He took careful aim and sent three bullets crashing in quick succession through the man's head.

The terrific impact of the bullets thrust the man's head backward. His mouth opened in a strangled cry and his huge body thudded to the floor with a crash that made the cabin shake. The hatchet blade buried itself almost at Carter's foot. The lean detective drew back from the fearful corpse of the Negro. The back of his head was almost blown away by the bullets.

Flames lit the cabin luridly now. The entire far wall was ablaze. Choking smoke whirled about him. Carter drew a handkerchief from his pocket, wiped clean the gun of fingerprints and hung it on the body of the man he had killed with the hatchet. He spun about and reeled from the cabin.

Circulation was rapidly returning to his feet now and the process of walking soon restored them to full efficiency. A glimmer of lightning lit the horizon fleetingly and the lurid red glare of the flames, spouting now through the flimsy roof of the cabin, sent their glare after him, guided his feet toward the road.

Suddenly Carter stopped, staring. Was an automobile parked there? Could it be that his captor had returned as he had promised? Suddenly the blinding light of a hand torch thrust into his eyes and the high giggling laugh of the giant smote his ears.

"Better stand right there," the voice said, "I got a gun in my hand and it might go off. That was a right nice piece of work you did back there in the cabin," and the giggling laughter rose again. "Saved me having to split up money with them."

Carter could see nothing of the man behind the broad gleam of the flashlight.

"Now 'spose you turn your back toward me," the man went on behind the light. Carter had no choice but to obey. "Now lie down on your face."

Anger stirred in Carter. There was muck beneath his feet. His shoes sucked in it when he moved.

"You might as well do it," the high voice went on, "or I'll have to smack you down and do it anyway."

Fairly trembling with anger, Carter finally obeyed, flopping down upon his knees and then upon his chest in the oozy mud. Instantly a weight flung upon his back, driving his face into the wet slop, smothering him. He held his breath, struggling, but the weight of the man upon his back was overwhelming

Face to face, Carter might have contended with him, but in the mud, with this huge weight upon his shoulders he could do little more than writhe. His arms were seized and bound, then his legs and, half strangled, he was carried like a sack of oats across the man's shoulder to the car and thrown upon the rear seat.

For good measure then, his captor strung a rope about the rear of the car and about Carter's throat, holding him securely in the back seat.

The man climbed in front, flashed the light back on him and tittered again his high mad laughter.

"I reckon that rope around your throat might be rather uncomfortable going to town," the man said, "but I reckon it won't kill you and I don't want you rising up behind me like you rose up behind that black boy in the cabin."

Uncomfortable? Good Lord, the rope would strangle him!

# CHAPTER THREE
# ARRESTED FOR MURDER

**THE ROPE** didn't choke him, but the ride back to town was a nightmare that Carter would remember all his life. Arms bound helplessly behind him, a rope tight about his throat, binding him to the cushion, and the light car bounding along the rutted road, bouncing him against the rope, jerking it tight about his throat, half strangling him, rubbing his throat raw until the mere touch of the rope was a torture.

A lesser man would have cried out in pain, but Carter grimly closed his mouth and resolved that the men behind this abduction should pay and pay heavily for what they had done to him. What was the reason behind it all he could not discover. But two had paid already, and the rest—

It was all utterly mad. First, Colonel Hartain stopping him in the lobby of the hotel, flying into a rage over his mere refusal to take the case; the Negroes about the building terrified by a ridiculous superstition; then, entering his room and having guns shoved into his face; being kidnapped—and all for no apparent reason.

Carter clenched his jaws, set himself grimly to stand the torture of that rope about his throat and waited. At last they hit the comparatively smooth streets of the city and Carter was driven to a house in the black quarter, into which his captor carried him. He dumped Carter on the floor, cut his bonds, and sprang back with a leveled gun.

The room was dimly lighted by an oil lamp. Carter rolled over. Wrists and legs were almost useless. A ring around his throat burned intolerably from the chafe of the rope.

He sat slowly erect, massaging his wrists. His clothing was thick with mud, his face smeared. His captor, eyes glittering, said, "You can wash up now, Mr. Carter, if you want to."

"Thanks so much," Carter said. His mouth was a thin line. He got up on numbed feet and threw a swift glance around. A bowl of water rested on the table against the wall. Carter inspected it and spotted a suitcase, his own, beside it. He frowned, whirled about. The giant was crouched by the door, the gun leveled

"There ain't no windows in here," the man said softly. "There's only this here door and I'm going to be outside it. As long as you stay in here, you can do anything you like. If you open the door, I'll shoot."

Carter glared at the man, saying nothing, and the giant whisked out the door. Ugly light glowed deep in Carter's eyes. His tall, broad-shouldered frame was taut with anger.

But he decided to make the best of the situation for the present. At least he could clean up.

He turned gladly toward the bowl of water, washed and quickly donned fresh clothing from his suitcase. In its bottom he found his two guns. Carter frowned; his peaked brow shot a glance toward the closed door. Swift examination showed the guns were loaded and in working order. He made his throat comfortable with a vaseline-coated bandage, put out the light and, guns in hand, tensed to the door. He snatched it open. The street outside was empty.

Carter's swift keen eyes searched the houses near by. No, there was no one watching. This was the queerest part of the entire kidnapping. Frowning heavily, Carter grabbed up his suitcase and, abandoning his dirty clothing, strode from the place, walked rapidly along the street until he spotted a taxicab, climbed in and ordered that he be taken to the Gibson House. He thought grimly to himself that he had had enough of the Royale to last him a long time. He was fond of good food, but there were limits to his endurance.

He deposited his grip at the Gibson without even waiting to look at his room, returned to his taxi and ordered, "Police headquarters."

He walked in and strode, grim faced, up to the desk.

He said, "My name is Kenneth Carter."

The sergeant stared at him with widening eyes in a fat, pasty face. He leaped to his feet and signaled two policemen lounging about the room and they crossed swiftly and closed in on either side of Carter. The sergeant's voice was shrill and excited.

"It's a lucky thing you decided to surrender, Carter," he said. "Fighting my men would be dangerous business."

Carter frowned. "Surrender? What do you mean?"

The sergeant said shrilly, "You'll find out what I mean," and came out from behind the counter, got on his uniform cap and called through a back doorway.

"Hi, Jeb, come on out and take charge here. Gotta take a guy somewhere," and with the sergeant ahead and the policeman on each side, Carter was marched out of the building.

"What's the meaning of all this?" Carter demanded. "I demand to know or I won't go another step."

**THE SERGEANT** turned toward him, his pasty face still excited and his voice shrill. He said, "I advise you, Mr. Carter, not to make any trouble. Maybe it's all a mistake. I don't know. But anyway, you got to go over here to be identified by a woman. If she can't identify you, it's all right."

Carter said, "I won't go anywhere until I know what this is all about."

The sergeant looked him up and down. He said, "I don't want to do it, but if you force me to I'll put the handcuffs on you, and there'll be a warrant, too."

Carter frowned, "What I'm trying to find out," he said, "is what the warrant would say."

"The warrant," said the sergeant, his shrill voice almost breaking, "will charge murder."

Carter sliced the air with the side of his hand. "You're completely mad," he said. "This is the damnedest, craziest town I was ever in in my life. I came here to report that I was kidnapped in my room, banged over the head with a gun and half strangled to death, and you say I've done murder. It's ridiculous."

"Ridiculous or not," said the sergeant, "you've got to go over and see this woman."

Carter slammed into the car. "Okay, okay, I'll go. But I warn you it's going to be a long time before New Orleans hears the end of this case."

He sat like a ramrod in the back of the car between the sergeant and one of the policemen, while the other cop climbed into the front seat of the flivver that bounced them over the streets.

The sergeant evinced interest in Carter's story of kidnapping, but the detective refused to say anything at all about the case.

"To hell with you," he said. "You've made the pinch, now see if you can make it stick. You're all going to look like fools before I get through with you."

The sergeant looked at Carter with eyes pale in a pasty face, but only leaned forward and spoke to the driver.

"The Royale, fast."

**CARTER CURSED** strenuously. He was fed up on the Royale. He was fed up on New Orleans and the superstitious blacks. He said vehemently, "I suppose that damned Devil's Hoof has kicked somebody in the slats."

The sergeant said softly, "Oh, you suppose that, do you?"

"Oh, go to hell," Carter sighed wearily and settled his broad shoulders back into the corner of the seat to rest. He touched his throat with solicitous fingers.

The police car whined a soft siren down Market Street, whirled into Fortescue, spun another corner and snubbed up short before the Royale.

Two police swung out and stood alertly, with their sharp eyes on Carter as he wearily stepped to the pavement. He went quietly toward the door with the sergeant at his elbow and the two guards trailing.

A Negro peered out with startlingly white eyes, whirled with a muffled shout and ran inward. Carter's eyes went ugly. He had had enough of this business. They marched on across the lobby and people's heads went together in whispers like the sibilance of a rising storm on the grass plains.

The sergeant ushered Carter into an elevator that creaked upward and the operator cringed away with shrinking shoulders from the nearness of Carter. The lean detective smiled grimly, his long face sardonic, and stepped nearer the Negro. Tremors raced over the boy's body.

He stopped the car, slammed back the gate and his sigh of relief at Carter's exit would have been ludicrous except for the mounting irritation that gripped the detective.

"How much longer is that mummery going to continue?" he demanded.

He got no answer, but the sergeant knocked at a door. A man's subdued voice called, "Come in."

The police stepped aside for Carter to go in first. He stared at each of them individually, then shrugged, put his hand to the knob and thrust open the door, took a long stride into the room, then another.

A girl started to her feet, jabbed a stiffened arm with a finger pointing at his face.

"That's the man!" she cried.

Her voice broke, but she stood white-faced and stared at him with black, hating eyes, the daughter of the man Carter called in his mind "the mad colonel," Jove Hartain.

Carter frowned at her.

"So what?" he demanded between his teeth.

"Do you deny that you quarreled with her father?" the sergeant demanded.

Carter looked slowly around the room. Colonel Jackson, with his pale face framed in white hair, his soft white mustaches and imperial, stood just behind the girl, looking at him with reproach. A diminutive youth with a wizened, freckled face and a rakish hat set on his head as if he never took it off, glared at him from the side of the room.

The frown on the detective's long face deepened. He ran his hand slowly up over the twin peaks of his forehead into his dull hair, as always when he was worried.

"Well, are you going to talk here or at police headquarters?" the sergeant demanded.

**CARTER WHIRLED** toward him, his demeanor unchanged except for the anger deep in his gray cool eyes. The two police suddenly snatched out pistols. He ignored them.

"Listen, Two-bits," he told the sergeant. "I've been pretty decent about this business so far. I came to you to report that I had been kidnapped and maltreated by three men, abducted from my room in this hotel. You immediately insisted that I come here and gave the lie to my story.

"Now you are making veiled threats. You can change your tone and act decently or I'll talk neither here nor at headquarters and you'll find yourself in the hottest water you've ever touched the tip of your finger to."

The sergeant bristled, thrust his well-fattened belly forward and glared at Carter, but there was nothing threatening in the detective's manner. He had spoken quietly with an air of being able to fulfill exactly what he prophesied, and the police officer hesitated. He blinked his pale eyes, screwed up his pasty face in worriment. Slowly the truculence vent out of him.

"It's just that you don't know the seriousness of the thing," the sergeant said finally.

The deep voice of Colonel Jackson cut in. "Mr. Carter is right Sergeant Knowles. You have no call to be so peremptory. Mr. Carter, though, I think you'd be wise to answer a few questions."

Carter bowed stiffly. "I'm not objecting to answering a few questions, but I do object to this—" he shrugged and let it go. "You were asking if I quarreled with Colonel Hartain. I most certainly did not. He stopped me in the lobby and assumed that I had come in answer to his telegram asking my help. I had come for a rest and told him so. I refused to take some case which seemed chiefly made up of Negro superstitions, and he became angry and tried to strike me with his cane. I took it away from him. That's all there was to that."

"My father believed this man had sold out to his enemies. I think he was right," the girl's low vibrant voice put in.

Carter turned toward her. Her small, shapely body was held rigidly. Her eyes still blazed with hate.

"I think I was quite nice about the thing, as a matter of fact," he told her. "Being a man of sentiment, I did not like to inflict my anger on an old man and especially—" he bowed with a grave face—"a man with so charming a daughter."

The girl took three swift steps forward and slapped Carter. Her face was livid with anger and Carter's matched it.

"Even though," he continued in an utterly calm voice, "I considered the man completely mad."

The girl slapped him again, clenched her fists and beat on his unyielding chest until Colonel Jackson, his kindly old face worried, took her by the arm gently and led her away. She burst into tears then, dropping her head against his shoulder.

"Frances is kind of worked up," the old man's deep voice intoned.

"So I gathered," said Carter dryly. "I considered her father mad because he credited some silly superstition or another about the Devil's Hoof, the sort apparently possessed by a super-Percheron which smashed the door of his stable and afterwards split the door of his room here.

"The Negroes apparently had become convinced of it, too, for from the moment that he spoke to me I could not get a boy to come within ten feet of me to carry my bags or for any other purpose."

He turned to Sergeant Knowles. "You must have noticed that yourself."

"I did," the police officer said grimly, "and I don't blame them."

Carter shrugged. "Apparently the whole town is mad."

The colonel shook his white head slowly. "No, my friend," he said. "You would not think anyone mad if you knew what has happened. The Devil's Hoof killed Colonel Hartain in his room a few hours ago."

Carter's face showed his incredulity. "A horse kicked Colonel Hartain to death?"

The colonel shook his head slowly. "No, the Devil's Hoof. The same one that smashed in doors, a huge thing too big for any horse that ever lived."

"Nonsense," said Carter sharply. "There must have been some human agency in the thing, then."

"That's right," said the sergeant sharply. "And you're it. I arrest you, Kenneth Carter, for the murder of Colonel Jove Hartain."

# CHAPTER FOUR
# THE ANGEL'S KISS

CARTER SPUN savagely toward the sergeant and the officer piped out, "Watch him, men!" in a voice gone suddenly thin. The two policemen sprang forward with drawn pistols, long barreled thirty-eights that they leveled at the detective's abdomen.

He glared at them, then laughed abruptly, throwing back his long head. It was not a mirthful sound.

"All right," said Carter, "if you're going to arrest me, I want a lawyer at once."

There was a telephone on a table near by and he crossed to it. The police started to interfere, but he looked at them, cold-eyed, above the mouthpiece of the phone and Colonel Jackson spoke in his gentle, deep voice.

"Surely, sergeant, you're not going to deny the man his just rights?"

"I want New York," Carter spoke rapidly into the mouthpiece. "Ellison Roberts, yes. His number is WIngate 9-8459. Yes. And put that through fast."

It went through fast and Carter swiftly outlined the situation to his lawyer. It took an hour for Roberts to arrange a writ of habeas corpus through a correspondent law firm in New Orleans and at the end of that time, Carter strode up to the sergeant's desk.

"I want to see Hartain's body," he said. "It is obvious that you intend to do nothing further about the case and if I'm to escape going through a ridiculous trial, I must catch the murderer myself."

Sergeant Knowles glared at him belligerently with his pale eyes. "You won't find the trial ridiculous," he promised in his thin voice. "Not when the jury finds you guilty and the judge puts on his black cap."

"Yes, yes," said Carter, "I've seen men sentenced to death, sergeant. Take me to the morgue, or give me an order."

The sergeant said grimly, "I'll go. I've been looking you up, Mr. Kenneth Carter, and I find many things about you I do not like. You have killed many men. You would not stop at killing one more if it meant money in your pocket."

Carter slapped the palm of his hand sharply on the top of the desk. "That will be enough of that talk, Sergeant Knowles. When I have killed, it has been to save my own life. And those I killed already had taken human life."

Sergeant Knowles was angry, but he controlled it well. He shrugged finally and stepped down from the dais on which his desk rested, picked up his uniform cap and growled, "Come on with me."

The police car moaned its siren again, the soft warm air of the Southern night fanned their faces and Carter suddenly realized that it was nearly daylight.

"Say, sergeant," Carter turned toward him, "how about a bite to eat before we go the morgue? I just remembered I haven't eaten since luncheon yesterday on the train. You must know some all-night place about here that serves decent food."

The sergeant eyed him suspiciously in the white rays of streetlights that zipped past, but finally nodded a grudging head.

"And something to drink, sergeant," Carter insisted. "I'm slowing down and I've a hunch I won't get much sleep in the next twenty-four hours or so."

"Listen," growled the sergeant, "If you're trying to get me in trouble—"

"Nonsense," said Carter. "You don't have to drink if you don't want to. And you can close your eyes every time I lift the flowing bowl."

**SERGEANT KNOWLES** still peered at him and Carter had about given up when Knowles leaned forward and spoke to the driver. They pulled up before a dark doorway on a side street. The man threw wide the door when he recognized the sergeant and Carter followed him down a dim hall into a room of shaded lights where a half dozen men elbowed a bar and tables in nooks held shadowed couples whose figures had but a single head.

Carter slid into one of the few empty booths and pulled the table aside to make way for the sergeant's belly.

"I will have," Carter pronounced "an Angel's Kiss."

The proprietor screwed up a mustachioed face, spread apologetic hands.

"I am so sorry."

"Don't know the Angel's Kiss?" Carter's voice reflected his astonishment.

The man pantomimed again. His plump, rosy face was distraught. He was sorry again.

"Nothing but the Angel's Kiss will do," Carter said, fuming to the sergeant. "Don't you think that would make an admirable antidote for the Devil's Hoof?"

The rosy face above them went blank. It remained bland, Carter saw, but a veil had been drawn across the eyes. So, here, too, the superstition of the Devil's Hoof was known.

Carter shoved the small table over so that it squeezed the sergeant red in the face.

"I must have an Angel's Kiss if I have to mix it myself," he declared. "I'll fix one for you, too, sergeant."

He shoved past the still gesturing proprietor, assuming a mildly tipsy air, and ducked under the bar, looked reflectively at the array of bottles behind it, picked up brandy and Cointreau for a start. He measured assiduously, shifted bottles so that even the bartender was puzzled over the movements, and finally drew down two tall glasses and poured the frosted mixture into them. He tasted it.

"Ah!" he expressed his satisfaction, ducked under the bar and marched back to the booth where the sergeant gazed in perplexity at the tall drink set before him.

"Taste it," Carter insisted, "and if you don't find it the antidote for anything at all, Devil's Hoof or not, then I have no further respect for the drinking judgment of the South."

The sergeant tasted it gingerly, moved his lips with little sounds, took another sip.

"Not bad," he pronounced. "Though I don't care much for mixed drinks. What's in it?"

"Chiefly flavoring," said Carter. "It's no wonder they don't know how to mix it. Your discernment will already have told you that it has a bit of brandy."

"Yes," the sergeant admitted, and tasted again.

The angels were generous. They gave the sergeant four more kisses. Carter handed him the fifth and he slopped a bit over on his hand and giggled.

"Believe I'm a little shpiffed," he said with slow difficulty.

"You? Nonsense," Carter jeered. "But I'll say this, sergeant, the Angel's Kiss is—"

The sergeant giggled again. "Yeah, I know. A good antidote for the Devil'sh Hoof." He leaned across the table, throwing out a haphazard arm.

"You know, s'funny thing, but you're not bad fell—fellow 'tall."

Carter bowed across the table with laughter that was not all pleasant in the depths of his eyes.

"You honor me, sergeant."

"No, no, don't." The sergeant wagged his head. "You're good fell—fellow. But I shtill think you know more about this Dev—Devilish Hoof n' you're telling. Negro boy saw you go into Hartain's room, said. Saw you come out leading big black horse. Shilly, that." He giggled to emphasize its silliness. "But he was shure wash you going out. Then poleeshmen took him to shtation, he got away. How you 'splain that?"

Carter's eyes were sharp. "Maybe his name was Mose," he suggested in a melodramatic whisper.

"Moshe? Moshe? Whash that got to do with it?"

"Was it Mose?"

"No," said the sergeant, " 'Smatter of fact was George, George LaFitte."

**CARTER SHOOK** his head. "Too bad," he said, "if it had been Mose, now, and he had lived on a street that began with Ch."

"C—Ch?"

"Yes."

The sergeant shook his head and giggled. "You're wrong again, lived on—on." He dug in his pocket and thrust a notebook, opened, toward Carter. The detective made a rapid mental note. "George LaFitte, 17 Romondo Street."

Carter returned the notebook gravely, his face expressing disappointment. "Then I can't give you any explanation at all for his escaping," he said.

The sergeant shook his head mournfully, raised his glass and emptied it. He started laughing suddenly, put his forehead down on the table and shook his shoulders with laughter. He straightened up and sang in a cracked voice. "Kish me again, kish me again."

Carter leaned across and clapped him on the shoulder. "That's good, sergeant. That's damned good," he told him energetically. "I'll fix you up right away."

He did, slid the tall, frosted glass in front of him and placed one for himself.

"Excuse me a moment," he said.

He walked across to the proprietor, spoke to him confidentially. "You'd better keep the sergeant here till he sobers up. He wouldn't thank you for letting him go out on the street like this."

The man nodded worriedly. "You are right, sir, and yet I dislike having him left here. Could not you, yourself—"

Carter waved a vague hand. The sergeant, he informed the man, had taken a sudden and violent dislike to him. He would understand how such matters were. He paid the bill and walked out. The sky was graying in the east and the police chauffeur behind the wheel was asleep. Carter did not disturb him. He walked swiftly toward a brighter street and succeeded in finding a nighthawk cab that took him to Romondo Street.

Silly, of course, to hope to find a Negro who had escaped from the police at his home, but there was no harm in looking. There might be something in the house that might somehow point to the murderer. Yet he had small hopes as he penetrated the crooked, black and unpaved street that was little more than an alley. The first light of day could not penetrate its narrowness.

Whoever had murdered the colonel had been infernally clever, had planted a clever frame-up against Carter. It would be absolutely impossible for him to prove an alibi; and if this Negro witness with his wild tale were found, it might help pile up incrimination.

Carter stumbled in the darkness and drew out a small flashlight that he flicked on the ground before him. The alley's floor was black mud, soaking wet from the rain earlier in the night. Carter's shoes sucked up and down in its stickiness, being nearly pulled from his feet.

He turned the white circle of his light on the house fronts and spotted almost immediately the nearly obliterated 17 that designated the home of George LaFitte. It was a dilapidated little one-story shack and its door hung agape.

Carter went up to it cautiously. Where, he wondered, were the police who undoubtedly must have been set to watch for the witness's return? He pushed the door and it swayed inward. Carter put his foot on two huddled objects on the floor and the chills ran cold up his back, raised his hair on end.

It was not that a policeman and a Negro lay dead upon the filthy floor. It was the way they had been killed. Their heads had been crushed as if by an enormous hoof, and the prints were deep, too, upon their crushed chests.

# CHAPTER FIVE
# A JOCKEY RIDES DEATH

CARTER CLOSED the door quietly behind him and stood over the bodies with the strong white glare of his light delineating every horrible detail of the men's deaths. The Devil's Hoof, for there was no doubt that this was what had killed the men, had struck the Negro square-ly in the face. The entire countenance was crushed in. Another had struck him on the chest and bits of rag were embedded in the wound.

In the case of the policeman, the first blow had come from the rear and the back of his skull was demolished. Carter, feeling faintly sick at his stomach, hair still tingling along the back of his neck, suddenly whirled and flashed the light behind him. Nothing there.

He swept the minute circle of white over the entire room. No, nothing there, nothing to fear. Carter crossed back to the door and shot home a bolt that was woefully fragile. It could not stand a single blow of the Hoof. Then Carter began a minute inspection of the room. There were chewed up places in the floor such as might be made by the cleats of a horse.

The room was bare and scantily furnished, but Carter went over the place conscientiously and in a drawer he found two small round sponges about the size of a silver dollar. He stared at them and his eyes narrowed. He put them slowly back in the drawer, took a final glimpse of the bodies and, unbolting the door, strode out into the early morning sunlight.

Within the lightless interior, he had not realized that the sun had risen, but the air was gloriously fresh with dawn, a mockery to the grisly death that lay within. Striding back up Romondo Street, Carter carefully obliterated every footprint he had made in the mud. He saw there were no hoof marks.

Carter walked five blocks before he found a cab. Grimly he ordered that he be taken speedily to the Royale. He grinned mockingly at himself. If the Negroes knew now what he knew, they would flee even more swiftly from his approach than they had on his two previous visits to the hotel.

He did not pause at the desk, but strode straight across and entered an elevator. He looked at the Negro steadfastly and the man began to roll his eyes.

"Up, Rastus," Carter said softly.

The car jerked into motion and the door opened with alacrity, slammed almost on his heels and he strode down the hall and knocked at the room of Frances Hartain. He had to rap three times before he heard a soft footfall within and the girl's low voice, "Who is it?"

Carter muffled his mouth with his hand, "From the police."

"Just a minute," the girl's voice retreated and presently he heard a key fumble in the lock and it was thrown wide. Carter stepped in and shut the door behind him.

"You!"

Anger contended with fright in the girl's voice. Carter began to talk swiftly.

"Listen, Miss Hartain, I'm not here to do you any harm, but I had to practice the deception to get in. I think I have a clue to your father's murderer."

The girl had straightened from the first retreat of fear and stood angrily straight, her head thrown back proudly, her black eyes flashing, her young body stern beneath the shapely severity of a white silk negligee.

"Get out of here," she ordered sharply.

Carter fought down his rising impatience.

"Did you ever hear of a Negro named George LaFitte?" he asked.

**THE GIRL** said bitingly, "You should know, he's one of the stable boys you drove away with your Devil's Hoof. Colonel Jackson gave him a job."

"Did your father run a crooked stable?"

The girl's eyes darted about the room. She took two quick steps and picked up a bookend. "Will you get out of here or must I force you to leave?"

Suddenly Carter smiled. He rarely did, but when he wished to, it made his face charming. Even his crinkling eye corners joined in it.

"Miss Hartain," he said, "I admire your courage tremendously, but—" he suddenly became serious—"you are being misguided now. I had no hand in your father's death, but I am going to find out who did. It is a necessity, since if I fail they will try me for his death. Won't you give me a little help in running down these murderers?"

The girl looked him over carefully, the heavy bookend still ready in her hand.

"Honestly now," Carter said again, "if I were the murderer, what earthly reason would I have for coming to see you like this? I would only be inviting trouble. I came because I thought you might give me information as to these enemies of your father, with whom he apparently thought I was in league."

The girl still eyed him, but thoughtfully, now and finally she put the bookend down and moved slowly back across the room toward the chair into which she sank.

"You are right, I suppose," she said. "I am behaving unreasonably, but I suspect everyone now. Evidence does point strongly to you, but I have looked over some letters my father received from friends in New York that spoke of you in the highest terms. What do you want to know?"

"Who are your father's enemies?" Carter asked swiftly.

The girl shook her head.

"His race track enemies?" Carter persisted. "I am convinced that this entire thing centers around the race track."

The girl shook her head heavily again. Her face was pale, drained of color, and her black hair was like a funeral veil.

"You are undoubtedly right about that," she said. "About the race track angle, but I can't help you. I know that father was threatened if he did not promise either to sell his horse or to agree to pull it up in the big race tomorrow so that it would lose. They promised good money if he would, death if he wouldn't. They knew father needed money, but we expected to get it from the race. We will get it from the race. Plurius can beat them easily." She stopped a moment, went on more slowly.

"Father," the girl choked on the word, "father got these letters anonymously. They told him if he agreed, to put a certain ad in the papers. Father flew into a rage. These people gave him to understand that every other horse in the race had been framed to lose, through its owner, trainer, or jockey.

"Father's helpers were incorruptible. He trained the horse himself. And our jockey was too loyal to be reached. It wouldn't do to kill the horse. Plurius must run to keep the odds on their own entry long, so they can clean up on bets."

"But which is their horse?"

"I don't know," the girl said, "I can't see—"

A hoarse shout that was almost a scream rang out in the hall. There was a terrific thump against the wall and Carter plunged across the room, yanked open the door and charged out. A huge black shape flitted down the hall silently and as Carter pursued, disappeared. He stared at the stone wall through which the thing, whatever it was, had apparently disappeared and the hackles of fear rose on his neck.

**CARTER WHIRLED** back up the hall and saw the crumpled figure of the diminutive youth Carter had seen before, the night when he had been confronted by Frances Hartain and accused of murder. Over the boy, the girl bent solicitously. Carter strode up to him. A hurried examination showed he had been merely knocked unconscious, despite a raking scar on the side of his head from which blood oozed darkly.

Remembering that terrific thump against the wall, Carter glanced up and there was outlined a hole in the plaster, the complete imprint of the Devil's Hoof!

Carter stared at the thing, remembered the huge dark shape flitting down the hall and frowned heavily. Some horrific plot was under way. That much was obvious, but the means of death, and that strangely disappearing shape....

He stooped and lifted the light body of the boy and bore him swiftly into the girl's room, laid him on a couch. The hall was thronged with people now and Carter was forced to slam the door in their faces. It was the work of a few moments to revive the youth.

The girl leaned over him, pale-faced.

"How are you, Johnny?" she asked anxiously. "Oh, please be careful of yourself, Johnny."

The boy sat holding his head in his hands. "Don't you worry, none, ma'am," the boy said. "I'm going to take care of myself for that race tomorrow."

"What happened?" Carter threw in swiftly.

The boy glanced up and, seeing Carter for the first time, reared uncertainly to his feet.

"What the hell are you doing in here?" he demanded in his sharp, high boy's voice.

The girl answered him, assuring him that she was convinced that Carter was working for their good, and the boy finally subsided, growling.

"What happened?" Carter repeated.

The boy raised his thin shoulders in a shrug. "I don't know," he said. "I was walking along the hall on my way to see Miss Frances, and suddenly I got scared, not for any special reason, just scared. I turned around and saw a big black shape and then something hit me."

"You didn't see what it was?"

The jockey shook his head slowly.

"Didn't see nothing."

"What hit you," said Carter slowly, "was a glancing blow from the Devil's Hoof. If it hit you squarely, you'd be dead now."

The jockey stared up with his wizened, freckled face at Carter and said nothing for minutes. Finally he spoke up, "Well, that black shape I saw was big enough to be a horse, but this is the first time I ever heard of a horse on the fourth floor of a hotel."

Carter said softly, "And I, too."

Abruptly the boy whirled toward the girl. "Miss Frances, what I came to tell you is George LaFitte was killed by the Devil's Hoof this morning some time. And they're looking for this guy Carter, here, because a taxi driver took him there just before dawn."

Carter's mouth was a grim line. "That will be the sergeant getting his revenge. I got him drunk," he explained with a slight twitching of his lips that could not be called a smile, "and got LaFitte's address from him. He said the boy had reported seeing me leave the room of your father and then the Negro had escaped from the police. I went to see him just before dawn, to see if I could learn something from him of the persons that made him tell that lie and I found their bodies, those of LaFitte and a policeman."

"Yah, you ain't expectin' us to believe that, are you?" the boy jeered.

Carter looked down at him. "Johnny," he said gravely, "I have long ago given up caring whether people believe me or not. I don't care now if I am not hampered in my investigation. If you don't mind, Johnny, we won't tell the police where I am right away."

The girl turned toward him, and the boy as well, staring fixedly into his face. Frances said finally, "I don't see what's to be gained one way or another by telling."

The jockey got to his feet, "Well, I do," he said shrilly and ducked past Carter and bolted to the door, dodged out before the detective's long stride could take him, slammed the door.

Carter grabbed the knob and suddenly there was a scream of wild terror in the hall. He yanked the door, but it would not open. The slamming had locked it and Carter lost precious time fumbling with the lock. The door yielded suddenly, almost throwing him into the floor. He darted out into the hall.

Jockey Johnny lay crumpled on the floor, his skull horribly crushed by the Devil's Hoof!

# CHAPTER SIX
# THE DEVIL DIES

CARTER TOOK one glance, then, thrusting Frances back into the room, closed the door.

"What is it? Oh, what is it?" the girl demanded. She stood wringing her hands, staring at Carter with her eyes large in a white face.

"Nothing we can help," he told her. "Listen, Frances. I want you to keep tight hold of yourself for the next half hour, for our capture of the man who killed your father depends upon it. Will you try?"

The girl continued to wring her hands. Her effort at control was almost physical in its intensity, but gradually her posture became natural, her hands dropped to her sides and her face became dead calm.

"It got Johnny, I suppose?" she asked listlessly.

"Yes," said Carter. "Now here's what I want you to do. I want you to go out in the hall and declare that you saw the murder, that you know how it was committed. Be a little hysterical about it, then rush back in here and dress and rush out again, very determined. You have a gun?" The girl shook her head and Carter took the small automatic from a side pocket and gave it to her. "I'll be near you. I don't care where you go. Go to Colonel Jackson's suite at the Gibson. That will do."

The girl's face now had become determined, her full sweet lips set. "In other words," she said, "you want me to serve as bait for a new attack in which we will capture the murderer?"

Carter nodded, "That's it precisely. Are you willing?"

The girl said very quietly, "More than willing."

"Okay," said Carter, "I'll duck out when you go into the hall, but I'll be near by. Remember, slightly hysterical, but get away before the police arrive."

The girl nodded again, opened the door and rushed out. The hall was filled with people and Carter had no trouble slipping out unobserved.

"I saw it! I saw it!" Frances cried, a shrill edge on her voice.

People whirled toward her, a white ripple of faces.

"I saw him killed," Frances cried again. "I know the murderer!"

Colonel Jackson was among those clustered about the crumpled body of the jockey. He pushed through the crowd toward Frances.

"Who was it, Frances?" he demanded, his voice vibrant. "Come, we'll tell the police, catch the murderer."

The girl, playing her hysterical role, stared up into his white-whiskered face as if she had not recognized him. Suddenly she whirled and ran to her room, slammed the door. The colonel knocked on it. Carter shoved up to his side.

"Did she say she knew the murderer?" he asked swiftly.

Jackson nodded his white head. "She did and now she has locked herself in her room. I'm afraid she may harm herself in some way."

"But this is important," Carter declared vehemently. "Let's get to a phone and call the police. We can go in the next room here."

**JACKSON LOOKED** at the door. "I don't like to leave for a moment," he said. "Something, anything might happen now. Why, she is in actual danger if word gets to the murderer."

"Right," said Carter, "but I'm armed. I'll stand guard here and won't let her out until you get back."

The colonel hesitated. "I reckon you're right," he said finally, and actually ran toward the door of the next room, knocked and thrust at the door. It yielded and he went in. Carter heard him shout over the wire.

He knocked softly at the door. "Frances," he called. "It's Ken Carter. You'll have to leave this second."

The door opened instantly and the girl slipped out, fully dressed. Carter strode with her to the elevator, standing empty, and sent it creaking down himself.

"Colonel Jackson was about to gum the works by holding you there until police came," he said. "You'll have to hurry. I think if I were you, I'd still go to Jackson's rooms. It's the last place he'll think of looking for you."

"You'll be with me?"

Carter said, "Yes, but not at once. I've got to go up and collect the colonel so he won't crab our game with the police."

The girl slid her hand into the pocket of her sports coat. Carter saw the outline of the gun. He smiled at her with tight lips. "Brave girl," he said, whirled on his heel and was gone. He strode swiftly across the lobby, met the colonel plunging from the elevator.

"Where is she?" he demanded.

"She came out of her room and short of holding her physically, I couldn't stop her. She had a gun." Carter was speaking swiftly. "She wouldn't let me get in the elevator with her and when I got down here, she was gone. I think she has ideas of avenging her father herself."

The colonel stood with his fists clenched at his sides. "That is what I would expect of Frances," he said softly.

He stood for a moment staring down at the floor. "Well, that being so, I reckon there's nothing else for me to do. I'll be getting back to my rooms. Sallie will be wondering what's happened to me."

He moved off slowly. Carter darted to a side door and grabbed a taxi, sped swiftly toward the colonel's hotel. His forehead frowned in thought, his eyes narrowed. He took off his hat and ran a swift hand up over his dull hair. Then, abruptly, he leaned forward and tapped on the glass.

"Faster, faster!" he ordered.

The taxi did two-tire whirls about corners, slid to a halt before the Gibson. Carter was out instantly, tossing a bill to the driver. His stride across the lobby seemed unhurried, but it covered space rapidly. The elevator droned upward to the fifth floor. Carter ducked into the entrance of a stairway and waited tensely.

A few seconds later a giant Negro stalked down the hall, his coat swinging loosely from enormous shoulders. Carter knew that giant, the man who had kidnapped him! The man walked up to the door of Jackson's suite of rooms and, as the door opened, Carter ran swiftly forward and jabbed his gun into the man's back, went in with him and shut the door.

Jackson's gorgeously red-headed wife stared from one to the other of them with green eyes that were startled. Her hands pulled the smooth green silk of her negligee more closely about her.

"What's the meaning of this?" she demanded coldly. "Why bring this Negro here?"

Carter asked swiftly, "Is Frances Hartain here?"

The redhead nodded.

"Fine," said Carter. "This Negro was here to kill her. He is the same one that kidnapped me from my room last night, just after I had talked to you and the colonel. I think he is the one who wields the Devil's Hoof."

**THE WOMAN** shrank back, her tapered hands spread white against the green pressed to her body. Her eyes went wide on the Negro's face. Frances stepped out of the door leading to the next room. She was pale and the pressure of her lips dampened their curve.

Standing behind the Negro, Carter nodded his head slightly toward the prisoner, then winked.

Frances let out a small cry, pointed her hand rigidly at the Negro, then ran back into the other room. Mrs. Jackson saw her and her eyes went wide. Suddenly the door of the suite was flung wide and Colonel Jackson strode in.

"You here, Carter?" he asked puzzled.

"I managed to trail Frances' taxi and rushed over to protect her. I just got here in time. This Negro was ready to murder her, too, and Frances has identified him."

Mrs. Jackson ducked her head in a swift nod. She no longer crouched, but stood to the full height of her mature loveliness.

"That's right, Whittier," she said slowly.

"The dog!" The colonel cried out and his hand snatched a gun from his pocket. Carter struck it up.

"No summary justice, colonel," he said coldly. "We'll turn the man over to police for proper action. This lynching business never did appeal to me." Carter's gun was completely in charge of the situation.

He raised his voice. "Frances?"

The girl showed herself in the doorway.

"Go out the door of the other room, go downstairs and summon the police. Bring them up with you when you come," he directed.

She whirled and was gone. The sound of a door closing floated back.

"I'll go with her," Mrs. Jackson said suddenly, and moved toward the door.

"You'll stay where you are." The colonel's deep voice was abruptly harsh.

The woman stopped by the door. She was against the wall, a brown, dark wall that outlined her exquisitely in her green silks. Her eyes narrowed.

"Watch yourself, Whittier," she said sharply.

"I reckon I can watch myself, and you, too," the man said in a slow, flat voice. "I should have started that long ago, long before you made me—"

"Shut up, you fool."

Carter stood quietly, gun in hand, and let them talk, eyes flicking from one to the other. The Negro stood impassive in the midst of this and the colonel moved on heavy feet to his side. He said something in a swift undertone and the Negro started as if pricked with a needle.

Carter sprang forward with leveled gun.

"Hands up, Jackson," he ordered.

Behind the white-headed old man, he saw the Negro's giant form get into action. He saw his arm swing wide, gripping a huge hammer. Mrs. Jackson screamed clear and loud, a shrill cry of absolute terror, and ducked for the door. Another scream started, but was cut short. There was a sickening crunch as the hammer struck. Carter darted to one side, aiming at the Negro.

The colonel fired first. The Negro's crouched body straightened with a grotesque surprise and the colonel fired again, slowly. Carter looked down at his own pistol with grim lips and did nothing. He held it ready.

The Negro's body rose on tiptoes, his face twisted about with fear and hate and surprise mingled upon its gross features. "Colonel—master," he mouthed hoarsely and fell dead. Furniture quivered with the weight of his fall.

Carter said quietly, "Surrender your revolver, colonel, it's all over."

The old man turned heavily on his feet toward the detective and his shoulders were bowed.

"Yes," he said slowly, "it's all over."

**THERE WAS** a sudden commotion at the door and Sergeant Knowles thrust in with Frances and other police.

The sergeant's shrill acrimonious voice rose sharply:

"Arrest Carter!"

"No," said Frances swiftly. "He didn't do it. It's a trap that he—"

Suddenly she saw the crumpled bodies on the floor and her voice stopped in her throat.

The sergeant said hoarsely, "Good Lord, the colonel's wife."

Jackson was staring at Carter with haggard eyes. "So it was all a trick, Carter?"

The detective said briefly, "Yes. How in the world, colonel, did you ever allow yourself to become entangled in a thing like that?"

The man's lips twisted beneath his white mustache. "Just an old fool, Carter. I loved her, God help me, and there was no money. She would have left without it. She planned the whole thing, gave the orders. I fought at first, but later it was easier just to drift.

"Well, she has paid now, as she should, by her own device. You checkmated me, Carter, when you sent Frances from the room. I thought that she had identified the Negro, that she knew the whole thing. Killing you would have done no good unless she could be put out of the way, too."

He gestured toward the Negro where he lay crumpled with his hand still on the hammer. It was a huge thing with a mushroomed end shaped like a horse's hoof and with a horse shoe welded to it. The Negro had carried it looped under his arm and the huge breadth of his shoulders had concealed it.

"Michael was my blacksmith," he said, "built the special shoes I use for my horses on the track. He made the hammer for Sallie after she read some legend about a knight a long time ago who used some such weapon for murders and spread superstition to cover it up."

The colonel turned his weary face, his weary body, toward the sergeant of police. The girl moved, stumbling, across to Carter and buried her face on his shoulder, her shoulders jerking with sobs.

"Sergeant," said the colonel, "I confess the murders, through this man, Michael, of Colonel Hartain, of his jockey, of a Negro stable boy called George LaFitte—we were afraid he would weaken in his identification of Carter after we frightened him into it—and of a policeman who was guarding him."

"I understand all except that shadow in the hall," said Carter.

The colonel smiled tiredly. "A stereopticon focused through a slot in the hotel room door, throwing a big black shadow. We swung the thing to one side and the shadow appeared to flit down the hall. We cut it off and the shadow vanished."

He looked them all over slowly, shook his head sadly at Frances' crying.

"And now is there anything else?" he asked.

"Yes," clipped out the sergeant, "You're under arrest, Colonel Whitter Jack—Stop! Stop!"

The old colonel had straightened as the words drummed on his ears. Abruptly, but unhurriedly, he raised the pistol to his head. He squeezed the trigger even as the sergeant rushed forward to stop him.

"**YOU SEE**, sergeant," Carter explained an hour later, "when I checked over the persons who knew of my little altercation with Hartain, and who knew the cause, that they knew I might be framed for murder by the kidnapping, the only persons I could think of were Jackson and Miss Hartain. And Miss Hartain had neither the strength nor the servant who could kill as these people were killed. The Devil's Hoof had frightened all her servants away."

The sergeant shifted in his chair on the other side of the table and raised a tall, frosted glass to his lips, smacked his lips appreciatively. He took it down and looked pensively into the pale purple drink.

"Then, when I went to LaFitte's cabin," Carter went on, "I found there two small sponges such as crooked stables sometimes thrust up a horse's nostrils to hamper its breathing so it can't win the race. And I found out LaFitte was at the time of his death a stable boy of Jackson's, which indicated he ran a crooked stable. Then, too, that wife of the colonel was surely not his calibre. I've met too many of her kind in New York. That gave a hint of the motive.

"But there was no evidence against him, so I rigged the trap."

The sergeant set down his glass reluctantly. It was empty.

"A nice job," he said.

Carter shook his head. "I've done better."

The sergeant shook the glass, "Better than this? You're crazy. It's the best Angel's Kiss you ever mixed."

Carter threw back his head and laughed.

"So you're going to forgive me for that little affair." The sergeant screwed up his pasty face, but his pale blue eyes were cheerful.

"On one condition."

"And that?"

"Show me," said Sergeant Knowles, "how to mix an Angel's Kiss."

# THE SINISTER EMBRACE

KEN CARTER HAD NO USE FOR INSPECTOR LITTLEMAN. AND THE INSPECTOR HATED CARTER'S GUTS. BUT THEY MADE A STRANGE BARGAIN—WHEN THAT STRANGE CORPSE WAS FOUND, FOR THE HEAD OF THE CORPSE WAS NOT THAT OF A NORMAL MAN. NO LIVING MAN HAD EVER HAD A HEAD LIKE THAT. AND THOSE WHO HELD THE CLUE TO THAT GRISLY SPECTACLE WERE HUSHED BY HANDS OF HORROR.

# CHAPTER ONE
# A LONG CORPSE

**K**EN CARTER kept a wearily wary eye on the black warehouses of Thirteenth Street past which the taxi crept. Close clouds absorbed the weak light of the first dawn. Carter, sprucely erect as always despite the sultry weight of the night that dampened even the cocky spryness of the nighthawk driver, watched with deliberate purpose.

Quivering through his body, as if it were sensitized to sinister radio waves, rippled a warning of death. The feeling was not unknown to Carter. Used to sudden murder in the night, accustomed always to be on the alert, it was not strange that he should develop a sensitivity to danger. Dogs, closer to the primeval world where the ability to sense and avoid death alone kept animals alive, had the same faculty. They bayed outside houses where men lay dead, even when there was utterly no way for them to know that the gaunt, robed reaper had turned his eyeless sockets that way.

Carter, feeling the cold, skin-tightening tingle of that telegraph of death, sat more erect in the melancholy cab, stared about with sharper eyes. In the shadow of a doorway, he caught a flutter of white and dropped back sharply in the protection of the car's steel body. The taxi boomed on. No shots came.

Ahead the two-globed lights of Fifth Avenue grayed the darkness. Then Carter, tense with the electricity of warning, heard a dog howl.

The howl was long-drawn and it quavered. It reached up into the sky and died on a drooping minor key, unspeakably mournful, unutterably frightened—and for Carter, fraught with sinister meaning. It was the death howl.

Abruptly the cab slid from the darkness into the half-illumination of Fifth Avenue. Carter rapped sharply on the glass and the cab drew to a halt. A cluster of blue-coated men stood in the middle of the street. Far up the avenue a siren moaned softly and the red eyes of an ambulance blinked.

Ken Carter sailed into the gunner.

But none of these things stopped Carter. It was the sight of a lean, tense-striding figure, the alert bundle-of-energy inspector of police, Littleman. If he was abroad at this hour, it meant something serious. Carter had a thin-lipped smile beneath the strong, long line of his nose as he briefly told the driver to wait and turned his long-legged stride loose on the distance that separated him from Littleman.

Littleman jerked up his head and scowled. "You, eh? Well, I don't want you here. Get out."

Carter's thin smile tightened. Beneath the brim of his expensive borsalino, his gray eyes were bitter. Hate between these two men—the hatred of a fair fighter like Carter for the unscrupulousness of the police inspector. Hatred of the inspector for Carter's keen-minded strength that plucked the criminal from security while Littleman still ran in circles.

"Get out!" Littleman snapped again.

Carter, with the memory of that dog's howl, with the keen telegraph of warning still tingling down his back, sensed that something important was here.

"What's the matter, Littleman?" he asked softly. "Afraid to let me know what has happened?"

**LITTLEMAN SNARLED** something inarticulate, spun on his heel and strode toward the cluster of blue-backed men. Between their knees now, Carter spotted a shrouded white huddle. Littleman thrust angrily among the men, shouldered them aside and turned his dark, angry face toward Carter.

"I'm very sorry, Mr. Carter," he mocked. "I sent one of my men to call you as soon as I found this. But you must have been out."

Carter replied nothing, but walked slowly toward the huddle covered with white. Close at hand now an ambulance drew to a halt. Two white-coated men climbed down. Carter looked down at the long, white-covered object. Here, then, was the cause of that feeling of death. Here was why the dog had howled.

Carter stooped slowly and pulled down the cover from the face. If it had not been for his control then, for the consciousness of Littleman's leering eyes, Carter would have dropped that cover quickly back over that horrible face. As it was his hand seemed frozen to the cloth. Over his body the muscles tensed and rippled and the cold of horror gripped his heart. For the head was not that of a normal man.

It was long from chin to forehead, much longer than any living man's head had ever been. Forcing himself to bend closer, Carter stared into the distorted features and saw then that the skull had been crushed. It was not as if someone had struck a heavy blow against one side of the head, but as if it had been placed in a vise and squeezed; and on the forehead, about the hollows of the eyes, which thrust horribly from their sockets, were several needlelike punctures.

Carter drew in a deep breath and straightened. He deliberately pulled the cover off the rest of the body, and the horror that gripped his heart spread slowly throughout his entire body, as if some chilling hand had thrust anesthetic into his being.

"Pretty, ain't it?" jeered Littleman. "Can you tell us, Mister Detective, what killed the man?"

Carter said nothing, staring down at the body. It was shapeless, and spread out like a blob of jelly. It did not seem to have been crushed, but it looked as though there were no bones in it at all. It was nude. The flesh was horribly bruised, broken in some places.

"Please, please, tell us, Mr. Carter," Littleman jeered. "Did the Empire State Building sit on him?"

A policeman guffawed appreciatively. "Looks more like it jumped up and down on him."

Carter found something horrible in their callousness to death. He had seen many men die, but was never able to get over the shock of living men deprived of all consciousness, stripped of life. He had slain men himself, but they were those who deserved to die. And this man was obviously the victim of some foul, terrible death.

Carter fixed his eyes upon Littleman's. "Yes," he said, "I can tell you what caused the death."

"The hell you can," Littleman growled. "What is it?"

Carter smiled at him slowly, turned on his heel and strode back toward where he had left his cab.

Littleman was after him immediately, a heavy hand clamping on his shoulder. Carter spun. "Take your hands off!" he ordered, and the inspector's hand twitched away as if Carter's shoulder had been a red-hot stove.

"Listen, Carter," the inspector growled, "you're going to tell me what killed that man."

Carter's mouth corners drew down mockingly. "A steam roller," he said.

Littleman frowned. "A steam roller," he echoed, obviously puzzled. "A steam roller would flatten a man out."

"Would it?" asked Carter. He laughed out loud, spun on his heel and strode off again. Behind him the police inspector's curses writhed in the air.

Carter brought up suddenly. His cab was gone. A policeman on the curb grinned at him. "Reporter grabbed it," he said. Carter shrugged and looked around. Not a cab in sight. He had to cross back to Sixth Avenue.

He started swiftly along, striding long-legged into the darkness, and suddenly he remembered that dark doorway and the movement of white within it. He glanced keenly into the darkness. The doorway was just ahead. The lights from Fifth Avenue did not penetrate here, and Carter hesitated to use his flash. No use attracting the attention of those police.

He moved warily toward it. Then, far up toward Sixth Avenue he spotted a cab. It had turned into Thirteenth Street and now was puttering along. Carter stood and waited. But he did not signal the cab. He kept his eyes on the doorway and watched, until the lights of the taxicab flashed into it. His eyes narrowed then and he strode into the doorway.

"Why," he asked impersonally, "do young ladies in evening gowns hide in dark doorways and keep out of sight?"

A low cry squeezed out of the girl at his first word. Now the white shadow wavered a little, and suddenly high heels were beating a frightened tattoo up the street toward Sixth Avenue, the girl's white face straining back now and then over her shoulder. Carter pursued, not too fast, on soft-fleeting toes.

As they neared the corner streetlight, he had a chance to admire the silvery cloak fluttering from her shoulders and the red gold glint of her hair. She skittered about the corner almost off balance, and Carter was instantly upon her.

"Just a minute," he called softly. His breath was quick from running.

The girl twisted her white face about, saw escape was impossible, and confronted him.

"Why—why can't you leave me alone?" she got out between gasps. Her head was thrown back, a firm round chin was tilted, and about her face the slightly disordered hair snared vagrant light.

Carter stood on straddled legs before her and bent his head so that he peered closely into her face.

"Why were you spying on the police?" he asked, breath still quick.

The girl jerked her head from side to side. "I wasn't spying on the police. I wasn't."

Carter said softly, "I wonder if Inspector Littleman would believe that."

He saw the girl's hands were clenched at her sides. She said low, as if strangling, "Oh, you are one of those police!"

Carter smiled slightly, presented his card. The girl turned slightly, held it to the light. A gasp tore from her. She whirled to face him, fright and horror in her face, and began backing away slowly with little steps.

Carter said, a little impatient, "Oh, come, come. I'm not as bad as all that. It's true I eat babies for breakfast, and slightly older girls for supper, but it's breakfast time now, so you're quite safe."

A stiff smile quivered on the girl's lips for a moment. "I was just surprised. I was out on a lark I had been warned against, and being accosted by a strange man in a very dark place and then pursued—" she looked down with a semblance of coquetry at the small white hands clasped before her—"while flattering is scarcely soothing."

Carter regarded her steadily, a frown still on his forehead. "Go on from there," he said.

"I'm afraid I'll have to," she laughed. "Go, I mean. It's quite late. You see, some friends and I were driving down Fifth Avenue and we saw the body in the street, so we drove around the corner to the home of one of the people and the men notified police and walked out to where they had found the body. They wouldn't let me go and I slipped out and followed them."

The girl spread her cupped hands in a small gesture. "I just wanted to see the police come."

Carter said, "I understand perfectly. Now let me take you to this friend's home, before some other detective gets after you, a detective who eats slightly older girls for breakfast."

The girl laughed uneasily and looked down at her white hands, again clenched before her.

"You just won't believe me," she complained, as if it mattered very much indeed, "but I won't bother you any more. The house is just around the corner."

She smiled again, and she had a sweet mouth. Her eyes were pools of brightness beneath the shadows of her brows. Carter reached out for her arm and she shrank back, then laughed uncertainly and allowed him to lead her down Sixth Avenue. "Twelfth Street?" he asked.

The girl hesitated. "I'm pretty sure it's Twelfth. I'm not sure. I've never been to this house before."

Carter laughed softly.

The girl stopped and faced him. They were under the corner streetlight now. The gray in the east had widened and reached almost to the meridian, and the dirty light made her white dress tinsel, like the decorations of last night's party. But the vitality of her face, the brightness of her hair, dominated.

"You don't believe me," she said accusingly.

"Who am I to doubt a lady's word?"

The girl said rapidly, "You know how it is. We were at a party and these people had a car and offered to take us home. Then, on the way, we saw this body and stopped at these people's home instead. I really don't know where it is."

Carter murmured, "You do meet the funniest people at parties."

The girl made an angry little gesture and Carter said soothingly, "All right, all right," took her elbow and guided her across the street and on down toward Twelfth. They turned the corner and the girl began to peer up at the building fronts.

"That man in the street was dead all right, wasn't he?" she asked, elaborately casual.

Carter said grimly, "He was."

**THE GIRL** twisted around, stared at him a moment, then back at the houses. There were autos parked here and Carter asked, "What kind of a car were you in?"

The girl, still staring at the houses, said absently, "I didn't notice. A sedan."

They walked along in silence, Carter's heavier tread and the sharp beat of the girl's shoes filling the street. The slow, heavy clop of a milkman's horse was behind them and the rattle of his bottles.

Carter said, "Maybe it wasn't Twelfth Street."

The girl shrugged. "Maybe it wasn't," and stopped looking at buildings and looked down at her feet.

"This dead man," she said, "What did he look like?"

Carter, watching her, said, "Like a jellyfish." The girl cried "Oh!" low in her throat and shuddered.

"Think you might know him?" Carter asked quietly.

She jerked her head in a violent negative. "No, no, I couldn't possibly bear to look at him."

"Do you think you might know him?"

The girl dumbly shook her head, and her eyes, meeting Carter's, were frightened, a little hunted. "Why should I know a man whose body was found in the street?"

Carter said, "Why should you be standing in a darkened doorway, spying on the police when they found the body?"

The girl caught her breath, her lower lip in the white grip of her upper teeth. "You won't believe me?"

Carter shrugged. "Look at it my way," he said. "Here's a murdered man in the street. I walk up along a dark building and there in a doorway is a young lady in evening dress, hiding. I speak to her and she runs away.

"When I finally stop her, she is very much agitated. She says it's all a lark, that she left a party of friends around the corner. We can't find the friends, she can't remember the kind of car she came in—it all seems pretty vague. But," he said suddenly, "I think my friend Inspector Littleman would be very much interested in talking to you."

The girl cried, "No!" and her voice was so hoarse the word was hardly recognizable.

Carter spread his hands, mouth corners drawn down cynically. "I must do my duty as a citizen," he said.

The girl got out a little laugh. It was uncertain and vague. She laughed again, with a little more confidence, and after a moment laughter actually bubbled from her mouth.

"Oh—oh, you were joking."

Carter had never heard such utter relief in a person's voice before. She said energetically, "It's been awfully nice of you to bother so much with me. If we can find a taxi, I won't bother you any more."

"But we were getting to be such good friends," Carter protested.

There was no smile on the girl's mouth now. She said slowly, "I am afraid I really must."

Carter repeated his formal bow and signaled a cab. Around the corner a motor whirred and a taxi whanged into view, spurted toward them and screeched brakes. Carter handed the girl in, started to follow, but she shook her head and held out a small white hand in farewell.

"No, you really mustn't. I can't bother you any more."

Carter smiled slowly, his eyes half closed. "You're afraid I'll change my breakfast diet?"

The girl's smile was warm now, her eyes were—nice. She said, "No," and looked at him straightly, seemed suddenly weary. "Please," she added.

Carter clicked the door shut and leaned upon the open window, his eyes traveling swiftly over the interior, and then he stepped back.

The girl's white hand came quickly through the opening, clutched his arm. Her face for a moment was framed in the dark opening, and it was deadly serious.

"If you value your life," she said rapidly, "stop this investigation right now."

She jerked back inside and said, "Hurry, driver. Straight up Fifth Avenue."

The cab sprang into motion, almost throwing Carter off balance. He stared after it with pursed, puzzled lips, his half-closed eyes amused. He pulled a notebook from his pocket and jotted down the figures 2879, the taxi driver's permit number.

## CHAPTER TWO

## VANISHING TRAIL

**K**EN CARTER strode swiftly back along Twelfth Street to Sixth Avenue and down to an all-night restaurant at Eighth. He thumbed a phone book, went into the booth and zipped the dial, calling the taxi driver's garage.

"Is the manager there?" When a rough voice grated in his ear, he asked, "Will you have taxi driver 2879 call Mr. Kenneth Carter at 122 1/2 Broadway when he comes in?"

His grip tightened on the receiver and his eyes glared unbelievingly at the mouthpiece. "Where was the crashup?" he demanded. "Twenty-Eighth and Fifth Avenue, eh? What happened to the girl?... You didn't hear anything about a girl in the accident?... The other guy get away?... He did!... What hospital?... Thanks."

He slapped up the receiver, dropped another nickel and dialed police headquarters.

"Listen, in the accident at Fifth and Twenty-eighth, was there a girl in it?... No girl, eh?... How badly hurt is the taxi driver?... Hell, he won't be able to talk for a week."

He slammed up and stood with clenched fists resting on the shelf on each side of the telephone. Abruptly he caught up the receiver again, called his office. Before he had a chance to give orders, his assistant spoke. Carter's eyes narrowed.

"So the Press wants me to check up on it, eh? Fine. I was going to anyway because of a certain police inspector.... Yes, Littleman, and because of a certain— Listen, Jordan, a girl was in a taxi accident." And Carter ordered an intensive search for the girl. "I'll check on the taxi driver and Bellevue Hospital."

Carter went thoughtfully out of the booth, found he was hungry, and sat down to eat. He ordered coffee, a couple of scrambled eggs, soft, and some toast, and, eating it, thought deliberately over the trail he had followed. It was obvious now that the girl had a much bigger part in that man's death than she had indicated.

He had guessed as much, but that taxi crackup had knocked his plans into a cocked hat. He wondered with suddenly narrowed eyes if the accident had been accidental, or whether someone concerned in the murder had rammed the taxi to get the girl?

"Damn!" Carter said out loud. He slapped coins on the counter, plunged for the door, shouting, "Taxi!"

The driver whined off toward Bellevue Hospital and Carter perched on the edge of his seat, gray eyes staring unseeingly ahead, fists clenched on his knees.

Across Eighth, on uptown on Fifth, the taxi whizzed. It was full daylight now and people moved sluggishly about the streets. The cab spun up to the main door of Bellevue. Carter stalked up to the information desk, whisked out his notebook for the taxi driver's number.

The frizzled blonde at the switchboard turned around, looked him over cynically. "Well, if it isn't Little Lord Fauntleroy!"

Carter laughed at her for all the tension within. He could handle this kind, too. "How did you know?" he asked.

She looked at him again and her hand patted her hair self-consciously. She stopped chewing gum and smiled. "Oh, I'm good that way. What did you want?"

Carter spoke swiftly. "A taxi driver was brought in here a while ago and all I know is his license number. Reckon you can find out what sort of shape he's in? I'd like to talk to him."

"What was the number?" the girl asked. Carter gave it to her. A man walked toward the counter, a man in a derby, rather flashily dressed. He stood waiting patiently. The girl turned back.

"His name is Paganini," she said, "and you can't talk to him."

Carter asked, "Why not?"

The blonde yawned, her mouth a red, artificial circle. "Because he's dead."

Carter pounded his fist softly on the counter. "Was there a girl brought in at the same time?"

"I'm getting awfully tired of this," the blonde said. "Who do you think I am, your secretary or something?"

Carter knew the answer to that one, too. He beckoned the girl away from the derbied man. "How much does your favorite candy cost?"

The girl brightened. "Only two dollars."

Their hands touched and the girl bent over the chart of emergency cases.

"They only brought in two women all night," she said. "One was alcoholic and the other jumped off a subway platform."

Carter nodded brief thanks and strode off down the hall, took an elevator to the morgue floor, paced down the dim corridor.

**IT MIGHT** be imagination, but you could always tell when you got into the morgue itself. There was a dankness, a coldness about the place. There were only a few lights and they were dim, and the far shadows of the halls and grim rooms always seemed to hide something. And there was a sense of death, bodies lying row on row on porcelain slabs, bodies cold in death, and colder from the refrigeration that preserved them.

Carter strode down the hall and his heels made heavy noise. Unconsciously he softened his steps, turned in at a door where a man sat under a single green-shaded lamp.

"Hello, Pop," he said.

A little old man who kept the morgue records raised a wrinkled, weazened face.

"Hello," he growled.

It was not a cheerful voice. Everything about this place had a funereal aspect. Shadows in the corner were like black crepe. Carter leaned elbows on the desk.

"What do you want?" Pop grunted.

"Unidentified body picked up 13th Street and Fifth Avenue this morning, looked like a steam roller had met him on a dark street."

"Oh, him," grunted Pop. "The undertaker came and carted him away an hour ago."

Carter said excitedly, "Undertaker?"

Pop bent over his records. "Guy named Zeiwitz over on Second Avenue."

Carter went out, fast. He sprinted down the hall. The door slapped behind him. Like an echo, guns began to racket. A black sedan at the curb spurted lead. Carter skated to the left, hopped to a buttress beside the steps, and jumped.

There was a two-foot well in front of the basement windows. It was walled in concrete. Carter went into it feet first and flopped on his face.

The guns continued to racket. Flakes of brick flew from the wall behind him. Off in the distance a police whistle shrilled. The motor of an automobile roared, whizzed away and died.

Carter poked up a cautious head. No more shots. The big black sedan was gone. Carter turned about. The wall was pitted by lead in a dozen places. He heard feet slapping the pavements, whirled to look into a cop's gun.

"What the hell is going on here?" he demanded.

Carter's face was grim and an ugly light lay deep in his eyes.

"I'm playing pussy in the well," he spat out.

The cop sputtered, "Don't crack wise at me. Come out of that." He had beady eyes squeezed up by fat cheeks.

"Are you a mind reader?" Carter growled and scrambled out. He dusted his knees.

"I heard shots."

"Think of that now," Ken Carter jerked down his hat brim and strode off.

"Hey!" the cop shouted.

Carter jerked his head about. The cop's gun was up. Carter strode back. He showed his badge, but the cop's beady eyes remained truculent. He puffed out fat cheeks explosively.

"An auto backfired," Carter said pleasantly, "and I'm nervous."

The cop was still angry, but the badge had punctured his truculence. "Didn't sound like backfiring to me," he muttered.

Carter said, "Get your ears tested," and strode off across the street, ignoring the cop's yell. He knew the cop wouldn't shoot.

The girl had warned him danger threatened if he pursued the investigation, and here it was. The murderers were losing no time, but how had they picked up his trail so quickly?

He remembered suddenly the man in the derby leaning against the information desk when he had talked to the blonde. Maybe he was the tipoff, had heard him ask questions about the taxi accident.

Carter found a taxi cab by the elevated stairs, shot uptown to Thirty-eighth Street.

**THE FUNERAL** parlors of Zeiwitz were unelaborate and dusty. A thin, stoop-shouldered man with a big nose came out lathering his hands.

"Vat can I do for you, sir?"

"Did you get a body from the Bellevue morgue this morning? A man all mashed up?"

The undertaker looked at him with eyes owlish on either side of that big nose. His face was impassive, yet a touch of swift horror writhed in the depths of those eyes. He said solemnly:

"I don't know vat you talk about."

"I am a private detective," Carter said swiftly, and showed his badge.

Zeiwitz blinked a moment in silence, looked frightened, shrugged his stooped shoulders. "Ja, I got him."

"Good," said Carter. "Who told you to get the body?"

Zeiwitz scratched the end of his long nose. "A young lady."

Carter said quickly, "Twenty-three or four, about five feet six, reddish hair?"

The undertaker nodded. Carter slapped his right fist into his left palm. "Fine! She got away!"

The undertaker blinked again and said, "So vat?"

"Never mind," Carter rubbed his palms together. "You got the girl friend's phone number or address?"

The man lifted his hands sideways. "I think maybe I should not tell you."

Carter strode up to him. "Listen, Zeiwitz, maybe you forgot what I told you. Don't get gay with a detective, or else—"

The thin undertaker nodded presently, started toward the back room. The front door opened and Carter whirled with the memory of those pinging, whining bullets at the back of his head.

Two men drifted in. They were flashily dressed, tight-waisted coats. Carter's eyes narrowed. Neither was the derbied man he had seen at the hospital, but he didn't like their looks. He turned to Zeiwitz. "Maybe you'll give me that address?"

The undertaker ignored him, but walked to meet the two, lathering his hands again.

"So vat can I do for you chentlemen?"

One of the men began to talk in an undertone to Zeiwitz, and the other moved along the wall, glancing casually at caskets. He dug out a cigarette and put it in his mouth, began to fumble around, looked over and saw Carter, sauntered toward him.

"Got a matchth?"

Carter's eyes did not leave the man's face. It was blue-jowled, strangely at odds with that lisping voice. Carter said bluntly, "No."

The man fumbled in his pockets again. There was a sudden gleam of metal in his right hand and the ugly snout of a bulldog pistol thrust at Carter.

## CHAPTER THREE
## THE STOLEN CORPSE

THE MAN with the gun said lazily, "Okay," then, "Upstairth and keep 'em up."

Ken Carter raised his hands slowly, eyes flicking from the gun to the other man still talking to Zeiwitz. The undertaker's hands were up and trembling. He backed slowly.

The guns pushed the two of them into the rear room. There was a basket on trestles. Carter bumped against it, darted a look and started, the beginning of horror tingling in his scalp as he saw it contained that horrible, jelly-like body.

"Handth behind you, mug," the gunman growled.

Carter jerked his eyes back. The man's blue-shaven, talcomed face was thrust close to his.

"Ever try Listerine?" Carter asked gently.

The man's fist flashed up. Numb pain surged over Carter's face and there he was on the floor. His hands were wrenched behind him, bound with biting ropes. His head was jerked up by the hair and adhesive stripped across his mouth.

The blue jowls were grinning.

"Why don't you crack wisthe again?" the man jeered.

He crossed swiftly to a side door, jerked it open, revealing the gleaming black sides of a hearse in the driveway. He said, "All right, Frank."

The two gunmen picked up the basket with the victim of the strange and horrible death. There was a clatter as some instrument fell to the floor. The two staggered, breath whistling, to the hearse with their burden. The door closed, an engine sputtered, crescendoed, and faded.

Carter rolled his head, peered about, spotted the instrument that had fallen. It was a long embalming tool, a hollow blade used to pump formaldehyde into deep organs. He hitched over to it, picked it up with cramped fingers.

A half-hour later his bonds parted. He massaged wrists and ankles, cut off the undertaker's ropes. The man ripped off his gag and began to emit shrill little piping yells.

Carter said savagely: "Shut up!"

"Mine hearse! Mine hearse!" the undertaker wailed. "Two t'ousand dollars it cost!"

"Shut up," Carter repeated. "Listen, the police are friends of mine. You get me that girl's address and I'll phone the police. They'll get your hearse back."

The man blinked at him a moment, then eagerness crept into his face. "Ja, ja, you phone police!"

He scuttled off. Carter crossed to the phone and talked into it, but kept down the hook that disconnected the line. He had a purpose in keeping the theft secret for the present.

He turned away from the phone to see Zeiwitz hurrying back to him, waving a slip of paper.

Carter grinned and took it. "I've called police," he said.

"Frances Smith," he read from the slip and disappointment darkened his eyes. It sounded false. There was an address and phone number attached. He called the phone and drew, "I'm sorry, sir, there is no such number."

There was no Frances Smith at the address she had given, either, Carter found after a taxi excursion, and he ordered the driver to take him to police headquarters. He jammed into Inspector Littleman's office without ceremony.

Littleman jerked his head up and stared out of hostile eyes. "And what do you want?" he demanded curtly.

It galled Carter to be forced to come to the police officer, but in this case he had no alternative. He stared straight and hard into Littleman's small dark eyes, an equal dislike chilling his own.

"I want to make a deal with you," he bit out.

A small smile twisted the dark lean face of the inspector. Enjoyment glistened in his eyes.

"Always glad to help," he said, mealy-mouthed. "You have been so helpful to us. But it may be that regulations—"

Carter spat out a single curse.

"I'm not asking favors. I know better than to put myself under obligations to an insect like you. I came prepared to buy—"

Littleman snapped to his feet, hands white on the desk. "Bribery, eh? Carter, you're under arrest."

**CARTER LAUGHED** shortly, plunged on, "To buy the information I need by giving you information you haven't got."

The two men glared into each other's eyes and finally Littleman allowed himself to sink into his chair. He dropped his gaze to the desk.

"You deliberately misled me," he said sourly. "And bribery isn't beneath you by a damned sight."

Carter's fighting grin was savage. "Nor is accepting one beneath you."

Littleman roared out in anger, springing to his feet again. Carter shrugged and spun on his heel toward the door. The inspector was instantly at his side, glaring up into his face, half blocking his path.

"Okay, okay," the man snapped. "I'll take your deal. I can't allow personal feelings to interfere with my duty."

"Congratulations," Carter murmured.

The men, moving back toward the middle of the office, were like stiff-legged circling wolves ready for battle. After a curt, still angry discussion Carter stated his needs, to inspect the list of missing persons and, in exchange, told Littleman of the theft of the body.

Littleman grew apoplectic. "I never gave permission to bury that body!" he yelled. "Something is crooked here."

Carter was quietly amused. "You wouldn't fool me, would you?"

Littleman grabbed his phone and bellowed orders, ordering the radio patrol to watch for the hearse, ordering men to call Zeiwitz and get the number of the missing hearse, to get a description of the men who stole it, to find out where orders for releasing the body had come from.

Then, his dark face still suffused with angry blood, he escorted Carter to a room full of filing cabinets and ordered the clerk, "Give this guy what he wants."

Littleman started to walk out, then changed his mind and settled into a chair to watch Carter. The detective went rapidly through the lists of missing men and still was working a half hour later when a policeman shuffled in and reported the missing hearse had been found near Harlem River—but without the body.

This had been Carter's real reason for coming to the police, knowing that their vast organization could locate the hearse quickly. The files had been only an excuse to remain.

Littleman started from the room, stopped and glared at Carter. He gnawed his lip and finally gruffly invited Carter to join him. The detective declined briefly, but as soon as Littleman slammed out, he followed and took a taxi to the Harlem River!

Police were already dragging the river for the body. Small boats moved systematically back and forth across the muddy water and Littleman prowled up and down the bank. Carter concentrated his search not upon the river, but upon neighboring buildings and High Bridge, stretched from hill to hill across the Harlem, a former aqueduct on which nothing but foot traffic now was allowed.

Carter let his glance range slowly over it, caught a glitter as of glass near the middle and screwed up his eyes to see better. He made out a girl, elbows on the rail, apparently using binoculars to watch the police dragging. Carter circled the police and moved swiftly toward High Bridge.

Down the steep hill, a flight of myriad steps sliced and Carter attacked them energetically. He soon slowed to a panting labor. When he reached the top, his chest was laboring.

The girl with the glasses no longer leaned on the parapet, but he spotted a girl hurrying across the bridge toward the opposite end. Carter's long, bent-kneed stride ate up the distance in her wake, but he was nearly a hundred yards behind when she left the bridge.

She went up a short flight of steps, hurriedly around a large brick building. Carter ran, took the stone steps three at a time, panted to the curb in time to see a taxi pull off. His glance searched the street, but nowhere could he see the girl. He grabbed another taxi.

"Follow that blue cab ahead."

**THEY WOUND** into the Bronx. Streets of shops gave way to apartment houses, apartment buildings to a quiet residential section where large homes graced elaborate lawns. Into the roadway of one of these the blue taxi curved. Carter, leaning forward as his taxi coasted by, saw a girl with red gold hair alight. He paid off his driver, went through the gate of the high iron fence around the lawn and strode toward the house under graceful trees.

A spreading verandah, deep windows and old-fashioned recessed door. Carter jabbed a black button beside it and a bell jangled. Silence within for long moments, then footsteps of slow dignity. The door opened narrowly. An austere but somehow furtive face peered out.

"What is it, sir, that you want?" A butler's voice.

Carter, silent, thrust the door heavily. It jarred against the man's shoulder, sent him reeling and flung wide. Carter strode in. The butler's yip of alarm was sharp in the dark, dim hall. Carter faced him and said harshly:

"The young lady who came here a moment ago. Get her down here quick!"

The butler drew up stiffly. His chest swelled. "If you do not leave immediately, I shall call police," he got out.

"Help yourself," Carter snapped. "In fact, if you don't call them, I will. But meantime, get the girl down here."

The butler blinked, demanded his business in a slightly altered tone. Carter said sharply, "Never mind that. Tell her Kenneth Carter is here."

The butler hesitated, then indicated a small parlor at one side of the hall with a disdainful gesture.

Carter said grimly, "I'll wait here," and finally the butler, as full of offended dignity as a ruffled hen, stalked away heavily up the stairs.

A girl called, "Never mind, Hawkins, I'll come down."

Carter's eyes twinkled. She'd been listening all the time. He peered up the stairs, saw trim feet and ankles, a swaying gray skirt, and then met her scornful eyes.

"I thought you were a gentleman," she said.

The same girl, all right, the same red gold hair.

Carter bowed with a slight smile, removing his hat with a small flourish so that the high twin peaks of his forehead showed. He straightened then and gestured toward the reception room.

"Won't you come into my parlor?" he asked gravely.

The girl watched him from her vantage point on the bottom step, her face troubled. One hand resting on the balustrade, gripped it painfully. Carter moved toward the door and looked back at her expectantly. She lifted her shoulders in a small shrug and walked after him.

She crossed the threshold first and turned in the middle of the room. Carter walked in and heavy red drapes swayed shut behind him. There was little light and much furniture, typically Victorian. Carter glanced casually about, made sure that the only entrance was the door he had just entered, and turned his side to that.

"Now listen, child," he said, "I'm tired of playing hide and seek with you. I want the truth about this business and I want it now. You know the man whose body was found in the street. You had an undertaker take it from the morgue with a forged police order and when the undertaker had it, the body was stolen."

The girl spread her hands in a pleading gesture. "You must understand, Mr. Carter," she said. "Any publicity on this matter would be absolutely fatal. My life wouldn't be worth a nickel, even if they identify the body that was found in the street."

"So it's blackmail," Carter said softly.

The girl fell back a half pace.

"I didn't say so," she cried. "I didn't say so."

"You didn't have to," Carter assured her. "Now come on, tell me all about it."

"Oh, but you can't do that to us, you can't." She walked toward him, laid a small white hand on his arm. "Can't you see," she pleaded, "if the police find out about this thing, these—these terrible people will kill us all. If you find out about it, you'll be doomed, too."

Carter looked down at the small white hand on his arm and from it to the troubled face so close to his own. The red lips were trembling, the blue eyes starry. He said finally, "It's all right about me, child. I can stand a little doom."

His face grew slightly grim. "Some of the boys took a shot at me this morning, and I'm not forgetting them.

They overheard me asking for you at the hospital desk. How did you get away from the taxi smash-up anyhow?"

"Saw it coming and jumped."

Carter patted her hand on his arm.

"Good," he said. "What's your name, anyway?"

She took her hand away, but she smiled slightly.

"Josephine Parsons."

Carter smiled. "Jo," he said. "All right, Jo. I'm in this with you. I don't want to tell the police. I don't want to say anything until we've solved the whole case. But you can't let these blackmailers do things without punishment. They'd take everything you have and kill you in the end. Now tell me all about it and let me help you."

She shook her head slowly. "It would mean death—death!" she insisted.

The red curtains swayed in the doorway and Carter sprang suddenly toward them. As his left hand touched them, a narrow-chested man thrust a big gun between the curtains and pointed it at Carter's face. The thin man had eyes that slanted down at the corners. They were unpleasant.

The girl cried out sharply, "Oh, don't, don't!"

## CHAPTER FOUR
## EMBRACE OF DEATH

**K**EN CARTER raised his hands slowly, his left against the curtain, and talked.

"You certainly have effrontery, breaking into a house like this. You're going to get in trouble with the police. You'd better hand over that gun right away and let me—"

He jerked with his left hand and the red curtains tumbled down on the man with the gun. Carter threw himself sideways. The gun roared and the bullet plucked his coat. The girl screamed this time and started forward.

Carter seized the man's wrist and threw his entire weight upon it in a wrench. The gun came away in his hand. He sprang free, leveling the weapon.

"Get up," he rasped.

The little man fought angrily free of the drapes and reared up.

Carter shook the gun like an admonitory finger. "Little boys ought not to play with big guns," he said with grim amusement.

"Either you get out of this house," the little man snarled, "or I'll have you arrested for forcing an entrance."

Carter stared at him unbelievingly, and the girl came up to his side and put her hand again on Carter's arm. She said softly, "This is the son of the man whose body was found on Fifth Avenue."

The little man whirled toward her. "Now you've told everything," he shouted. "Now we'll all be killed."

"In your case," Carter said gently, "that would be a great loss; I might say an irreparable loss."

Anger screwed the little man's face into a tight knot, but there was more fear there than anger.

The butler's haughty face showed pale in the doorway suddenly, and he made way for two tall, angular women with white hair.

Jo said softly, "These are Miss Ellen and Miss Anne. The man who was killed was my uncle, and these are his sisters."

Carter bowed grimly to the women and put the gun in his pocket.

"Aunty," the girl said, "this gentleman thinks we ought to tell the police."

One of the sisters buried her head on the shoulder of the other and began to sob. "Oh no, no, they'll kill us all as they did Edward, and as they will Silas if we don't pay them."

Carter demanded swiftly, "Who is Silas?"

Absolute silence fell over the room, a silence broken only by the gentle sobs of the old woman, and the excited pacing back and forth of the little man.

Carter said softly, "So they've already kidnapped another of you, have they?"

The little man stopped squarely in front of Carter, peering up with his down-slanting, unpleasant eyes.

"Look, I'll give you five hundred dollars if you'll keep your mouth shut and stay out of this."

Carter took an angry stride toward the man, who fell back hurriedly. Once more Jo's hand was restrainingly on Carter's arm.

"You mustn't," she said, "really. Can't you see that they're all terrified to death? Why can't you be kind and help us?"

Carter turned toward her. "Jo, I'd like to. That's what I came here to do. But you don't want help. You're being hostile, and this man—"

He turned to the little man, who cried eagerly, "Then you'll promise to be quiet about this thing?"

Carter said grimly, "On one condition. If you'll let me help capture these extortionists, I'll keep quiet. But I won't unless you do that."

The women were whispering together now and the little man was staring into Carter's face. He said slowly, "All right, on those conditions, then. You're not to talk, we're to let you help us."

Carter nodded. "That's it. Until you want to talk."

The two older women walked toward the little man with gesturing hands, talking. Jo was silent with her hand still on Carter's arm.

He said, "Jo, you tell me about this thing, now." The girl shook her head. "I have something to attend to. I'll take my aunts with me and Henry will tell you what there is to know."

She walked toward her aunts and smiled back at Carter over her shoulder and he saw suddenly that her face was very tired. When they were gone, the man called Henry and Carter walked to two opposing chairs. Carter sat down heavily. He realized suddenly that he too was very tired. No sleep since the day before.

"My father—" Henry Parsons began.

**CARTER STOPPED** him. "Wait a minute," he said slowly. "Your name is Henry Parsons and your father is Edward Parsons, isn't he?"

The little man nodded.

"The same Edward Parsons that quit the circus business last winter?"

Henry Parsons nodded again, his down-slanting eyes slightly narrowed. "Yes, why?"

Carter stared at him without expression. He shrugged. "Just a matter of identification."

Parsons said, "Oh," softly, waited a moment, toying with two shark teeth charms that dangled from a heavy gold chain. He looked up again and went on with his story.

"My father," he said, "was threatened with a horrible death if he did not give these extortionists a hundred thousand dollars. He was stubborn, but we persuaded him not to tell the police because the extortionists had threatened to wipe out the entire family if we did that, and I believe they're capable of it.

"My father refused to alter his way of life or to carry a gun. He went about just as usual, and one day he disappeared. They told us there was no way of saving him, because of his obstinate behavior. They told us where to hide the body, Fifth Avenue and Thirteenth Street. Jo had gone there when you saw her. Silas and I let her go so we could protect my aunts."

Carter was looking down at his hands. "Jo your sister?" he asked.

Parsons looked at him a moment, said, "No, my half-sister."

"Then Parsons wasn't really your father?"

"No," Parsons said, then added plaintively, "I don't see what that has to do with it."

"You wouldn't," Carter said. "Get on with the story."

The man blinked, he crossed, then uncrossed his neatly creased gray trouser legs, shrugged and went on:

"My aunts are insisting on paying, but Silas and I did not like the idea. They demand three hundred thousand dollars now. It would bankrupt us. But now Silas has been kidnapped and I don't know what to do. He started to work this morning and we called his office and he hadn't reached there. Also there was an anonymous call that said he, too, would be killed by this horrible death—God only knows what it is—if the three hundred thousand dollars was not paid.

"They haven't told us yet how we're to give them the money, but this time we have no choice. We must pay."

Carter ran his hand slowly up over his peaked forehead, smoothed his dull hair. "Yes," he said, "you'll have to do that, but when you do, we'll capture these criminals."

Suddenly Carter stiffened, leaped to his feet.

A woman's shrill scream, Jo's scream, rang through the house!

Carter dashed to the hall. "Jo!" he called. "Jo!"

No answer.

The scream was cut off as if a strangling hand had shot down upon her throat. Carter raced through the building, found the back door wide open, plunged through it.

There was a dark gray sedan in the drive. He saw a girl's frantically gesturing hand in the window, then the machine jerked into motion down the drive.

Carter raced across the smooth old lawn, hurdled the hedge. A Packard roadster stood in the garage, a chauffeur unconscious beside it.

Carter leaped to the running board. The key was in the ignition lock. It was the work of an instant to start the motor, whirl the car in a skidding run, and scoot down the driveway after the gray sedan.

The car that carried the girl was traveling at top speed, taking corners on squealing rubber. Carter flung the roadster after it, shot up the wide, two-laned Grand Concourse with blaring horn, jamming through the crowded traffic of Fordham Road, streaking on along the Parkway.

The gray car, swooping down grade, was being driven wide open. Carter snapped a glance at his speedometer. It registered 75 miles an hour. Luckily it was mid-afternoon and traffic was light. Carter heard police sirens screeching behind him and pressed a little harder on the accelerator. The speedometer needle wavered at 75, crawled up to 76, 78.

A cop stepped out in the road ahead of the gray sedan, brandishing a revolver. The car swerved, headed straight for him. He leaped, sprawled to safety just in time, and rolled over, threw up his revolver and banged away. The gray car already was two hundred feet away, sweeping into the Boston Post Road. Carter flashed by, tires moaning on the bricks as he took the turn. Then he settled down to driving.

**POLICE SIRENS** died in the distance behind him and his speedometer needle stood at 79. The heavy car seemed to hug the road, but it heaved and heeled on the turns. He could not gain on the gray sedan, but neither could it pull away from him. It was a matter of endurance.

If the police managed to stop the car ahead, well and good. They would have some of the extortionists, and Jo would be safe. But he doubted that the group ahead would surrender without a battle. A battle might mean punctured tires and a crackup at that speed would probably kill everyone in the car. For the same reason, Carter made no attempt to use a revolver.

They swept out into lonelier roads now, roads that swept up and down rolling hills like a switch-back. On the crests the heavy Packard lifted like a sea-sled, bounding from the top of a wave. When it shot down grade, the needle hovered around 85; the next grade would shove it back to 71 or 72 and always the gray sedan was cresting the ridge just ahead.

Then, almost imperceptibly, the distance seemed to widen between him and the car he followed. Carter's eyes shot to the heat gauge and saw that it was at the peak. He cursed, low water or low oil.

He jammed the accelerator down and gave the Packard everything it had. He must overtake the gray car within the next few miles or all would be lost. The sedan was perhaps three-quarters of a mile ahead now, whirled around a turn.

Carter skidded the Packard into the curve. A rise ahead was empty. He swept over it. The hill beyond was empty. Carter began to curse monotonously, steadily, in a low voice, pushing the Packard, watching the heat gauge out of the corner of his eye, the speedometer needle wavering below 75.

He swept up the next rise, topped it with a lift and suddenly jammed on brakes and whirled his steering gear. Two huge red moving vans were parked close to the right-hand side, but were so wide they nearly filled the road. Carter, with tightly clenched teeth, swerved the swaying Packard around them, skimmed past and jammed the accelerator wide open.

He topped the next rise and ahead was a long straight stretch of three miles or more. It was empty. There wasn't a car on it, except a Ford coming toward him.

Carter frowned. The car ahead couldn't possibly have covered all that three miles. And yet level, treeless land stretched on either side of him. No chance to turn off. Carter lifted his foot from the accelerator. The engine was boiling now, steam spurting. He would have to stop for water.

A gasoline station caught his eyes, and he snubbed the car to slower speed, rolled up to the gas tank and halted. He piled out. The station attendant, leaning lazily against the pump, straightened and ambled over to the car.

"Did a gray sedan go by here at around 75 an hour a little while ago?"

The man grinned, wrinkling his face. "The only fast thing I've seen around here was this Packard of yours," he said. "The way you came over that rise back there, I could see blue sky between your tires and the road."

Carter frowned and stared at him. "You're sure nothing else went by?" "Not a darned thing. Yours is the first car in half an hour." The Ford Carter had spotted from the top of the hill rattled into the filling station and he repeated his question to its driver. No gray sedan had been seen on the road. Carter twisted off the radiator cap, filled up the panting radiator, whirled the Packard, and shot back the way he had come.

As he sped along, the two huge moving vans he had so nearly smashed into crested the rise, bellowing in low gear, and trundled down the grade. Carter pulled far over to the edge to let them go by, then ran slowly back toward town, searching the roadside for spots where the gray sedan might have turned off. But he could find no trace, no clue of it. Finally he gave up and started for the Parsons' home, avoiding the roads where the frantic police had trailed with squealing sirens. He slammed around a corner to the quiet, tree-shaded street where the Parsons lived and suddenly clamped on brakes, bringing the Packard to a halt within its own length. The now familiar prickle of cold horror ran over him.

For the body of a man sprawled in the road. It was nude, and it lay on the hot asphalt like a blob of jelly, boneless, crushed to a pulp.

# CHAPTER FIVE
# THE MURDER WALL

**H**IS TEETH clenched, eyes narrowed half in anger at the brutality of the crime, half in reaction to its horror, Ken Carter circled the Packard around the body. He stared at the body and cursed softly.

It was in every way a replica of that which had been found on Fifth Avenue. Every bone in it had been crushed, even the skull was elongated and flattened. In spots the flesh was broken as if by extreme pressure, and one shoulder was lacerated jaggedly. Suddenly Carter stepped on the gas and sent the Packard skidding on and into Parsons' driveway. The tires popped on the gravel.

He leaped out, raced toward the house, through a kitchen where two startled servants stared at him, and into the front room, where Henry Parsons was seated with his head in his hands.

He started to his feet as Carter plunged in and glared at him hostilely.

"Did you find her?" he demanded.

"I didn't find her," Carter answered. "The car disappeared as though it had been swallowed up in sand. I chased them away out on the Boston Post Road, going 75 and 80 miles an hour. We had half the police in town on our trail, but they got away."

Parsons opened his mouth to say something, but Carter cut in again. "There's another man's body up here, naked, crushed to a pulp, lying in the middle of the road."

Henry Parsons groaned, and dropped back into the chair. He said, "It's Silas, I know it's Silas."

"Where's your phone?" Carter snapped.

"No, no!" the little man sprang after him. "We don't dare phone the police."

He dug into his pocket and brought out a piece of paper that he thrust into Carter's hands. Carter looked at it with a sinking feeling in his heart. Somehow he knew in advance what it would say.

His hands trembled slightly. Pencil smudges covered the gray dirty surface, with crudely crooked letters:

> You have waited too long to pay the ransom for Silas, as you waited too long for your father. Pay tonight or you'll find that girl's body tomorrow. Won't she be pretty with all her bones crushed?

The message was unsigned. Carter crumpled it in a clenched fist, glared straight ahead of him.

Henry Parsons spilled words. "Don't you see now why we can't claim Silas's body? We were going to get father's body secretly, and we had nothing to do with stealing it.

"The kidnapers must have done that. We knew if the body was identified, the police might get the thing out of us, and they stole father's body and threw it in the river to stop that. We can't phone police about Silas's body."

Carter said curtly, "No."

"There's only one thing to do," Parsons raced on, "That is pay the money. It will take every last cent we've got, but we've got to save Jo."

Carter said savagely, "If you don't save Jo, I'll break every bone in your body worse than these extortionists would."

The telephone tinkled and Carter whirled. "Where's that phone?" he grated.

Parsons was before him, his quick feet hurried him across the room, dashed into the hall with Carter at his heels, across the dim, dark hall, into another crowded parlor.

Parsons grabbed a phone from a small table and with the instrument at his mouth and ear hesitated. He gulped and said, "Hello." He waited a long time and said, "Yes," and then, "All right."

He put the phone slowly back on its cradle and turned heavily toward Carter. "You've got to leave the house," he said.

Carter's frown lifted his brows. "Who says so?"

Parsons nodded toward the phone. "They do. They say you've got to leave the house at once or they'll kill you as well as Silas, and they say it will be bad for Jo, even if we ransom her, if you don't go."

Carter said savagely, "That's all nonsense. They're afraid of me because I chased the car."

Parsons stared at him for a long time. "How about Jo?" he asked.

Carter glared at him, fists clenched at his side, his tall, wide-shouldered body tense. He opened his lips to speak, closed them again, and finally got out hoarsely, "I guess that settles it. Have you got the money for her ransom?"

Parsons glanced at his watch. "I've got to go to the bank to get it," he said dully. "I'll have trouble because it's in Silas's name."

"Right," said Carter, "you and I are going down there together."

**WHEN DARK** night fell upon the Parsons' mansion, Carter was crouched in a rented car in the driveway of an untenanted house across the street. His Hispano Suiza would be too conspicuous for tonight's work.

He had eaten, but he hadn't slept and he was weary. He settled himself as comfortably as possible in the car. In the deep shadows of the trees it was invisible and it was ready to dart either way on the street when the chase should begin.

Parsons had refused to tell Carter anything of the plans for paying the ransom, but Carter was sure it would require some trip outside of the mansion and he was going to be ready when that time came. The Press was after him for some sort of story, but Carter had refused flatly to say a word until the case was wound up. The paper knew Carter. It had yielded.

But these thoughts were not uppermost in Carter's mind now. Nothing mattered except saving the girl.

Carter smoked and time dragged heavily past. He was sleepy, yet dared not close his eyes lest fatigue overcome him and he be asleep when Parsons started out with the ransom money. He got out and crept over behind the hedge and did some calisthenics to help keep awake. He got two big rocks and put them in the seat and sat on them, hoping the discomfort would help him resist.

It was a terrific but losing struggle, but just as Carter's head was nodding into sleep, a large black car rolled out of the Parsons' drive. Carter's head jerked up. The man was coasting down the drive with a dead engine, stealing a march on any watchers around the house.

It was the Packard Carter had driven in the afternoon. It drifted down the driveway with only the gravel crumbling under its tires, coasted out into the street, and then its motor started. As it muttered off, Carter let his own lighter car roll down the inclined drive and the chase was on.

The Packard droned on through the night, with only dim lights burning, following much the same course that

Carter had pursued that afternoon, up Grand Concourse, across Fordham Road, along the Parkway and into the Boston Post Road.

When they reached the main highway, the Packard began to pick up speed. Carter trailed at a distance of half a mile. He didn't want to get too close lest the kidnapers know Parsons was being followed.

He was a half-mile back when the other car suddenly spurted ahead at full speed. Carter stood on his own accelerator, but the lighter car had nothing like the pickup nor the speed of the Packard. If only he had dared drive his Hispano tonight! Soon, topping a high rise, he failed to see the Packard. What he did see were the red and green lights of two huge moving vans lumbering along.

He cursed softly to himself, sent the car scudding down the road. His headlights showed the dull red paint of the vans. They were exactly like those he had seen earlier in the day. Two autos had disappeared in succession, and each time those huge moving vans had been on the road.

There was suddenly an eager light in Carter's eyes, but his mouth was grim. He gave the little car all it would take, put distance between himself and those strange trucks.

Ahead Carter saw a red warning sign, spotted an underpass. He exclaimed aloud. This was his chance. He ran the car into deep woods, hurried back to the bridge, where he crouched below the parapet.

It was a moonless night and the air was like soot. Carter raised only the top of his head above the walls of the bridge, crouching, waiting for the trucks to come. He heard the rumble of their motors grinding up the rise long before he saw the green and red lights along their tops and their headlights boring whitely into the thickness of the night. They swooped down a grade, began to moan up the hill that led under the bridge. Their speed was reduced to a walk.

Crouching low, Carter moved over to the uphill side of the bridge. He let the first van groan under him, then climbed up on the edge of the parapet and as the second truck thrust its snout out from under the bridge, he let himself hang by his hands and dropped the few feet remaining to the top of the second van.

He threw himself flat and waited. He had dropped well toward the rear of the truck so that the noise of his fall would be as little noticeable as possible. The roar of the motors was unceasing and the grinding toil up the hill did not check. Nevertheless, Carter held his breath, waiting, listening for some alarm from the sound of his fall.

There was nothing, however, and he hitched forward along the swaying top. Far at the front of the van, just back of the seat where the driver and his helper sat, was a small trapdoor. Carter fumbled around on it, discovered no padlock, and hitched it upward.

A red burst of fire came out of the darkness below and a bullet whizzed past Carter's ear. The explosion echoed hollowly. Carter flinched back from the opening.

**EXCITED SHOUTS** came from the truck ahead and from the seat of the one on which Carter crouched. If he perched up here, they would pick him off like a fat turkey in the dark. The truck lurched to a halt and now, from below, he heard a woman's moan, a muffled, strangled sound, as if someone sought to get words through a gag.

Carter's heart leaped up. That must be Jo! He must reach her, set her free. A slim chance, with a gun waiting for him in the darkness, but there was nothing else to do. The moan below had seemed to come from the extreme forward part of the truck. Drawing his own gun, Carter crouched at the opening, sprang into the air, and dropped feet forward into it.

Plunging down into the pitch blackness, he threw himself prostrate on the floor. The darkness burst into flame again as a gun spoke. Carter rolled rapidly toward the gun. Something struck his back. He threw out an arm, grasped a man's leg and jerked. Another bullet tore into the blackness. Lead smacked the floor.

The man fell on top of him. Carter groped frantically in the dark, grabbing for the man's wrist to wrench away that perilous gun. He found the man's chin instead, and struck heavily, once, twice, with the flat of his own gun. There was a little moan and the man collapsed. Carter wasted no more time on him. He crouched and called softly, "Jo?"

A muffled moan answered him and he felt through the dark until his hand touched the girl. He found she was bound and gagged and worked loose the knots, caught her up in his arms.

"Poor child," he murmured. "Did they hurt you?"

Jo, free of the gag now, spoke with difficulty.

"No, they didn't hurt me. Just locked me up in this horrible hole with a man to watch me," she whispered. "It wasn't because they were afraid I'd escape. There's something else—something I don't know about."

Carter said soothingly, "There, there. You stay right here. There is a full magazine in this gun, more bullets in my pockets."

He moved off through the truck to a spot opposite the girl, so that if the men above fired at his gun flashes, she would not be hit.

"You're not leaving?" her voice was tense.

He whispered, "No," into the darkness toward her, crouched against the back wall of the small forward compartment in which they were imprisoned. The opening in the roof was a square of paler black, that was all. Pistol pointed toward the opening, Carter waited.

Nothing happened. Shouting continued outside, but not in so loud a tone. There seemed to be fumbling noises under the truck. Carter leaned against the wall and waited, waited with every nerve pitched to the nth degree, with muscles as taut as piano wires.

Suddenly he was aware of movement. Not human movement. The wall behind him was pressing against him, thrusting forward. Carter thought his tension was fooling him, but no, there could be no doubt about it, the wall was opening like a door that swung toward him. Carter bounced away from it, crouched beside the girl, and trained his pistol on those moving walls.

"What is it?" she whispered.

"Those walls over there, those walls are opening."

The girl screamed. It was a throat-splitting, ear-splitting scream. It jerked at Carter's heart.

"Help!" she cried. "Help!"

"Jo—what's the matter?"

She gasped, "We've got to get out of here. Get out of here quick or we're dead!"

Carter stared at the spot where those two walls were opening. Somewhere deep within him horror coiled like a pale, cold snake, thrust up toward his heart.

"But what is it, Jo?" he asked hoarsely. "Why did you scream like that?"

She moaned. "There's something horrible back there, horrible, unbelievably horrible. What it is I don't know, but it's what killed my uncle, that's what they've been threatening to kill me with if Henry didn't come with the ransom money."

Carter said, "Oh, tommyrot." But he knew she was right.

Then, in the blackness where the wall moved, Carter saw two round glowing spots. They were like red fire. Carter gasped. The girl screamed again and again, filling the dark hole with an agony of horror.

## CHAPTER SIX

## FRESHLY KILLED MEAT

A **MAN'S** voice above them at the opening lisped, "There'th a rope ladder. Come up if you want to, but come up with your handth up."

"Come on, Ken," the girl panted, sprang forward toward the rope and Carter saw her sway upward toward the lighter black of the opening above.

But Carter did not go. He crouched against the wall and watched those two round points of fire, the gun with its full magazine clenched in his hand. Those two balls of fire did not flicker. They were like two unblinking eyes, and Carter became aware of a musty odor.

Suddenly fear gripped him, fear such as he had never known before in all his terrific adventures. He pointed the gun and squeezed the trigger. A bullet bounced into the darkness. He ripped open the blackness with powder flame. His ears rang with the explosions. Then Carter did a thing he cursed even while he did it, a thing he could not help. Wet with a sweat of horror, he flung his empty gun after the bullets and dived toward the ladder.

"I surrender! I surrender!" he shouted.

The ladder was hauled up to accelerate his climb. He was yanked out and the cover clamped down upon the opening. A bar clanged into place and fastened it.

Something thumped against the under side of the cover, heavily, so that the lid vibrated against the bar. Bump—bump—bump!

Carter stared at the lid and cursed in a low undertone. His chest labored. Slowly he fought his way back to calmness, conquered the cold thing that writhed within him. Somewhere near in the blackness, Jo sobbed:

"What is that Thing with the red eyes?"

Her sobbing went on and as if it would never end. Men laughed.

One with a lisping voice said, "Maybe you'll have a chanth to find out, Missth Parhonth."

The muzzle of a gun was jammed into the back of Carter's neck. He was searched hurriedly, then bound.

"Wheretth your gun?" the man with the lisp demanded.

"I threw it at Red Eye," Carter said. The man with the lisp cursed suddenly.

"Hell," he said, "where'th Frank?"

"He was out cold," Carter said.

"Quick! Get to the portsth!" the man ordered.

They piled down the sides, but one stood guard over Carter and the girl.

Carter heard someone yell. "He's safe!" and there was silence.

Finally the men came creeping back on top again, grasped the brace across the trapdoor and lifted it. Carter stared narrowly at the opening, but nothing happened. The rope ladder was dropped down inside again and one of the men went down and helped up the man Carter had struck down.

Another man with a flashlight stood over the opening, and the face that came up through it presently was white as the moon, beaded with sweat that stood out on his forehead.

He stood swaying a moment, glaring at Carter, then strode forward and struck him heavily in the face, struck him again and again. Carter swayed backwards, fell. His head jarred against the top of the truck. He heard voices faintly, felt himself lifted and lowered. Ropes bit into his arms and legs, a gag suffocated him.

"Want somebody to stay here with them?" a man called beside him.

The man with the lisp replied from above. "No," he laughed. "If the doorsth open again, it doesthn't make much differenth."

Carter saw a man's body sway against the light, then the light went out and a lid clattered into place. The darkness was so thick about him it could be cut. Suddenly he realized he had been put back again into the dark pit with the Horror.

**COLD FEAR** trembled over him. He felt sweat start from his pores, then he remembered that apparently the Horror had been shut into the back of the truck. But where was Jo? Carter heard dim voices behind the wall against which he lay and pressed his ear against it.

He heard the man with the lisp, but what he said was a hissing mumble. Listening acutely, Carter finally began to catch words.

"There wouldn't be any point," the voice was saying, "in giving them to Oloo Thay Wah now. It would be much better if they were freshly killed when we dump them out in whatever town the chief dethides to work nexth."

"Freshly killed!" Carter felt an inward shudder. As if he and that lovely girl were so much meat for the butcher.

Carter moaned into the darkness and heard an answering moan. His heart leaped. Had they put Jo with him? He rolled toward the sound and his face brushed her hair. He mumbled into the gag, but could not frame words. At last he thumped around until his bound hands were against hers. Then he began to work on the knots.

It was slow, tedious work and the feeling was half gone from his hands because of the pressure of the bonds, but after half an hour he succeeded in freeing her, and it was a matter of moments then before both were free, and able to talk.

Carter put an arm about the girl's shoulders and together they sat down and leaned back against the sides of the truck. Carter waited only to make sure she was reasonably calm, then he felt around and found their ropes.

He whispered to Jo, "I'm just going over and tie shut the door opening into the back of the truck. It might force someone to come down in here and give us a chance."

He walked as silently as possible across to the back wall. There were no staples or other things to tie shut, but finally he located the heads of two or three nails. He tied the rope on these, but had small hope they would keep out that lurking horror. He crept back to the girl and lied.

"The rope will hold," he said. "Now all we have to do is wait."

It was two hours later that the truck stopped and feet scraped against the side and over the top. Carter and the girl hurriedly restored their gags and lay on the floor as if bound. A man came in with a flashlight in one hand and a large knife in the other. He went directly to the girl and the back glare of his torch showed his grin.

"I hate like hell to do this," he chuckled, bent over her and began to rip off her clothing with the knife.

Carter rose cautiously to his feet, slammed his fist under the man's ear and grabbed the hand torch, used it as a club. The man went down and out. Carter flashed the light on, searched him hurriedly. He was unarmed except for the long knife. Carter took off his coat and gave it to the girl and she buttoned it about her.

"I think," she said slowly, "that they were getting ready to open the doors."

"Not much doubt of that," Carter said grimly. "Get over in the corner."

He put on the cap and coat of the man he had knocked out, bound him with his belt, then, muffling his voice with his hands so that it would be unrecognizable, yelled for a rope. The man above did not investigate, but snaked the rope ladder down and Carter, clutching the flashlight, swarmed up it.

The odds must be five or six to one up there, he knew, but if they opened the door and let in that horror, Carter knew the odds would be millions to one. He climbed upwards to battle.

# CHAPTER SEVEN
# HORROR IN THE DARK

**K**EN CARTER kept his head bent forward, so that no glimpse of his face would betray him to the men above before he got firm footing on the top of the truck. One man jeered at him coarsely, asking why he had taken so long to get the girl ready.

Carter made no reply as he climbed upward. He held the heavy flashlight in his right hand, in his left he grasped the knife, concealed in his sleeve. The sky was graying in the east and a dim dirty light filtered into the darkness.

As Carter straightened on top the truck, he saw that four men confronted him. One of them glimpsed Carter's face and with an oath cried out, "That ain't Mickey!"

He grabbed toward his pocket and Carter leaped upon him, the flashlight swinging in a short, brutal arc. It caught him above the ear and he went down like a ten-pin. He rolled once and flopped over the edge to the ground.

Carter whirled upon the other three. One man had his gun out. He was too far away for Carter to club. He threw the flashlight with all his force and it caught the man squarely on the face. A hoarse cry tore from him and he pitched backwards, did a head-first dive to the pavement.

Carter did not wait for the other two to attack, but charged headlong into them. He felt steel tear at his shoulders and struck savagely with the knife. There was a gasping cry. The knife was wrenched from Carter's hand and another man fell. He did not roll off, but lay there, a helpless, sodden bundle with his hands clenched to his belly.

But the blow that had felled him had dropped Carter to his knees. The remaining man towered over him, a broad-shouldered man with a blue-jowled face. He gripped a club.

Carter sprang forward and grabbed the man around the legs, tripped him.

As he fell, the club flew wide and Carter hurled himself bodily upon the man, striking at his chin. The man made no effort to guard, nor roll Carter off, but reached out long arms with talon-like hands and seized him by the throat.

His fingers were like steel. They bit painfully into Carter's throat. The man had ducked his chin against his chest so that the blows did no more than batter against his face and did not daze him.

Blood began to pound in Carter's temples, his lungs seemed to swell and his staring eyes glanced about frantically in search of help. They were only a foot away from the edge of the truck.

Desperately Carter threw his entire weight sideways. He toppled off into space, dragging the other man with him. They turned over once in the air and Carter landed on top. The terrible grip on his throat was broken and he sprang free. The man staggered up dazedly. Carter swung savagely at his jaw. He connected and the man reeled back, but did not fall.

Instead, he ducked his head savagely and charged again. He ignored the blows Carter rained on him and clasped bear-like arms about his waist, got his head under Carter's chin and began to squeeze, bent him backward. Carter gasped with pain. He knew he couldn't outlast many minutes of that punishment.

Striking out desperately, he managed to trip the other man and they fell to the road together. They were on the edge and Carter's frantic fingers found a heavy piece of stone. His spine was strained, arched far back. He felt that at any moment it might snap. Desperately he seized upon the stone and slammed it with all his strength against the back of the man's head. He felt the impact up against his own chin where the top of the man's skull rested.

The arms about his back relaxed slightly and desperately Carter slammed the stone again and again against the man's head. The arms came loose and Carter sprang erect, reeled drunkenly and leaned against the side of the van. His breath came in labored gasps. His entire body ached and his shoulders sagged.

A horrible scream rang out. Carter stared up toward the top of the van, outlined more conspicuously now against the further lighting of the sky. Once more that horrible scream rang out. It was Jo, calling his name. His heart turned over.

Carter sprang toward the front of the truck. A wooden ladder led up the side and he scrambled up it, chest laboring. The ladder seemed to stretch interminably, but finally he reached the top, sprawled across the roof toward the opening where the girl's screams rose.

"Oh, Ken! Ken! Hurry, or it will be too late!"

**CARTER DROPPED** the rope ladder, saw the girl's white face sway upward toward him, reached down and snatched her to safety. Together they seized the trapdoor and clapped it over the opening, searched for the bar to lock it in place.

Carter felt his body was bathed in sweat. There was a white terror within him like nothing he had felt while battling against the heavy odds of human enemies. That he could face, but what was below in the darkness was not human.

The sudden sound of a shot hitting the roof whirled Carter around and he saw another man scramble over the edge and plunge forward, a gun in his hand.

"Throw up your hands, both of you," the man shouted.

Carter plunged toward him instead, hands over his head. The blast of flame from the gun muzzle singed his face. Then he closed with the man. He struggled with him, chest to chest. He heard the girl scream again, but could not turn.

"Look out, Ken!" Jo screamed again.

Pain seared his leg as if a dozen teeth were clamping into it at once, and he felt himself hauled irresistibly back by that grip, falling down into the blackness of the truck, into that horror of darkness.

Desperately he held on to his enemy. The man fell with him into the darkness and the hold on Carter's leg was broken. He scrambled erect, snatched for the gun in the other man's hand. It exploded again, then the gun flew from his hand and racketed to the floor.

A scream mingling horror and pain and terror unspeakable tore from the man with whom Carter struggled. Something hard and old, terribly strong, struck Carter and hurled him aside. Its very touch made his flesh crawl. He cried out hoarsely. The man's screams continued, one on top the other, without pause for even breath. Carter shrank back against the wall, saw the rope ladder come tumbling down.

"Hurry!" came the girl's panting voice. "Oh, hurry, Ken!"

Carter seized the rope, swung himself desperately upward. He reached the roof, clambered out, and sprang to his feet, glaring about, searching for a weapon.

"A gun, Jo! A gun! I must find a gun!" he said.

The girl cried, "Let's get away. Oh, let's get away!"

Carter shook his head. "We can't leave any man to die as that man is dying."

Screams tore from below, but they were fainter. Carter scrambled down the side of the truck. The girl came after him, and searched frantically on the bodies of the men, still stretched there unconscious. No weapon was upon them and in the half-light he could not spot anything on the ground that might be a pistol.

He ran toward the other truck, halted a few feet away. The door stood open in the back. He clambered in. There was a car inside with runways so that it might run from the truck down to the road. He recognized instantly that it was the Packard that Henry Parsons had driven away from the house that morning.

He went hurriedly through its pockets. There were no weapons there. He scrambled into the driving seat of the truck. Finally, beneath it, he located a pistol, and ran heavily back toward the other truck. The pain was beginning to eat into his leg now and warm blood trickled down into his shoe. His breath came in gasps, and the girl, seizing his arm, helped him along.

"Did you recognize that auto?" she cried. "It was ours, ours! Cousin Henry must have driven out here after me."

"He drove out here," Carter told her between panting breaths, "but not to ransom you."

"What do you mean?" the girl asked in a low, strangled voice.

Carter only shook his head, grabbed the ladder leading to the top of the other truck, swarmed up it. He had a flashlight he had taken from the truck ahead and he sent its cold white beams flashing down into the horrible darkness below. He glanced once and threw up his gun, then stopped and switched off the light. The girl was at his shoulder.

"Oh, tell me what it is," she asked.

"I'm going to shoot," said Carter "it would be better if you didn't see."

"But I must!" she cried. "Don't you see, I must know!"

She snatched at the flashlight in Carter's hand and he let her have it, but kept his hand on her shoulder. The sun pushed up above the horizon and its red light bathed the world, touched the golden red glint in her hair.

"Listen, Jo, believe me! Don't look down there."

She looked wide-eyed into his eyes for long minutes. Horror crept into her face. She turned and stumbled away.

**CARTER FLASHED** the light again through the opening, face grim, mouth a thin hard line. He knew now that "Oloo Thay Wah" was Ulu-Sawa. And Ulu-Sawa was a huge snake, a Malay or Regal python. It lay below, its coils straightened out fully thirty feet long, its back a weaving of rich yellow, brown, and black, like oriental tapestry.

Iridescence glowed on the high lights of the folds, but the mouth was stretched horribly, and it engulfed the head of a man.

The man's head had vanished completely within the jaws, which were being stretched now to take in the narrow shoulders. The body was crushed like a blob of jelly.

The dead man, who had used the snake to kill others, to terrorize the family into giving up its wealth, was Henry Parsons, murderer of his stepfather and half-brother. Carter raised the revolver slowly and fired until the hammer clicked on an empty shell casing.

There was a monstrous crashing within the van like a dozen sledgehammers being hurled about at once. Carter reeled to the edge of the truck and clambered slowly to the ground.

He led Jo back to the front truck and began painfully to rig up the slanting platform that would permit him to drive the Packard out of the truck and speed home. Working side by side with him. Jo asked anxiously, "What made that horrible noise in there, in that other truck?"

Carter said slowly, "I just executed the murderer of your uncle and cousin, a big snake. They probably got it from some disbanding circus, maybe your father's. They kept it and starved and prodded it to viciousness. That snake was what they were planning to throw you and me to, to be crushed to a pulp, and dropped on the street of some new city as a forerunner of horror.

"After that, the gang planned to approach some wealthy family and demand money on pain of suffering the same death, the same horrible, unexplainable death that you and I almost had suffered."

Carter added grimly, "I suspected the leader from the moment I laid eyes on him. Fear alone could not have made him try so hard to keep me off the trail, and when you were kidnapped, he did not seem excited, did not seem to care. He must have hated you all terribly."

"But who is it?" Jo ask excitedly.

"Someone you didn't know at all," Carter said slowly.

They finally got the runway rigged and backed the Packard down. "Aren't we going to wait for the police?" asked Jo, "to tell them what's happened?"

"No, my child," said Ken Carter, laughter in his tired gray eyes. "I'm going to let my friend, Inspector Littleman, read about this in the newspaper."

# SATAN'S SIDESHOW

IT WAS A HOUSE OF HORROR TO
WHICH KEN CARTER CAME THAT
STORM-NIGHT. FOR CONGREGATED
THERE WERE THE HUMAN
MONSTROSITIES THAT MADE UP
MILT ROSS'S SIDESHOW, AND ONE
OF THEM, CARTER KNEW, HAD
MURDERED THE OLD MANAGER
WITH COLD STEEL. BABBLING
PINHEAD, SNAKE WOMAN,
MALFORMED DWARF OR THE
GIANT MAN-MOUNTAIN, JOSEPH—
WHICH ONE WAS WHAT HE HAD
TO LEARN. AND THE ONLY CLUE
LAY IN ROSS'S DYING PLEA—
"WATCH OUT FOR LILITH!"

**K**EN CARTER bounded from the taxi and went striding on long legs through the slashing rain toward the porch of the boarding house, his topcoat kiting back from his shoulders where it swung like a cape. He rapped the door hard with his big knuckles and stood shifting from foot to foot, a slender man with a narrow, long face. He had a cane tucked under his left arm, thrusting back his coat like a sword.

All about him the night crowded close. A fresh wind, blowing rain, plucked at his coat and flattened the brim of his soft brown felt. He reached up his hand to knock again and the door faded away under his knuckles. Within, the light was dim and for a long moment he stood motionless, lifted a little on his toes, staring into its half-light, hand still outstretched…. He cursed low in his throat and felt cold needles prick along the back of his neck.

He jerked back his hand and slid it subconsciously to one of the twin automatics that jutted from inside his belt. What—what, by all the gods, was this thing that stared at him with vacuous idiot's eyes, its thick lips slobbering, its head— A shudder he could not resist plucked at Carter's muscles—its head rose to a high conical peak like a dunce's cap!

Ken Carter laughed shortly. Imagine a man as old in the show business as he was, being taken in by a circus freak that was obviously what the creature was, one of those horrible monstrosities that made awful the sideshows of traveling carnivals. But even recognizing the creature for what it was, Ken Carter had to force himself to stride forward. The pinhead fell back awkwardly before his advance.

"Where's Ross?" Ken Carter asked, speaking very slowly, very distinctly, as was necessary with these half-imbecile creatures.

The pinhead looked at him through a long, vacuous moment, slobber dribbling from its lips, then it lifted a limp left hand toward the dark hallway that led to the rear of the first floor.

"Back there," it articulated vaguely.

Ken Carter went past, long bony face scowling, his striding legs carrying him swiftly along the hallway. Strange that Ross would allow his freaks to wander about the

From his elevated position he thrust desperately for the giant's right eye.

house this way. Usually they were confined to their rooms, closely watched, closely cloaked until the hour for the show. Ken Carter felt a sharp, inexplicable dread. Something, he told himself, was wrong with Milt Ross! His mind flashed back to the message he had received at his hotel tonight.

"Milt Ross needs you. Come quickly!"

Ross must be in a bad spot indeed to send such a message. He had always been so utterly self-reliant in the old show days when he and Ken Carter had traveled the vaudeville circuit in companion acts—Carter as a magician, juggler and tight-rope walker—Ross, a snake charmer. He had one act with a big cobra that no one else could ever handle. A small, reminiscent smile curved Carter's long, straight lips. Lord, the times they had split their last dollar together, he and Milt Ross, companions in distress and in rare plenty, until Ross had turned to the more lucrative work of running a freak show and Carter had followed his natural bent for man-hunting and become a detective.

**LIGHT THAT** lay in a pale oblong on the floor marked the narrow opening of a door and Ken Carter hesitated before it, rapping softly. No one answered his knock and Carter waited impatiently. He looked sharply behind him, but the pinhead was no longer in sight. There was nothing in all the dim, high hallway except himself and this narrow beam of light. Impatiently, he thrust open the door and, stepping inside, stopped in his tracks, dark, intelligent eyes narrowing. The smile that had formed to greet Ross tightened off his lips.

Milt Ross lay upon a bed, his face pallid and weak beneath the great shaggy head of hair, his eyes dark bulges beneath closed lids. He opened them slowly at the sound of the door's opening and his lips moved faintly. It might have been intended for a smile, but it was pitiful to Ken Carter, who had known Ross in his hearty-strength. He reached the bedside in two choppy strides, throwing his eyes in a sharp challenge to the two other men in the room. Carter knew neither of them. He kept a watch on them out of the corner of one eye as he bent over Ross, hat in his cane hand, coat still caped across his high, slightly stooped shoulders.

"What the hell's the matter, Milt?" he asked, his voice oddly resonant and deep, vital in that room of subdued light and life.

Ross's heavy hand lifted languidly, clasped the lean, strong fingers of Ken Carter.

"Thanks for coming." Ross's voice was a ghost whisper. "Thanks, Carter. I... need you."

Carter felt something like pain tugging at his chest. Why, damn it, he and Ross had been... partners.

"That's what I'm here for, Milt," Carter said, his voice vibrant. "Just tell me what you need and it's yours."

His eyes lifted deliberately to the other two men in the room, one beside the bed, the other leaning stout, bare forearms on the foot-board. The latter caught Carter's eyes first, a stocky Italian with glossy black mustaches that drooped over his upper lip. His liquid dark eyes met the keen grey gaze of Ken Carter speculatively, unwavering. Carter looked to the other man, standing at Ross's side and a curse caught in his throat. Another of those confounded freaks!

Damn it, it was hellish to meet such monstrosities at the sick bed of a friend. This freak was natural enough aside from a claylike pallor, and one other thing. From the middle of his chest, a—a *thing* sprouted. Something caught in Carter's throat. Damn it, the thing was a little man, complete except for a head, a figure at least seventeen inches long that sprouted by its neck out of this man's chest. It was dressed completely in a little suit of dress clothes. The man with this motionless abortive twin growing out of him regarded Carter unwinkingly. He had his hands on this—this other body—stroking its dangling hands absently with his palms, running his fingers down over the thing's knobby wrists.

The sight of it stirred something hot and angry within Ken Carter, made him feel a little sick. He jerked his eyes away from the freak to look down again at Milt Ross.

"What is it, old man?" he asked gently. "Just tell me and I'll do my damndest to help you out."

The man at the foot of the bed said: "Somebody stabbed Ross in the back. Doctor says he doesn't stand a chance."

Ken Carter said roughly. "Shut up, you fool!"

He glared at the impassive face of the Italian, feeling horror and incredulity tug at his heart—horror at the man's callousness, disbelief…. Why, Milt Ross couldn't be dying. And stabbed in the back! He heard himself demanding hoarsely to know who had done this to his friend, but no one answered. The freak stopped stroking the mannikin's hand and began wiping a dribble of blood from a corner of Ross's mouth. Ross's eyes were on Carter's face, pleading with him somehow, yet burning with some dark, unfathomable emotion. By the gods, it was… *fear!* The recognition of the thing that lurked in his friend's eyes stirred something deep within Carter. He leaned his cane carefully against the wall, his long lips thin against his teeth.

"You two get out of here," he said softly.

**THE FREAK** was stroking the hands of the monstrosity on his breast again. The Italian straightened and took his muscular forearms off the foot-board.

"Why should we?" he asked deliberately. "Me, I am his manager. Fritzie here is his friend. We do not know you."

Carter's coat swirled behind him as he took a long stride forward to confront the Italian. "Ross used to be my partner," he said. "He sent for me tonight. You two will leave the room."

Ross called out sharply: "Ken! Ken!"

Ken Carter whirled toward his friend, eyes anxious. There was death in the face of Milt Ross. Carter had looked too often into the vacant skull sockets of death when his own bullets had brought down men not to recognize it on sight.

Ross said faintly: "Ken, watch out for Lilith—"

"Of course, I'll watch out for Lilith for you," Carter said. "And I'll do more than that. I'll catch the guys that did this to you. Who did it, Milt, old man?" Once more he was conscious of dark fear creeping into Ross's eyes, and he was aware of something else, a sound that came from the floor above. The pattering of small, rapid feet, too firm and regular for a child's, yet light and somehow happy.

Carter strangled a curse. Another of those damned freaks, of course. The boarding house, one of a hundred Ross used in his swing about the country, would be full of them. It was a fearful thing for Milt Ross to be dying here like this, surrounded by monstrosities instead of friends. Who was this Lilith of whom he had spoken?

Ken Carter straightened his gaunt, flat-muscled body and turned again to the two men who stood like black vultures beside the bed of the dying man. He stood stiffly as a soldier, coat like a military cape.

"You two will get out now," he ordered shortly.

The Italian looked from Carter's face to that of the man on the bed, then he ducked an absurdly graceful bow and swaggered toward the door, broad shoulders rolling like a sailor's. "Come on, Fritzie," he called.

The freak walked out with great dignity, still stroking the motionless hands of the twin that sprouted from his chest. Carter blew out a long sigh of relief and spun to his friend, drawing a chair close to the bedside. Ross's eyes were closed, his breathing was shallow and rapid.

**KEN HUNCHED** over the bed, rounded shoulders a little weary, narrow face intent. He waited hopefully, conscious of queer creaking sounds that drifted over this ancient boarding house where Ross had stabled his congress of freaks. Carter heard a snuffling, slobbering noise at the door, as if an imbecile were crying. The little feet kept running jubilantly back and forth upstairs and once there was another slow, slithering sound.... Carter felt his muscles stiffen, his hands were tight upon his cane. He could not sit here and listen to those monsters move about the house, all of them waiting, waiting for Ross to die. One of them had thrust a knife deep into their promoter's back. No doubt of that in Carter's mind. It was in the fear that lay in Ross's eyes whenever he tried to get information from the wounded man. Always there was that fear and an excited, "No, no. Watch out for Lilith—" Now Ross was unconscious. It was doubtful if he'd ever awake from his coma.

Ken Carter sat motionless beside the death-bed of his friend and stared with bitter eyes at the darkness outside the window, a strong, gaunt man with a face of harsh, angular lines. He gave an impression of lean power, of stamina as he sat there, chin on his chest, dark, deep eyes that could be very kind, staring, staring at nothingness. The cape remained about his shoulders, his big, bony hands clasped his cane. Two long hours dragged past before he bent with sudden sharp suspicion over the still figure of his friend, feeling a stab of pain in his throat....

And then he knew. Ross was dead.

Carter straightened heavily. He had known that Ross would die. It had been written plainly on his white, weakened face, but the fact that he was dead struck him heavily, a blow between the eyes. He put out a big uncertain hand to the wall and stood, looking down at the dead face of his friend. His breath came, heavy and sharp, in his throat. He said nothing at all, but his thin-lipped mouth was straightened and hard, and his eyes were cold when finally he went to the door.

**A SHADOW** raised up from a corner and the idiot eyes of the creature with the misshapen head peered up at him. The pouting lips were still slobbering and a slow shudder swept over Carter's hard muscles. Somehow death amidst these... these things seemed doubly terrible. His hand shut grimly over his cane. He jerked the brown felt down over his brows and strode past the idiot pinhead toward the front hall. At the foot of the stairs, the Italian was waiting. He stood squarely in Carter's path and stared up at him with round, black eyes.

"He is dead?" he asked flatly.

"He is dead," Carter agreed, watching with his keen, dark eyes. The two men regarded each other steadily.

It was the Italian who spoke first. He lifted a hand to his mustaches. "I am Tommaso," he said. "I am the knife thrower in the show. I am also Ross's assistant. I do not need your help."

Carter's long lips curved slowly and the movement seemed to tighten his narrow, long face. "So you are the knife thrower," he said softly. "And being Ross's assistant, you probably inherit the show also."

Tommaso folded his arms across the barrel of his chest and lifted his head. "Yes, is now my show. I not need your help."

Carter poked a long, hard finger against the man's chest. "Listen, Tommaso," he said, his words clipped and ringing. "Ross was my friend. He asked me to do a certain thing for him. And I shall do it. And more—I shall find the man who killed him, and when I do—" He lifted his hand before Tommaso's face and closed the big, strong fingers stiffly. "When I do, the man'll pay."

Tommaso's face remained imperturbable. "I hear what he ask you and I can do it myself. I shall watch out for Lilith."

Carter's lips still smiled. "It looks as if Lilith would have plenty of protection, with both of us on the job."

He turned his back on Tommaso and went up the stairs with a balanced, smooth stride that revealed the power of his lean-muscled frame. He did not look behind him, but he was aware of the hard, round gaze of Tommaso. He did not pause at the head of the steps, but turned to the room directly over the death room of Milt Ross. As he listened before the door, he felt his anger rise and wash over him in a hot tide. Damn it, Milt Ross was dead, murdered, and behind this door might be the man....

With the same brittle smile on his lips, Carter opened the door and stepped in. His dark, brilliant eyes swept the room. On a bed against the left-hand wall, a woman lay. She wore her freak's costume, tights and a high bodice of pink, but her clothing was curiously shapeless upon her body. Her legs were horribly twisted. Beside her was a man from whom a childish, strangely artificial sniveling came. He had buried his face upon her shapeless shoulder and his whole tiny body shook with his sobs. He was a midget.

On the couch against the right-hand wall, two men sat. Fritzie stroked the dangling hands of the monstrosity and beside him sat a man without arms, scratching his cheek with one of his bare feet.

"What can we do far you?" asked Fritzie gently.

Carter looked them over slowly, conscious of the hard stares of the men. The midget's sobs kept rising thinly into the silence.

"Ross is dead," Carter said, deep-voiced. "I'm looking for Lilith."

The midget's wails rose higher and the armless wonder said in a thick guttural voice: "So Ross is dead."

The man stroking the mannikin's wrists said quietly: "Well, there's still Tommaso. He can run things."

Carter whirled toward the man. "Where is Lilith?" he demanded sharply.

Fritzie looked at him calmly, his pallid face frowning slightly. "I suppose I may as well tell you. You'll find Lilith in the room across the hall from here."

**CARTER LEFT** the room without another word. There wasn't a person in that room who was sorry Ross was dead, unless it were the wailing midget. Yet Ross had always been kind to those poor misfits, kinder than anyone else had been in all their lives. There must be something about being a freak that distorted the mind to match the body. What sort of brain would that Fritzie have, with his second, headless body? And Lilith? What sort of being was this woman-creature Ross had named? His hand, reaching out for the door of the woman's room, hesitated. A slow, cold chill of apprehension crawled up the ridge of his spine. Ken Carter cursed himself and rapped sharply on the door. A woman's voice, so soft, so pleasant that it startled Carter, called out: "Who is it, please?"

For a second, Carter could not force himself to speak. Then, hurriedly, he gave his name and explained his connection with Ross.

The woman's voice was broken when she spoke again. "I'm going to open the door," she said distinctly. "But I'm warning you that if there's any trickery, I'll turn Milt's cobra loose. He won't harm me, but anyone else—"

Carter choked down a wild, rising laugh. Here was another madness, added to this nightmare house. A woman with a pet cobra. He forced himself to calmness, fought the anger that was his body's reaction to budding fear. He said sharply: "What trickery could there be? For heaven's sake, keep that snake shut up."

The door opened a crack and, through it, Carter glimpsed a woman's golden hair. He took off his hat and bowed, his coat swinging from his shoulders. "If you are Lilith," he said softly, watching her face, "I would like to talk with you. Ross said he wanted me to look out for you—"

He saw that the girl's eyes were young and that there was a tracery of tears across her cheeks. She looked at him for a long moment, then opened the door wide. She was fully dressed, even to her blue serge suit coat and hat of stiff black straw. She turned her back on him and walked across to a large green trunk against the wall. The trunk had holes cut in it on all sides and was labeled—*Danger! Handle Carefully. Snakes!*

Carter said with a lightness he did not feel: "Where is that cobra? I want to be sure I don't let him out accidentally."

The girl shook her head and Carter saw that her shoulders were shuddering. "It's in the trunk—with the rest," she said in a strange, muffled voice. "And its fangs are pulled—every month."

She sat down on the trunk and turned toward Carter, dabbing at her eyes with a scrap of lace handkerchief, and Carter saw that her face was pale beneath the white gold of her hair, saw that her hand was trembling. Carter didn't know exactly what he had expected to find behind the door, but certainly it was not a girl as lovely as this.

He said: "You're a very lovely young lady to be a snake charmer. Is that why Milt asked me to watch out for you?"

Lilith caught her sobs. "Milt was awfully good to me. He knew all these damned freaks were in love with me. He always took good care of me. But of course—"

Carter studied the girl with careful eyes, nodded abruptly. "Listen, Lilith," he said. "It looks to me like every one of these freaks—not excluding Tommaso—want to keep me from finding out who killed Ross. I haven't been able to ask any questions at all and get decent answers. You tell me about what happened."

"We just found him," Lilith said, her voice almost inaudible. "We all came back from the show together and found him in the hall, stabbed in the back."

The words seemed painful to her and Carter felt his anger rising at the picture she conjured up. Ross lying there in the darkness, dying, with a knife wound in his back. He said tightly: "All of you together?"

Lilith nodded. "All of…. *Ohhhh!*"

Lilith's scream was high and piercing, quavering with fright. She flung up a pointing arm and Carter pulled his head down upon his chest and pitched forward. Metal streaked silvery across the room, struck him between the shoulders with a muffled thud, then the door clapped shut and all over the house was silence—except that Lilith's scream still shivered in the air.

**CARTER STRUCK** the floor and bounced to his feet again in a moment. He whirled and stooped his gaunt body to snatch up a knife that lay upon the floor, a long, gleaming weapon with a keen six-inch blade. He weighed it upon his palm for an instant, then tossed it to the bed.

"Did you see the person who threw that?" he demanded as he strode toward the door. In place of his previous uncertainty, a vast coolness had settled upon him. Knives and physical violence were things he could meet, tangible things.

Lilith gasped. "Oh, oh! I thought you were dead—"

Carter pulled open the door. "Did you see who—"

"No, no! I didn't."

Carter threw his long body at an angle through the door, his topcoat held before his face like a shield, but no one was in sight, no one attacked, and he went down the steps in long, bounding strides. He punched open the front door, sprang out into the rain in a dash for the street and heard an automobile motor roar up half a block away. His taxi was still waiting and Carter flung into it with a sharp cry. "That car ahead. Catch it!"

The taxi driver's motor was sluggish and the other machine was two blocks away when the cab at last ground forward in low gear, then the two cars were racing down the dark, rain-swept road. The windshield wiper sloshed liquidly. Rain drummed with hard, nervous fingers on the roof and the tires whined with suction. Carter drew his two automatics from his waistband and examined them carefully, though he was already sure they were in perfect condition. He was frowning tightly, his long face dour with drawn-down mouth corners. This just didn't fit in, this attack upon him while he was in Lilith's room, unless—unless the girl knew something that they feared to have him know. Even that was no explanation, though. The murderer, whoever he was, could not continue to kill every person who came to question Lilith about the murder of Ross.

Carter leaned sharply forward and rapped on the glass. "Turn around!" he shouted. "Turn around and get back to that house! Fast!"

The taxi driver pulled a white, startled face about on his shoulder, then kicked brakes and spun the wheel. The taxi came around in a lurching skid that almost slammed the wheels against the curb. The moaning suction of the treads took hold and sent the car rocking ahead just in time.

"Fast!" Carter yelled. "Fast, man!"

Either the murderer was a bungler and had attempted to kill him, or this had been a deliberate attempt to get him out of the way while they removed Lilith as a possible witness against them. Perhaps Milt Ross had known that she could identify his murderer and had sought to give Carter what information he could in the presence of others he might not trust.

But either way, Carter was certain of one thing. If he got back to the boarding house before the man who had fled through the rainy night, it would be easy for him to discover which of the show people had left the warm comfort of the boarding house. Any man or woman absent from that place at the moment would necessarily be the one who had attacked him. The taxi driver palmed his horn, kicked his brakes and fought the crazy rocking of the car. Carter was thrown forward on to his knees by the violence of the skid, but he had a moment to glimpse what was in their path before his forehead slapped against the back of the front seat and half stunned him.

The man who had stepped squarely into the path of the racing taxi was over eight feet tall! His great, heavy body was lurching forward, straight at the car, in a hulking, pounding run. The taxi's brakes took hold, threw the machine to the left in a shrieking skid and the huge man stepped clear of its racing doom. But the car was out of control now, swinging and skating about on the wet asphalt of the street while the driver, almost standing erect on his brakes and wrenching at the wheel, fought to keep it from crashing.

**CARTER HAD** only a moment to realize that the giant must be one of Milt Ross's freaks, when the auto leaped the curb, snapped a small tree off short and bounded up the wooden steps of a bungalow that stood close to the road. The taxi wallowed through a thicket of evergreens, skated sideways again and teetered over gently against the steps.

Carter just had time to wrap his head in his arms before the glass from the doors came in upon him and he was thrown against the cushions. While his brain still rang with the force of the impact, he was scrambling out of the uppermost door, leaping to the ground. The taxi driver evidently had jumped before the crash. He sat now on the green lawn, motionless in the lashing of the rain, dimly revealed in the diffused rays of the blazing headlights. Carter became aware that his automatics still were in his hands and he thrust them back into his belt while he stared about, searching the black wetness of the night for the giant who had caused the wrecking of the cab. The man had vanished.

A ragged curse forced itself from Carter's throat. Damn it, he was six blocks from the boarding house. Anyone who had left the house would have time to double back…. Carter reached the driver's side in long strides and heaved him to his feet, a hand beneath each arm.

"Geez!" the man gabbled. "I seen a giant. A giant, I tell you. He was as tall as a telephone pole and—"

Carter thrust a small roll of bills into the man's hand and started at a hard, pelting run back toward the boarding house. If he could get back there quickly, he might still be in time to tell which of the freaks had left the place, fleeing in that racing car which the taxi had vainly pursued. Perhaps the giant might know something. Certainly, the wrecking of the taxi had seemed deliberate. If he could force the giant to talk—Carter's harsh laughter forced itself up against his teeth as he ran on, feet slipping and skating on the wet pavement. Force that creature to talk! Why the giant could tie him in knots, strong though he was.

Carter whirled around a corner, saw the dim lights of the boarding house diagonally across the street and threw back his head for a hard sprint. The rain slashed into his face, its drops cold on his eyes. If only he were not too late— He slammed open the door so that it hammered back against the wall, took the stairs in long strides. He pushed directly into the room where all the freaks had assembled before. He looked about the chairs, the bed and the couch. All, all of them were here as before, but this time the Italian, Tommaso, and the giant were here, too.

The giant's clothing was damp, his shoes black with rain as he stood in the middle of the room, head bowed against the ceiling.

The man's size was stupefying. He stood fully eight feet, four inches tall, great fists swinging at his sides, eyes small and bright, his entire face dwarfed by a huge, protruding jaw. The man would weigh fully seven hundred pounds, his arms could almost span the room.

Carter stalked up to him, anger swelling within him. "Where have you been?" he demanded, his voice deep and hard. "You've been out in the rain!"

The giant looked down at him, blinking eyes that seemed tiny in his big, heavy-jawed face. "I just went out for a walk." he said, his voice contra-bass, slow and stupid. "A taxi damned near ran over me out there."

Carter cursed, spun toward the others. "Do you mean to tell me this man was not in the house when I was here before?"

Fritzie stroked the wrists of his other, smaller body dreamily. "My dear fellow," he said gently, "we're not telling you anything. You didn't see the lad, did you? And surely, you don't think we could hide that bulk under the bed?"

**CARTER SWORE** savagely under his breath. "All right," he said shortly. "Maybe you'll talk better for the police."

"Maybe so," said Fritzie, "but it might be a good idea for you to get ready your explanation as to why you delayed calling them so long."

The giant laughed, deep in his belly. "I think the midget is crazy," he said dully. The midget stopped crying and looked up at the giant with his sly, small face wrinkled curiously.

Carter swore at them, eyes flicking over the monstrosities that crowded the room, taking in the lax-bodied
woman on the bed. He knew abruptly who she was, the
one they called the snake woman. In some curious way,
she had been born practically without bones and her legs
and body could be tied in knots. Her eyes were as ma-
levolent as any snake's.

Carter laughed shortly. "It's easy to explain why I
delayed," he said. "I went to tell my fiancée about Ross's
death, and while I was there, I was attacked."

Fritzie's eyes became hard and interested for the first
time since Carter had first seen him. "You went to tell—
*whom?*"

"My fiancée, Lilith," Carter explained smoothly. "We
used to be engaged and that's why Ross called me to take
care of her. We've decided to renew the engagement."

Carter turned his back on the group of freaks and strode
across the hall, tapped on the door. Lilith opened it quickly
when Carter identified himself.

"Oh," she whispered. "I was so frightened." She clung
to his hands, her pale, fragile face lifted to his. "Are you
sure that knife didn't hurt you? It hit you right in the back."

"Quite sure." Carter told her with a little laugh. "Listen,
Lilith, I told the freaks across the hall a little lie. I told
them that you and I used to be engaged and that we'd
decided to renew it."

Lilith began to back away from him. "You, too?" she
whispered.

Carter laughed. "Listen, you fool. I only told them that
so that we can learn who killed Ross. You want to find
that out, don't you?"

Lilith stopped her retreat. "Yes," she whispered. "He
who killed Milt must be punished."

Carter nodded. "Exactly. And this is the way we can do it. I am positive now that Milt was killed out of jealousy over you. By one of these freaks. I have a pretty fair idea who's guilty, but an idea isn't enough. We've got to *know*."

Lilith came slowly toward him. "What do you want me to do?" she asked quietly.

Carter smiled, a hard excitement pounding in his chest. "Go with me to Milt Ross's room and do whatever I indicate. You won't mind if I put my arm around you?"

Lilith smiled dimly. "No, I won't mind."

Carter nodded. He adjusted his topcoat around his shoulders, thrust his cane under his left arm so that it held the cape-like coat out from his back a little. He put his right arm around Lilith's waist. "Now," he said, "we are ready. First, we are going across the hall to say goodbye to the freaks."

He felt Lilith sway back against his arm for a moment, then she went with him. Carter guided her across the hall and opened the door of the room where the freaks had congregated. They were no longer seated about the walls, but standing about the bed where the snake woman lay. The midget cowered down behind her lax, unmoving body, his sly childish face screwed up in fright. The giant spun about, lowering. Tommaso and the pinhead had left the room.

Carter scowled at them. "Lilith just wanted to tell you goodbye before we go," he said. "We're going downstairs for a last look at Ross, then we're going to the Standard Hotel. The police can find us there if they want us for anything."

Fritzie's eyes were glittering and green. "They'll want you all right, Carter," he said flatly. "They'll want to know how you got here so promptly after Ross was stabbed."

Carter ignored him and Lilith said weakly, "Goodbye to you all. Take good care of my snakes."

The giant came, fumbling-footed, toward them. "I'll take care of them, Lilith," he said. "You know I always loved you."

**CARTER DREW** Lilith out of the doorway with his arm around her, glared about the room, then went swiftly downstairs and back toward the room where Ross had died. Lilith shrank close against him.

"I'm afraid," she whispered. "All of them looked at me so terribly. As if I'd betrayed them. Do you think one of them did it?... Oh!" Her voice died.

Tommaso got up off his knees beside Ross's death bed, turned to glare at Carter with his round, hard eyes.

"What you want in here?" he demanded.

Carter eyed him from under his brows.

"Lilith and I came to say goodbye," he said softly. "We are engaged and we are going away together."

Tommaso said: "So? That is very good." He nodded as if in benediction and went out of the room.

Carter watched him until the door closed, then he left Lilith's side and went swiftly about the room, opening drawers and closet doors. There was no clothing in any of them. When Carter came back to Lilith, his eyes were glittering.

"In a few moments," he said softly, "the giant will come here and attempt to kill me. I will keep him from hurting me, but will make it seem as if he has overpowered me. I want you to go to him then and say that he is the one you really love and let him take you in his arms."

Lilith's blue eyes grew very large and her breath came roughly from her lips. "Oh, but I couldn't," she said huskily. "I just—couldn't if he killed Milt."

Carter nodded his head seriously. "He didn't kill Milt—he's just the tool of the killer. And you must do as I say. It is the only way we can catch Ross's murderer. Surely a lady who lets snakes twine about her neck will not mind if a man puts his arm around her for a little while?"

Lilith looked up at him and her eyes slowly widened. "You are making fun of me."

"Not at all," Carter assured her. "It is merely a matter of your cooperating a bit. I am showing you how you can help. Now remember, you must stop the giant from attacking me when I pretend to be overcome, and tell him that he is the only one you really love. And you must let him put his arms about you, but you must be sure that he faces the door when he does that."

Lilith looked down at the floor and a slow shudder shook her shoulders. "Very well," she said in a muffled voice, "but you must let me have a gun or something. In case—in case Joseph really hurts you."

Carter said: "So the giant's name is Joseph." He gave Lilith one of his heavy automatics, then tossed his topcoat into a corner with his cane, turned his back deliberately toward the door and put his arms about Lilith. He buried his face in the softness of her throat, whispered against it.

"You must pretend to be enthralled," he said, "so that the giant, when he comes, will be too angry to creep upon us. You must tell me when Joseph comes."

"All right," she said.

**CARTER FELT** the pulse leap faster in her throat, thrust her suddenly from him, whirled toward the doorway.

The giant, Joseph, had come in, the slobbering pinhead at his heels, and closed the door behind him. The idiot dropped into a chair against the wall, a vacuous grin on its drooling lips, as though about to be a pleased spectator at whatever was to follow. Joseph clutched a knife in his big, thick-fingered hand, holding it in his fist with its point downward. He made no attempt to throw it, but came slowly forward, shuffling his feet, his small, narrowly spaced eyes beady with hate. There was a low rumbling in his throat.

"You take Lilith from me," he said throatily. "Now I kill you."

He made a great awkward spring forward, but Carter ducked under the down-stabbing sweep of his arm and came up behind him. He planted his foot against the bend of the giant's knees and thrust violently. He had time to see that Lilith had shrunk back against the wall and thrown out both arms against it as if for support. Her violet eyes were watching the fight narrowly, not with horror, but with fascinated interest.

Carter's kick made the giant's knees collapse and he thumped down on them heavily, teetering forward almost off balance. He was not quite six feet tall now and Carter started a blow from the knees, pivoted on his left heel and put all his weight and carefully poised strength into a slugging smack just beneath the left eye. The giant tottered, threw out the hand with the knife and braced it against the wall. A deep-chested roar tore from his throat and he reared to his feet, started his big arms whipping about like windmills. The pinhead clapped its hands in an ecstasy of inane delighted approval.

**THE GIANT** stood with his head scraping the ceiling. His hands were twelve inches long and when he balled them into fists, they were like small hams. One blow would smash Carter's skull like an egg. Even though the giant's strength was not in proportion to his size, his enormous weight was a terrible weapon. Carter danced agilely about the man. He had snatched up his cane now and he used it like a sword, denting the giant's soft stomach muscles, lancing upward at his throat. Like all victims of overdeveloped pituitary, the giant was slow in his movements, a little blundering and heavy on his feet. It was only this that enabled Carter to keep out of his reach.

But Carter's blows had little effect on Joseph. They stung him, but none was capable of disabling him. Carter hoped that soon he would be able to swing at that other eye. The one he had struck was purpling and swelling so that the giant moved toward him with awkward right hand twists like a great, half-crippled crab. The small space of the room worked to Carter's disadvantage. When the giant spread out his arms, he covered almost the width of the room. Finally, the slow-witted Joseph seemed to realize this advantage and spread his arms wide, crouched a little and began to shuffle toward Carter.

The man's face, distorted by the swelling of his left eye, was terribly twisted, the lips pulled back from great white teeth, the eyes squeezed up to slits. He kept roaring from deep down in his chest and the noise of it shook the house. Still no one came to interfere. Carter realized abruptly that he had failed to take full account the man's colossal size or had overestimated his own agility. Unless he could close that other eye with his cane, slow the man down—

Carter's breath came painfully, raspingly through his throat; his chest pumped with his panting. He was driven to frantic dodging to keep out of the giant's clumsy way and the violent physical exertion was playing queer tricks with his mind. It was becoming fantastic, this battle with a giant in a room with a dead man, a half-wit malformed creature and a frightened girl for an audience. It was like something out of the dark legends of the past. Joseph seemed to swell in size until he filled the room. Carter realized abruptly that he was wasting his own strength in furious curses. He flung backward against the wall and stood there, cane drooping from his hand, eyes bleared with effort, watched the giant waddle toward him with those great outstretched arms.

With a shout that was almost hysterical, Carter flung himself toward the man, prodding violently with the cane. His weapon darted in and out like a shuttle, jabbing deep into the man's abdomen, cracking his knuckles, flicking up into his face. But he could not quite reach the eye without placing himself within the compass of those huge fatal arms. Carter's mad attack accomplished one thing, it drove the giant back a slow, heavy step. All that effort, and the man retreated one step!

Carter found crazy laughter was pumping up from his chest. He flung both arms high above his head and screamed with laughter and the giant paused for a moment, blinking at him uncertainly with his one good eye, twisting his head awkwardly to the side to see better. His arms sagged down. Carter ceased his laughter as suddenly as it had begun. Now, now. He must strike in this instant, or— Carter put his left hand on the foot-board of the bed where his friend lay dead and vaulted over it, sprang to the foot-board itself, balancing precariously with the half-forgotten skill of his days on the stage.

Joseph pulled down his huge head, swayed forward on his feet with his arms starting upward again and in that moment Carter struck. From his elevated position, he thrust desperately for the giant's right eye. The tip of the cane slid through before Joseph could get his windmill arms up and caught the giant squarely on the right cheekbone. At last! At last! He had succeeded in damaging both the man's eyes. Now it would be possible to carry through with the subterfuge he had planned with Lilith. Triumph surged over Carter in the instant he felt the ferrule slide home, but it was short-lived.

In making the thrust, Carter was forced to extend himself too far. The upward sweep of the giant's arm caught the cane and snapped it from his grasp. The jerk pulled Carter off balance and, with a despairing curse, he realized he was toppling directly into the giant's grasp!

**ONE MOMENT** in the grip of those mighty arms and he would be destroyed instantly. Joseph could fall upon him and crush him to death. Even if he only teetered for an instant, the man would reach out and take him. There was only one thing to do and Carter seized upon it in the same moment the realization flashed through his brain. He dived toward the giant, but a little to his left. He flashed under outsweeping arms, curled and landed on his shoulders, rolled immediately to his feet. He was near the door now and could escape. To remain without a weapon seemed fatal. Yet Carter did not flee. There was a hard set to his mouth, a cold glitter in his eyes.

He swept past the giant as the man turned lumberingly. He caught Lilith up in his arms, gripping her from behind, and walked toward the giant.

"Do your stuff, Lilith," he panted. "Come on, girl friend, if you love life—"

The giant completed his whirl in pursuit of Carter, paused dazedly as he glimpsed the girl coming toward him. Joseph's left eye was completely closed, his right was swelling shut from Carter's last blow.

"Hurry, Lilith," Carter whispered, "or it will be too late."

Lilith raised a voice that had no quaver in it. "Joseph, darling," she called. "Take me in your arms!"

The giant hesitated, rumbling deep angry noises in his throat. He swayed, peering about the room to find Carter with his one fast-closing eye. Then he lumbered forward, arms outstretched toward Lilith. One of his great hands brushed her shoulder and her dress tore.

Suddenly, without warning, a muffled shot rang out in the room.

"He attacked me," cried Lilith. "He attacked me!"

A startled, whimpering sound rose from the giant and his hands closed upon Lilith's shoulders. Lilith's gun kept on banging, two, three, four, five shots. The hands dropped from Lilith's shoulders and Carter set her down on her feet gently, lightly. The automatic belched twice more and there was a crashing, splintering sound as the giant fell heavily backward upon a chair and smashed it to the floor, while the idiot pinhead bubbled with delight. Joseph did not stir after he slumped down.

Carter laid himself gently down in the corner where his topcoat lay and twisted his arms and legs grotesquely, as if he had been hurled there violently by the giant, his half-shut eyes were on the door and his right hand held the second automatic, which he had eased from his belt. Lilith stood firmly, staring down at the dead hulk of the giant, and the door opened and Tommaso came in. He looked at the dead giant with an expression of satisfaction, gazed at Carter's motionless form and smiled.

"Good work, Lilith," he said. "Now, there is no one to tell on us. That driveling pinhead in the chair couldn't tell anything even if he did know what had really happened. We can say the giant murdered Ross and you killed the giant when he attempted to attack you after confessing. Carter was killed defending you."

Lilith spun around and stared at Carter, jerked her head toward Tommaso.

"Shut up, you fool," she snarled, her voice far different from the hesitant, gentle thing it had been. "Carter is just shamming."

Tommaso's round eyes grew large and Carter lifted himself up on his elbows and grinned at him. "Quite so, Tommaso. I was just shamming, but you have confessed your crimes now. It is just as I suspected. You killed Ross by throwing a knife into his back, so you could take the show and Lilith too. Lilith was Ross's wife. The cobra that no one but Ross could ever handle was in Lilith's room and I searched there and found none of Ross's clothes at all. If you two tried to hide that from me, you didn't succeed very well. When were you planning to marry Tommaso, Lilith?"

**WITH A** snarl, Tommaso snatched the gun from Lilith's hand and pointed it directly at Carter's head. Carter only smiled, did not even raise his own automatic that he held close to his side.

"You're too damned smart," Tommaso snarled. "I—"The automatic clicked emptily.

"Yes, it's empty." Carter said gently. "I counted the shots when Lilith emptied them into Joseph over there. You see, Tommaso, it was very easy to figure out. All that Ross could tell me in your presence was to watch out for Lilith? That could have a double meaning, you see. It sounded as if he asked me to protect her. Actually he was warning me against Lilith. When I learned she was his wife, it was obvious she was party to the plot. That meant a love affair. She couldn't have been in love with one of the freaks, so it must be you, my dear Tommaso. I saw that as soon as I figured out she was Ross's wife, but it was necessary to force the two of you out into the open, which I accomplished by giving you an opportunity to frame someone for the murders. I'm sorry about Joseph. You used his love for Lilith to set him against me. I thought I could save him—"

Tommaso stooped swiftly and caught up the knife Joseph had dropped, whipped it forward in the same motion, its point traveling arrow-swift and straight for Carter's throat. He had been expecting it and he lifted his topcoat before him. The knife failed to penetrate it and dropped harmlessly to the floor. Carter laughed harshly.

"Lilith," he said, "you were wondering why the knife Tommaso hurled didn't kill me in your room—and incidentally, Lilith, that was something else that proved you were a party to the plot. You couldn't have failed to see the face of whoever tried to knife me. The light was right in his face. But to get back to why I wasn't killed. This coat is lined with bullet-proof silk, a little precaution of mine against just such murderers as Tommaso."

Tommaso bit out a curse and sprang at Carter with the automatic reversed in his hand. Carter's long lips tightened against his teeth as he shot Tommaso twice through the heart.

# SILK DOPE

*We liked the story but we were frankly skeptical about Ken Carter's cape when Norvell W. Page sent "Satan's Sideshow" to us. It smacked more than faintly of those wonderful magic garments that used to thrill us as a youngster in the pages of Hans Christian Andersen and the fairy tales of the Brothers Grimm. "Oh-oh," we said to ourselves, "here's another one of those things that go in the same bracket with deadly but hitherto undiscovered poisons so rare that even the Indians of the upper Orinoco aren't just sure what they are all about." We expressed these doubts to the author and he came right back at us with the following. Now we're more than convinced of the error of our ways and as a result you readers have a new fictioneer on your thrill docket.*

*Here's the dope on bullet-proof silk as Mr. Page shot it at us—*

When you expressed doubt about the bullet-proof silk cape which saved Ken Carter's life in "Satan's Sideshow," I realized that the strength of the silk was probably not generally known. As a matter of fact, it is actually stronger than manganese steel!

I'm not just talking. I can quote page and paragraph to back it up. During the war, the United States government made all sorts of experiments with the use of modern body armor to protect its men and silk was one of the materials tested. The British government for a while made a silken necklet standard equipment for four hundred men in each division. Later it was abandoned because the devices cost too much, $25 each, and because of their deterioration in trench mud.

I'm going to quote, now, excerpts from *Helmets and Body Armor in Modern Warfare* by Bashford Dean, who was in charge of United States experimentation and tells the results in this book. Major Dean (or Doctor Dean; he bears both titles) went back into history for the first examples of silken armor. He cited the fact that the Japanese used padded silk, frequently reinforced with iron plate, from the Seventh Century up until 1870. He finds it also was used extensively in Germany and Russia. Major Dean quotes from William A. Taylor, a British experimentist (*Helmets and Body Armor, etc.,* page 288 footnote). "The only material that gives materially better results than manganese steel is pure woven silk which, against shrapnel bullets up to a velocity of 900–1,000 foot seconds, has a distinct advantage, weight for weight, over steel."

As compared with the silk's resistance to velocities of 900 to 1,000 foot seconds (I quote from the same book, page 298), a forty-five caliber Army automatic pistol, admittedly one of the hardest shooting American sidearms, has a foot second velocity of only 802 when the muzzle is against the target! And that figure is less at increasing distances. It's easy to see, then, how Ken Carter's cape stood up against a knife attack. Don't suppose, however, that the silk mentioned here is the thin artificial stuff of which many women's dresses are made. It was pure, usually raw, and placed between layers of weather-resistant cloth. That, mentioned by Mr. Taylor as being superior to manganese steel, had a weight of almost eleven ounces to the square foot. Ken Carter used a lighter composition, but even so his cape weighed a little over 20 pounds as against approximately 15 for a heavy overcoat.

*There you are, just in case you too, wondered about the impregnability of the silkworm's product. We shouldn't have been so skeptical if we'd read the following about Mr. Page's newspaper career. He was a good reporter, and good reporters get their facts straight—even in fiction. Now meet the man himself—*

I don't know why it is, but men who aspire to write the Great American Novel always become newspaper men. I did, too, and for the last twelve years have been sliding about the country doing one dirty job after another. I didn't know, when I was patting corpses familiarly on the shoulder in the morgues, that it was all going to come in mighty handy someday. In fact, when I began to write fiction finally, I chose the one part of these United States I knew absolutely nothing about: the West. I wrote Western stories and, what's worse, sold 'em.

One day the editor who purchased them looked at me sourly and said, "Why don't you write about something you know… like gangsters." Well, he paid for that remark—for I've been writing detective stories ever since. Amazing how many midnight murders can chill your blood after a lapse of years when at the time they happened it was "just another stiff." And we newspaper men grumbled about leaving our cans of coffee in the press room and pushing out into the night. We thought that was *work*. I could get wistful about newspaper work and I could swear that when I sidle into a police headquarters press room and whisper, "I'm an old newspaper man myself," my voice is positively *mournful*.

www.ingramcontent.com/pod-product-compliance
Lightning Source LLC
Chambersburg PA
CBHW031152050726
47495CB00019B/1600